Praise for *The Torah Codes*

"As I read, it became a very viable blockbuster film because the writing enabled me to visualize the story so well. The biggest issue I had was my inability to put the book down to sleep. Don't buy *The Torah Codes* unless you have a job that allows you to stay up all night! Yep, it's that good."

—Allison Bliss, contributing reporter for the *Oakland Business Review* and *Alameda Business* newspapers.

"*The Torah Codes* roars along for quite some time, driven both by plot twists and—of far greater importance—a superb main character. Nathan is smart, odd, witty, and a bit world-weary. He's a great character to tag along with. The pages seem to turn themselves."

—Jonathan Berman, partner at Jones Day.

"I plowed through *The Torah Codes* in record time. Nathan is likable and often very funny, and the action kept me turning the pages. Do I believe prophecy is encoded in the Torah? Doesn't matter. It was fun and crazy and I look forward to Barany's next thriller."

—Melydia, a remarkably ordinary woman.

Also by Ezra Barany

The Torah Codes

6 Short Stories of Suspense

36
Righteous

A Serial Killer's Hit List

EZRA BARANY

Dafkah Books

For Beth.

*You're all the
good I need.*

Note from the Author

This story was inspired by the biblical tale of Jacob fighting with an angel in the city of Jaboc. A part of this story was also inspired by a typo in Ernest Hemingway's "A Clean, Well-Lit Place," one which English teachers insist was not a typo.

To address any inaccuracies, we wish to point out that aspects of a national landmark have been fictionalized to protect U.S. national security.

Thank you for choosing to read *36 Righteous: A Serial Killer's Hit List*. We know you have a choice of books and on behalf of the author and the 10,000 voices in his head, we would like to thank you for reading our book today, and we hope to see you again in the next book. In the unlikely event of a loss in pressure, we regret to inform you that no oxygen masks will fall from the ceiling.

Unless you're reading this in a plane.

Yeah.

Then you're good.

36
Righteous

A Serial Killer's Hit List

Chapter 1

Winneba, Ghana

Disarming a bomb isn't so hard. What's hard is disarming a bomb that hasn't been found yet.

On an early afternoon in my darkened living room, I sat at the desk beside a squat lamp carefully working one of the wires of my device into a perfect ninety-degree angle.

There are so many different ways a bomb might detonate. By timer, by pressure, by proximity. But if it's triggered by a remote signal from a cell phone, the bomb's location doesn't matter. All that matters is that the cell phone's signal doesn't reach the bomb.

The phone call to trigger the bomb would be sent in two minutes. I had to line up everything on my device just right or else my device's signal wouldn't cancel out the cell phone's signal. Or worse, my device would trigger the bomb *before* the phone's signal.

Outside my cement house, the growl of a large vehicle idled into silence. I followed the slice of daylight that cut between two pieces of sheet metal covering my window, and peeked through the slit between them. An unfamiliar van was parked out front. David Moore, my friend and the vice-president of my company, stepped out of the van and spoke to two men in hospital uniforms as he pointed at my house.

Something was wrong.

Were they orderlies? Nurses? David's stature always reminded me of a dwarf from a Tolkien novel. Now his expression conveyed a determined dwarf getting ready for battle. They knew I was close to finishing my device and wanted to stop me. That didn't worry me. I knew how to handle them.

Keeping the lights off, I squatted in a dark corner of the living room. A moment later, a knock sounded at the door.

In a sing-song falsetto voice I called out, "Who *is* it?"

"Nathan," David shouted. "Open up. It's important."

"More important than taxes?" I used my regular voice.

"Nathan, please."

"I'm not home right now. Please leave a message after the beep. *Beep.*"

"Nathan, open the door."

I said nothing.

"Nathan."

Some voices muttered outside and then came a loud crunch against the door. A piece of the wood frame cracked.

"That's okay," I called out. "I've been meaning to get a new door. One of those lovely hand-carved things with stained glass."

The next kick came, busted the frame entirely, and the door flung open. The men stepped in, shadowed as silhouettes by the daylight behind them. They paused, probably to get accustomed to the darkness.

I pounced high and landed with my elbow into the first orderly's face. His nose made a cracking sound, and he fell backwards. The second orderly came at me from behind, but I elbowed him in the gut. Glancing behind me to double-check his position, I placed a kick to his shin and he dropped to the floor as well.

"Nathan, stop!"

I raised my fists to my face ready for the third attacker, and froze when I saw it was David.

"Nathan, why do you think I called them?" By the daylight seeping through the front door, David's face actually showed concern. Was he bluffing? "What would be in it for me?"

"You're just trying to stop me from deactivating the bomb."

"What bomb?"

Anger spilled into my voice. "You know damn well what bomb. The call to trigger it will be made in about fifty seconds."

"Nathan, you're just having one of your delusions." David's bushy eyebrows practically lifted off his forehead. "Alright, just for the sake of argument, let's say there is a bomb. What specifically clued you in to its existence?"

I thought about it. There had to be a specific clue, a precise piece of evidence that made me aware of the threat.

Thirty seconds.

The more I tried to grasp that clue, the more I realized the evidence was never there. The knowledge of the bomb just came to me.

Twenty seconds.

The information came like dream knowledge. When I dream, my dream knowledge can reveal facts true to the dream but false in reality. Someone I might have never met before can be my brother. Someplace I might have never seen before can be my old high school. On rare, treasured occasions, my dream knowledge lets me have a dream of a world where my girlfriend Sophia doesn't exist, and I don't feel so alone without her.

In this case, my dream knowledge told me to beware of a bomb. The problem? I wasn't dreaming.

Five. Four. Three. Two. One.

No explosion sounded anywhere.

David gestured to the living room mirror. "Look at yourself. You're a mess."

In the low light, I checked the broken mirror. A fractured reflection of my unkempt brown hair reached past my long neck. My eyes puffed out signs of sleepless nights. My T-shirt had more stains than my driving record. Though the mirror couldn't reflect it, I imagined my scent wasn't much better to bear.

David put his hands on his hips. "I got no pleasure from calling the mental hospital, but I had to do it. I mean, really. What would I gain from putting you there?"

"You'd take over my position as CEO." But as I said the words, I knew that would never be his motive.

"I'd be honored to become CEO of the company, but you know me. I don't play corporate dog-eat-dog games just to get a promotion."

I nodded. He was right.

David sighed. "Think about it. Think about how you've been handling the company lately."

I considered each puzzle piece of my reality. The way the employees scrutinized my every move, the enemies I had at the local supermarket and bank, the barber's sinister plot against me, the bomb out there somewhere. The pieces of my jigsaw didn't fit. The puzzle pieces for David's version of reality fit well. I had stopped taking my meds several months ago, and during that time I discovered more and more enemies. But now, considering it this way, I realized all my enemies might not have been enemies at all. The only true battle I had left to fight was against my own paranoia.

Crap. Fighting people was easier.

"Alright," I said. "Let's go."

I followed David through my broken doorway and squinted at the bright daylight. The orderlies trailed behind, one limping, the other holding a handkerchief over his bloody nose.

Chapter 2

Berkeley, California

*C*rash!

"Did you hear that, Shoshana?" Rabbi Elihu Silverman asked his wife. The bedside clock's red numbers glowed 2:47. Three hours ago, he had wished her goodnight. He flipped on the bedside lamp.

"Hear it?" She said, "I thought it was a bomb going off!"

"Bombs don't sound like broken glass," Elihu said. "I think someone's in the house. They knocked over the flower vase by the window, maybe?"

"Quick," she whispered. "Call the police."

"Shoshi, if a stray cat is what makes the noise downstairs, we should call the police?" Elihu lifted himself from the bed without a sound. "I'll see what *mishegoss* is going on downstairs."

"Be careful," Shoshana said. Before Elihu left the room she added, "Take a weapon."

He scanned the room, then picked up the flashlight he kept by his dresser. The heavy baton took two size-D batteries. It should do.

At the top of the staircase, Elihu paused. From the rustling of papers, someone must have been rummaging through his office downstairs. So it was not a stray animal. A person had broken into their home. Why ransack the office? The intruder thought Elihu had something of value to steal, maybe? There was nothing of value in the house. No jewels, no cash, no stocks or bonds.

But having someone in the house wasn't the worst of it. The worst was that the intruder made no attempt to be quiet about it. Like when the Nazis looted Jewish homes during the war. The German soldiers had no concern for consequences. If the Jewish owner tried to stop them, he would be shot. This intruder downstairs, whoever he was, would not run. More likely, the man would kill Elihu and his family, and keep searching until he found what he wanted. For Elihu, getting out of the house now took priority. There was no point in calling the police. They'd be too late.

Chapter 3

Elihu padded back to the bedroom entrance. "Shoshi, come quick," he whispered. "Fetch the children. We're leaving the house and going to Samuel's place."

"What? What is it?" Shoshana slipped into her bathrobe.

"It's like 1939 all over again. Let's get the children."

"*Mein Gott!*" Shoshana rushed to the children's bedrooms.

Together they sneaked across the upstairs hall and one by one shushed their nine children as they woke them up. Shoshana carried the baby while the rabbi carried Seth, the youngest toddler. At the top of the stairs, he told his children, "We are all going to go very quietly downstairs and leave the house."

A bit too loud, one of his sons asked, "Why, *Aba*?"

"Shuh, shuh, shush," Elihu whispered. "It's a game. "

Their quiet descent down the stairs sounded more like a carpeted marching band.

Shoshana reached for the front door.

A voice behind them said, "Your father's right. It is a game."

A young bearded man in black burglar clothing pointed a gun at Shoshana's chest. The stranger also gripped a hand-crafted book that Elihu had hidden in his office. The book contained a list Elihu had made over the years.

"Please," Elihu said. "Take what you want and let us go."

The man set the book down on the hallway table, removed a silencer from his jacket pocket, and screwed it onto the end of the gun. "I'm afraid I can't—"

A spray hit the intruder's face. The man screamed and dropped his gun to scratch at his eyes. Shoshana was holding up a pepper spray can.

Elihu thanked God for providing him with a clever wife, and opened the front door. A few of the children laughed at the funny faces the man made and the two eldest pushed him to the floor. The younger children must have thought the intruder was play-acting.

Elihu's son Yakov held the man's gun by the long end where the bullet comes out. "I got his gun, Aba. Do I win? Do I win?"

Elihu maneuvered his one-year-old son, Seth, to one hip to extend a free hand. "Give that to me, Yakov." Yakov handed it over. "Everyone, time to go!"

Without any more fuss, they hurried out of the house, leaving the intruder moaning inside. As they crossed the yard into the night, Elihu threw the gun into the bushes. The younger children giggled amongst themselves agreeing the man was very funny. The older ones kept quiet.

Elihu and his wife hustled the children down the street a few houses. Still carrying Seth on one hip, Elihu rang the doorbell.

Without waiting, he plunged his finger into the doorbell again.

The children asked all sorts of questions, now. "Is Uncle Samuel also playing?" "Who was that man?" "Can we go back and play some more?"

Elihu rang the bell again.

And again.

The porch light switched on and the door opened revealing a squinting, balding man he was glad to see.

"May we come in, Samuel? It's a matter of life and death."

"Life and—? Yes, of course. Come in. What's wrong?"

After the children trudged inside, Samuel turned the lights back off at Elihu's instruction, save for one dim lamp. Elihu told Samuel what had happened, and had this been a *drash* or sermon at his synagogue, there would have been dramatic embellishments. *This* story, Elihu completed in record time.

"Please, Samuel. Can you help us out?" Elihu squeezed his hands together.

"Anything you need." Samuel placed a comforting hand on his shoulder.

"Thank you. My children should get back to sleep, and I need to make a phone call."

Samuel nodded. He showed Elihu to the phone, and then helped Shoshana and the older children set up some beds.

Elihu dialed the fifteen-digit phone number.

The phone on the other end of the line rang its foreign tone once. Twice. A message machine picked up after the third ring. At the tone, Elihu said, "Nathan, it's Rabbi Silverman. My whole family is in grave danger, but it's worse than that. Someone stole the list. In case I die, you must protect these people."

Elihu recited the names and locations of the world's last hope for survival.

Chapter 4

Two months later
Winneba, Ghana

Having spent two months at the mental hospital, I got David to agree to take me home. Now that I rode in his car, however, I didn't feel much gratitude. The car jerked and tossed like a ship on the high seas.

"Thanks for coming to get me out of my cage," I said to David. I gripped the passenger-side car door handle to stay upright. "But I was hoping to leave with my life."

The four-wheeled shaker spent most of its energy moving in every direction except forward. Fortunately, the net vector direction *was* forward, so we did seem to make progress in that direction.

"I take it you're back on your medicine?" David swerved around a corner, throwing me against the door.

In a moment of calm, I removed a bottle of meds from my coat pocket and shook it in front of his face. He pulled back his head. I probably would have made it out of the hospital much sooner if the doctors hadn't tested a slew of alternate medicines to see if I had a better response to them. The side effects of delirium, welts, and dizziness gave me reason to stay until they found the proper drug and dosage.

"The meds may take away my super powers." I put away the bottle. "And I may no longer be able to see things that are invisible to everyone else, but there's something to be said for sanity."

"Hear, hear." David braked hard at a stoplight. I put my hands against the dash to stop the momentum from throwing me through the glass. "Listen. I just want you to know it's good to have you back."

I said nothing.

"I missed you."

I said nothing.

"Setting up the water-filtration plant the way you did, it wasn't just a stroke of genius, it was more than that. You helped the people here get the water they needed. I…" David glanced at me, scowled at the road in front of him, and shrugged. "You inspire me."

"Do you have any breath mints?" I asked.

"No, why?"

"I want to have a minty fresh breath for when you start kissing me."

David accelerated into a sharp left turn that pressed me against the car door again. "All I'm saying is you've done some amazing things for these people, and the world owes you. You're an inspiration to everyone who knows about you."

With all the newspaper journalists and TV news reporters that came to see me when I got the desalination plant up and running, it was true that there were hundreds, if not thousands, of Americans who probably knew me not by name, but as the man who purified water in eleven African countries.

"Just what I need," I told David. "A bunch of high school kids whining because they have to write a stupid essay about me."

We drove along the dirt road for a silent spell until David asked, "So…uh…any conclusions from what you… from your experience at the hospital?"

"What the hell kind of question is that?"

"I don't know. Forget it."

David's face turned a slight shade of red. I peered out the side window. *My experience at the hospital? Yeah, I can conclude that I'm still sick in the head. I can still have hallucinations and delusions. Ultimately, I can't trust myself to be safe around others.* My throat closed up and my gut felt hollow.

"Yeah, I've got a conclusion." The words were hard to say. "I've concluded that the less I'm around people, the better."

"Well, that's pretty much been your daily schedule here."

"True, but I can't keep leading Sophia on."

"Your girlfriend in America?"

"Yeah." I pushed against my throat to get the words out. "It's time I cut ties with her once and for all."

David drove past the clustered homes where privacy didn't exist. His car kicked up dust behind us.

He said, "Long term relationships never work."

He didn't sugar coat the truth. I appreciated that. I had expected him to say, "Aw, don't break up with your girlfriend," or "Aw, but love knows no bounds." Instead, he spoke his mind from an objective standpoint. It's what made him such a good VP of the company.

Twenty minutes later, David pulled up alongside my place and shut off the engine. I hopped out, grabbed my duffel bag from the trunk of his car, and bent down to speak to him through the open driver-side window.

"Thanks for the lift. I hope you never drive me again."

David smirked, used to my way of saying thank you.

I walked to my door, and groaned. "You gotta be kidding me." In place of my busted door was a brand new one. With stained glass windows. I turned back to David.

He called out of the car window, "You said you wanted one."

I checked out the stained glass. Flowers, a rainbow, and was that a unicorn?

David threw some keys out of the car in my direction.

I laughed and shook my head. "Go away."

I snatched my new house keys off the ground. My friend chuckled and drove off.

I unlocked the pretty door and entered. The place felt as humid as I had left it. On top of that was a smell. Probably the milk gone sour. I'd forgotten to tell David that when he went back to get me clothes for my stay at the hospital, to also throw away the milk.

After abolishing the milk, I peeled the sheet metal from the windows. The welcome sunlight spilled into my living room.

Letters hugged the walls. My correspondence with Sophia. Each letter always signed, "With the love from all my heart, Sophia." I plucked them off the walls, one by one, unable to look at them. Taking the letters down wasn't so hard. Throwing them away was.

When I finished, I lay back on my bed. The bed springs whined under my weight. The walls were empty now. No trace of anyone beside me.

Chapter 5

Berkeley, California

In her tiny apartment, Sophia Patai lay on her bed frowning at the day's news in the newspaper. Glad to be distracted by the buzz of her intercom, she rose and pressed the "Talk" button.

"Yes?"

"It's me," Miriam's cheerful voice crackled its reply over the intercom.

"Come in." Sophia pressed the other button, the one marked "Door," to let in her good friend of seven years.

In under a minute, a knock rapped at Sophia's door. Sophia gave the stubborn door her usual hefty tug to open it and Miriam bounced in with her coy grin and raven curls and ruffled dress. The aquamarine, sleeveless dress had a flattering V neckline. Miriam always did know how to show off her beauty in a modest yet stylish way.

"That's a beautiful dress," Sophia felt the material at Miriam's shoulder. It was softer than cotton.

"It would look better on you. Where did you get your gorgeous blonde hair?"

Sophia smiled. "My mother's Scandinavian ancestors. Listen, I'm glad you're here." She motioned for Miriam to sit on the bed, the only seat in the studio apartment. "I need your thoughts."

"On what?" Miriam sat and smoothed the dress over her knees.

While standing, Sophia leaned against the marble countertop by the fridge. "I have these…visitations I guess you could call them. It's like someone is speaking through me. But I'm usually unconscious at the time."

"What do you mean?"

"You know I have epilepsy?"

Miriam nodded.

"Sometimes during my seizures, I say things that people standing around hear but I'm not conscious as I say them. Like talking in my sleep."

"Weird." Miriam twirled a lock of her midnight hair.

"Actually, it's something that happens to many people with epilepsy."

Miriam scowled. "Then you're *not* strange. That is, aside from the quirky person you are, there's nothing else strange about you."

"There's more. The things I say…" With no easy way to tell Miriam what was happening to her, Sophia took a deep breath. "It's like the Shekinah is saying it through me."

"*The* Shekinah? The female aspect of God? Don't let the ultra-Orthodox Jews get wind of that."

Sophia tensed. "Why? You think they'll kill me for claiming the Shekinah speaks through me?"

"Worse. They'll stop talking to you."

She exhaled. "Funny."

Miriam shrugged. "Maybe your subconscious likes to pretend you're God. Everyone's entitled to a god complex once in a while."

"I'd like to think you're right, but..." Sophia went to the brown cherry nightstand and removed a piece of paper from the top drawer. She handed the piece of paper to Miriam to show the series of news headlines she wrote. "Take a look at this."

Miriam read Sophia's note. The headlines said things like, "Giants Slay Dodgers in Close Game," and "Two Killed in San Francisco Apartment Fire," and "Construction Worker Pleads Guilty to Oakland Bank Robbery."

"So?" Miriam looked unimpressed.

"These are the messages I got from the Shekinah, most of them I wrote down after having a seizure and having people tell me what I said during it."

Miriam read more of the headlines. "So I don't get it. What are these phrases?"

"Keep in mind I wrote these over the course of the last two months."

"Okay."

Sophia handed her a newspaper. "Look at today's paper."

Miriam scrutinized it. Her gaze went back and forth between the headlines Sophia wrote and today's headlines.

Miriam's eyes widened. "You're saying you predicted today's news?"

"I'm saying the words that I said while I was unconscious are the same as today's news headlines."

Miriam shook her head as if she didn't believe it, and squinted at Sophia. "Suppose these phrases you say *are* coming from the Shekinah. Why would She have you say these words?"

"I thought about that. It might have something to do with how I dismissed my unconscious words. I've been trying to convince myself these are just random phrases I say during my seizures. It could be the Shekinah is trying to prove otherwise."

As Miriam stood and continued to examine the headlines, Sophia's cell phone rang.

"Hi, Sophia." It was Frank, a friend of Miriam's. Sophia had met him several months ago. "I hope I'm not interrupting anything."

"It's okay, Frank. What's up?"

"I'm holding a surprise birthday party for Miriam, and I wanted you to come. It's tomorrow night. Do you think you can make it?"

Sophia smiled at how Miriam didn't know about the party and at the same time stood nearby.

Miriam whispered, "Why are you smiling?"

Sophia scrunched her nose and shook her head, *It's nothing.*

"You're talking to Frank?" Miriam mouthed.

Sophia nodded.

Miriam faked a swoon and fell on Sophia's bed. Sophia choked a laugh.

"What's so funny?" Frank asked.

"Nothing." Sophia waved at Miriam to be quiet. "I'm watching South Park."

"You hate South Park," he said.

"Family Guy?"

"Cute. So can you come or not?"

"Yeah, that sounds good." Sophia smiled, still looking at Miriam.

"Great. Oh, and what was that weird email about?"

"What weird email?"

"Yesterday you sent me an email. Like a transcript of a dialogue."

"I didn't send you an email yesterday."

"Yes, you did."

Sophia thought maybe she did it during a seizure. Terrific. Like sleepwalking, except in this case, writing that message was more like sleep emailing. "Ignore it, Frank. I was probably asleep when I sent it."

Frank was slow to reply. "Whatever. I'll see you at Miriam's surprise party though, right?"

"Right."

Sophia hung up and pulled out her laptop from underneath her bed.

"What's the matter?" Miriam asked.

Sophia set the heavy thing on the bed and turned it on. "Apparently, I sent Frank an email yesterday, but I must have been having a seizure or something because I don't remember doing it at all."

Sophia clicked on her sent folder in her email account and saw what Frank was referring to. According to her history, she sent an email to Frank in the early afternoon.

She opened it up. Both Miriam and Sophia gasped when they read:

-Listen, I'm glad you're here. I need your thoughts.

-On what?

-I have these visitations I guess you could call them. It's like someone is speaking through me. But I'm usually unconscious at the time.

-What do you mean?

-You know I have epilepsy? Sometimes during my seizures, I say things that people standing around hear but I'm not conscious as I say them. Like talking in my sleep.

-Weird.

-Actually, it's something that happens to many people with epilepsy.

-Then you're not strange. That is, aside from the quirky person you are, there's nothing else strange about you.

-There's more. The things I say. It's like the Shekinah is saying it through me.

Chapter 6

I woke up to the phone ringing. Was it Sophia? Then I remembered. We didn't use the landline to connect. We used the internet, snail mail, and my cell phone.

The surrounding barren walls made me feel like I had slept in a stranger's house. Now that I had decided to end my relationship with Sophia, would I never hear her voice again? My body cemented stiff at the thought, but the phone continued to ring. I had to unload the heaviness of my troubles if I wanted to answer it. I rubbed my gritty eyes, broke out of bed, and shuffled to the living room to stop the phone from nagging.

"Hello?"

"Hi, is this Domino's Pizza?"

Anger burned inside me. "Listen, you. This is the fifth time you called my place asking for Domino's Pizza."

"Really? Sorry about that. I guess I dialed the number wrong."

I clenched my hand around the handset. "How do you dial a number the same wrong way five times? I mean, do you realize how statistically improbable that is?"

"I'm sorry, okay?"

"If there were just one number difference between my phone number and Domino Pizza's phone number, the chances of you reaching me would be one in ten."

"I'm sorr— wait, one in ten? That's not so bad."

I snatched up the base of the phone and paced the living room, the phone cord following behind me. "That's if there were only one number difference. But I know there's a helluva lot more differences between my phone number and Domino's because you're calling from where? Fresno?"

"Uh…New York."

"While you're calling from New York, I'm trying to get some sleep here in Ghana freakin' Africa! We've got a whopping five more digits on our phone number for you to even reach me. So tell me, Cletus—"

"It's Jason."

"When you're making a phone call to Domino's, how the hell do you dial the extra numbers to reach me? The same ones? I mean, do you think you're at one of those business phones where you have to dial extra numbers just to get a dial tone?"

No response.

"Cletus?"

No response. Kid probably hung up. Didn't blame him. I looked around still holding the phone to my ear. The walls were so bare without Sophia's letters.

"I am so madly in love with you, Cletus," I said. "I want you to take me in your Domino's Pizza arms and squeeze all the cheese out of me."

"Uh…What?"

Oops! I slammed the phone down. My ears itched. Never pretend to flirt with someone you can't stand.

The answering machine message light blinked. Two blinks at a time. Two messages. I pressed the "Play" button.

The female voice droned, "Saturday May 12th, 2:42 a.m." *Beep.*

Great. These messages were two months old.

A man's voice came on. "Uh…hi. Is this Domino's Pizza?…Hello?"

Eat me.

The female voice chanted, "Saturday May 16th, 3:17 p.m." *Beep.*

A man's voice I immediately recognized sounded breathless. "Nathan, it's Rabbi Silverman. My whole family is in grave danger." I listened carefully to the message. He recited names of people he thought were in trouble.

"Number thirty-four is Cole Montgomery. He lives on Millchester Lane in Oakland. Number thirty-five is Rabbi Gerald Katz. I believe he lives on Brochetta Avenue in Oakland. And number thirty-six, Nathan, the last name on the list of the thirty-six righteous is your friend Sophia Patai."

Chapter 7

I **played the message again and wrote down** the thirty-six names and their locations. Not entirely sure what the rabbi meant by them being in danger, I figured the international spider had something about it. I turned on my computer and accessed the world wide web. In the search engine, I checked the first name on the list along with his home address.

A few obituaries came up. Poor guy had a heart attack. *Okay. That one's no longer in danger.* I dug deeper into his obituaries and short articles about him. Seemed he was a big deal in his community. According to an article on a small Jewish website, his grieving widow revealed that he had often made anonymous donations to charities. His Jewish community showed no surprise in learning of his generosity.

Anyhow, no need to worry about him. Probably ate too many fatty steaks.

I did a search for the next name on the list. A chill sliced through me. More obituaries came up. Also a heart attack. A coincidence?

I skipped to the fifth name. More obituaries. Heart attack. The tenth name. Another heart attack. All of these men died within the past two months.

What the hell was going on?

I jumped down the list to check Sophia Patai. Typed in her name along with her address. My finger hovered over the "Enter" key. I couldn't press it. Thoughts of discovering her grave suffocated my body into stillness.

I shook my head empty and before letting the thoughts come back, I tapped the "Enter" key. Most search results come up in under a half-second. All the horrific thoughts of finding her dead came pouring back during that half-second. The longest wait of my life.

Nothing came up.

That is, no obituaries came up. But the lack of an obituary didn't guarantee she was alive. The search results listed her social media affiliations, her professional listings as a tarot reader, and other sites mentioning her memberships.

I went to one of her social media pages. Her last post read, "My horoscope says I should stay home today. Screw that! I have a birthday party to go to! …But I will be extra careful. ;-)" I checked the date and saw it posted four hours ago. Seemed she was okay.

I pushed out a breath I didn't realize I had been holding.

In the search engine, I tried the name before Sophia's— Rabbi Gerald Katz—along with his address. No obituaries came up. Made me feel a helluva lot better. I figured that rabbis always got obituaries. From their congregation, if not from their family.

I decided to do a complete search for each and every name. On a pad of paper, I wrote down the name, how they died, and when they died. An unsettling result emerged. A span of at least twenty-four hours passed between each death. The first fifteen names on the list all died by a heart attack. The ten following names were killed in what could be called dangerous areas. Dark alleyways, sketchy neighborhoods, that sort of thing.

After those, I learned that the next seven were also dead. Only four left living on the list. Three before Sophia.

The way those last seven died troubled me. Two in drive-by shootings, four shot answering their front door, and one stabbed on a crowded subway train. It was as though the murderer started out cautious, the heart attacks turning up no investigation into their deaths. Afterward, the murderer steered the blame onto bad neighborhoods. But lately, as the list dwindled, the murderer felt bold enough to kill in any setting and by any means.

Thirty-two dead. Three left before Sophia.

Chapter 8

Elihu brushed his teeth. All the children were lying down to sleep, some sardined on the guestroom bed, and others on floor mats. *Baruch HaShem*, thank God, his wife was asleep too.

Elihu paused his brushing and stared at his reflection in the mirror. The horror of seeing his six-year-old son Yakov with the gun. It's unthinkable what might have happened.

What was it he should be doing? How could he be sure the family, they were out of danger?

What about the children? How would they mentally process the experience when they got out of this whole ordeal? *If* they got out.

The image of Yakov with the gun popped into his head again. Elihu shivered.

Yakov. A name that meant *to follow* but whose root also meant *a crooked path*. Like Yakov in Genesis who was on a crooked path descending into his own personal hellish *Gehenna* after cheating his brother out of his birthright, and after lying to his father when his blind father asked, "Who are you?" All to claim the family power. The guilt consumed the biblical Yakov so much that while he was alone, he fought a man or angel. But there was no man or angel. Yakov fought his own inner demons. It was no coincidence that *Yakov* confronted his past in a town called *Yavok*, and that when he was "alone" he wrestled with a man. After he owned up to his dirty past, Yakov's name became Yisrael, a word that meant *to struggle with God*, but whose root also meant *a straight path*.

Elihu remembered his own struggle with God from the time of his college years. The memory of overcoming the pain and coming to terms with God inspired him to believe he could get through this struggle his family now faced with the intruder.

He released a sigh that seemed to come from deep within and seeped out like a dying breath. How was it he should be dealing with this? How could he convince the police of the danger? The whole family had seen the intruder's face. Would such a man want Elihu and his entire family dead?

A chill of truth pierced Elihu. The family would only be safe when the intruder believed he was no longer at risk of being identified.

Maybe I could talk to him. Maybe I could tell him that we promise not to speak of who stole the list. Maybe I could convince the man that I understand how it wasn't such a terrible, terrible crime. It was just a book, after all. Not like gold or jewels or cash, he stole. Maybe the intruder would understand. Maybe the intruder would agree to leave us alone.

But Elihu knew such thoughts were fantastical. Convincing the man was not an option. Besides, how would he contact the intruder?

Perhaps the man would not come after them when he believed Elihu and his family no longer threatened his freedom. If he believed Elihu wouldn't contact the police, then perhaps he would leave Elihu's family alone. Now what situations would allow that to happen?

One possibility? If the intruder were in prison, there would be no point in stopping Elihu from saying anything. It would already be too late.

Another possibility? If no one ever knew where Elihu and his family stayed, then the intruder could rest assured knowing no one would learn of how he broke into Elihu's home. But that solution would just be an extension of what the family was already doing. Hiding out.

A third possibility? What if someone could stop the intruder? Someone like Nathan. Maybe Nathan got the message. Maybe Nathan could help out.

Elihu returned to the task of brushing his teeth with brisk, energetic strokes.

Chapter 9

Sophia **took a bite of the angel food cake** pretending not to notice the guy with steely blue eyes watching her as the hard rock music roared. Cake wasn't usually her thing—she didn't like overly sweet stuff—but she knew Miriam would be pleased to see her eating some of the bright yellow birthday cake, and Frank would be happy to see her participating in the festivities.

Sophia glanced at the stranger who kept his distance. Yep, the man still stared at her. His cute face and admiring glances and unspoken promise of possible futures only served as a reminder of how much she missed Nathan.

She twirled the ring on her finger, the one Nathan had given her before he left for Africa.

Frank's house dwarfed the size of her apartment, but then, any house or apartment or voting booth was huge compared to Sophia's place. The house didn't look well cared for. It posed as a guy's place, with posters instead of paint, beer cans instead of decorations, and mismatched couches without throw pillows. She liked it.

She couldn't make out the colors of the living room because the lights were set low to enjoy the music and to give the feeling of intimacy. Some couples danced, and like every party, one of the dancers looked adorable at pretending he could dance. Perhaps the low lights helped reduce any insecurities he had about his dancing skills, or lack thereof.

Some cute guys hung around which, by itself, made Sophia happy. In fact, if they all just stayed where they were, the party would be perfect. The last thing she needed was the temptation of handsome men coming on to her, especially Mr. Blue Eyes.

Uh, oh. I jinxed it.

She acted as if she didn't notice the gorgeous stranger approaching her gripping a bottle of beer in his hand. Mr. Blue Eyes. He had arrived at the doorstep the same time she had. What was his name? Sophia couldn't remember. She had been too distracted by his gray-blue eyes, dimpled cheeks, and kissable lips when he introduced himself.

Nathan, I wish you were here.

"How's the cake?" He had a sensual smile.

"It's hot—I mean, good." She felt her face flush.

"How do you know Miriam?"

"We were in the same English class at Cal." Sophia thought about the way Miriam looked when she first met her. Miriam had been wearing a fun yellow sundress with red trim, and sandals that just made her sparkle. After class that day, the two of them ate lunch on a grassy hill enjoying the sun barefoot. They had shared girlish silliness and secrets and solace.

Blue Eyes kept one hand in the back pocket of his jeans as if reaching for his wallet.

Sophia brushed a lock of her blonde hair behind her ear. "How about you? How do you know Miriam?"

"We go to the same *shul* together. The same synagogue."

"I know what a shul is," Sophia chuckled. "She goes to Beth Israel, right?"

"Right."

"What is that? Conservative?" She fiddled with her cake fork.

"Modern Orthodox." He removed his hand from his back pocket and scratched the back of his neck.

"Modern Orthodox? Isn't that an oxymoron?"

The guy's laugh revealed a set of charming crooked teeth. "It means women play a bigger role in being a part of the services without breaking any orthodox laws."

Yeah, whatever.

Miriam appeared arm-in-arm with a young woman. "Sophia, there's someone I'd like you to meet." Miriam turned to the guy and said, "Hi, Guy."

Blue Eyes nodded to Miriam.

His name is Guy? Oh, yeah. I think that's what he said at the doorstep.

"Sophia, this is Leah. Both Guy and Leah go to my shul. And Leah has been dying to meet you."

"Oh? Why's that?" Sophia smiled at Leah. Leah had auburn hair under a beret, and a round face dotted with freckles.

Miriam squeezed Guy's arm. "I hope you don't mind, Guy, but could we shoo you away? We want to have some boring girl-talk time."

Guy showed off his dimples. "No problem. I'm going to try the cake."

Miriam watched Guy retreat in his tight jeans and whispered, "Isn't he dee-vine?" She rolled her eyes back and licked her lips.

Sophia laughed. "I know! If I were a nun, my habit would be on the floor by now. Thanks for saving me from such temptation."

"So, I know you didn't want me to, but I told Leah about your visitations."

Sophia tightened, bending the paper plate in her hand. Her cake fell to the floor.

Leah crouched and helped Sophia pick up the crumbled pieces. "I know Miriam wasn't supposed to tell me, but don't blame her. I told Miriam about a problem I'm having and asked for her advice. She said she couldn't think of anything but I saw some hesitation in her, so I begged her to tell me what she had on her mind."

Sophia still couldn't believe Miriam had talked about her visitations. How many others did Miriam tell?

Leah walked beside Sophia to throw away the crumbs in the living room's rectangular trash bin. "Anything. I would try anything to solve my problem. She still wouldn't tell me what she was thinking so I pleaded with her. Reluctantly, she told me about you and the Shekinah." She wiped her hands free of crumbs on her floral-print skirt.

"We don't know it's the—" Sophia glanced around the room to make sure no one else listened to their conversation. Thankfully the music blared, but she didn't want to take any chances. She grabbed both Leah and Miriam by the arm to the bathroom and shut the door. Being in a man's bathroom felt a bit intimate. The electric razor and the aftershave and the blue toothbrush and large hair-brush…it made her miss Nathan even more. "We don't know it's the Shekinah. I have epilepsy. I black out every once in a while."

"What about that time when Miriam was at your apartment?" Leah asked.

Sophia glared at Miriam who turned her head away, eyes to the floor.

"I don't know what that was," Sophia said. "And even if it was the Shekinah, there's no way of knowing whether the words She says through me mean anything."

Leah gripped Sophia's hands. "I'm at the end of my rope. If it turns out that what you do doesn't help, that will be just as good as everything else I've tried."

This was exactly what Sophia didn't want. She didn't want to give false hope to people. *Why did Miriam tell Leah about my visitations?*

"Please," Leah said.

Sophia gently tugged her hands out from Leah's grasp. Leah clearly needed help and seemed okay if Sophia's attempt to help her didn't work out.

Sophia sighed. "What's the problem?"

Chapter 10

Winneba, Ghana

The way I see it, death by fire is one of the worst ways to die. And though most people caught in a burning building die from smoke inhalation, not from the fire itself, the smoke is actually a useful part for us. It functions as a warning sign. Where there's smoke, there's fire. The smoke, absent of all oxygen, causes the throat to gasp and constrict, triggering a coughing reflex. It wakes up potential sleeping victims, exposing them to the threat. They can then rush out of the building, safe from danger.

But for these thirty-six righteous, there were no warning signs. No indications that they were in danger. Like a smokeless fire. A dangerous situation without any indications or warning signs. My job was to warn the remaining people on the list that they were in a smokeless fire.

I picked up the receiver, ready to call Sophia. She needed to know the peril she could soon face. She needed to get away from her apartment, out of the city, out of the state, hell, out of the country, if possible.

I paused.

What could I say to her? Thanks to my bipolar disorder, I have a complete resume of experience in crying wolf at times when the wolf turned out to be just another delusion. If Sophia was smart, and I knew she was, she'd ignore my urgent warnings and chalk it up as another one of my paranoid delusions.

Besides, I hadn't communicated with her in over two months. I already made the decision to help her move on and drop me out of her life. There had to be another way I could help her.

I knew what to do.

I phoned David, the VP of my company. He answered on the first ring.

"Hey, David. Nathan here. I'm quitting."

"What?"

"I'm quitting the company. You're the CEO now. Congratulations!"

"What?"

Damn phone reception. I put the mouthpiece closer to my lips, "CAN YOU HEAR ME NOW? I SAID I'M QUITTING THE COMP—"

"I heard you the first time!"

"Then how come you—"

"Nathan, why are you saying that? What makes you want to quit all of a sudden?"

Did I really want to tell him why? No. But I needed to. "It's Sophia. She's in trouble and needs my help. I gotta get back to the U.S."

The line went quiet. Then I heard David say in a small voice, "Okay."

"Okay?"

"Yeah, okay." David sighed. "You built the desalination plant, got it running smoothly, and now the whole system is automated. The ugly truth is we don't need you anymore."

"Exactly."

"I get it. You need anything for your trip?"

"No, I'm good."

"I'll miss you," David said.

"Shut up." I hung up the phone and imagined the smile he always had for my rude behavior.

Chapter 11

Berkeley, California

Sophia watched Leah put the lid of the toilet down to sit. Leah scrunched her brow collecting her thoughts. She kept her dark curly hair partly hidden under a beret that Sophia guessed was a part of the orthodox Jewish way of doing things. Religious Jews expressed modesty by covering the hair, along with wearing a long-sleeved shirt and long dress. Leah looked subdued and serene and beautiful.

"It's been very hard," Leah said at last. "Ever since I found out my sister Yochevet has lung cancer, I've been determined to find a cure. And there are lots of cures out there." She laughed with no joy in her voice. "We've tried chemotherapy, magnets, electricity." She sighed and added as an afterthought, "Prayer."

Leah twisted the thin fabric of her flower-patterned dress.

Sophia waited for Leah to continue.

"I remember when Yochevet and I would play tricks on Papa. He used to smoke a pipe, and Mama encouraged us to hide it whenever we could, to help him cut down on his smoking. For fun one morning, we woke up early to play a different trick. We took all the yarmulkes from their drawer and placed them all over the house where Papa would find them when he woke up. He found them in his sock drawer, in his shoe, in the pill cabinet, and even in a cereal box like a toy surprise." Leah gave a light laugh, her eyes looking at a distant past.

"Each time Papa found another yarmulke, Yochevet and I looked at each other and giggled. The whole breakfast was filled with giggles as our papa talked about finding so many yarmulkes like an unexpected treasure hunt. Yochevet's laugh was infectious. She had a Woody Woodpecker laugh through plump cheeks." Leah's faded smile turned into a grimace. "You should see her now. She's so thin. She's at the hospital all day, and can't even get out of bed without assistance. I wonder if I'll ever hear her laugh again."

Miriam slipped an arm around Leah's shoulder.

Sophia's heart clenched. "I'm so sorry." She crouched in front of Leah so that she was eye-level, and gripped her hands in her own. "I want to help, but I'm not sure what I can do. What are you expecting?"

"Anything. Any words from God, from the Shekinah, to help me know what I can do to save my little sister." Tears fell from her cheeks.

Sophia dropped her gaze to the floor. "I can't exactly just talk to Her at any time and ask questions. But give me your phone number and if something happens, something that seems to relate to you and your sister, I'll call you."

"Thank you so much." Leah wiped her cheeks. "I can't thank you enough."

Sophia searched the bathroom counter, then tugged off a few squares of toilet paper and handed it to Leah. "Isn't it just like a guy not to keep a box of Kleenex in the bathroom?"

Leah blew her nose and laughed through her sniffles.

Chapter 12

My flight connection from New York to San Francisco landed ten minutes early. All my possessions I had taken to Ghana fit in one carry-on. Though height is often considered a positive attribute, I had to keep my head bent low as I exited the plane with my duffel bag. Planes were meant for one thing only. Flying. They were not meant for entering and exiting. As such, by the time I exited the plane and found my way to the gate, I arrived exactly according to the arrival time.

Everyone else plodded to the baggage claim to get their luggage from the turnstiles. Fortunately, I didn't have to go through that inconvenience. Unfortunately the crowd was so thick I wouldn't get to Customs until the herd ahead of me got their luggage off the turnstiles. A siren light twirled and a heavy buzzer sounded signaling the start of the turnstile's rotation.

I craned my neck and assessed my path to Customs. A boy scowled at me. He then gazed toward Customs as if he could discover what I was searching for. I decided to follow nature and go the path of least resistance.

Placing a hand on the boy's shoulder, I said, "Don't do this."

I scanned the area to make sure no security guards were looking, climbed onto the moving turnstile, and ran along it using it like an angled escalator, slipping most of the way. It was every bit as fun as it looked.

At Customs, I had the privilege of being one of the first passengers to arrive. To my surprise, the government worker at the booth was wide awake. I didn't realize Customs workers could ever be anything other than half-asleep. Maybe he'd just started his shift. I gave him my passport.

"Name?"

"Nathan Yirmorshy."

"It seems you've been gone for quite a while, Nathan."

"About nine months."

He studied my passport. "Are you here for business or pleasure?"

I had to think about that. I wasn't here on business. David had that under control in Ghana. Was it pleasure? Definitely not.

"Sir?"

"Funeral," I decided. It was the closest thing to accurately describe neither business nor pleasure. After all, I did fly here because of deaths.

"Sorry to hear that." He stamped my passport. "Here you go."

***

Sophia relaxed in her bed rereading the best parts of Nathan's last letter. The letter arrived three months ago, but the words still stuck to her core.

> *You should see the walls of my bedroom. They're covered with your letters. Seems like the more letters I put up, the closer I am to you, and the more this godforsaken place feels like home.*
>
> *I know I'm not there to help you out if you need it. But whenever you're lonely and troubled, whenever you need to be heard, just look up at the sky and think to me about how you feel. Know that I am under the same sky. We are still connected.*
>
> *In your last letter, you mentioned how concerned you were about us changing. Being apart, we may steer down different paths, discovering different interests, and we may become different people. But know this, no matter who you choose to be, I will always want to fully devote myself to you and have you in my life. Whether you choose to be a giver or a taker, weak or strong, cruel or kind, all I ask is that you be true to yourself, and be mine.*

Sophia snagged a tissue. She checked her email on the iPhone that Nathan had given her. Still no word from Nathan. What happened to him? Sophia sighed.

Her stomach growled.

"I know, right? He usually sends letters snail mail and then emails if he's been late with his letters. So what gives?"

Her stomach growled again.

"I hear you." She rolled onto her belly, reached out, and opened the fridge. One advantage to living in a tiny apartment? Everything was in easy reach.

The chilling fridge turned out to be as desolate as she felt.

She opened the memo function on her iPhone and hit the record button.

As she scanned for the missing contents of the fridge, she recited, "I need lettuce, tomatoes, cucumber, apple juice—" Her head felt dizzy. What was she doing? Oh, yeah. She was recording the grocery list. "Uh…bagels and cream cheese." Enough food for one, she thought. *For one.* When would she see Nathan again?

She turned off the record button and grabbed her keys to go to the grocery store.

Leaving Customs, I sought the exit and made my way down the long path to the point of no return. Leaving airports always felt that way. No turning back. At the exit, people waited for their loved ones, their lost ones, their family ones, their friendly ones. No one for me.

No time to let loneliness feed on my gut. I needed to make an untraceable phone call. Hmm. Finding a pay phone at an airport. Not an easy task in this day and age of cell phones. After asking a clueless bartender and then a savvy security guard, I became victorious in my treasure hunt. I fed the pay phone a couple of coins. That's about the time I realized American pay phones didn't take coins from Ghana.

I found a kiosk that advertised phone cards. Though the man at the counter seemed friendly and honest enough, I wasn't about to use my credit card. Call it a bad habit, but when I had paranoid delusions, I trained myself to avoid leaving any money trail that could be traced. Though my state of mind now functioned properly, I still preferred to do all my transactions in cash.

At an ATM, I pulled out the maximum withdrawal in a single transaction. My bank dispensed a maximum of forty bills, so I took out eight hundred dollars in twenty-dollar bills. Sure, there were some transaction fees, so it cost me more than eight hundred dollars, but having the cash handy gave me a sense of freedom. Freedom to do anything I wanted.

I put the cash in my large wallet, along with my passport, social security card, and California driver's license, keeping a twenty handy to break. I went to the nearest store in the airport. A bookseller. The girl at the register looked fresh out of high school.

"May I help you?" she asked.

"Yeah, can you break a twenty?"

"I'm sorry." The clerk made a poor attempt at sounding sincere. "We can only give change for purchases."

Figured. I searched for gum or candy or any cheap item I wouldn't mind chowing down. Plenty of cheap stuff on the counter. Nothing I wanted. My eye caught sight of one of the paperbacks for sale. Something called *The Torah Codes*.

"What the hell is that?" I pointed to the book.

"It's a thriller. Like a Jewish version of *The Da Vinci Code*."

"Just what this world needs. More knock-offs."

This was a waste of time. I grabbed a bag of overpriced peanuts and slapped the twenty on the counter. I specified that I wanted five of the dollars back in quarters. After she gave me the change, I left to find the nearest phone.

The clerk called behind me, "Sir, your nuts!"

Tell me about it.

I ignored her and returned to the pay phone. Plugged in the coins and got set to dial Sophia's number to let her know I was on my way to see her.

Decided against it. My plan was to protect her from an assassin, but also to spare her from my manic episodes. I could do both better from afar.

I had to call the rabbi. No way around it, if I wanted his phone number fast, I needed to turn on my cell phone and check the database. Still, my call had to remain untraceable, so I stuck with the pay phone. Clutching the receiver to my ear with my shoulder, I checked the rabbi's number in the database and tapped it into the pay phone. I turned off my cell, and waited for the rabbi to pick up. Noticed the throng of tired faces dragging luggage behind them, walking to and away from the gates, new beginnings and lost vacations. With each ring, my chest felt heavy. No one picked up.

He and his family might already be dead.

***

Richard Stone handed off a file to his assistant when the phone rang. The phone display's readout indicated it was an interoffice call. He picked up.

Over the phone, his coworker said, "I did a check on all noteworthy behaviors and financial transactions of the eight people you mentioned."

His coworker was referring to the known associates to the remaining targets of the thirty-six righteous. There were eight known associates. Most of them were family members of the targets, others were lovers. Ever since the assassin stopped using caution when carrying out his assignments—shooting the targets instead of making the targets look like victims of heart attacks—Richard needed to be extra careful about making sure he wasn't implicated. He needed to avoid any complications from external sources, sources like the known associates of the remaining thirty-six righteous.

"Go on," Richard said.

"Going over the past two months, only one stuck out."

"Who?"

"Nathan Yirmorshy. He took a flight from Ghana to San Francisco."

Richard tapped his pen on his desk. Nathan Yirmorshy was a known associate of the last name on the list, Sophia Patai. Could this Yirmorshy jeopardize the mission?

"Sir?"

Richard cleared his throat. "Thank you. Keep me posted for any other activity." He hung up.

His gaze fell to the framed photo of his daughter. Holly had been seven years old when the picture was taken ten years ago. Richard admired her blonde hair, those huge innocent eyes, and her toothy grin. She had no idea of the mission he had taken upon himself. That mission needed to be completed.

It would be best to remove Yirmorshy from the equation. Just in case.

Chapter 13

Sophia parked her car in the Berkeley Whole Foods lot. She loved this grocery store. It prided itself in having a healthy food court so that you could buy a hearty meal. You could eat it at the tables by the windows, and then go shopping on a full stomach. For those still thirsty, a booth offered customers an opportunity to taste wheat grass. The store featured vitamin supplements, cereals sweetened with fruit juice, and a slew of aisles devoted to what Nathan called "free-range organic, biodegradable, vegetarian meats." He had hated the store saying the food there had no artificial sweeteners, no artificial colorings, no artificial flavorings, no MSGs, no Dhts, and no XYZPDQs.

Still sitting in her car, Sophia twirled her ring at the warm memory. She sighed, padded across the sunny lot, enjoying the heat on her body. She stepped through the automatic glass doors and cold air slapped her skin. She glanced around the store.

All the clerks were either tall, lanky guys uncomfortable in their bodies, or else lesbians with tattoos, tongue studs, and body piercings.

With a moss green grocery basket in hand, she found several items she needed but she couldn't remember everything. She pulled out her iPhone to play back the recorded memo. When she saw the most recent file she had recorded, she gasped. The file displayed its length as thirty-six minutes long.

That made no sense. She knew she had turned the recording off after reciting her grocery list. And if she hadn't, the darn thing would still be recording, wouldn't it?

She hit play and heard her own voice. "I need lettuce, tomatoes, cucumber, apple juice.... Only her death can save her. Only her death can save her. Only her death can save her. Only her death can save her. Only her death can save her..."

I ducked into the back of a taxi with my duffel bag and told the driver the rabbi's address, off by a few numbers. Again, a habit of paranoia. Have the taxi drop you off a block or so away from the destination, and there's no trail of where you went. Plus you can approach the place on foot with caution.

The taxi smelled like vanilla, a manufactured scent, but still favorable. Until I detected the added scent of sweat among the seats.

The driver called over his shoulder, "Thees your first veeseet to Amereeca?"

"You're kidding, right?"

"No. I tell by accent you are foreigner."

"What accent? I was born in Oakland."

"Really? You sound like from Ghana. You know where is Ghana?"

How in the hell?

"Never heard of it," I lied.

"Great country."

"Do they have peanut butter cup ice cream? Because I don't go anywhere that doesn't have peanut butter cup ice cream."

"Ha, ha! You joking, yes? Ha, ha. You crazy man."

I examined his license. His name was one of those names so over-Americanized, you know it had been changed to make you feel like you're with an American. Like calling tech support and chatting with a Pakistani man named Jimmy.

I wondered if the rabbi was okay. Would he greet me with a smile on his face? Or would I discover his body among the bloody corpses of his many children?

The driver had a folded picture attached to his taxi ID. Showed a kid about eight years old standing next to him with a woman's arm resting on the boy's shoulder. Beside that photo was a headshot of an attractive lady.

"Is that your wife?" I nodded to the picture of the attractive lady. His eyes looked back at me in the rear-view mirror.

"Oh, yes." He pointed to the attractive lady. "We married almost two years now." He tapped the photo of the boy. "And this is my son. From first wife. I am lucky man."

I nodded. Though I didn't know the condition of the rabbi's situation, I found comfort in knowing the driver had a good family life.

He drove in silence and the late morning sun shone warm through the windows. In about twenty minutes, we entered the lower level of the Bay Bridge heading out of San Francisco and toward the East Bay. The above alternating lights of the bridge mesmerized me. Left, right, left, right. We tunneled through Treasure Island, and then the bridge opened up to the East Bay landscape, Berkeley's arm on the left, Oakland's arm on the right. The arms spread wide to welcome me. The taxi hurtled across. Seeing the familiar old roads and buildings hit me to my heart. Made coming home more visceral than I had expected.

When we got off the freeway in Berkeley, the driver pulled over at a spot nowhere near where I had asked.

He turned off the meter and unbuckled his seat belt. Opening his door, he turned to me. "Stay here. I be right back."

He left the car and entered a store. I couldn't believe it. I checked my watch, eager to see to the safety of the rabbi.

I waited a minute.

Two minutes.

This was stupid. I unbuckled my seatbelt, but as I did, the driver exited the store.

He climbed back in carrying an ice cream cone and handed it to me. "Here." He nodded to the cone. "Peanut butter cup ice cream."

I laughed and took the ice cream.

"Welcome to Amereeca." He flipped the meter on and continued to drive me to my destination.

Chapter 14

Sophia stood still in the Whole Foods grocery store listening to the recording. Though surrounded by people passing her, no one paid any attention. She might as well have been standing on her own lonely island. The memo played the same words over and over. *Only her death can save her.*

She sat on the hard floor, ignored the looks people gave her for sitting down, and listened to rest of the memo.

Could this have been a message for Leah? Could it have been for anyone else? Sophia considered all the people she knew, all the troubles and worries her friends had. The more Sophia heard the words, the more she became convinced. The message was for Leah.

After a half hour, she neared the end of the recording and listened closely.

"Only her death can save her. Only her death can save her…uh…bagels and cream cheese."

Oh, yeah. That's what I forgot. Sophia's thoughts were still clouded from the shock of the Shekinah's visitation. *Bagels and cream cheese.*

***

When the cabbie dropped me off at the upper-class neighborhood, I thanked him and gave him enough of a tip to buy a few buckets of peanut butter cup ice cream, in case he ever had the yen. I jogged past single-story houses with manicured lawns, and made my way to the rabbi's home. I dropped my duffel bag on the porch, and pounded on the door.

"Rabbi?" I shouted. "Rabbi? It's Nathan Yirmorshy, open up." I rang the doorbell a few times and hammered at the door some more. "Rabbi?"

No response.

I stood back and peered through the windows to search for any signs of life. Anything.

The house was dead.

I checked the lock to the front door. A regular bump key would do. They're easier to use than lock picks. I took out a set of bump keys I made in Ghana when I had fears that "they" would break into my home and change the locks just to play games with my head.

The laws on breaking and entering were pretty much the same all over the world. It's illegal. By using the bump key I wouldn't be breaking. That would bring down my sentence to entering. Technically, the correct term was trespassing, but I liked *entering* better. In front of a judge, I could always claim I didn't know there was anything illegal about entering.

The second bump key I tried fit into the keyhole. All I had left to do was jolt the pins out of their position so the key would turn. I touched the edge of the head of the key and applied a little pressure to turn it. With my other hand, I picked up a stone at my feet and tapped the key in. It took some doing, but eventually the tap or "bump" jolted the pins, and the key turned freely.

I brought my duffel bag inside, closed the door behind me, and locked it.

Around me lay the same scene I saw the last time I had been to the rabbi's place. Toys lay on the floor, and bookshelves lined every wall filled to overflowing with fat religious tomes. The family didn't move out. This was still their place. The question was, did I happen to arrive while they were all on a picnic?

What do people do daily? Brush teeth.

I bolted upstairs to the bathroom and checked for toothbrushes. Couldn't find any. Relief washed over me. That meant they were away, but more important, they were alive.

Could be on a trip. A vacation, perhaps. The next question was, what do people always take with them, especially for trips? Maps? Passports, if they leave the country.

What else?

My eyes scanned the master bedroom, but didn't land on anything helpful. *Luggage.*

I opened a few closets to look for luggage, but as I did so, I realized that the only helpful result would be if I found no luggage. That would tell me they were likely on a trip. If I did find luggage, it could be the family took a day trip, or that they took other luggage with them and left behind whatever luggage I came upon.

I found luggage in the hallway closet. Didn't help me reach any conclusion. Not sure what to do next, I moved to the children's bedrooms.

The beds were unmade. In fact, all of the beds were unmade. I went back to the master bedroom. There also. The bed covers were tossed and disheveled. Who goes somewhere with their toothbrush and leaves their bed a mess? Made no sense. If they left in a hurry, they would have left their toothbrushes, too.

Unless…

I went downstairs and out the front door. A man peeking through a window across the street hid behind the curtain to his house when he spotted me. I grabbed my bag and closed the door behind me. Wiggled the doorknob to be certain the door was locked. Jogged across the street to the neighbor's house.

I pounded on their door. Though I couldn't be sure, I had a pretty good idea of what happened. The man from behind the window answered. A balding, plump man. Probably retired.

"Where are you keeping the rabbi?" I asked him.

"Who?"

"Rabbi Silverman and his family from across the street." I felt myself lose control of the rising anger in my voice. "They were in danger and left the house, abandoning everything. They came to you and later, perhaps the next day, they needed some belongings from the house. Believing it safe enough to retrieve things from the house but not safe enough to return to live there, someone came to collect the needed items. Things like toothbrushes. While they were away, they asked you to keep an eye on the house in case any more dangerous people came. That's why you, and only you, noticed me enter their house. Now where are they?"

"I - I don't know what you're talking about. I—"

A familiar voice from behind him said, "Samuel. It's okay."

I peered around the rotund man. The rabbi stood on the staircase leading to the second floor.

"Nathan." The rabbi motioned for me to enter. "It's good to see you."

Chapter 15

Sophia arrived back at her apartment. In one hand, she carried her Psychic Institute canvas bag filled with groceries, and in the other her jangling keys. She closed the door with a firm bump of her hips and placed the bag on her bed. She had to call Leah and pass along the message she heard on the memo.

It took just a few minutes to put the groceries away. Sophia sat down on the bed and took out her iPhone. She rolled the phone over in her hands a few times, then decided to play a quick game of Angry Birds.

After twenty minutes, she closed the game and grabbed Leah's phone number from her backpack purse. Using her phone's email application, she scanned her inbox. Still no messages from Nathan.

She spent the next forty minutes answering other emails and finally closed the email app. She checked Leah's number and dialed.

The phone rang and rang. Sophia decided to hang up if she got the machine.

"Hello?"

Sophia's stomach churned. "Hi, is this Leah?"

"Yes."

"This is Sophia. We met at—"

"Did the Shekinah contact you?"

Sophia traced the seam of her blue jeans. Her restless fingertips glided across her leg. "Look. I don't know what happened, but I did say something. Probably while having a seizure. I happened to have a recorder on so it picked up what I said."

"And what did you say?"

"I don't know if you want to hear this."

"Sophia, I've been through so much lately that nothing you say could cause me any more grief. I am at my lowest right now. Please tell me."

Sophia sighed. "I or the Shekinah or whatever it was said, 'Only her death can save her.' "

There was no response.

"Leah?"

"What do you think it means?" Her voice was quiet.

"I don't know, exactly. But if it does have anything to do with your sister, then I think the message is that it's your sister's time to pass on."

Sophia tried reframing the message, using religious words Leah would connect with. "Maybe the only way for peace to take place, hers and yours, is if you let life take its course and accept her going back to God."

Leah said nothing, but Sophia thought she heard her crying.

"Leah?"

"You're right," she sniffled. "Or She's right. I have been holding on too much. Yochevet is in such pain, and I've only been telling her not to give up. To hold on. And maybe," Leah exhaled a deep breath. "Maybe I haven't been making it better for her. I've only been making it w—"

Sophia heard sobs from the other end of the line. Her throat closed, and Sophia wiped the tears that fell down her own face.

Chapter 16

I sat drinking instant coffee with the rabbi in Samuel's kitchen, out of view from the street windows so we couldn't be seen. The kitchen tiles were the size of old 3.5-inch floppy disks. They had an impressionist sprinkling of fruits. Grapes, bananas, peaches, limes. I examined the backdoor, visible from my vantage point. It had a deadbolt, and a chain lock. I asked Samuel to secure the bolt and the chain. Neither could stop a guy who knew how to open locks, but they slowed an intruder down long enough for the people inside to notice and escape. Hard to enter from the outside, easy to unlock from the inside.

I tasted the coffee. It was horrible. Like sucking on old gym socks.

The rabbi told me what happened the night of the break-in two months ago.

"What happened to the gun?" I asked.

"When the coast was clear, I returned to the house to get Seth's blanket, our medicines, toothbrushes, and other toiletries. The gun had disappeared. Someone must have picked it up."

I nodded. "Probably the attacker. No way a guy like that would leave without his gun. What did he look like?"

"Let's see." The rabbi stroked his beard. "He had a very nice haircut. Dark hair."

"Age?"

"He looked to be in his twenties or thirties."

"Was he left- or right-handed?"

"He was right-handed. I know because he held his gun in his right hand."

"Okay. Anything else? Distinguishing marks?"

The rabbi rubbed his forehead. "He had a beard, but most men I know have beards."

"It's a start." I waited for more, but the rabbi looked like he was trying to solve a set of complex differential equations. Time to move on. "Tell me more about this list he stole."

"Nathan, I've told you before how I'm one of the few Jews who believe in the *lamed-vav tzadikim*, the thirty-six righteous."

"Yeah. You mentioned that legend when Sophia and I first met you about a year ago. As long as the beating hearts of thirty-six good people exist, God will spare the world from complete destruction. If one righteous man dies by natural causes, another takes his place. Kind of like vampire slayers."

"What?"

"*Buffy the Vampire Slayer*. A TV show about vampires that…. Never mind."

"Buffy?"

"Anyhow, you said that if the thirty-six are killed, the world would be destroyed."

"Exactly. But there is something I must tell you. You see, Nathan, in the late 1100s, when King Amalric besieged the Egyptian town of Bilbays, many Jews were taken captive. The astronomer and physician, Rabbi Maimonides, also known as the Rambam, believed that the righteous ones were among King Amalric's captives. The Rambam feared that should the Jewish captives be slaughtered, King Amalric might inadvertently destroy all civilization. The Rambam took steps to negotiate the release of the captives, and with a ransom, he succeeded in convincing the Crusaders to free them."

"How does this relate to what's happening now?"

"I'm getting to that. After the narrow escape of the Jewish captives, the Rambam remained haunted by the possibility of someone killing the lamed-vav tzadikim. He took it upon himself to assign one of his students the task of finding the righteous ones and monitoring their safety. Should they be in trouble, the student was to notify the Rambam immediately, and he would coordinate some plan to save the vulnerable righteous. That student sought out the ones who seemed to directly experience the Shekinah, the Divine Presence. He found the very people he believed were the lamed-vav tzadikim and monitored their safety from afar. Years passed, and when he realized he could not forever watch them, he entrusted his son with the task. He wrote down the names of the thirty-six righteous and gave the list to his son."

I saw where this was going.

"Over the generations, there have been new righteous ones, and over the generations, there have been new observers keeping a careful eye on them. The list became pages of lists and were assembled into a book."

"You're the current observer."

"Yes, Nathan. That book was entrusted to me by my grandfather. I kept it protected by locking it away in a hidden part of my desk."

"But Sophia? She couldn't be one of the thirty-six righteous men. She's a woman."

"No, Nathan." The rabbi waved a finger. "The thirty-six righteous can be either gender. Male or female. I'm worried that whoever stole that list is thinking of killing all thirty-six."

"Can you think why anyone would do that?"

"That's the thing. I can't think of a single reason. All it does is bring world destruction."

Something about that sounded familiar.

"Rabbi, there's something you need to know."

"What is it?"

"The first thirty-two on that list of yours are dead."

The rabbi said nothing. His lip trembled and his eyes looked vacant.

"They all died within the last two months."

His hands curled into fists. "Then there's no time to lose. We must warn the others."

"Hold on a second. I don't think anyone would believe us. And for reasons I don't want to go into, I'm trying to avoid contact with Sophia. So who's number thirty-three, a Yoseph somebody, right?"

The rabbi asked Samuel for the white pages. After Samuel placed the hefty telephone book on the kitchen table, the rabbi licked his fingers and flipped through the pages.

"Here he is. Yoseph Schwartz." He read me the address. "Is that far?"

"Not at all. You can walk it. It's two blocks south of this street."

"Okay. I'll go find Yoseph. Call me if you need anything." I gave him the number to my cell phone. "Don't go back outside until this is over. If they want you dead, they won't rest until they succeed."

The rabbi gulped.

I was being harsh, but he needed to be scared. Acting over-cautious could save his life.

Chapter 17

Idashed with my duffel bag to Yoseph's neighborhood where the foliage grew so thick it was hard to see the houses. Yoseph's house turned out to be more of a cottage than a house. The front presented a well-tended garden of tall plants. I crossed the cobblestone path to the door and buzzed the doorbell. A woman answered, wearing a shawl over her hair. The shawl didn't do much to hide her tresses. She seemed too young for the streaks of gray in her brown locks.

"Is Yoseph in?"

She glanced at my duffel bag. "Are you a friend of his?"

"Friend of a friend. I just need to see him."

"He's not here. He went on his weekly night out to Yael's Kosher Diner."

I scrambled through my knowledge of the area trying to come up with the locations of nearby kosher restaurants. Couldn't think of any. Didn't keep a mental database of kosher places to eat.

The woman twisted the fringe of her shawl. "He likes to have some alone time. I guess that means some alone time away from me." A quivering smile troubled her face. "I suppose I should talk to him about it, and I will sometime soon. I'm sure it has nothing to do with me, but it's good to know for sure, right?"

Did I have a sign on my forehead that said therapist? "Where is the diner?"

"Yael's? Just straight down Shattuck Avenue, one block past the park."

I thanked her and scurried away, cutting off any opportunity for her to tell me more about her relationship concerns.

Ira Hughes turned off the engine. The target he had been tailing, number thirty-three, had entered a diner, but the crowded diner offered too many witnesses. Ira had to wait for the target to leave. The waiting was the hardest part.

Somewhere inside that diner, the target unknowingly ate his last meal. Ira removed the .22 caliber revolver from his holster and slid a round into each chamber. He preferred his Glock over the revolver, but mixing up the weapons helped keep the homicides look unrelated.

He had waited in front of the target's house and had wanted to complete the job while the target was away from his wife. No longer necessary to make the targets on the list look like victims of heart attacks, Ira still had to be cautious. He could use his firearm, but he had to be sure he wouldn't be spotted. After all, his superior, Richard, probably hadn't appreciated the way he handled target number thirty-two. Target thirty-three had walked from a small house to the busy diner, a place where passersby could spot Ira if he tried firing through the diner window, so it was best to wait this one out.

With his firearm fully loaded, he pushed the cylinder into the frame. A colleague in training used to flip the cylinder shut as if he were a cowboy in the movies. It didn't take long before he had his ass chewed out for mishandling the revolver. Flip the cylinder closed enough times and you could bend some parts jamming the weapon or making the cylinder too loose to function. Ira listened to the radio. Several of his favorite Christian rock songs kept him company.

Where was the target? It had been an hour and a half. Was he reading?

Ira put on sunglasses and his Oakland Athletics baseball cap, got out of his car, and did a casual walk-by along the deli windows. With subtle glances, he scoped the customers sitting at the red booths.

Didn't see the target.

Ira walked into the diner, stopped a waitress, and flashed a photo of his target. "Do you happen to know this man? Yoseph Schwartz?"

"Sure. Great tipper. But he's always going on and on about how great his wife is."

"Where is he?"

"I just finished cleaning off his table. He went out the back. Said something about a shortcut home."

Damn!

His phone rang. He recognized the number. "Richard, how are you?"

"What the hell was that?" Richard sounded angry.

Ira lowered his voice so the nearby customers and employees couldn't hear his conversation. "What was what?"

"You stabbed number thirty-two in a crowded subway?"

"Believe me. I carefully assessed the situation and the risk. With my ball cap and sunglasses on during the hit, no one could recognize me."

"I told you, I want to avoid police involvement for as long as possible."

"There are just a few targets left. Don't worry, Richard. I've got this."

"You'd better."

Ira ran out the back door and saw a glimpse of the target in his black coat turn the corner.

Inside Yael's Kosher Diner, I asked a waitress if she'd seen Yoseph.

"Like I told the other guy, he went out the back."

"What other guy?"

"Guy with a beard. Asked the same thing you just did."

Damn. "Which way did he go?"

"He went out the back, I assume to catch up with Yoseph."

Chapter 18

Ira followed the target through the back parking lot to the edge of a park and thought it the best place.

"Yoseph!"

The target stopped and turned.

Ira put on a smile and gave Yoseph a wave as he trodded along the grass to catch up with him. The target had a confused expression, but matched Ira's smile all the same, as though he were happy to see a stranger.

When Ira caught up to him, he cheerfully brought out his revolver and pressed it against the belly of the target. "Why don't we move into the park?"

The target still grinned, probably thinking this was a joke because of how Ira spoke to him.

"Is that real?"

Ira dropped his smile and hissed, "Shut up and get in the park."

The target complied with a pale face and put his hands in the air.

"Keep your hands down. Just walk like we're taking a pleasant stroll." Ira turned him around, and pushed him forward keeping the short barrel to the man's back. Soon they arrived at a secluded location. "Stop here."

"What do you want?" The target remained facing away and stood stiff.

"The Rapture. I am sorry, but this must be done." He pointed his gun to the head and fired into the temple of the target. The man's head snapped to the side, and the target collapsed.

Objective accomplished.

Chapter 19

I exited the back of the diner. No sign of anyone. I jogged down the most reasonable path Yoseph would take. The path of least resistance to Yoseph's house. Kept looking down remote locations, the park and alleyways.

Some feet stuck out from behind a trash bin in the park. Not a great place for someone to rest. And the shoes were too nice to belong to a homeless person.

I ran closer and in the darkness of the night saw the hat and curly locks of an Orthodox Jew lying on his side. Probably Yoseph. Didn't see any blood. I dropped my duffel bag and got on my hands and knees on the wet grass. I felt for a pulse on his neck. Nothing.

Dammit.

Rolling him over on his back revealed a small gunshot wound on the side of his forehead.

I searched the area for clues. Some of the grass near him shined wet. Probably blood. A quick examination of my hands showed I had touched it. I wiped my hands on the grass to get the blood off me. Taking out my cell phone, I dialed one of the emergency numbers in my call list.

A lady answered the phone. "Berkeley Police Department."

"I need to report a shooting at Live Oak Park." I gave a specific description of the location.

"Who did the shooting?"

"I don't know."

"Who was shot?"

"Yoseph Schwartz." I ran a hand through my hair.

"Is he breathing?"

"He's dead."

"And your name?"

I hung up. I needed time to stop these murders. Being called in for questioning would be damn inconvenient.

Chapter 20

After the sun sank behind the Berkeley hills, Detective Bobbie Graff arrived at Live Oak Park off of Shattuck Avenue. The siren lights colored the trees in red and blue light. The DO NOT CROSS yellow and black tape encircled the crime scene, and the forensic scientists stooped over to canvass the area for clues.

Detective Jimmy Belmont greeted Detective Graff at the scene. "So much for your theory of Berkeley Homicide being quieter than Oakland. You still glad you transferred?"

"Quit shooting your wad. What do you got, Belmont?"

He shook his head and got down to business. "We've got a mugging. Guy shot in the head. Looks to be shot by a .22 or other small-caliber bullet. There's an entry point, but no exit wound. The bullet probably bounced around inside the vic's skull until his brains were scrambled."

"Let me see him."

Belmont took her to the vic and nodded to the coroner to uncover the body.

Graff grimaced at the victim's curly locks and yarmulke. An ultra-religious Jew. "Either the perp is very clumsy or a professional. This wasn't a mugging."

"What do you mean?"

"You didn't find the wallet?"

"Right," Belmont said.

"So what happened here? This religious man, respectful of avoiding violence at all costs, tried to fight an armed mugger, so the mugger shot him? I don't think so. Anybody in their right mind confronted with a gun is going to give up their wallet and thank their lucky stars they weren't hurt. Unless this vic turns out to be a gung-ho risk-taking Jedi knight who roams around undercover as an Orthodox Jew, my guess is the perp shot him for who he was, not for his wallet. I'd bet my bones this homicide was pre-meditated."

One of the forensic scientists stood from his crouching position and snapped off his blue gloves. "Detectives."

"Yes?" Graff hoped for some good news.

He wiped his forehead with the back of his hand. "We've got fingerprints."

Got him.

Chapter 21

I **headed** **down** **Shattuck** **Avenue** **toward** downtown Berkeley, called the rabbi, and broke the news to him. He gasped and choked on a sob. I couldn't imagine what he was going through. He had made a list of people he thought were the legendary thirty-six righteous, the people whose very existence supposedly was enough to convince God to spare the Earth. Now that very book with the list had been stolen, and the list had become a hit list. If the rabbi never wrote down those names, they'd still be alive.

The rabbi must think their deaths are his fault. Truth is, they are. And Sophia's life is in jeopardy because of him.

I kept my anger in check. Number thirty-three was Cole Montgomery. I asked the rabbi for Montgomery's address. The way the rabbi responded so fast, he must have known the address by heart.

"One thing I don't get, Rabbi. Why do you think all the thirty-six righteous are in one area? Wouldn't it make sense to have them spread out all over the world?"

"How would you hide your jewels? Would you spread them out all over your house or keep them hidden in one safe location?"

"That's different. The Bay Area isn't exactly a hidden location."

"Three of my children enjoy playing those hidden object games. You know how they look for the objects? They scan the entire picture, and when they find one object, they move to a different part of the picture. Do you know why?"

"Because they think the rest of the objects are hidden elsewhere. I get your drift. While the objects seem to be at random places in the picture, the truth is they're pretty evenly distributed. It's not random at all."

"Exactly."

I said, "So if the killer happened to find one of the thirty-six righteous in the Bay Area, he'd probably move on to another area and search the rest of the world for the other thirty-five."

"Exactly."

"It's only because of your list that the killer knows all the righteous live here."

The rabbi didn't say anything. It was cruel of me to say, but I had to speak the truth.

"Bye, Rabbi." I hung up the phone before waiting for an answer.

I headed toward the Downtown Berkeley Bay Area Rapid Transit station. I felt dizzy. The sidewalk curbs undulated.

Not good.

I hadn't slept since the flight, and the lack of sleep could bring on an episode. Having bipolar disorder brought on all sorts of unique experiences, but there was never a suitable time to have a hallucination. I could go straight to Mr. Montgomery and make sure he was okay, but I wouldn't be much use to him if I had a paranoid delusion and believed him to be the assassin.

If I got a night's sleep, I'd be more effective at helping out. Truth was, none of the murders had happened within a twenty-four hour period of each other. As much as I hated to admit it and run the risk of losing another on the list, I had to accept that everyone would be better off if I grabbed some shut-eye.

I found a slummy motel off Shattuck on University Avenue, about ten blocks from the park. The old man at the counter looked me up and down. Probably saw the blood on my pants from where I bent down to check Yoseph's pulse.

He grimaced. "You gonna be any trouble?"

I scanned him from his straw fedora to his flying eagle belt buckle. "Are *you*?"

He licked his teeth as though they needed moistening. "Two hundred per night."

"The sign says ninety."

"Two hundred. Take it or leave it."

I shrugged. Got out two hundred dollars from my wallet, and slapped it on the counter. A few streaks of blood showed on the bills. My hands were still dirty with Yoseph's blood.

"Got someplace to clean up?"

He put the room key on the counter. "Do it in the room."

I took the key and brought my duffel bag upstairs to 207, the room number noted on the leather tag attached to the key.

Once inside, I flung my bag on the bed and turned on the bathroom sink's cold water. The pipes screamed as I scrubbed the blood from my hands. Twisted the water off, and the pipes stopped their moaning. My fingers were stained pink. I wondered if the blood or my memory of Yoseph would ever wash away.

I flopped onto the bed. The springs squeaked. On my phone, I checked Sophia's social media status.

It read, "Why is it that what your friend needs to hear most is often what they don't want to hear?"

Updated twenty-seven minutes ago. She was alive. And would stay that way as long as Mr. Montgomery stayed alive, too. In the morning, I'd make sure he wasn't the next fatality on the list.

I stared at the ceiling. For a moment, just a brief moment, I swore I could feel Sophia's arms around me. The moment vanished, and I sunk into the sand of sleep.

Chapter 22

In the early morning, I paid for another night's stay and left my duffel bag in the room. Bay Area Rapid Transit always impressed me with how fast I could get from one place to another. The BART train took under fifteen minutes to go from downtown Berkeley to the Rockridge station with a quick transfer at MacArthur station. Mr. Montgomery's house was a pretty nice two-story outfit in the Rockridge area, right near the train station. I climbed the front flight of stairs and rang the doorbell.

A young woman with long, light brown hair parted directly down the middle answered the door. She looked as fake as a model in a magazine.

"Hi. Mrs. Montgomery?"

"Yes?" She had a stunning smile.

I noticed her necklace had a crucifix. A mixed marriage, perhaps? "Uh…May I speak with your husband?"

"Certainly." She turned to the living room. "Hon? A gentleman's here to see you." She faced me. "Is there anything I can get you?"

That was an odd offer. Usually people only asked that to familiar guests. Not strangers at their doorstep. "No, thank you."

A middle-aged gentleman appeared wearing a white sweater and cleft chin. The kind of chin a guy wears just to show off how handsome he is and to make you feel ordinary.

He whispered to his wife, "Thanks, Sweetie," and gave her a kiss.

There was nowhere to throw up.

Cole Montgomery gave me a smile as if proud of me. "What can I do for you, sir?"

"My name's Nathan Yirmorshy. Rabbi Silverman sent me."

The man scowled and seemed to be waiting for me to explain further.

"You know Rabbi Silverman, right?"

"Actually, no. We're Catholic, so we don't know many rabbis." He called out into the house, "Sweetie? Do you know a Rabbi Silverman?"

I could hear a "No" from the kitchen.

He put his fingertips together as if praying. "I'm sorry."

I stepped backwards and checked the numbers beside the door. Right address. The man I thought was Cole looked amused at how I checked the address.

I scratched my head. "You are Mr. Montgomery, right?"

"Yes."

"Cole Montgomery?"

"Oh. Cole is our son." His eyes widened. "Wait a second. Did you say Rabbi Silverman?"

"Yes."

"Did he say our son was one of the world's righteous?"

"Yes."

"You'd better come inside."

Chapter 23

We sat in Montgomery's living room, the early morning sunlight piercing through the windows. The wife had served me fresh brewed coffee. Black. The way I liked it.

They introduced themselves as Brad and Heidi. Their saccharine smiles made them look like they were the all-too-perfect parents from a Disney movie. I sat in a comfortable lazy chair as the parents sat together on the couch.

Heidi took Brad's hand. "We adopted Cole from an agency when he was two years old. When we learned he came from a Jewish home, we raised him Jewish. We sent him to Jewish Sunday school, had him join a Jewish youth group, and sent him to Jewish summer camp."

They brought him up to be Jewish? "I don't understand. Don't you want to raise him Catholic? No disrespect, but as I understand it, according to Catholic beliefs, he would go to Hell for not being Catholic."

Brad nodded. "We believe Heaven has a place for everyone." He paused as if trying to work out how to phrase his next words. "When Cole was eight years old, he became very depressed."

Heidi leaned into Brad, gazing at the floor looking lost in her memories.

Brad continued, "He wouldn't tell us what bothered him, and we feared he might cut off all communication with us. We knew he needed Christ in his life to find joy again, but we also knew that the best way to lead him to Catholicism was to embody the love of Christ. We made sure we were always there for him, supporting him and loving him through whatever pain he struggled with. We also knew that he would only come to us after fully connecting with his heritage."

Heidi nodded.

Brad glanced at Heidi and said, "It's true that we want Cole to embrace the Catholic faith, but we felt he needed to fully experience his Jewish roots before considering Catholicism. We knew that no matter how he grew up, there would come a time in his life that he would want to learn about his heritage, and we wanted to respect that. Better that he get the full experience of his Jewish heritage rather than feel we removed him from it."

I froze, then took a sip of the coffee.

Heidi squinted at me. "Is something the matter?"

"No, it's just that I don't think I've ever met anyone as amazing as you two."

They smiled and shared a loving glance.

"Now about that rabbi you're talking about." Brad shifted on the couch. "One time I received a call from a rabbi, he said he knew Cole from synagogue and wanted us to know that Cole was one of these thirty-two or thirty-six righteous. It sounded very…"

"Unbelievable," Heidi chimed in.

"Right. We didn't tell Cole about the call because he can be pretty sensitive to things that are outlandish."

"So you don't believe he's one of the thirty-six righteous?"

Heidi laughed. "He's a great son, and I love him dearly. We both do. But I don't know that he's one of the best in the world."

I swallowed the last of the delicious coffee. "I understand. And the truth is, I don't believe it either. I think the rabbi got so caught up in his own beliefs that he acted on them."

Brad nodded.

"However…" I tried to work out a way to say this without upsetting them. Did they really need to know their son was in danger? Would they even believe me? I could show how most of the people on the list of thirty-six righteous died, but heart attack was hardly a cause for concern. *Who knows? They might even call the cops on me. Telling them could just complicate things further.* "I think there's someone out there who believes the rabbi is right. And because of that, I just want to be sure that Cole isn't… harassed by this other person."

"Who is this person?"

"I don't know, yet."

Heidi looked at her watch. "Hon, you need to finish getting ready for work." She stood and picked up my empty coffee cup. "Nathan, was it? If you want to talk to Cole, you can find him at the MacArthur BART station. He likes to skateboard there."

Skateboard? How old was this kid?

Chapter 24

Detective Bobbie Graff ran a hunch. She checked her computer database for all California homicides within the last few weeks and pulled up the names and faces of the vics. Names and profile images plastered her screen. What she sought out made it easy to eliminate the irrelevant. Easy, but not fast. Applying the process of elimination would eat up her time.

She looked at the profile images of each victim. The ones with the black hats, beards, and curly locks of hair hanging by their ears caught her eye. After two hours and forty minutes, she narrowed her list of vics to three.

All religious. All Jewish.

I hiked to the MacArthur BART station and wandered up to the entrance that sat below a freeway. The sun split the freeway as though it wedged a spike through the interstate and sprayed a stripe of light across the middle of the station entrance. Reminded me of the sheet metal I had used back in Ghana to board up my windows, the sun making its way through the narrow slit. At the BART station, boxes of grass made an attempt to adorn the entrance, as did a statue that didn't resemble anything at all.

MacArthur BART station didn't have my vote for the ugliest station around, but it had a stale essence of urine about it that kept it in the running.

There were skateboarders. Three of them. All of them in their early teens. I guess you didn't have to be an adult to be one of the righteous.

Having met the parents, I spotted their son without any trouble. The only one with sandy-colored hair and a cleft chin.

The kid with sandy hair called out, "Hey, Cole!"

"Yeah?" A kid with spiked black hair, eyeliner, and a leather jacket skidded his skateboard to a halt. Oh, yeah. Cole was adopted.

"Watch this." Sandy Hair jumped up, his skateboard flipped full circle, and he landed back on the skateboard as if he'd been riding it the whole time.

"Cool," said the kid named Cole who didn't look anything like his parents.

A street beggar in a ragged overcoat said something to a middle-aged man in a brown business suit who had just exited the BART station. Probably asked for spare change.

Brown Suit's veins popped at his neck. "Get out of my face, piss-breath!"

Everyone turned to see the shouter.

Cole rode his skateboard toward Brown Suit and "accidentally" knocked him over.

"Sorry, man." Cole offered a hand.

Brown Suit glared at him from the ground. "What the hell? Why don't you look where you're going, ass-wipe?"

"I'm sorry. Let me help you up." Cole brushed the suit off in a manner that looked more like a spanking than a cleaning. Did Cole just pickpocket the guy?

The businessman shoved Cole away. "Leave me alone."

"Okay, okay." Cole raised a hand up in surrender.

This was one of the righteous?

As Cole rode his skateboard away from the suit, he sneaked the bills from the wallet and, while passing the beggar, slipped the bills into the beggar's pocket without the beggar noticing. Cole squatted on his skateboard and placed the wallet on the ground.

The businessman patted his pockets. "My wallet. Stop that kid! He stole my wallet!"

Brown Suit ran after Cole, and Cole took off on his skateboard leaving his friends laughing and giving each other a high-five.

Terrific. I gotta babysit a kid who thinks he's Robin Hood.

Chapter 25

Richard sat in his office, going over the papers for a project that only he and two others were allowed eyes on.

His cell phone sounded out a single ping.

"Yeah?"

"It's done," the voice said. Richard recognized the voice immediately. "Ira took care of number thirty-three. Only three left to go."

Richard tapped his desk. "Jonah, I still don't like the idea of one of our own processing the objectives."

"Why not? He was the perfect choice, especially since he already lived in the area. There are only three left on the list. It doesn't really matter now if the crimes start to be recognized as murders with the same profile."

"He's sloppy. He's not properly trained in handling assigned terminations. He even broke a billion-dollar weapon designed to make the victim appear to have had a cardiac arrest. Anyone from the Green Berets would be better than Ira."

"The one Green Beret we had has completely removed himself from the Order ever since Project MEG."

Richard rolled his eyes. "Don't get me started on Project MEG."

"What do you mean?"

"It was a waste of time, money, and resources. The process took generations. Project 36 can at least be completed in a matter of months—"

"Or in this case, with only three left to go, a matter of days."

"Right," Richard said.

"So what's the problem?"

"Like I said, he's getting sloppy."

"He can afford to be sloppy," Jonah said. "He's got thirty-three down without raising any suspicion. The police don't suspect a thing."

Richard shook his head. "Not true. A detective investigating number thirty-three has pulled the files for three of our previous targets. Probably working up a profile on Ira as we speak."

"What? What's the name of this detective? I'll take care of it."

"Don't. The last thing we need is an entire police department investigating the death of one of their own."

"Fine. Let me know if he ever becomes a problem."

"She. She's a woman."

"Okay. Then it should be easy to stop her if we ever need to. What's her name?"

"Detective Bobbie Graff."

Chapter 26

Sophia returned home from giving tarot readings near the UC Berkeley campus. She sidestepped through her front door, steering the portable table through the doorway. With a hip sway, she bumped the door closed. After leaning the folded table against the wall, she shrugged her backpack purse loose from her aching shoulders and onto the bed. It felt good to kick off her shoes. The summer day turned out to be a hot one. She ran a washcloth under cold water, lay back on the bed, and draped the cold rag over her face. Sweet sleep began weaving its web inside her consciousness.

Her cell phone rang.

Keeping the soothing cloth on her face, she answered the phone. It was Leah.

"I just wanted to let you know, my sister passed about an hour ago."

"Oh, I'm so sorry to hear that." Sophia sat up on her bed, letting the wet towel fall to her lap. "How are you feeling?"

"That's why I called. To let you know that I'm at peace with it. After I spoke to you, I went to the hospital. I told Yochevet what you said and that she didn't have to worry about me. I would be fine." Leah took an audible breath. "When she heard me say that, she smiled. It was the first smile I've seen from her in months."

Sophia listened carefully.

"Fifteen minutes later she passed."

After those words, Leah said nothing. Sophia joined her silence, being with her but without talking, the way good friends just want to be connected to each other. Maybe some good did come from these strange visitations she had.

"What pleases me most," Leah continued, "is that I saw peace in her face, too. So thank you."

"You're welcome, Leah. I'm so glad to hear that you feel at peace."

Chapter 27

Isuspected Cole planned to lay low after having stolen the businessman's wallet. Finding Cole would be tricky. But if finding him was problematic for me, it would also be problematic for the killer. Cole might have been on his way home. I could either run around searching for him, or I could let a few hours pass and meet up with him at his house. By the grumbling of my stomach, spending the next hour eating lunch won first place for Best Idea of the Moment.

At a nearby sandwich shop, I was enjoying my pastrami sandwich when a customer hobbling with a cane asked if he could join me. Didn't know what his angle was. Empty tables surrounded us. Still, it could be amusing. I pointed to the empty chair.

"Thanks." He set down his cane and scratched his clean-shaven chin. "You work around here?" He took a bite of his tuna sandwich.

"Nope. Just visiting. Why, do you work around here?" I sipped my lemonade.

The man shrugged. "You're from out of town?"

"You could say that."

"Visiting a friend? Family?"

"I do have a good friend here, but I'm not visiting her. What's your excuse?"

The man smiled to himself like he just thought of an old joke. "If you're not here visiting friends or family, what are you doing here?"

I put down my sandwich. "I don't get it."

"What do you mean?"

"I'm answering all your questions, and you seem to be avoiding mine. Who are you?"

The man snorted and shook his head. He wiped off the mustard from his mouth with a napkin, stood up, leaned over the table and put his face directly in mine.

"You listen and you listen very carefully, Mr. Yirmorshy." The man spoke with an angry whisper. "If you want to stay alive, you stay away from Sophia Patai."

At the mention of Sophia's name, I froze. I needed to get him to talk. Find out more about him. Best if I didn't look scared. Keeping my eyes glued to him, I chewed the last of my sandwich and washed it down with lemonade.

I placed my cup on the table. "Who are you? A jealous boyfriend? Cause if you are, don't waste your energy. I'm breaking up with her." I pointed to his sandwich. "You gonna finish that?" Before he could respond, I picked it up and had a bite. Tuna fish. Not bad.

"Breaking up with her? Smart decision. Now go back to where you were this morning and catch a flight back to Ghana."

I picked up his bag of chips. He knew I lived in Ghana and came from the airport this morning. Pretty neat trick. I ate one of the chips. BBQ-flavored.

I cringed and threw the bag of chips back on his tray. "How did you know where I was this morning?"

He staggered over to where I sat, yanked me out of my seat with a strength I didn't expect him to have, and pushed me face-first up against the wall, twisting my arm behind my back. He thrust my arm upwards as though trying to twist a wing off a fly. His maneuver drilled pain at my shoulder's joint, and I winced.

"You still don't get it, do you, Mr. Yirmorshy? I know where you are at all times. There's nowhere you can hide. And if I find that you're even in the same zip code as Sophia Patai, I will personally place a bullet between your eyes."

He forced my hand to make a fist around something. Felt like a wooden handle of a tool.

"What are you doing?" I asked.

"Insurance."

I heard the rustling of plastic. He pushed my arm back further and I bit my lip to fight against the scream trying to escape me. Didn't want to give him the satisfaction.

I took a deep breath. "I could have the police on you in a second. What you're doing is against the law."

"Who do you think I represent? I am the law." He released his grip and the pain fled from me. "You enjoy your sandwich, now." He picked up his cane and hobbled out of the store.

The young employees stared slack-jawed. Were they just standing there watching the entire time?

"Thanks for all your help." I flung the remains of the tuna sandwich at them and stomped out the door.

Eric Redding hiked away with his cane at a steady pace. Having completed the assignment, he couldn't ignore how different this job had been compared to his other assignments. Usually, his superior officer gave him tasks involving explosives. But getting an order to scare a citizen out of the area, and obtain the man's prints? Very odd.

He shrugged it off and returned to his car. Inside, he shoved the ice pick wrapped in plastic into the glove compartment.

Chapter 28

Graff's office phone rang. "Detective Graff."
It was the lab. "You requested the results of the fingerprints found on the body of Mr. Yoseph Schwartz."

"Yes, did you find out whose prints they were?"

"Sure did. We were able to ID the prints in CODIS."

"Good news." Graff picked up her pen. "What's the name?"

"One Nathan Yirmorshy."

"Yirmorshy?" She dropped her pen. "That's impossible. He's in some godforsaken country in Africa."

"Could it be a computer error? Maybe the prints belong to someone else."

"Or Yirmorshy is back in town." She couldn't believe her bad luck. Back when she first met Yirmorshy, he was the victim of some serious whack jobs. He was not a killer. If the prints did belong to him, it wouldn't be the first time she'd have to bail him out of trouble. "Thanks. I'll look into it."

She slammed down the receiver.

***

I stormed down San Pablo Avenue with its bargain-baiting store fronts, its chain-link gated parking lots, and its asphalt-piercing weeds. *There's nothing I hate more than being bullied.* I clenched my fists, ready to punch the first person who talked to me. Took a deep breath. Noticed the time. A half-hour left before Cole might be back at his place.

I stopped at a dimly lit bar. Rock music fought against the sounds of clinking glass and chatter. When my eyes adjusted to the darkness, I saw how much of a walk-in closet the place was. With a wall on the right and the bar on the left, I walked forward. The place had just a few patrons. Made sense for the lunch hour on a weekday. Odd artifacts hung on the wall, labeled with a short description of their origin. Artifacts like a voodoo doll and a porcupine's penis. I went deep into the belly of the bar and sat down.

Ordered a Heinekin. I burned at the memory of that handicapped stranger pressing my face against the wall. He wanted me to stay away from Sophia? I had planned all along to stay away. I didn't want to stir up old feelings with her. She deserved someone better than me. With my bipolar disorder, I was broken. I'd just be a burden for her.

Dammit! Staying away from Sophia felt like I was giving in to the bully's demands. It made me want to see her just to spite him. But I had to treat this whole thing logically because I risked more than a relationship. The stranger knew where I had spent my morning. He said he was the law. If he was telling the truth, it would make sense that he knew about my flight. Police have access to such information. The murders of the righteous weren't just a whim carried out by a serial killer. This attack had organization, with powerful people in charge.

The bartender placed the beer in front of me. I took a sip. The cold taste was a welcome friend. Hadn't had a beer this good in months. Took another sip and felt my whole body relax.

Seeing Sophia again would do more than cause trouble with her emotions. If they had eyes on me twenty-four seven, visiting her could threaten her life. Whichever way I cut it, I had to avoid meeting up with Sophia.

I listened to the song playing on the radio. The power of the words hit home.

Remember the first time we met?
You were the first day of my life.
Ever since then, I thank the heavens
For revealing you, my bride, my wife.
Remember the first time we kissed?
That was the kiss that awakened me.
Like a fairy tale, my love was so frail
Until you shared your love with me.
Why is there a distance
Keeping us apart?
Why is it I miss you
Deep inside my heart?
We've so much love to take,
And so much love to send.
I want to kiss you for the first time,
For the first time, again.

An interlude began with a crying guitar. The song pierced my heart with its every note. I tried finding solace in the beer. The singer sang more, the words twisting the knife in my chest.

Remember the day we wed?
That is the day I cherish.
All that we do, for me and for you
Could never perish.
Why is there a distance
Keeping us apart?
Why is it I miss you
Inside my heart?
We've got so much love to take,
And so much love to send.
I want to kiss you for the first time,
For the first time, again.

I slapped money on the wet counter and left the bar. It was too much to bear. Still too early to go to Cole's house, I considered heading toward Samuel's place to check in on the rabbi. But with eyes on me all the time? Visiting the rabbi could reveal his location and put him in jeopardy.

There was only one thing left to do.

Chapter 29

I plodded down the sidewalk of slimy businesses, passing 99-cent stores, liquor stores, bail bonds stops, and tire shops. Many of them kept their security gates half-closed as if expecting a riot to happen at any moment. I steered myself into an electronics store.

Before anything else, I needed to drop off the grid.

Inside the store, I asked the clerk who had all the expensive electronic gadgets behind her, "How do I activate those prepaid phones?"

She pointed to a few phones behind her. "These can be activated online." She gestured to other phones along the back wall. "Those are preregistered. Once you get one of those, you activate it by just turning it on. Then you're all set."

I checked the price. "I'll get three. And I'll take that Swiss army knife."

She took my cash and as soon as I left the store, I opened all the boxes, threw out the plastic, and said a prayer of apologies to the landfill gods. Keeping the phones off, I slipped them and the army knife into my pocket. I took out my cell phone, turned it off, and removed its battery. Slipped the pieces in my coat. No credit card use, no personal cell phone use, no contact with known associates. I was off the grid.

Detective Graff had to confirm that Yirmorshy was in the country. She found the fifteen-digit phone number to Yirmorshy's office on his company's website, punched it in, and got an answering machine.

Damn! Of course they were closed. Ghana existed on the other side of the globe.

She left a message to have Yirmorshy call as soon as possible.

The next step involved calling CBP.

A lady with a syrupy voice answered. "Customs and Border Protection. How may I help you?"

Graff introduced herself as a detective for the Berkeley Police Department and gave her badge ID. "I'm calling to see if a Nathan Yirmorshy was on a recent flight from Accra."

"I can check that for you. Please hold."

Graff waited to the sound of silence. Thankfully, she didn't have to listen to elevator music or an advertisement while on hold.

The lady came back on the line. "Yes, he was on the connecting flight from New York with Delta Airlines, flight 430, and arrived this morning at 9:06 a.m."

"Thank you."

Either Yirmorshy had nothing to do with the vics killed over the past month and was only responsible for last night's homicide at Live Oak Park, or—more likely—the deaths of the previous vics alerted him to try and prevent the Live Oak Park homicide, but he arrived too late. How did he know who the next vic would be? And what role did he play in all this?

Time to locate him.

Chapter 30

I returned to Rabbi Silverman's hideout and Samuel welcomed me into his home. He brought me to an upstairs bedroom. The rabbi's wife stood by a dresser folding her children's clothes. The rabbi sat on the bed and looked ragged, his eyes red from wear.

"Rabbi, about what I said over the phone."

"No, Nathan. You're right. If I hadn't written down the names of the righteous, or if I kept the book under better protection, then none of this would have happened. I'm responsible for their deaths."

"Rabbi, I need you to focus right now and help me save the remaining people on that list."

His gaze fell to the floor. "The Talmud teaches us that whosoever destroys a soul, it is as if he has destroyed an entire world."

I clenched my fists. I didn't have time for this.

His wife took his hand. "The Talmud also says that whosoever saves a life, it is as if he saved an entire world."

She caressed his face as he looked up to her. "Listen to Nathan. Help him save those lives."

He sighed and finally nodded. "What can I do to help, Nathan?

"I need to see your phone."

"Why?"

"We need to get you untraceable."

I took his ancient-looking candy bar phone. Slid the back off and plucked out the battery before handing the phone's shell back to him.

"And your children's electronic devices," I said.

The rabbi collected them and handed them to me. I picked the portable video game consoles that required an internet connection, and removed their batteries. The kids whined. Their mother shushed them.

"Same thing with these." I returned the hollow cases of the children's game consoles to the rabbi. "You need to wait before putting the batteries back in, otherwise, you can be traced by your children's user name or game ID." I handed him one of the burn phones from my pocket. "In the meantime, use this."

He examined it and managed to turn it on.

"We can communicate this way. The number isn't connected with a name so all calls, though traceable, don't have a name associated with them. To make sure there's no electronic trail when you call me, is there some sort of way we can communicate in code?"

His eyes lit up. "I know just the thing! Have you heard of *Atbash*?"

"Sounds familiar."

"It's a type of code used in the book of Jeremiah. Remember that Jeremiah lived at a time when the Babylonian king overran Jerusalem, near where Jeremiah lived. In his writings, Jeremiah mentions the city of Sheshach. When you apply Atbash to the name of the non-existent city, the name becomes Babel, the Hebrew word for Babylon."

"I remember now. Atbash is a simple replacement code. The Hebrew equivalent of A is replaced by Z, B is replaced by Y, and so on until Z is replaced by A. It's not going to work, Rabbi."

"Why not?"

"It's a simple code to crack. Any guy who solves cryptogram puzzles in the newspaper can solve that code."

"Exactly. Which is why in the late 1700s, the kabbalist Rabbi Abraham ben Jechiel Michal HaKohen presented a code wheel to make Atbash personalized and indecipherable."

"A code wheel?"

"Yes. Come see."

The rabbi took me downstairs to Samuel who sat in the living room with the curtains closed.

"Samuel," the rabbi said, "you wouldn't happen to have a copy of *VeShav HaKohen*, would you?"

Samuel stood with a grunt and moved to a corner of the bookshelf. "Here, Elihu."

"Thank you." The rabbi flipped through the book's pages. "Ah! Here it is."

He showed me a page with an illustration of a wheel with Hebrew letters on it.

"You see?" The rabbi pointed to the page. "There's an inner wheel and an outer wheel. You can imagine spinning the inner wheel so that the inner letters line up with different letters on the outer wheel. If you spin the wheel at every word, you can get it so that a different letter replaces the letter Aleph each time."

I saw his point. With a constant change in the decryption key, a coded message could quickly become too challenging to decipher. Like having a safe that changed its lock combination hourly. Still, the wheel had Hebrew letters.

"Rabbi, what would be the English equivalent of this?"

"Excellent question." The rabbi asked Samuel, "Do you have some paper and a pen?"

We followed Samuel into the kitchen where he snagged a pen and a pad of paper from beside a telephone. Rabbi Silverman sat at the kitchen table and I took a seat next to him. The rabbi drew out a code wheel similar to the one in the book using English letters instead of Hebrew.

I examined his drawing. It made sense.

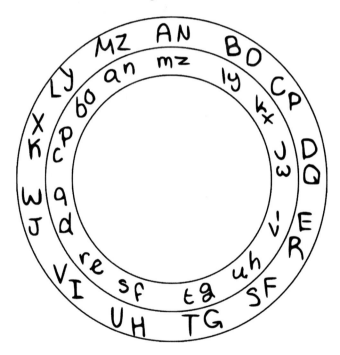

"I must make an identical one for myself." The rabbi drew another wheel. "There! Now if we agree to spin the inner wheel two places at every word, that should make it impossible for anyone to know what we're talking about."

"Not impossible," I said, "but difficult enough to cause headaches trying. Good. Let's communicate by texting each other using this code."

Time to go. I realized another obstacle to overcome. "Rabbi, do you have a car I can borrow?"

"Of course!" The rabbi extracted a set of keys from his pocket and removed one of the larger keys on the key ring. "Here. We won't be needing it until this whole thing passes."

"Thanks." I took the key, threw my coat back on, peeked outside the curtain to see if any vans or any other suspicious vehicle hung around nearby. "Remember, Rabbi. Don't go out of this house and don't return to your home to pick up any more items."

The rabbi nodded his agreement.

I bid him, his family, and Samuel goodbye and left. I'd say that I felt like a spy on his first mission, but really, all my delusions felt like spy missions.

Unfortunately, this wasn't a delusion.

Chapter 31

On the sidewalk outside Samuel's house, I checked the time. A quarter after three. If Cole had skateboarded or taken a bus straight home, he'd be home by now. I called his house using the burner phone.

"Hello?" It sounded like Heidi.

"It's Nathan Yirmorshy from this morning. Is Cole there?"

"No, he isn't."

A chill grabbed me as I realized that if the puppet master, whoever he was, put a trace on my cell phone, who's to say he didn't also put a trace on Cole's phone and kill him this past hour? I took some comfort in knowing that the killer always seemed to wait at least a day before moving on to his next victim. If he stuck to his pattern, Cole would be safe until the evening.

Heidi asked, "You didn't see him at the station?"

"Just missed him. Any idea when he'll be back?"

"He always comes home around six."

Good to know. But if Cole finds out about me, he might think I'm a cop or someone investigating his wallet stunt earlier today. "Could you do me a favor and not tell him I've been asking about him?"

"Are you afraid he'll think you're out to get him?" She chuckled. "Yes, he can be touchy about those things. Don't worry. Your secret's safe with me."

I thanked her and hung up. Just under three hours before six o'clock. Enough time for me to completely disappear.

I crossed the street and searched the driveway for the rabbi's car, but all I saw was a minivan.

Oh yeah. Nine kids. So much for being inconspicuous.

I hunkered down inside and after adjusting all the mirrors and seat placement for my tall bulk, I drove to the San Francisco Airport.

Chapter 32

Sitting on her bed, Sophia picked at the crumbs of her poppy seed bagel from her plate. Knowing that Leah had come to peace with her sister's death made Sophia feel good, and useful, and all because of those cryptic words she had recorded herself saying while making a shopping list. Sophia used to believe the phrases she muttered during her epileptic seizures originated from her twin sister who died at birth, as though her sister was calling out to her. But this recent seizure had directly helped Leah. Perhaps the Shekinah did truly control her words. Wherever the words came from, be it her sister or the Shekinah, or just some random trigger of her seizures, the visitations might not have been a curse, after all.

Her phone rang. She set the plate of crumbs down on her bed and answered. A woman with a stern voice spoke on the line.

"This is Detective Bobbie Graff of the Berkeley Police Department, and I'm trying to reach Sophia Patai."

Oh, no. Images of Nathan's body being discovered worried her mind. "This is Sophia."

"I'm calling to find out when you last had contact with Nathan Yirmorshy."

Sophia stood up and paced beside the bed. "Is something wrong? Is he okay? He's in Ghana now."

"We have reason to believe he's in the Bay Area."

That couldn't be true. "If he were here, why wouldn't he have contacted me?"

"I don't know. That's why I'm calling. I—"

"No, that can't be right. He would have called."

"Is there any reason he might not contact you? A fight perhaps?"

"We don't fight." Sophia raised her voice. "We're not even in the same country to fight."

"Is there anywhere else he might be staying? A motel he used often? Another friend?"

"Nowhere else. Just me. He just knows me. And I know he's not in the US. He's in Ghana. Do you understand? Do you even know where Ghana is?"

"Okay. I apologize for disturbing you. Thank you for your time." The detective hung up.

Sophia couldn't understand it. She shuffled through her address book and found Nathan's home phone number, the one she should call only in the case of emergencies. Usually, the connection was so bad and expensive, they had better results using chat and email instead.

Sophia dialed the number. She had to wait several seconds for the line to connect. When it did, a strange tone pulsed slowly, the African version of a ring tone.

Whenever she felt lonely and wanted to pour all her thoughts into pages and pages, she'd write via snail mail.

She ended up writing letters three to four times a week. He answered every time with a letter of his own.

The line on the other end purred its rings. There was no answer.

She tried his cell phone, but like so many times before these past few months, he didn't answer it. Maybe he forgot to charge his phone?

Sophia tried calling his Skype ID. Computer to computer, face to face with cameras.

He didn't answer that way, either. He might not have been near his computer.

Sophia navigated to Facebook. Nathan was still listed as being offline. She checked his status for online chat, but again, he was listed as offline. She sent a personal message via two routes, one by Facebook and one by email. She waited fifteen seconds and couldn't stand the wait. She tried Nathan's landline again, maybe he was asleep and her persistent calls could wake him up.

It rang and rang, not even rolling to voice mail. She listened to each ring, not willing to hang up.

"Where are you, Nathan?"

Chapter 33

I stepped inside the air-conditioned terminal of the San Francisco airport. True, I was off the grid and couldn't be traced by any cell phone, but phone calls weren't the only way to track a person. I may have been a needle in a haystack, but I wanted to make it impossible for others to find me.

I found a comfortable seat near the check-in desks. One good thing about having paranoid delusions, they give you the incentive you need to plan for emergencies, like setting up an emergency bank account with $50,000. I made a note on a piece of paper, then sought out the airport's nearest business center. Finding one, I sauntered over to the copy machine, and copied the hell out of my note. As I paid for the copies, I handed one to the cashier.

"What's this?" she asked.

"It's a great gift I want to spread around."

She read aloud, "Dear kind stranger, I had the recent privilege of coming into a large inheritance. To honor my father's name, I wish to pass on his generous nature. Below are the credit card number, expiration date, and three-digit card security code number to the account that holds the inheritance money. Please feel free to use the below credit card number under the name Nathan Yirmorshy for any purchases you'd like up to $100. Enjoy!"

The girl scowled at me. "Is this for real?"

"It's not for fake. Enjoy!"

She gushed her thank yous as I made my way out of the store. I left the copies at the entrance of the airport's food court.

The only thing harder than finding a needle in a haystack is finding a particular needle among a haystack made of needles.

Yes. Now I was completely off the grid.

Richard's focus got disrupted by a knock on his office door. "Come in."

Anderson from Surveillance entered. That potbelly of his was so round, the guy looked like he'd swallowed a beach ball. Richard tried to ignore his sorry shape. Anderson had been hired for his brain, not his brawn.

"Sir, we've lost Mr. Yirmorshy's phone signal."

"He turned off his phone?"

"Must've."

Richard sighed. "Fine, just keep me posted on his financial transactions."

"Yeah. About that."

"What's wrong? Has he stopped using his credit cards?"

"Not at all." Anderson checked a yellow sticky note. "We've got 326 online book purchases, 748 electronics purchases, stereos, TV, game consoles, and two down payments on cars. A Camaro and a DeLorean."

"Sounds like he's spending his entire fortune."

"That's not the problem."

"What is the problem, Anderson?"

"The purchases were made all over the world, some simultaneously."

How was that even possible? "You're saying he wasn't the only one using his card to make purchases?"

"Sir, as far as we know, he may be the only one *not* using his card."

Dammit!

Chapter 34

I returned to Cole's house just after six o'clock, though with the way the sun was still shining this late during the summer, it felt like mid-afternoon.

His mother greeted me at the door. "Brad and I are making dinner. You're welcome to join us."

Since pleasant conversations made me sick, I usually didn't accept offers to dinner, but staying would give me the opportunity to keep an eye on Cole.

I forced a smile. "That'd be great."

"Wonderful. We're making spaghetti with meat sauce. I hope you're not a vegetarian."

"I'll eat anything that isn't still moving."

"Perfect. Come in. I'll go get Cole."

Soon after I stepped inside, the same spike-haired kid I'd seen at the BART station appeared. Now, with his jacket off, I could see his black T-shirt. The shirt flaunted a picture of a burning skull and the words, *Hell on Wheels*.

"Your parents let you wear that?"

"Hello to you, too." He squinted as though sizing me up. "Your parents let you wear *that*?"

I instantly fell in love with the kid.

"Who the hell are you?" he asked.

I introduced myself as a friend of Rabbi Silverman. "Know him?"

He shrugged. "Sure."

"How do you know him?"

"I met him at synagogue." He said it as if it were the most obvious thing in the world.

It still amazed me how his Catholic parents raised him Jewish. "You've got some damn good parents."

"Best I could ever have." Cole shifted to his other foot. "So what's up? The rabbi okay?"

"He's not, actually. He's fine for now, but you're in more immediate danger. It's a long story. I should probably tell you someplace private so your parents don't get worried. Can we talk outside?"

"We can go to my room." He turned and waved his hand for me to follow him.

"Your parents trust you to be alone with a stranger?"

He chuckled. "After seeing the self-defense moves I learned in my Krav Maga class, my parents are convinced I can take care of myself."

As we passed the kitchen, Cole's father greeted me wearing an apron over his suit. "Dinner will be ready in fifteen minutes. Can I get you anything? Tea? Coffee?"

Coffee sounded good, but by the forest of pots and pans, it looked like they were too busy with dinner. "I'm good. Thanks."

Cole called back, "We'll be in my room, Dad."

He took me to the basement door and started downstairs.

"Weren't we going to your room?" I asked.

"This *is* my room. And, yes, by choice. I could have kept my old bedroom upstairs, but now I prefer living down here."

Downstairs in the basement, I did a double take. The bed was made, the rug was clean, the books on the shelf were tidy, but the walls were plastered with photos, newspaper clippings, lines drawn connecting articles to pictures and handwritten words all over. Was this kid crazy? Then I realized my walls probably would have looked the same way in Ghana if I hadn't had Sophia's letters plastered everywhere.

Chapter 35

In Cole's basement, a puppy greeted me with his tongue falling out. The yellow Labrador's paws were so big he kept tripping over them, his big ears flopping up and down.

"Who's this?" I asked.

"That's my best friend Echelon. Check this out. I always know where he is because of this."

He showed me a GPS unit, the kind that someone could mount on their car's dashboard. After turning it on, the screen displayed a map of his neighborhood with a red dot over his house.

"See that? I got a chip put in him, so I'll never lose him."

"Nothing says 'I love you' more than a GPS implant." I scratched his dog's neck. "You know, you didn't seem very surprised when I said your life's in danger."

"See all this?" He gestured to the newspaper clippings and photos on the wall. "I realize it must look crazy, but I'm unlocking the truth. These secrets and conspiracies show the way things really are. A lot of powerful people don't want this information known. You say I'm in some kind of danger? Discovering these truths has put my life in danger for the past several years. Which danger are you talking about?"

I told him about the legend of the thirty-six righteous, the list of names the rabbi made, that the list was stolen and that most of the people on it were now dead. I told him his name appeared next on the list.

He didn't say anything. Just nodded.

I scrutinized the room. One wall displayed images of the Kennedy assassination along with lines drawn to a picture of Oswald and other photos tied to the event. To the left of that mess was a collage of UFO images. The wall to the left of the UFOs charted out a host of names I didn't recognize. The names were arranged and linked like a tree.

"What's that?" I pointed to the tree of names.

"The New World Order."

"Which is?"

"A group of people, a cabal, from all sorts of places in power intent on achieving the End Days."

"Sounds fun. So what has all this 'truth' done for you? Put a merry spring in your step?"

"I've learned the basic strategy the government uses to fool everyone."

"Oh? What strategy is that?"

"Distract, confuse, and deceive. With Kennedy, the distraction was easy. Everybody had their eyes on Kennedy. The government then confused the onlookers by firing shots from different places. Then they deceived everyone by saying Oswald did it. Another example, the Army-Air Force publicly dropped crash-test dummies from the sky and confused everyone when they forced down an ETV with strong radar signals."

"ETV?"

"Extraterrestrial Vehicle."

Oh, brother.

He pointed to an old photo on the wall of a military officer holding up a male mannequin. "The Army-Air Force deceived everyone by claiming the extraterrestrial bodies witnesses saw were just crash-test dummies. Distract, confuse, and deceive."

"You really think you can take down a flying saucer with radar signals?"

"I can prove it. I got this off the FBI Freedom of Information Act website."

He handed a sheet of paper to me that looked like a poorly photocopied memo. It read, "An investigator for the Air Force stated that three so-called flying saucers had been recovered in New Mexico. They were described as being circular in shape with raised centers, approximately 50 feet in diameter. Each one was occupied by three bodies of human shape but only 3 feet tall, dressed in metallic cloth of a very fine texture. Each body was bandaged in a manner similar to the blackout suits used by speed fliers and test pilots."

I checked the memo. It was from someone named Special Agent Hottel written to the director of the FBI. The date read March 22, 1950. The director back then was J. Edgar Hoover.

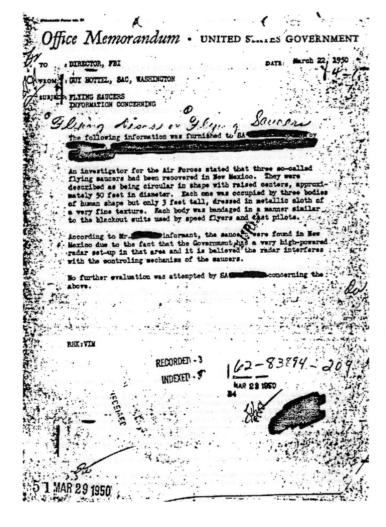

Office Memorandum • UNITED STATES GOVERNMENT

TO : DIRECTOR, FBI   DATE: March 22, 1950

FROM : GUY HOTTEL, SAC, WASHINGTON

SUBJECT: FLYING SAUCERS
INFORMATION CONCERNING

Flying discs or Flying Saucers

The following information was furnished to SA ▓▓▓▓▓▓ by

An investigator for the Air Forces stated that three so-called
flying saucers had been recovered in New Mexico. They were
described as being circular in shape with raised centers, approximately 50 feet in diameter. Each one was occupied by three bodies
of human shape but only 3 feet tall, dressed in metallic cloth of
a very fine texture. Each body was bandaged in a manner similar
to the blackout suits used by speed flyers and test pilots.

According to Mr. ▓▓▓▓▓▓ informant, the saucers were found in New
Mexico due to the fact that the Government has a very high-powered
radar set-up in that area and it is believed the radar interferes
with the controling mechanism of the saucers.

No further evaluation was attempted by SA ▓▓▓▓▓▓ concerning the
above.

RHK:VIM

RECORDED - 3
INDEXED - 5

162-83894-209

MAR 29 1950

5 1 MAR 29 1950

I continued reading. "The saucers were found in New
Mexico due to the fact that the Government has a very
high-powered radar set-up in that area and it is believed
the radar interferes with the controlling mechanism of the
saucers."

I released an exasperated sigh. There's nothing worse than hearing someone's conspiracy theories which aren't your own.

I sat at a table by his bed. "Do you have any beer?"

"Sure." Cole crouched at his basement fridge. "But I only have Heinekin."

"You're my new best friend." I didn't think he'd actually have beer. My attempt at making a joke backfired with fruitful consequences.

Cole took off the bottle caps, stood on a stepladder, and pressed the caps into the corkboard that lined the ceiling. I hadn't noticed all the caps that peppered the ceiling. Quite festive.

"So you're what, thirteen years old?"

"Fourteen."

"And your parents let you drink beer?"

He stepped down off the ladder. "Like I said, I have the best parents. Besides, they know I'd never abuse the privilege. I know my limits." He grabbed a deck of cards and sat down across from me at the table. "Don't take a drink, yet. Let's play a game."

"I hate games."

He smirked. "Then you'll love this one. It's especially designed for game haters."

"Yeah, that sounds like my kind of game."

He shuffled the cards. "Here's how it works. The first guy who gets a turn has the chance to ask the other guy three yes-or-no questions. If any of them are wrong, the player can't continue asking his set of three questions. The three questions have to be in the form of guessing something about the other person. Their likes, dislikes, histories, deviant behavior, that sort of thing. If the player gets a question right, instead of saying 'yes' the other player has to take a drink from the beer."

"And if all three questions are right?"

"Then the asker has the option of drawing a card."

"And?"

"If the card's red, he gets to ask anything about the other player. Not just a yes or no question."

"And if the card is black?"

"The asker has to *answer* any question."

I didn't quite follow all the rules, but I knew it didn't matter. I'd pick it up as I played. "What's this game called, anyhow?"

He put the deck of cards between us. "It's called *You Suck*."

I gave a snort. "I now officially like this game."

"I go first. Here's my first question. You don't really care about me. Are you making sure I stay alive for a reason that has nothing to do with my safety?"

I grinned. I took a drink of the beer.

"Is someone paying you to protect me?"

Nope. "My turn." Coming up with a question hurt my head. What could I ask? *Do you always use dental floss? Did you ever steal matchbox cars?* This game was stupid. "Were you ever raped?"

Cole's jaw dropped.

I shifted in my seat. "Look, I'm not good at playing this kind of game. I don't know what to ask."

He looked away. Then took a sip.

Chapter לו

Detective Bobbie Graff dragged her worn, weary body home from work and climbed up the amber-colored wood stairs to her bedroom. The bland evening did not promise rest.

There were two fatal things in this world, death and dating.

Tonight loomed a blind date set up by Scarlet, her older, well-meaning sister. Bobbie made a mental note. *Whenever dear sister calls to discuss dating men, ignore her by singing the national anthem out loud.*

Bobbie Graff stripped out of her slacks, blouse, and underwear, and took a shower.

The hot, pleasing water washed away the grisly crime scenes of the day. She visualized the copper blood of the vics she had witnessed, imagined it washing off her body and pouring down the shower's drain. This one calming picture helped her deal with all the brutal suffering she had seen during the day. She exited the shower, yanked a towel off the towel rack, and whisked her hair, drying off with rough strokes.

She fastened on a black lacy bra and slipped into some dressy, matching panties. She lay a black restaurant-appropriate dress on the made bed. That dress was the fanciest she owned. It was her one good dress, though having run it through the wash several times, she had to admit her dress looked as worn out as she felt. It was time to invest in a new one. She set her black pumps next to the bed. She needed new shoes, too. Her only pair of pumps with high heels had been worn so much their surface was scratched and scuffmarks lined the sides. Still, they remained the only pair she could wear with the dress. It was an ensemble so old the audience had left the theater.

She had promised her sister she'd wear makeup. How in the hell did she let herself fall into the trap of promising such a chore? Makeup was reserved for special occasions, like getting a personal tour of Thor's home planet with Thor as the tour guide.

She stepped back into the bathroom and took out a red metal toolbox from the bottom drawer. Stuffed inside the toolbox lay a bunch of makeup sticks wrapped in a rubber band. The rubber band looked tired. She had to peel it off and it broke in the process, having completely lost its stretch. If her memory served her, the last time she wore makeup was on her last date. Was it that long since she'd been on a date?

She picked out the blush, applied the soft brush to her cheeks, and let the remaining makeup sticks clack and roll along the bathroom counter top. Not convinced the brush would get enough on there, she pressed the brush harder against her face bending the bristles. The handle poked her cheeks.

She applied the lipstick. The bizarre coloring caked her lips, but she had to admit, the red lips did give her an overall softer, more feminine look.

Weird.

Now the part she hated. The eyes.

She picked up the mascara, pulled out the wand, and stroked the lashes of her left eye. She moved onto her right eye.

Why was Nathan Yirmorshy back in town? What was his connection to the homicides?

"Ow!" A gob of mascara dribbled into her eye.

She recited all the obscenities she knew and came up with a few new ones. *That'll teach me to let my mind wander while applying makeup.*

Checking herself in the mirror, she had to squint one of the eyes. It hurt too much to open it.

Damn. Eyeliner was supposed to go on *before* mascara. She angrily picked up the eyeliner and applied it to her left eye. That wasn't so difficult. The right eye, however, squinted too much to get good access to the edges of the lids. She made more lines across her eyelid and the pouch under the eye than at the edges.

She chanted a few more cuss words and walked out of the bathroom throwing the makeup sticks in the trash. The doorbell rang.

That must have been him. Lee Crawford.

Using her commanding police voice, Graff shouted, "Just a minute!"

She wiggled into her dress, putting her arms through the spaghetti straps and twisted her feet into the heels.

Grabbing a large purse, she stuffed in her keys, mace, a notepad, and pen. She stopped and looked around.

"Will he be naughty or nice?" She shrugged and added her pistol and condoms.

She stumbled down the top few stairs, catching herself with the banister.

After checking the remaining stairs, she said, "The hell with it."

She swung a leg over the banister, and slid down the rest of the way. Climbing off the banister, she wobbled to the door, opened it, and through her good eye she saw Mr. Crawford's strong jaw, cleft chin, auburn hair, and lean build—a relatively handsome guy.

"It's good to finally meet you, Lee." She offered her hand.

He took it. "Hi, what happened to your eye?"

"Let's not ruin the moment." She turned her back to him. "Can you zip me up?"

Chapter 37

I couldn't believe it. Guys don't get raped, right? Or do they? I guess kids got molested. Was there a difference between molestation and rape? I didn't know. Who would molest Cole? A man or woman?

"Was it a man?"

Cole looked at the floor. Took a sip.

"Your father?"

He shook his head. "Doesn't matter now, anyway. The guy's dead. Heard it was an STD. There's poetic justice for you." He set his beer down on the table. "My turn. Do you have a girlfriend?"

I took a sip.

"Is she one of the people on the hit list?"

I took a sip.

Cole thought for a long moment. Something seemed to be chewing at him.

"Is she still alive?"

I took a sip.

He grabbed a card and flipped it over. It was red. He got to ask any question he wanted.

"Then why aren't you protecting her instead of me?"

I sighed. "I planned on breaking up with her when I was in Ghana because long distance relationships don't work, but then this came up so I'm trying to stop the killings without having to see her. After all, there's something wrong with saying to her face, 'I'm breaking up with you because long distance relationships don't work.'"

"So you're going to wait until you're back in Ghana to use that lame-ass excuse to break up with her?"

"Nuh-uh. No more questions. My turn to ask the questions."

I wondered whether I should pursue the whole rape thing. Clearly he didn't want to talk about it. Wondered if anyone else knew about it. Women go through tremendous amounts of shame and humiliation for being powerless. Can't imagine what it's like for a guy who's supposed to always be in power. Women who are overpowered are considered victims. Men who are overpowered are considered wimps.

If he never told anyone, that could be a problem.

"Am I the first person who found out?"

He took a sip.

Damn. He needed to talk it out. Make it less of who he was and more of something that happened to him. The more he told the story, the less power the experience would have over him.

"Do you think it would help you if you talked about it with someone?"

He took a sip.

Well, that was a start, but I didn't want to force him into talking about anything before he was ready. With something like this, it didn't make sense to dominate him. I gave him his power back.

"Do you want to tell me about it?"

He gave me a type of smile that said, *Thanks for giving me an out.* "My turn."

Cole looked at the ceiling as if he were searching for his next question. He must have found one. "Is there a more significant reason why you're breaking up with your girlfriend?"

I had to think about that for a second, but I realized the truth. I took a sip.

"Is there someone else you're shtooping?"

"My turn." I decided to let go of the whole rape thing. "Do you think it was wrong for the rabbi to put you on the list of the most righteous people in the world?"

He took a sip.

"Is it because you don't consider yourself very righteous?"

He took a sip.

I thought about what to ask next. Supposedly, one trait of the righteous that separates them from the rest of us was their connection to the Shekinah.

"Have you seen the Shekinah?"

He studied me as if I had asked a trick question. He took a sip.

I grabbed a card and turned it over. It was black.

"Yes!" Cole fisted the air. According to the rules of the game, the black card meant he got to ask me any question. "What's the real reason you're breaking up with your girlfriend?"

How to put this? "I have bipolar disorder. I thought that I was in control over my episodes, but I found out in Ghana that I still can't trust myself to be responsible about taking the meds. Once I'm off those meds, I can be a danger to everyone. The truth is, I may be a physical threat to Sophia if I were to live with her. By breaking up with her, I'm giving her the freedom to find someone else. Someone she can trust to keep her safe and feel safe with."

Cole rolled his eyes. "Yeah, I'm sure she'll be happy about that. It's still my turn. Do you want to see her?"

I took a sip.

"Do you think she wants to see you?"

I took a sip.

"Are you usually this stupid when it comes to relationships?"

I shrugged and took a sip.

He flipped a card. Black.

This time, I already knew my question for him. "What happened with the whole Shekinah thing?"

He released a heavy sigh. "The day after my eleventh birthday, my parents told me who my real mother was. They were going to wait until I turned eighteen, but they found out that she was struck by a car and might not survive much longer. She was in a coma."

I didn't say anything.

"It was weird finding out what my real last name was. I mean, my birth mother never married, so if I wanted to change my name to match my real parents, I guess I would take *her* last name."

"What was her last name?"

"Hirsch. So that makes me Cole Hirsch." He sipped his beer. "I went to the hospital and found her room. They let me sit by her as long as I wanted. I just sat and didn't know what to say, so I held her hand. What bugged me the most was that she could never answer all my questions. It's one thing to know you'll one day have the answer to a question, it's another knowing you'll never have the answers. Anyhow, a nurse entered the room. She asked me, 'Are you Cole? The patient's son?' After I said yes, she said, 'It's good you're here. A lot of people think the patients can't hear them. The truth is, they hear everything. And knowing you're here with her in her last moments makes her very happy.' "

Cole fiddled with the label on his beer, and I said nothing.

"I asked her whether she knew anything about my birth mother. She picked up the chart and read off of it, 'Born in Phoenix, Arizona, thirty years old, lived in Phoenix until she was sixteen, ran away from home, lived without any clear address, skipped out on an appointment with an abortion clinic. That's probably why you're here today. Took classes at Cal with a major in Social Health Care, and worked part time at a dentist's office. She left a will made out to her son. That would be you. Her preferred hospital foods are peaches.' It was kind of funny when she said that, because I love peaches, too. The nurse said, 'She loved you, Cole. Still does.' "

Cole's eyes swept across the table as if he were picturing it all in his head. Playing it out before continuing to speak.

"She returned the chart to the bed and left. I went to

see what else the chart said, and that was the weird part. The only things on the chart were the injuries, name, birth date, and social security number. It didn't say anything else. When I went out to find the nurse, she was gone. I asked another nurse if they had seen her. I remembered her nameplate read, Shekinah. They said they didn't have a nurse by that name." He shook his head. "Anyhow, I don't know what happened. Life can just be so weird."

"I'll drink to tha—"

Shots rang out upstairs. Gunfire. Seven shots.

"Mom!" Cole ran to the stairs.

"Get down!" I grabbed the kid by the collar and pulled him down to the ground. The shooting stopped, but footprints plodded above us. My gut felt like lead. It was too late for his parents. From all the gunfire I heard, they must have been dead.

Since the footsteps were still clomping above us, I knew the killer came for Cole and wouldn't leave until he searched the whole house. *Chances are he'll first check Cole's bedroom, which he'll think is on the second floor like I did.* I waited until the footsteps were no longer audible. That meant he was upstairs.

"Where's the basement exit?"

"There is none. We sealed it when we made this my room."

So much for plan A. Time for plan B. I motioned with a frantic hand. "Come on. We need to move."

Cole grabbed his puppy first.

"Now!" I pressed.

We stole up out of the basement. Cole's parents lay dead in the hallway. I peeked and saw the gunner at the top of the second floor stairs. Cole didn't notice the gunner. He cried out and ran to his parents.

I reached out to stop him, but the gunner fired four shots and Cole fell clutching his side. His dog ran to the back of the house. Cole screamed. He must have been hit in the arm.

"Go, Cole! Run!" I stayed where I was out of the gunner's line of fire. "I'll deal with this guy."

"Take care of Echelon."

"I'll get your dog and meet you at the Campanile. Just get out now!" I kept my sights on the gunner. Through the corner of my eye, I saw Cole skateboard down the street clutching his arm.

Chapter 38

With the assassin at the top of the stairs and me down below, I was at a disadvantage. Height always had the advantage. Every time.

I peeked out, he fired two more shots. I ducked back, though some bits of wall splattered in my face. That was thirteen. The gun looked like a Glock 22. Unless he had another magazine, he probably had only two bullets left. Waiting here was stupid. Perhaps I could escape the back way.

Past the kitchen revealed the back door. Such a door would have been a welcome sight, if it weren't bolted shut requiring a key to open it. Dead end. I examined the windows. Two gunshots fired. I ducked. Glass from a small window pane spilled outdoors. That was fifteen.

I dashed back into the kitchen and stayed low. Tried my luck and glanced at the gunner. I heard a click. His gun was empty. I braved a longer look at him. Young guy with a beard. Probably the man who broke into the rabbi's home. He reached behind to his back pocket and extracted a knife. That was good. No more bullets. He had a knife, but so did I.

I snagged two carving knives from the cutlery stand in one hand and grabbed a broom in the other. Thrusting the broom down against my raised knee, I snapped off the broom's handle. I yanked the kitchen's phone cord out of the wall and disconnected it from the phone. Tied the knives onto each end of the handle with the phone cord. Instant double-sided bayonet.

When he treaded into the kitchen, he paused, eyeing the makeshift bayonet. Then he came at me.

I thrust the bayonet toward his chest, but he parried it. He thrust the knife at me and I blocked it with the broomstick. An idea came to me. I slammed the broomstick down against my raised knee cracking it into two halves. Now in each hand I carried a stick with a blade at the end. I twirled them in my hands. If I kept a confident posture, it might instill fear in the assassin, enough to have him make a mistake.

I pounced on him, and he threw me off. In the process, one of the blades slipped from my grip.

I tried recovering with a thrust at his chest, but he grabbed the base of my remaining bayonet and yanked me toward his knife. I let go of the bayonet, and kneed him in the gut. I got a hit in, but it also meant releasing my grip on my lone weapon.

He had me. I didn't have a weapon. He still held his.

He thrust his knife at me, I dodged and scissored my arms on his knife hand, bending it back.

He cried out and dropped the knife.

He no longer had me.

Having the moment, I glanced around the room. What else could I use to my advantage? I saw the answer.

"Do you want fries with that?" I threw a pan of boiling water on his face.

He screamed in pain holding his face.

I said, "You mess with Rabbi Silverman or Cole again, and more than just your face will burn."

I ran out of the house, jumped into the van, and peeled out toward the Campanile to meet Cole. Peeling out is not easy to do with a minivan.

Chapter 39

Detective Bobbie Graff kept her balance in her high heels, walking beside Lee to get from his parked car to the restaurant. She brushed aside her long hair wishing she had kept it in a pony tail the way she usually wore it. She caught herself from falling. *These damn heels.* As she regained her balance, she peered out through her working eye to see where she was headed.

Lee took her arm. "Why don't I help you?"

Graff jerked her arm out of his grasp. "I got it."

The restaurant turned out to be a plush place. Fancy and swank. She had never eaten there before. She was more the burger-and-fries kind of person, not really interested in having cooked vegetables infest her plate.

When the waiter showed them to their table, Graff gasped a quick intake of breath at the table settings. The red tablecloth was an actual cloth. Even the napkins were linens. Polished silverware surrounded plates with fancy designs. She didn't know what half of the utensils were for. When the waiter pushed in her chair as she sat, she was too distracted by the place setting to be upset at the waiter's condescending gesture.

Instead, Graff picked up the tiny horizontal fork at the plate's twelve o'clock position. "Look at this cute little fork."

"That's the shrimp fork," Lee said.

"Oh, I can't eat shrimp. I'm allergic to shellfish."

"We probably won't be using all of these utensils."

Graff picked up a tiny spoon. "What's the little spoon for?"

"That's the dessert spoon. For ice cream or some other creamy dessert."

"Oh, we're definitely using that one."

Lee bellowed out a hearty laugh.

The waiter bent stiff at the waist with a quick jerk as he presented the menus.

Graff took the menu. "Oh, good. I'm so hungry I could eat an elephant and the ship it came on."

She scanned the menu. The items she wanted instantly pinged off in her head.

Roasted chicken with red potatoes and dill. Ping!

A glass of White Zinfandel wine. Ping!

Oh! The appetizers looked good. The goat cheese and fig jam bruschetta with mint leaves. Ping!

She set the menu down beside her plate. "Ready."

"That was quick."

"A cop doesn't have time to debate the choices. I'm used to making quick decisions. Even if they're the wrong ones." Graff smiled. Lee returned the smile. She admired the way his eyes squinted when he smiled. *Yeah, I'd be willing to spend the rest of my life waking up to that.*

While Lee continued to browse the menu, Graff eyed a dish of walnuts in their shell in the center of the table.

Fun! She grabbed a nut from the dish and searched the table. No nutcracker. She picked up her butter knife and wedged the blade into the shell.

"What are you doing?" Lee asked.

"They forgot to leave us a nutcracker." The butter knife by itself proved useless.

Lee looked at the other diners. "I think those are for decoration only. But if you want, we can ask for a nutcracker."

"No, I got it." With the knife's blade wedged in the groove of the nut, she tapped on the other end of the knife with the palm of her hand. She still had no luck. Maybe if she had a hammer or something just as heavy. She opened her purse and found what she needed.

To hell with protocol.

Pulling out her pistol, she whacked the nut with the butt of the gun. The nut broke into pieces and she picked at the meat. It tasted stale.

Lee seemed shocked.

"It's not loaded. See?" Graff pulled back the slide revealing the empty chamber.

The rest of the patrons screamed and ducked under their tables.

"Oh, sorry," she said to everyone around her. "It's okay. I'm a police officer." She held the butt of the gun by her thumb and finger, and demonstrated she was putting it away. "Sorry about that."

Chapter 40

I met Cole at the Campanile clock tower on the UC Berkeley campus as darkness was making its bed. Since it was after hours, it meant breaking into the tower with a bump key. Not easy to do while holding a puppy. After I had escaped the gunner, I had found Echelon by driving slowly around the block.

Working the bump key into the lock, I cut my finger but managed to open the door. I sucked the wound on my index finger clean. Inside the tower, I waited an interminable amount of time for the elevator. Some advice? If you've got adrenalin coursing through your veins from fighting a killer, don't schedule the rest of the day waiting for elevators.

The elevator was a tiny thing that took me up to the only floor available. The doors opened to the observation platform where Cole stood staring at the view.

The tower looked out over college kids bouncing along lamp-lit paths to buildings. Each one of them had their night class to go to, their time to get there, a schedule, a map, a plan. None of them knew the other's plan, yet everyone seemed to function with organization. I looked at my cut. How does a cell know to go to a cut and turn into a skin cell? How do the primitive cells know to turn into bone cells if a bone breaks? Random people. Random cells. None of them knowing the others' plans, and yet still functioning as a cohesive whole.

Cole clutched at his arm but he seemed to be fine.

"Listen," I said. "On the way over, I stopped at a pay phone and called the police to report what happened."

I waited for a response, but didn't get any.

"I didn't tell the police who I was, and didn't tell them about you. I can't say for sure who's behind all this, but I know whoever they are, they're powerful. You might be safer avoiding any attention from the police."

Cole still remained silent. I held Echelon, scratching the dog's neck. The puppy wagged its tail.

"Got your dog." I held up his puppy. Felt stupid for saying that.

Cole didn't meet my eyes. "My parents are gone."

I took a deep breath. "No. They're not gone."

"What do you mean?"

I nodded to the sky. "See those stars? They're so far from us, that it takes a long time for their light to reach us. What we're seeing is the past. We're seeing how those stars *used* to look. Many of them have burned out centuries ago, but their light still shines in our night sky and will continue to shine for thousands of years."

Cole didn't say anything.

"Your parents are just like those stars. They may not be around anymore, but their memory will burn bright for a long, long time."

Cole gazed at the sky with wet eyes. We stood side-by-side at the clock tower for over a half hour before he said anything.

"What do we do, now?"

I considered our options. Only one made sense. "We wait as long as possible, then get a motel room."

"Why wait as long as possible?"

"The shooter will try to find us at all your possible haunts."

"And will also check the motels to see where we decided to spend the night."

"The longer we wait before making a decision—"

"The less time he'll have to figure out where we are," I said.

He nodded. After gazing outside some more he asked, "So what should we do to kill time?"

The way he phrased the question made me think of how time could be killed. Literally. I thought about the inseparable bond between space and time. Thought about how making changes in space—curving it, warping it, twisting it with mass and electricity—also made changes to time, slowing it down. Thought about how if the gravity were strong enough, like looking at something that edged close to a black hole, time stops completely, effectively killing time. And also ripping to shreds the idiot that thought it was a good idea to take a vacation near a black hole in the first place. But figuratively speaking? What could we do to kill time?

"We talk." I let Echelon down onto the floor. He scampered away along the platform. I didn't worry. The observation deck was circular, so there was no way we'd lose the dog.

"Talk about what?"

"Why do you have pictures of the Twin Towers on your wall?"

"They weren't destroyed by planes," Cole said.

I was headed into another of Cole's conspiracy theories, but I figured it a good way to get his mind off of his parents. "What do you mean? Everyone saw the towers get knocked down by the planes. The planes hit the towers, the towers fell down."

"Yeah, well by that logic, check this out. The world's birth rate has been rising. At the same time, the number of video stores has been decreasing. You think we can stop overpopulation by opening up more Blockbuster video stores?"

I smirked. Score one for him. In making me smirk, that is. "So why don't you think the planes knocked down the towers?"

"Get out your fingers," he said, "cause you're going to need them to keep count of all the reasons."

I sighed. Cole was probably one of those guys that found little inconclusive pieces of evidence and decided that since there were so many, the conclusion must be true.

I stood my ground. "Just give me scientific evidence. None of this, 'he said she said' crap."

"I wouldn't have it any other way. First of all, at what temperature does steel melt?"

"2750 degrees."

"And at what temperature does jet fuel burn?"

"Yeah, yeah. Jet fuel burns at 1400 degrees, but burning point and melting point are two different things. You don't need to melt the steel to make the building fall. You can heat up the steel to 1400 degrees and make it bendable. The steel will collapse at that temperature."

"True. So how come reporters saw pools of melted steel? Never mind that thermite, an explosive found at the scene, burns at over 4000 degrees."

I wanted to tell him he was crazy, but I supposed a page in Ms. Manners's Book of Etiquette read, "On the day when a child's parents are murdered, it is impolite to call him crazy." Truth was, I had a low tolerance level for conspiracy nuts. I swam in plenty of my own imagined conspiracy waters, but at least I could blame it on my bipolar disorder.

I shook my head. "I'm not convinced."

"Not good enough for you? Alright, try this. You're standing at the top of a tree." He leaned against the low wall of the observation deck, vertical iron bars protecting him from falling. "Which way would you rather jump down to the ground? Straight into the air where there's no branches beneath you or down where there are a lot of branches beneath you?"

"I'd jump where there were branches even though it would scratch my silky-smooth feminine skin."

"Good. Why would you jump that way?"

"It would slow down my fall. And the longer it takes for me to fall that same distance, the less injury I'd feel. I probably wouldn't even get all the way down, because once I got to the sturdier branches, my fall would stop, and I could climb the rest of the way down."

"And what if, for some reason, there were no bigger branches? Just dead twigs all the way down?" Cole pointed to the ground.

"I'd still jump down that way. The twigs would cause a tremendous amount of resistance, slowing my fall and reducing the pain of impact."

"If the top 20 floors of the South Tower were dropped in air from their original height of 1300 feet, how long would it take to land?"

"From 1300 feet? That's what, about 400 meters?" I did the calculation in my head. "About 9 seconds."

"Right. And what if the floors were dropped through iron?"

"The same distance?" The numbers bumbled inside as I figured out the acceleration of a steel object falling through iron, based on their different densities. Once I calculated the miniscule acceleration, I figured out the time it would take. "Over a minute."

Cole made an over-dramatized face of being impressed.

"Right. But that top piece of the tower went through 90 floors of steel and concrete in under 15 seconds."

"That's not possible," I said. Now he was just making stuff up. "You must have your time all wrong."

"Don't like that? Okay, try this. You drive a Volkswagen bug head-on into a parked school bus. Who wins?"

"The bus."

Cole touched his nose. "Right. Maybe the bus driver is a little injured, but little Annie in the back of the bus is safe and your car is totaled. Turn that picture on its side so that the front of the bus is pointed to the sky. If you drop your car downward head-on into the school bus, why would the physics change so that now little Annie gets crushed by your car?"

I saw where he was going with this. The car represented the top twenty floors of the South Tower, and the bus represented the rest of the building. The top part of the building should have lost energy with every floor it hit. Unless the laws of physics decided to take the day off, there's no way the support force should have vanished as it must have done for the towers to fall.

Cole waved his hands around like he drank too much coffee. "Isn't it odd that the bottom floors of the towers, so used to holding up the entire building, instantly pulverized when the top twenty floors hit them? Isn't it odd that the leaseholder of the towers bought terrorist insurance six weeks before the attacks? Isn't it odd that the trusses passed fire endurance tests but still failed to hold the towers up in the fire? Isn't it odd that thermite incendiaries and explosives were found in the steel and dust?"

I wasn't sure what bothered me more, his whole conspiracy attitude or the idea that he may have been right. Planes couldn't demolish towers. Planes could knock them over, maybe. Could even start a fire, leaving a skeleton of a building left over. But demolish? Nuh, uh.

Cole listed on his fingers. "The planes hit the towers, distraction. The towers fell, confusion. The government blamed al-Qaeda, deception."

"Just shut up," I said at last. He looked hurt, and I was sorry I said it.

Chapter 41

Bobbie Graff **wished she could take Lee by** the arm and lean against his side as they walked to her doorstep, but she knew it was not to be. When they stopped at her front door, she shrugged. "I'm sorry it didn't work out. I'm probably not the girl you want to take to a public place."

"Are you kidding? That was the most enjoyable dinner I ever had. When I think back on all the times I ate at that restaurant, they're a blur. I will never forget tonight. If spending time with you is always this memorable, I want to do it again."

"Really?" Graff tried to check for signs that the guy was lying and just wanted to get into her pants. No red flags waved, no mental warning sirens blared.

"Really. Can I see you again tomorrow night?"

Graff smiled and nodded.

"Great. Don't worry about makeup."

She realized she was still squinting through her right eye and laughed. "Just call me Rocky."

"Okay, Rocky. I'll see you tomorrow at the same time."
He kissed her cheek.

She closed the door feeling warm all over. How long
had it been since she felt this way? Too long to remember.

Cole and I collected my duffel bag from the first motel I
had stayed at. We checked into a motel on University Avenue in Berkeley at 11:40 p.m. Inside the room, I unloaded
Cole's puppy out of my arm onto the bed, and I dropped
my bag in a corner.

Our room was plastic. Plastic drawers, a plastic TV,
a plastic bathroom with plastic shower, hairdryer, and
cups for water, a plastic shower cap and plastic bottles of
shampoo and conditioner. The only exception seemed to
be the hotel clerk's smile. His smile was the genuine article.
By the way he interacted with his golden retriever at the
front desk, the clerk's love for his dog probably triggered
his joyful disposition.

I checked the drawers. The standard stationary, the
standard local maps, the standard coupons for nearby
restaurants and museums and coffee shops, the standard
Bible. In the drawer with the Bible, I found a ball of twine.
That was new. Probably left over from one of the previous
customers.

Cole slept in one bed, his puppy slept on mine. I stood
at the window keeping an eye out. My line of vision stayed
on the parking lot, so I could tell if anyone pulled in. I
could also see the office in case any others checked in late.

I saw the stars. I watched them spill their light upon us from millions of light years away.

After fifteen minutes, I lay down beside the puppy and reflected more on the stars, Cole, and his parents. The more I thought about them living on, the heavier my lids felt.

Darkness took over.

Chapter 42

Sophia awoke to the phone ringing. What time was it? Just after two a.m.? She sat up in her bed and snatched the phone.

"Nathan? Is that you?"

It was a woman. "You bitch! You killed my sister. You killed her."

"Leah? What the hell are you talking about?"

"You were wrong. The doctor called and said some tests came back showing it wasn't lung cancer after all. She had blastomycosis, a fungal infection that is treatable and curable. If I hadn't listened to your poisonous words, I wouldn't have given up on my sister, and she wouldn't have given up, and she would have been alive."

"Leah—"

"Because of you, she's dead. You killed her. You murdered her. I hate you!" Sobs drained out of her. Then the phone clicked silent.

Sophia remained still, holding the phone to her ear. The only other person who had hung up on her was her mother.

That conversation, from years ago, was the last time Sophia heard her mother's voice. The memory made her shiver.

Sophia pressed the red "End Call" button, put away her phone, and lay down. Back when she had read tarot cards to make her decisions, she could blame her problems on the cards. She still did readings for others, but had stopped her habit of using tarot to make her decisions. Now, she accepted the responsibility that this fiasco with Leah had been produced by her own decisions. Her own decision on what the recorded words meant, her own decision to share her interpretation with Leah, her own decision to tell Leah to let go of her sister. Though she told herself that Leah ought to shoulder the responsibility for all the actions Leah took, Sophia knew Yochevet's death was also her own fault.

It hurt, the tugging of that responsibility upon her heart. She wanted so much to return to the tarot cards, but this feeling—this pain of taking responsibility for her own decisions—was something she knew she had to face.

Chapter 43

The sun shot its first fists across the sky. The pain of the boiling water still sizzled Ira's face as he approached the front door to Rabbi Katz's house.

Who the hell was that guy at Cole's residence? Damn him!

Ira knew his wish would come true and that man would be damned. Whoever threw the hot water in his face would go to Hell and be damned for eternity. Still, Ira savored the idea of destroying the man's friends and family. What was it he said? *You mess with Rabbi Silverman or Cole again...* Sounded like a good plan. Ira might not know who the man was, but at least he knew the man's friends.

For now, only two targets were left, and who knew what dreams may come? Ira smiled at the Shakespeare quote in such a religious context.

Ira pounded on the door and waited.

No answer.

Rabbi Katz usually busied himself at home at this hour, right? The only time he ever left in the mornings, according to the intel, was to pick up groceries at the Safeway store down the street.

Ira hit the sidewalk. He adjusted the baseball cap he wore so that the majority of his blistering face remained shaded.

What an insignificant life the rabbi must have led. A single man spending all his time at home, in a synagogue, or at the grocery store merely promised day after day of monotony.

Ira weaved through the cars in the parking lot and stepped through the store's automatic doors. The produce section seemed the best area to scope first. The rabbi was likely a health nut.

Ira didn't see him.

He strode past the cash registers, peeking from aisle to aisle, and found him scrutinizing the cereals.

"Rabbi Katz," Ira called out, reaching for his gun.

The rabbi turned and scowled as if trying to recognize him.

Ira fired three shots into the rabbi's chest, and the man went down. *Another one bites the dust.* As expected, people screamed their heads off. Ira couldn't figure out why they bothered screaming. If a gunman were to kill someone near you, screaming didn't do a damn thing except give away your location. The best plan of action for these shoppers was to just shut up and duck for cover. Not that Ira had any intention of upping the body count. His job here was done.

Ira's shoe stuck to the floor. Lifting his shoe off the linoleum revealed a stretch of pink gum.

Son of a bitch!

He swung his fist and struck a sale display of cereals off their shelf. The boxes scattered onto the floor. For the moment, the cops were too far away to catch up with him, but he still had to leave right away. He'd poke off the gum later.

Only one more target left.

Bobbie Graff answered her phone.

"Hey, Graff. It's Denton."

"Well, well. How's my old partner doing? Still getting the 'best cases?' " Graff had switched precincts because she hated when the vics were kids, a too-common part of Oakland Homicide. Not as bad as San Francisco, according to the stats, but enough to want to move. Denton always played the optimist, even if it meant describing the cases as the best cases a detective could hope for.

"There's been a shooting in a grocery store on International Boulevard."

"That's Oakland. Out of my jurisdiction now, remember?"

"Yeah, but didn't you have an Orthodox rabbi killed in your area?"

"He wasn't a rabbi. But what about it?"

"Well this one was a rabbi. Shot in the chest three times."

Damn.

Chapter 44

I woke up and found a note from Cole scrib-bled in a familiar handwriting. "I've taken a bus to the Toys R Us in Thanan."

Where the hell was Thanan? I took out the motel room's map of the Bay Area. I copied the directions to the town. Glanced at the cut on my finger from when I broke into the Campanile the night before. Seemed to be healing well.

I took the map with me out of the motel. In the van, I followed the directions and the freeway signs to this place. The town of Thanan had all the appeal of a busted hole in the wall. Toys R Us stood out like a sore finger that would take a lot longer to heal than the cut on mine. The parking lot looked abandoned. I pulled into a parking space a good distance from the toy store and hiked on over to the establishment. The place was desolate. They only needed a single person at the registers. Probably because it was a weekday.

The short man at the register didn't even seem to be working. Just laughing. He stared at the television set hanging in a top corner of the enormous room. The TV played a SpongeBob SquarePants cartoon.

I got the clerk's attention. "Hey! You see a kid with a skateboard come through here?"

He just pointed with his thumb over his shoulder and kept on watching the cartoon.

I went to the back of the store. Followed the grinding sound of a skateboard streaking along one of the aisles. Found him quickly enough.

He flipped the skateboard with his foot into his hand, and scratched his head with an over-dramatized confused expression on his face. "Who are you?"

"Don't you mean *how* are you? I'm fine."

"You're fine? Really? Coulda fooled me."

The shelves were covered with skateboards, replacement wheels, and other board accessories for any skateboarder who wanted to stand out among his friends.

He grinned. "I love this place."

"I can see why."

"So why are you protecting me and not Sophia?"

"As long as you're alive, Sophia is safe. That's all that matters."

He snorted. "Why don't you just go straight to her and protect her?"

"This again? It's complicated."

Cole said nothing. He just raised an eyebrow.

"Okay, so it's not complicated. But the reason why I'm breaking up with her is complicated."

"You think long distance relationships don't work, huh?"

I groaned. "Okay, so maybe that part wasn't complicated, either. But there must be some part of my whole thing with Sophia that is complicated and thereby warrants no further discussion about it."

"Yeah. Keep on dreaming." Cole dropped the skateboard, stepped on, made it flip, and landed back on it without a hitch. "So why keep it long distance?"

"What?"

"Why not come back to Berkeley where you can see her all the time and not have a long distance relationship? Make it short distance."

"They need me in Ghana," I lied.

"For what?"

I put my hands in my pockets. "I'm the CEO of the company that provides water to people in many African countries."

He teased me with a mocking tone. "Ooooo. Check out Mr. Look-at-me. The world needs me so I can't have a relationship. I'm irreplaceable."

"Okay, so I'm not needed. I just can't be with Sophia, okay. I can't do that to her."

"To her, or to yourself?"

I balled my hands into fists. "What do you mean?"

"What might you lose if you got into a close relationship with her?"

What the hell kind of question was that? One I didn't want to think about.

I gave in. "With great love comes great pain. Every time. All love comes with pain and I don't want that. Not for Sophia, and yes, not for myself."

"I see. So what you're saying is that you're a wuss."

I smiled. Score one for Cole.

I saw a Magic 8 Ball toy on the shelf. Ask the liquid-filled ball a question, shake it, and a twelve-sided die with engraved responses on each side floats to the surface to answer your question.

I picked up the toy. "Let's ask the all-knowing 8 Ball," I said. "Should I get back together with Sophia?"

I shook the ball, and it read, "Try again."

"Should I get back together with Sophia?"

I shook the ball, and it read, "Try again."

"It's broken." I set the toy back on the shelf.

"You're doing it wrong." Cole picked up the ball. "What's my favorite color?" He shook it and said, "See?" He showed me the 8 Ball's response: Yes.

He put the toy on the shelf. "You're in a smokeless fire."

Before I had a chance to ask what he meant by that, I got distracted by a news report on the TV. "Rabbi Gerald Katz was shot in an Oakland grocery store on International Boulevard. This, right after the shooting of another Jewish victim at Live Oak Park in Berkeley."

I recognized the name. Rabbi Katz was number thirty-five on the list. I was an idiot. *Why did I think the killer would stay in the order of the hit list? He'll just go on down the line and come back for Cole last.*

The next one on the list was Sophia.

I ran for the exit and waved Cole over. "We got to get back to Berkeley. Now!"

Chapter 45

Sophia managed the front desk of the Calico Apartments, spending the final hour of her morning shift slipping the residents' mail into their cubby boxes. She had only worked there for two months and loved it. Though the pay kept her just above broke, she had virtually no duties. She had the freedom to chat with any friend at the front desk or on her cell phone as much as she wished, and she could even read to pass the time. Her only tasks were to sort the mail, answer the few phone calls that came in, and make sure no transients or solicitors sneaked past her.

As Sophia finished sorting the mail, her friend Miriam leaned on the counter across from her. Sophia felt grateful for the company. She told Miriam about the message she received from what may have been the Shekinah, how she passed the message on to Leah, the way Leah appreciated the message until the diagnosis of her sister changed, and how Leah now accused Sophia of killing her sister.

Miriam gasped. "I am so sorry, Sophia. I should never have told her about your visitations."

Sophia almost agreed with her, but caught herself. "No, Miriam. It's not your fault. It was my decision to connect with Leah and follow through with her wishes. It's just… why do you think the message turned out to be so wrong?"

"I'm not sure. Shall I try some NLP on you?"

Sophia smiled. "Taking that Neuro-Linguistic Programming class with you was one of the best decisions I've ever made. Let's do it."

"Okay. What do you want?" Miriam asked the first question NLP practitioners always started with.

Sophia leaned on the counter. "I want to know what the message means."

"What will having that do for you?" Miriam leaned on the counter, mirroring Sophia's posture.

Sophia struggled with that question. "Maybe it will help me understand why I'm experiencing these visitations in the first place."

"Once you have that, once you understand why you're experiencing these visitations, what will having that do for you?"

"Maybe the messages will become easier to understand so I won't mislead people like I misled Leah."

"What is the effect on you when you say you're misleading people?"

"It feels like people think I'm some sort of prophetess."

"What's so bad about that?"

"I might let them down, just like I let down my mom."

"You let your mom down?"

"It sure seemed that way, last time we talked. She got angry with me. In my last years of high school and college, she always seemed to be angry with me."

"What kind of relationship would you like with her?"

Sophia remembered her grade school years. Every few months her mom took her to the hospital to see a neurologist for her epilepsy and get blood levels tested. Sophia loved the attention her mom devoted to her on those days. As a reward after the appointment, her mom took her to the hospital cafeteria and let Sophia choose anything from the vending machine. Sophia always chose the sour cream and onion potato chips. At home, her family never had chips, and Sophia envied her friends at school who had a bag of chips everyday in their lunches. Those chips at the hospital cafeteria tasted like flakes of culinary gold.

What kind of relationship would Sophia like with her mom? "A pleasant one."

"I noticed you looked up and to the left into your past when you said that."

Sophia smiled. "I was thinking of a fond memory."

"Good. Now look from the upper left to the upper right and bring that fond memory from your past into your ideal future."

Sophia pictured her mom's attention on her, making her feel special. She let the emotion fill her heart and her breath and her dreams.

Miriam nodded. "Perhaps the message was meant for your relationship with your mother. You have great relationships with your brothers and father, but not your mother. When was the last time you talked to her?"

"It's been about six years, now."

"Maybe the death of her anger against you is the only thing that can save her."

"Sounds like a stretch."

"The only way to get out of a victim-perpetrator relationship is if the victim apologizes to the perpetrator."

Sophia didn't understand. There was nothing in NLP about apologizing to a perpetrator. "Don't you mean the other way around?"

"No. It's a practice I learned from my coach Bryan Franklin. The roles of perpetrator and victim are illusions. Apologize to your mom. It puts a counter spin on the abusive cycle and the perpetrator, your mom, will wake up from the illusion long enough to recognize what's going on and can do something about it."

"I don't know."

"Apologize to her, Sophia. End the cycle."

A tall Cal student wearing a crimson miniskirt stepped in to take over Sophia's post. The girl was a new employee of the apartment complex.

Miriam made a show of checking the time on the clock behind Sophia and posed as if ready to write something down. "I'm afraid our session is up. Shall we schedule another appointment for next week?"

Sophia chuckled, but still felt in a daze while reflecting over Miriam's advice.

Chapter 46

Ira decided to use the rest of the day to destroy the friends of the man who burned him. Getting the UPS truck and stealing a uniform was easy enough, and just what he required to track down Rabbi Silverman. Ira arrived at the doorstep of a house across the street from the rabbi's. The first four houses had been unsuccessful. His script had only extracted confusion among the homeowners.

When a plump man answered the door wearing a thin wreath of grey hair, Ira nodded a greeting. "I have a package for a Rabbi Silverman?"

"There's no one here by that name," the balding man replied.

"Yes, I realize that. He actually lives across the street, but I have specific instructions to get this high priority package to him."

"Why don't you leave it on his doorstep?"

"I'm afraid I require his signature. This is the third day I've tried making good on a next-day delivery service and, well, have you ever met a manager of a courier service?"

"No."

"Let's just say I hope you never do." Ira smiled and added a friendly laugh. "Do you happen to know where he may be so I can get this package off my hands and keep my job?"

The man seemed to think about it. "Would it help if I sign for it and when I see him, I mean, when he comes back from wherever he is, I'll pass it along?"

"Yeah, I just can't do that. It has to have his signature and as tempting as it is to just forge the guy's signature and leave it on his front porch, I can't let that evil side of me take over, if you know what I mean."

"I understand. Well, I'm sorry I can't help you."

"That's okay." Ira tipped his hat. "I'll try next door."

"Good luck." The balding man closed the door.

Ira pretended to leave the porch, then returned to see the direction the old man was headed. If anyone else were home, the man would tell them who was at the door. Through the front door window, Ira peered at the old man going upstairs. Was he meeting someone up there? Ira arched his back to see the upstairs window. A boy peeking through the window curtains quickly let the curtains fall closed again. Ira recognized him. When Ira had broken into the rabbi's house to obtain the book of thirty-six righteous, that boy had taken his gun and Ira had to retrieve it from the bushes.

The kid was one of the rabbi's sons.

***

Back from the toy store in Thanan, I dropped off Cole at the motel. "You stay here while I get Sophia."

"Promise me something."

"What?"

"Promise me you won't bring her here."

I didn't have time for this. "Why not?"

"I'm just thinking of you. It's a really bad idea."

"What, keeping the last two remaining people alive from the hit list in one space is a bad idea?"

"Righto."

I decided to ignore his request. "Makes sense. I'll be right back with Sophia."

"Asshole."

"Idiot."

Even though he smiled, I didn't understand why I felt bad leaving him alone.

The rabbi heard the door close and soon saw Samuel climbing up the steps. Elihu rubbed his hands together anxiously. "Who was that?"

"UPS. Were you expecting a package? It sounded important."

"I wasn't."

"Well, I hope I didn't do the wrong thing by sending him away."

"No, Samuel. You did exactly the right thing."

Yakov ran to his father and said, "Aba, he saw me! The funny man saw me!"

Chapter 47

In the early afternoon, I parked the minivan near Sophia's apartment in downtown Berkeley. The red brick building contributed to the old look and feel of Telegraph Avenue. I pulled out my key ring and found the keys to Sophia's apartment. Should I barge in? Better to just buzz her. I pocketed the keys and rang her number from the intercom.

"Hello?" Her voice still sounded sweet as it scratched through the speaker.

I didn't know what to say.

"Hello?" she said again.

What could I say? *Hey, it's Nathan from Ghana calling from downstairs. Open up.* Ridiculous.

"Hello?" she asked a third time, then hung up.

I used the key to open the front door of the apartment and climbed the steps to her floor. Used the key to her apartment and, remembering how the door required a hefty push to get it open, I burst in shoving the door open with my shoulder.

"Nathan!" Sophia cried, rushed over and kissed me. I kissed her back, taking in her scent. It was overwhelming. How could I have forgotten her scent? She held on tight like I was the only timber of a shipwreck keeping her afloat. My throat choked and my eyes burned. I didn't expect to feel this way.

I'll see you again, I had told her before leaving for Africa. *I promise.* The power of a promise fulfilled set my heart on fire.

I broke the hug. "Sophia, I—"

She shushed me and hugged me again.

It felt like a good ten minutes before she let me go, but she held onto my arms.

"Now I'm ready. Before you tell me why you're here, tell me how long you're here."

A good question. *Just until I stop the killer set out to hunt you down,* didn't seem like the right opening line.

"More than a month, less than a year." I realized I was no longer sure whether I wanted my stay to end sooner rather than later. Did I want to end it at all?

Sophia hugged me again without saying anything. I should have stopped her. I should have ended the hug and told her our relationship needed to end. But the hug became a kiss. The kiss became an embrace. The embrace became the code of my promise to see her again unlocked, undressed, and unending.

Chapter 48

Rabbi Elihu Silverman started when he heard the living room window crash downstairs.

"Get down!" Elihu ushered his children into the bathroom. "The bathroom is the only door with a lock. Come, children, Shoshi, Samuel. Quick!"

Everyone followed the rabbi's directions into the bathroom. Some of the kids climbed into the tub. All crouched down. Elihu turned off the lights and sat beside his wife clasping her delicate hand as she held the baby in her other arm.

Mein Gott! How awful, should this be the last time I hold Shoshi's hand.

Elihu could barely see his wife's face in the darkened room. "Do you remember when I met you?"

At first Shoshi seemed perplexed by the question. Maybe because of the timing.

Elihu persisted. "Do you?"

Her face softened. "The first time? When you had mustard on your face?" She nudged him. "You thought I was smiling because I had a thing for you."

"Yes, and I said to myself how striking and magnificent you looked. I right away felt you deserved the best. So I gathered up my courage, approached you, and told you, 'May you be blessed with the husband you seek, the family you desire, the home you want, and the happiness and health to live a long, good life.' "

"All with a yellow, mustard cheek. I remember."

"I must apologize. I haven't brought you to Israel. I haven't given you everything you desired. I couldn't afford the things that would please you. And now, I've put you and our children in jeopardy. I haven't given you the life you deserve. And I'm sorry—"

"Stop, stop, stop!" She squeezed his hand. "My dear *Bubbeleh*, don't you realize? As long as I'm with you and our children, I *am* living the life I always wanted."

Elihu's gut tensed, and tears fell from his cheek. He hugged her.

There came a noise from downstairs, like that of stepping on glass.

In the bathroom, the breaths and whimpering were too loud to hear anything more, so the rabbi said, "Shush!"

He held his breath, not daring to gasp. He heard padded footsteps up the stairs. He heard the bedroom door burst open.

There was silence.

And in that silence there was peace.

And in that peace there was hope. A hope that they would not be found. That they would be safe again.

Their baby, the one in Shoshi's arm, began to cry.

A heavy weight slammed against the bathroom door. The mother and children screamed. It was the criminal pounding against the door, possibly with his shoulder.

The door held, the wood cracked and splintered.

Then they all heard a cell phone ring outside the door.

The criminal answered it.

Through the door, they could hear his muffled voice.

"Yeah?"

Pause.

"I'll get right on that. Just finishing up some business."

Pause.

"I know. I just need to—"

Pause.

"Yes, but I—"

Pause.

"Yeah, okay."

Pause.

"I understand."

The conversation ended and there was a stretch of silence before a burst of gunfire hit the door. Everyone screamed. The gunman shouted a primal cry.

The gunfire stopped while everyone in the bathroom continued screaming.

Soon, Elihu yelled out, "Shush! Shush!"

His wife, children, and Samuel went silent.

They listened.

No sound.

They kept still and listened some more.

Elihu stood up hunched over, and placed his hand on the doorknob. Shoshi grabbed his arm to stop him, but Elihu gave her a calming hand gesture to show that it would be okay.

He unlocked the door quietly. His hand inched turns of the knob. He eased the door open and peeked out. No one was in the bedroom. He couldn't hear any intruder upstairs or downstairs.

The house seemed empty of danger.

Elihu returned to the bathroom standing up straight. "He's gone."

Shoshi asked each of the children, "Are you okay? Are you hurt?" She and Elihu checked them for blood. Everyone was unharmed. The bullets had flown above their heads. A miracle.

Elihu took out the code wheel, found a piece of cardboard packaging in the trash, scribbled on the cardboard what he needed to say, and pulled out the prepaid cell phone Nathan had given him.

Shoshi touched his arm. "Who are you calling?"

"Not calling. Texting."

Ira thrust himself into the UPS truck, frustrated that he came so close and failed. But Richard was insistent. Complete the mission. It was the only thing left that mattered.

He touched his face. The raised skin still tingled.

He understood where Richard was coming from, but missing out on the opportunity to get back at the man who scarred his face infuriated him. Any unfinished business would have to stay unfinished.

The world was coming to an end.

Chapter 49

I lay on Sophia's bed and smiled as I watched her get dressed. I kept silent the whole time.

"You sure are quiet." She smirked and threw my pants at my chest.

Truth was, I didn't want to ruin the moment by telling her what she needed to know. But holding out longer would only make matters worse.

I sat up. "There's something I have to tell you."

"Sounds serious."

"It is." That stupid song *Breaking Up is Hard to Do* came into my head. "You're probably wondering why I haven't been in touch lately."

"Really? I didn't notice." Her smile dimpled showing off teeth so beautiful, I wondered how I could have let myself be away from her so long.

"A couple of months ago, I stopped taking my meds. Figured, hell, if I have delusions or hallucinations, this African city of Winneba is too much of a pinhole in the wall for anyone to notice."

Sophia scowled, looking concerned, but said nothing.

"Sure enough, the delusions came back. I became super aware of my surroundings, able to detect what people were thinking, plotting, instigating, all by the telltale signs of how they put gari on their red-red."

She looked confused.

"Red-red is a kind of Ghana stew," I explained.

She sat on the bed and took my hand. "So what happened?"

"I got myself educated and trained in things like how to spy, martial arts, military strategies, all sorts of practical things everyone in Ghana can benefit from in their daily lives."

"Gosh." Sophia fluttered her lashes with mock dreamy eyes. "My Nathan. A regular double-oh-seven."

"Fortunately, the VP of my company had the good sense to get me to a mental hospital where I could recover."

"Let me guess. That took two months."

"Right." I checked her face for any signs of sadness or fear. No signs. She was handling this well.

"So what's the bad news?"

Now came the hard part. Why had I let our reunion become so passionate?

"I realized while I was in the hospital that I'm still going to have delusions and hallucinations. I'm not good to be around. I'm broken. That, and the problem with long distance relationships—"

"Stop, Nathan. That is not your choice to make. How I choose to spend my life is my choice, not yours. If you wanted to break up with me because you didn't love me anymore, that would be a whole different story. But ending our love because you think it's what's best for me? Nu-uh. No way. You think you shouldn't be in a relationship because you're bipolar? What about me? I have epilepsy. Does that make me 'broken'? We are stronger people because of what we have. I love you for who you are, Nathan. Never forget it."

I nodded, not sure what to say. Couldn't tell if the feeling of ropes tightening around my gut came from how sorry I was for making her angry or how happy I was for hearing her say she loved me.

My phone vibrated. It was a text message from the rabbi.

M cbo ujp rwsn oqtngjdp bw edt gjawu br nev npgzhgn-lulta enevpq cs m ZKS bjifa wlr inpo hcvvrf sx jfugjw tceeot qn apsx druj rdg ipxiveizki.

I took out the code wheel the rabbi made for me and worked on deciphering the code, making sure to spin the inner wheel two places at every word.

Sophia's intercom buzzed.

"Hello?" Sophia answered.

A voice crackled on the speaker. "UPS. Package for Sophia Patai."

"I'll be right down." She clicked off the intercom and heaved open the apartment door. "Be right back."

"Okay." I got as far as halfway through deciphering the text before my heart ran cold.

A man has been knocking on our doors in the neighbor-hood posing as a UPS agent...

Chapter 50

I **bolted down the stairs. "Sophia, stop!"**
Just as she turned the handle to the building's front door,
I yanked her back. The door flung open with an armed
UPS guy in the doorway. I thrust the palm of my hand up
at his chin.

"Go out the back way to the rabbi's minivan!" I yelled
to Sophia.

She turned and vanished. I punched the guy twice in the
stomach—a left, then a right. He doubled over. Grabbing
him in a neck hold, I dragged him into the building to
get him off the street. I recognized him. He was the man
who killed Cole's parents. Only now, he had horrible burns
on his face. He tried to pry my arm off his neck with his
hands.

Tightening my grip around his neck to hold him steady,
I said, "Who sent you?"

No response.

"Who sent you?" I yelled.

"Who…are you?" His grunts came with a struggle for air.

"I'm Nathan Yirmorshy, now who the hell are you?"

His eyes widened. "*The* Nathan Yirmorshy?"

"What do you mean?"

"Heard you got to witness...the presence of Jesus Christ in Israel....I'm sorry, sir. I didn't know....It's an honor to be in your presence."

Boy, did he ever get it bass ackwards.

"What's your name?" I kept him in a headlock.

"Ira Hughes."

"*The* Ira Hughes?"

"You heard of me?" he gurgled.

"When Jesus came down to speak to me, the dear boy said I would one day meet you."

"Yeah?"

"Yeah. Told me that when I did, to pass along a message."

"Yeah?"

"Yeah," I applied more pressure to the side of his neck, right at the arteries. "Jesus told me to tell you that he doesn't love you." The assassin's struggles weakened. "He just wants to be friends."

The assassin passed out.

Graff got ready. Another night with Lee, and this time no makeup. One less thing to worry about.

Now for the clothing. What would she wear? She only had the one outfit. Damn, it was too late to borrow a dress from a friend.

She put the same dress on. Maybe she could make it look different by just accessorizing it. After removing her police belt's attachments, she put on the belt and examined it. If she covered the arms…She donned a dark green cardigan sweater. Opening her toolbox, she found a bunch of necklaces tangled in a bundle. One of the necklaces had some green stones that looked like jade gems but weren't.

The doorbell rang. "One minute!"

One glance at her high heels made her nauseous. She grabbed some sandals and raced down the steps to the front door. She slipped her feet into her shoes. As she answered the door with one hand, she bent over fastening the sandal's straps.

"Hi." She smiled at Lee who looked fabulous in his navy blue pin-striped suit.

"Hi. Chinese? Italian? American?" He reached out for her arm to steady her.

"I've got a hankering for Kosher."

Chapter 51

After lugging the unconscious assassin up to Sophia's studio apartment, I set up a collapsible tray table in front of him while Sophia waited for me in the van. I tied his hands behind him to the back of the chair. My watch read nearly seven p.m. *This shouldn't take too long.*

I slapped the assassin's cheek to wake him. When the assassin opened his eyes and noticed his predicament, he didn't look too pleased. I sat directly across from him in another of Sophia's folding chairs.

"Good morning." I pointed his gun at him. "How about a beer?"

I stood and tucked the gun behind my back at my waistband. I took two beers from the fridge and uncapped them over the sink. The beers foamed, their caps tinkling in the sink.

I placed the bottles on the tray table, one for him and one for me.

He pierced me with angry eyes.

"What's the matter? Not thirsty?" I scratched my chin. "You know what? Let's play a game. That should put you into a better mood."

I got a deck of cards and set it on the table.

"The game is called 'The Interrogator and The Suspect.' Here's how it works. At least, here's my variation of it. We take turns interrogating. The interrogator asks the suspect a question. Any kind of question. Then the suspect answers. If the interrogator thinks the suspect is lying, the suspect has to drink some beer. If the interrogator thinks the suspect's telling the truth, the suspect doesn't drink any beer."

He gave me a look that I knew meant he wasn't impressed.

I continued, "After three questions, if the suspect has lied all three times, then the interrogator picks a card. If the card is red, the suspect has to drink the entire beer. If the card is black, the interrogator has to drink the entire beer. Doesn't that sound like fun?"

He didn't say anything.

"You know what? Let's make the game a little more interesting."

I moved to the bathroom and in the medicine cabinet found a toothbrush, toothpaste, headache medicine, flu medicine, cough medicine, sleeping pills, and a box of Band-Aids. I took out what I needed and checked the bottom cupboard.

Most of it was liquid death. Too immediate for my purposes. Liquid cleansers, lye, bleach. Then I saw the perfect thing. A box of rat poison.

Chapter 52

Bobbie Graff admired Lee's strong chin as he drove. She wondered if it was a trait from his ancestry, a cultural thing, or was his pronounced chin unique to him.

He glanced at her. "Something wrong?"

"Oh, nothing." Her cheeks felt hot.

The neighborhood changed from glitz to darkness as they approached the Live Oak Park area. Lee parked near the restaurant, and Graff let him walk her arm in arm.

Inside the restaurant, the hostess with curly bronze hair to her shoulders and a mocha brown dress guided them to a table. Several couples dined at the surrounding tables, men with yarmulkes and women in modest dresses. A few men wore black coats, hats, and long side locks of hair.

Once they got settled at the table, Graff stood. "I'll be right back."

She approached the hostess at the front counter. "Have you seen this man here?" She held up a photo of the vic.

The hostess checked the photo. "Sure. That's Yoseph. He comes here about once a month."

The hostess had the vic's name right.

"When you last saw him, did he seem in any kind of stress?"

She took a customer's bill and credit card. "No. He was his normal self. Very generous. Always leaves big tips, and makes sure to check in on each of us to see that we were okay." She stripped the receipt from the small printer and handed it to the customer with his card. "Last time, he said he'd find me a 'mensch' to marry."

"Thanks." Graff returned to the table. By the way the hostess described the vic, word of his death must not have reached her, yet.

"Everything okay?" Lee asked.

"Fine."

"Here are the menus." The waitress in a black dress and white apron presented large, laminated cards. "I'll give you a minute to decide what you want."

"Thanks. Oh, could you tell me if you've seen this man here before?" Graff handed her the photo.

Lee looked at Graff with a raised eyebrow.

Graff whispered to him, "I wish I could raise one eyebrow like that."

The waitress nodded. "That's Yoseph. He's wonderful. You know, you're the third person to ask about him."

"Really? Can you describe the other two?"

"The first one was a stocky man with a beard who asked me how Yoseph gets home. So I told him that Yoseph likes to leave through the back and take a shortcut through Live Oak Park."

That sounded like someone on the hunt. "And the second one?"

"The second man was tall, had a long neck, and curly brown hair. He seemed pretty upset when I told him he was the second man who asked about Yoseph."

That sounded like Nathan Yirmorshy. "That's it?"

"That's it."

"Thanks."

The waitress left and Graff picked up the menu but didn't read it. The words were not penetrating her mind. The suspect had asked about Yoseph with the probable intent on figuring out the best place to kill him.

"Well?" Lee asked.

"Probably the perp," Graff muttered.

"What?"

"Huh?" Graff didn't hear.

Lee sighed. "What was that about? You take your work with you?"

"It has to do with a case. Let's just order."

Before they finalized their decisions, the waitress rushed to their table. "I just remembered something about the first guy who asked about Yoseph. After he talked to me he got a call on his phone."

"Any idea who he was talking to?"

"Sounded like his boss."

"His name?"

The waitress shook her head *no* as she thought, then she looked up and pointed with her pen at Graff. "Richard. It was Richard."

Chapter 53

I returned from the bathroom holding the box of rat poison. The assassin's eyes bulged. From a kitchen drawer, I got the smallest spoon I could find and sat down.

"I admit, this isn't very strong, but here's how it works."

I took a spoonful from the very nearly empty rat poison box and sprinkled it into his open bottle of beer.

"Your beer is poisoned." I sprinkled a spoon into my bottle. "So is mine. Now whoever goes unconscious first, the other has to call the hospital. Hopefully, they'll get here in time to pump our stomachs."

I removed the gun from my waistband and pointed it at him. "You would do that for me, right? We would do that for each other. If I fall unconscious, you'll call the hospital, and if you fall unconscious, I'll call the hospital. Sound good?"

He said nothing.

I laughed. "Yeah, you're right. I wouldn't call the hospital for you. Why would you make the call for me?"

I stood and sliced through his bindings with a serrated

knife while keeping the gun pointed at him. "Time to play. You go first."

"Are you really Nathan Yirmorshy?"

I sat down. "Yes. That's one."

"The one who saw the Lord in Israel?"

"Yes. That's two."

"What did He look like?"

"Like my girlfriend," I said honestly. "Do you want to pick a card?"

"What?"

"You can pick a card. If you get a red card, I have to drink my entire beer. You pull a black card, you drink your entire beer."

He folded his arms. "I'm not picking anything."

"My turn, then. Who do you work for?"

"I don't know his name."

"Nope, you can only tell the truth, remember? Time to take a sip of your poison cocktail."

"What?"

"Drink a sip of your beer, or I shoot you right here."

He froze.

I shrugged. "Hey, if you prefer I shoot you because you think heaven won't take you if you commit suicide, that's cool with me."

I cocked the gun.

"Okay, okay, okay." He put up his hands. "It's Richard Swanson. Richard Swanson is in charge."

"Aww, if only you had said that earlier." I shook my head with mock pity. "You still have to sip your beer."

"No, please!"

"Tell you what, it's just a sip. You'll probably get a bellyache that'll pass. Take the sip and maybe you'll live to tell the tale." I moved the gun closer to his head. "Or I could always…"

"Okay, okay." He took a sip of the beer. Coughed.

"Great, now isn't this fun? So that was question one. Next question. Why are you doing this? Killing off the thirty-six righteous."

"To hasten the End Times." He coughed some more.

"Good man. I actually believe that. That was question two. Last question. Where is Richard Swanson?"

"I just know his phone number." He recited the number, and I noted it down.

"You know what? That answer was almost unsatisfying, but I still believe you. Good job. You survived the three questions. Now shall I pick a card? If I do, I could risk my life. Then again, I might get the fun in seeing you drink the rest of your poison, so I'll pick a card. Red you drink, black I drink."

I picked a card. Red.

I shook my head. "Oh, I am so sorry about that. You'll have to drink the whole beer."

"Please." He coughed, struggling to keep his eyes open. "I'll do whatever you want, give you money, anything."

"Don't be a spoilsport, Ira." I got up and stepped to the fridge. "Tell you what. Here's a pretty full half-gallon of milk. I'll give you the choice of either the gun, or drinking the full beer. If you drink the beer, there's something you should know. Poisons are usually acidic. But milk can neutralize poisons to some degree. Certainly enough to keep you alive for a hospital. So you drink the beer, and I'll let you have the milk."

He stared at the beer. Then looked at me. I aimed the gun. He got the message and chugged the beer.

I clapped his shoulder. "Alright, Ira! Way to make high school kids proud."

As he finished the beer, I set down the milk in front of him and he chugged that down. He coughed. Looked up at me with drooping eyelids.

"How you feeling, Ira? You look kind of sleepy."

"I thought you said the milk would stop the poison." His words were drawn out, as if he lost use of his tongue.

I shrugged. "Sure. If there were any poison to stop. But milk doesn't do a damn thing against a crushed sleeping pill."

He fell asleep.

Chapter 54

Bobbie Graff considered her next move for the Live Oak Park case. She stood from the restaurant table and collected her purse. "I need to make a call."

Lee Crawford leaned back in his chair. "Let me guess. Work related?"

She stopped in her tracks, then sat down. "I'm sorry, Lee. I should be focusing all my attention on you tonight."

He shook his head. "You should know something."

Sounded serious. "What is it?"

"My father was a workaholic." Lee scratched the back of his neck. "He left early and came home after dinner. Sometimes after midnight."

Graff said nothing. He had something to say. She wanted to hear it.

"On the weekends, he put his attention on my mother and me, but still had work on his mind. We could tell. So when I was eleven years old, my mother told him how much she loved his companionship and wanted him home more often. After that, my father agreed and worked regular hours, always home in time for dinner."

Lee looked down at his plate as if working out what to say next.

Graff said, "I think I understand. You don't want to be around someone who—"

"I'm not finished." He raised his eyes back to her. "My father never seemed happy after that. He did put on the air of a man grateful to be with his family, but I could tell he felt resentment for sacrificing his work." Lee paused, looking lost in his memories. "He divorced my mother when I was twelve."

Graff took his hand. His fingers were smooth to the touch.

Lee tightened his grip on her fingers. "The point is, your job is a helluva lot more important than me. I'm proud to know someone who makes such a difference to the city. If I'm going to date you, I want to know what your lifestyle is like, just in case."

"Just in case what?"

"You know. Just in case the relationship goes any further."

Graff got a chill. She had grown accustomed to the idea that no man could understand her commitment to police work. But Lee did.

She smiled and caressed his cheek. "I'll make this quick."

She weaved her way around the tables to the ladies room. Inside, while leaning on the sink, she called her captain.

"Hey, this is Graff."

"Detective?"

"Yeah. It's about the body in Live Oak Park with the gunshot to the chest." Graff explained how according to the waitress, the killer spoke to a man named Richard. "None of the suspects have a first name of Richard, but I think this lead warrants a higher priority of investigation."

"Alright, Detective. First thing tomorrow morning pull the vic's phone records and talk to his wife to see if anyone named Richard pops up."

"I think it's still early enough in the evening to call his wife now."

There was a painful pause. Graff held her breath.

"The last thing I want is an harassment suit on our hands." The captain paused again. "Fine. Call her now, but make it brief."

Graff exhaled. "Thanks, Captain."

She hung up and extracted her note pad from her purse. Flipping through the pages of notes, she couldn't find the number. *Where the hell is it?* Maybe she had written the number on the back of someone's business card. She returned her notepad to her purse and removed a batch of business cards she had collected over the past few weeks. A few of the cards had her scrawls of phone numbers on the back, but none belonged to the vic's wife. Graff flung the stack of cards back into her purse. She leaned against the sink. *Think. What were you holding when you wrote down the phone number?* She remembered. When she took out her notepad and turned it over, she found the phone number for the vic's wife scribbled on the cardboard backing.

She held her phone ready to dial, but the phone rang. It was the captain.

"Graff, don't call the widow. You are no longer to work on this case."

"What?"

"I don't know what you did or who you pissed off, but I just got word from the governor who just got word from a lieutenant general at the Pentagon to stop investigating this case."

"Captain, this makes no sense. I only just found out the name of the killer's associate two seconds ago. What's going on?"

"I don't know. I'm just passing the word along."

Graff hung up the phone. What the hell? Why would the Pentagon care about this crime? If the crimes were all connected, and there really was a serial killer out there, then maybe there was a team already investigating the crimes. But that would be handled by the FBI, not the Pentagon.

It was time to work her connections.

Graff called the governor's home. Back when she had helped get his daughter out of the hands of dangerous kidnappers, the governor had given her his home phone number saying "he owed her one" for whenever she needed help.

The governor himself answered.

"Hi, sir, this is Detective Bobbie Graff with the Berkeley Police."

"Detective Graff, it's a pleasure to hear your voice. What can I do for you?"

"I was in charge of investigating the murder of Yoseph Schwartz."

"You got the message to stay off the case?"

"Yes, sir. I just wanted to know why."

"I understand Detective, but unfortunately I was not informed of a reason. I only know the order came from high above, and that I'd get in some pretty hot water if the command wasn't carried through."

Damn! "I certainly don't want you to get in any kind of trouble, sir. Could you at least tell me who gave the order?"

"Yes. An officer named Lieutenant General Stone. Richard Stone."

Chapter 55

The sun was setting, escaping behind the pizzerias, bagel shops, falafel eateries, cafeterias, and burger joints on Telegraph Avenue. After I climbed into the driver's seat of the van next to Sophia, I took out my burner phone and called the phone number Ira gave me for his boss.

Sophia wanted answers. "What the hell was that all about?"

I got an automated female voice on the line. "We're sorry, but the number you are dialing has been disconnected or is no longer in service." I hung up.

Figured. A bogus number. I bet there's no Richard Swanson, either.

Sophia wanted to know what it was all about?

I said, "The reason I came." I tried to figure out how to explain it.

"Is this going to be a game of twenty questions, or are you going to tell me more?"

"Let me see your phone. It may give away where we are," I said, and she handed it over. I switched the settings to Airplane Mode and turned the iPhone off. "You remember when you and I first met Rabbi Silverman, and he talked about the thirty-six righteous?" I put the phone in my pocket.

"Yeah."

"Well, he thinks you're one of them."

She was silent for a bit, then burst into uncontrollable laughter. Made me smile.

"Me. Righteous."

"Yeah. Go figure, right?"

"What does that have to do with the guy who attacked us just now?"

I explained how the rabbi's list was stolen a few months ago, how nearly every person on that list had been assassinated, how I managed to save Cole but not the thirty-fifth person on the list.

Sophia grimaced. "Are you going to call the police?"

"Not yet. I need to figure out more about this Ira Hughes guy. If we turn him over to the police now, whoever is running this show will probably just send in another killer. We need to stop the leader of the pack."

"Now what do we do?"

I told her my plan, and then we sat in silence in the quiet of the night. Reflecting on my original intent to break up with Sophia, I knew in my heart she'd be better off without me. With all the delusions I had recently of people planting bombs nearby and playing tricks on me, I couldn't see how anyone would want to be a part of that. Two months of mental treatment in the hospital certainly helped.

Sophia turned to face me. "What's been going on in your life? Any fun delusions or hallucinations to share?"

"I checked up on those Torah codes."

"Let me guess. You think they're a bunch of hooey?"

I scratched the back of my neck. "Actually, the damn things are real. I now officially believe in God or a higher power or whatever you want to call it. It's the only way to explain how the codes are in the book of Genesis."

Sophia looked shocked. "My Nathan? The guy who doesn't believe in anything metaphysical? Mr. Anti-Religion himself believes in God?"

"I never said I was sane."

"So how come you're not wearing a yarmulke and have those cute curly locks of hair by your ears?"

"Just because God wrote the book of Genesis doesn't mean I'm about to follow all those crazy rules the rabbis made up."

Sophia laughed. "That's the Nathan I know and love. Skeptic to the end."

"What about you? What have you been up to?"

"Lately, I've been taking classes in NLP."

"What's that, Nature Lovers Porn?"

She smirked. "Neuro-Linguistic Programming."

"Sounds complicated."

"It's a way of using language to help re-pattern the neural pathways in the brain, so that we can have the change we want."

"Still sounds complicated. Do they have a book out? *NLP for Dummies*?"

"I don't think so. Wait, let me check." She scanned the

windshield as if she were looking at a bookshelf. "Nope. No such book."

I chuckled. "I guess I'm not the only one who can hallucinate. Can you do a demonstration of NLP?"

"I'm not supposed to practice on loved ones."

"Why not?"

"Just like psychiatrists shouldn't analyze and prescribe medicines to their spouses, change work is between a professional and her clients."

"How about you just practice instead. That way I'll see what it is."

"Okay." She settled in the passenger seat. "The first question we always ask is, 'What would you like?' "

The question, so simple, was for some reason hard to answer.

Sophia prompted me. "First thing that comes to your mind. What would you like?"

"To understand what's going on."

"Okay, and once you understand what's going on, what will having that do for you?"

"It will help me know how best to handle these guys."

"Once you know how best to handle these guys, what will having *that* do for you?"

"I'll know how to keep you safe."

She smiled. "You care about my safety? Now there's something we have in common." She winked. "What would let you know that you have that?"

"Never needing to look over my shoulder. Or over yours." The more I answered her questions, the more I realized I wanted to be a part of her life. Hell, even if it meant spending the rest of my life looking over her shoulder, I'd take that over being away from her.

"How would that feel, never having to look over your shoulder, or over mine?"

"Safe. And I could move on. We could move on." This future I imagined us having together felt good, and I warmed up to it.

She perked up. "We could move to Amsterdam."

I laughed. "Amsterdam, huh? If that's a professional prescription, I think I could get to like this NLP stuff." I leaned across the gear shift and gave her a kiss.

Chapter 56

Ira Hughes felt his face being slapped from slumber.

Someone yelled at him, "Come on, wake up!" The voice sounded deep and gravelly. "You can't be here."

Ira flinched from the slapping. "Where am I?"

"On the stairs. You can't sleep here." The man sounded like he had ruined his lungs from smoking too much.

Ira forced his lids open in a squint. "Who are you?"

"The manager of this building. Now get up. You have to leave."

His eyes still felt heavy, but with the help of the manager, he fumbled his way out of Sophia's apartment building and into the dark night. What time was it? The manager left him to fend for himself the rest of the way to the stolen UPS truck. Ira fought the temptation toward unconsciousness and found his keys still in his pocket. The truck started with a grumble. The dashboard read 9:36 p.m. Ira put the truck in gear and steered into the darkness. On his way across the Bay Bridge into San Francisco, he retrieved his cell phone from the glove compartment and dialed.

"Richard, it's Ira. Number thirty-six escaped with the help of Nathan Yirmorshy. Remember him?"

"Yeah. I tried to scare him off by having another operative in your area confront him."

"Whatever you tried, it didn't do jack."

"Where are they now?"

Ira forced his eyes to stay open. "All I know is they're using Rabbi Silverman's van."

"Hang on a sec. I'll pull up the DMV file on his van and locate its GPS."

Ira kept the cell phone to his ear and the other hand on the wheel as he waited for Richard to come back on line. About a half hour later he was still on hold. He parked his truck in a free space across the street from his house and climbed out of the truck.

"Got 'em." Richard sounded eager. "They just passed Ford St. and Price."

Ira tried wrapping his head around that one. "That's impossible. You must have tracked my truck, because that's where I live."

"That's where you live?"

"I'm there now." Ira managed to unlock his front door. "I just got here. I'm telling you, you tracked the wrong vehicle."

"You idiot! They followed you home."

"What the—?" He ran to the street and saw red taillights fading out in the distance. Richard's faint voice shouted on the phone, so he put the phone back to his ear.

"Ira, you there?"

"Yeah."

"Where's a good location for you to take care of them?"

"I don't know." He searched his tired brain. "The waterfront past Fisherman's Wharf, at Pier Two."

"Good. I'll steer them there. Just be ready for them."

"I'm on it."

Ira hung up, cursed, and climbed into his Jaguar still wearing the UPS uniform.

Chapter 57

Bobbie Graff let Lee take her arm as he accompanied her to her doorstep.

Lee scratched his chin. "Any chance I can see you tomorrow?"

"You betcha."

"Normally a guy brings flowers or chocolates to a date, but I'm not so sure you'd go for that sort of thing. Do you want me to bring you anything?"

"How about a complete set of steak knives? No, better yet, get me some of those…what are they called?"

Lee scowled. "Give me a hint."

Graff put on a mean face and pretended to swing the weapon around her waist and over her shoulders.

"Nunchucks?"

"Nunchucks. Get me a set of those. I always wanted a set."

"Where does one go to get a set of nunchucks?"

"You're a resourceful guy, you'll figure it out." Bobbie grabbed Lee by the collar and gave him a deep kiss. When she parted from his lips, both of them were panting, gasping to catch their breath. Lee seemed stunned.

"See ya." Bobbie raised her palm goodbye and slipped inside her home.

As I drove away from Ira's house in the inky night, I navigated the van's console menu to its GPS and punched in the address to the Berkeley motel.

I spoke my thoughts aloud. "Now we know where Ira lives. Half an ant's ass away from Nowhereville."

"Who do you think is behind this?" Sophia's quiet voice sounded distant, like she spoke from a different world.

"Not sure. Someone powerful. Someone who has the ability to track a cell phone."

She didn't say anything.

I drove in silence for a few minutes, keeping an eye on the directions for getting to the Bay Bridge.

Sophia stared out the window. I had no idea what she was looking at. The clouds painted the sky so dark, there wasn't much visible below them.

"Hey." I tried to get her attention. "You okay?"

She just nodded. I let her have this time to process all she'd been through and continued driving in silence.

Nearly half an hour passed before I realized the area looked wrong. We were nearing the ocean, somewhere close to Fisherman's Wharf. "That's weird."

"What?"

I scrolled through the directions on the screen. "There's nothing here about taking the bridge."

"What do you mean?"

"These directions. It's like they're not taking us back to Berkeley. They're taking us somewhere else."

"I know where we are." Sophia pointed. "The bridge is back that way. Turn right here."

I turned right even though the GPS said to turn left. After ignoring the screen's directions for several turns and having the GPS adjust to our new coordinates each time, I punched a few buttons and navigated out of the GPS screen.

Richard stood behind the surveillance officer watching the progress on the monitors. Working so late at night to track down Sophia Patai proved fortuitous. He had a skeleton crew of one. Richard would have encountered much more resistance if the entire surveillance team were present.

The tech piped up without looking away from his computer screen. "The vehicle seems to be ignoring the planted GPS data."

Richard cursed under his breath, then said, "You have the make and model of their vehicle, isn't that right?"

"Yes, sir."

"Which systems have E.C.U.s for that vehicle?"

"Electronic control units? All but the steering, sir."

"Disable the brakes and increase the gas flow."

The officer turned to Richard, an addled expression on his face. "Sir?"

"Can you do it?"

He frowned. "Well, yes, but they're in a pretty populated area and—"

"Do it. That's an order."

"Yes, sir." The surveillance officer slowly turned back to his computer and administered commands to the satellite.

Chapter 58

As we neared Pier 39, I got my bearings back on where we were. The streets were better lit and bore heavier traffic. At the stoplight, I stepped on the brake.

It didn't respond.

I had to weave my way around the car in front of me just to keep from crashing into it.

"Nathan, you just went through a red light."

"The brakes don't work."

"What?"

With my foot off the gas, at least we were slowing down. I stomped on the parking brake, but that didn't do anything, either.

"That's weird." Sophia leaned into me and checked the dashboard, perhaps to see if any warning lights were on. "Maybe you should pull over."

"It's not that simple. Both brakes aren't working."

The van sped up by itself.

What the hell?

"Whoa, Nathan. Don't speed up if the brakes don't work."

"It's not me."

We were driving at forty miles per hour. I steered my way through traffic, turning at the next stoplight to get away from the crowded streets. The van sped up to fifty miles per hour. *Dammit!*

"What do you mean, it's not you?"

"Somehow the van's being controlled by someone else." I shifted the van into neutral, but it kept running like I had it in drive. Sophia put her hands on the dashboard in front of her as if to brace for an impact. A hybrid in front of me slowed down at a stop sign. I squeezed by the hybrid, ripping off the side mirror of a parked car, and our van squealed when I made a sharp turn onto the cross street.

The van sped up to sixty.

Who could have the range and technology to hack into a van and control it? I maneuvered around a double-parked car. What could be overriding the van's acceleration and brakes?

I thought of satellite signals. "Let's get to the bridge."

Sophia knew the area better than me and guided me to the nearest on-ramp. I had to run through red lights and swerve away from on-coming traffic. Once we hit the freeway toward the Bay Bridge, the cars were fast enough to drive alongside at a safe clip.

The van sped up to seventy.

"What are you going to do?" Sophia sounded as scared as I felt.

"The van's probably being controlled by a remote signal,

like turning on a TV with a remote control." I changed lanes to pass a truck. "If it's exactly the same thing, then the van is being controlled by a light wave. You can't turn on a TV when there's a piece of furniture in the way."

"You think it's possible to stop the signal from reaching the van?"

"That's the idea. We'll get to test that theory on the bridge since we'll be driving on the lower level."

Eighty miles per hour.

The freeway curved closer to the bridge entrance. I maneuvered over to the fast lane, thankful it wasn't rush hour. The start of the bridge came to view at a distance of just a few yards away. I tapped the brake just to make sure. Still no response.

I steered into the bridge entrance. "Here we go."

We joined the rest of the traffic onto the lower level of the bridge, the upper level a solid metal ceiling above us.

Ninety.

"So much for my theory."

"Why isn't it working?" Sophia's voice got louder.

"High frequency. The signal can go through walls like a radio signal. They must be using a high-frequency carrier wave to make the signal go through the bridge's ceiling."

"So what stops a radio signal?"

Of course! "Sophia, I love you."

One hundred.

The engine whined. The steering wheel shook. We neared Treasure Island, a former military base the bridge passes through before reaching the East Bay.

From the corner of my eye, I could see Sophia clenching the dashboard tighter.

I tightened my hands around the steering wheel. "Just a bit further."

The van sped up to a hundred and ten miles per hour. We reached Treasure Island's tunnel that passed under a small, but solid mountain. Bright lights lit up the road inside the tunnel. Deeper into the belly of the mountain, the magic happened. Radio signals can pass through a wall with minor interference, but an entire mountain will completely disrupt the signal.

The van slowed down. Control of the brakes returned at my feet. I maneuvered to the slow lane and slowed to a crawl putting my emergency blinkers on. Cars behind us passed around us. I parked right there inside the tunnel.

Sophia let out a deep breath. I did the same.

Neither of us said anything for a few minutes. I don't know what Sophia was thinking, but I was too busy counting our blessings to talk. Sophia embraced me, and we stayed there for another few minutes.

When I let go of her, she tucked a thread of her hair behind her ear and straightened her blouse. "What now?"

"Now we enjoy an evening stroll."

Careful to avoid any on-coming cars, we climbed out of the van leaving the emergency blinkers on, and locked up. The tunnel lit the freeway well enough for drivers to see the van, and the blinkers helped indicate the van wasn't moving anytime soon.

I knew I had to work on figuring out who was after Sophia. I knew I had to come up with a plan to stop whoever was behind it. But at that moment, all I cared about was that we survived a near-death experience, and the grim reaper was too busy eating a snow cone or watching some Woody Allen film to notice.

Sophia and I sauntered along the narrow emergency pedestrian platform that ran beside the freeway. The thin path made it impossible to walk side-by-side, so Sophia walked in front of me. Once outside the tunnel, the path widened for pedestrians and bikers who traversed the expanse of bridge that stretched from Treasure Island to the East Bay. Since the path was closed for the night, we had it all to ourselves. We shivered in each other's arms, pressing our bodies close for warmth, and we gazed over the East Bay waters. The clouds cleared, the stars winked at my good fortune in love, and the waves below joined in with quiet claps.

Chapter 59

In the early evening, I enjoyed my stroll with Sophia across the bridge and to the nearest bus station. We made it to the Berkeley motel from the stalled van in under two hours. Echelon flopped over to me with a happy tongue hanging out the side of his mouth. I scrunched my nose. The smell of his healthy, functioning endocrine and digestive system greeted me. Poor carpet.

Cole wasn't there.

The damn kid ran off again.

I picked up the dog and handed it to Sophia.

"Aw, who's this adorable creature?"

"That's Echelon, Cole's puppy."

"Cole?"

"The kid I told you about. One of the so-called thirty-six righteous."

"Ah!" Sophia got caught up in getting the puppy to stand on its hind legs. She didn't notice my concern over Cole's disappearance.

My eyes were heavy, but I didn't feel right sleeping while Cole was still out there.

I snagged a coat hanger from the closet. "Stay here. I may be awhile."

"Where are you going?"

"To find Cole."

She tapped her lips reminding me that I couldn't leave without paying the proper toll.

I gave her a kiss. "Don't wait up."

The parking lot was only half full. The best part about second-rate motels? The renters often have older cars without computer chips and advanced electrical systems. Seven doors down from our room, I spotted an old Mustang.

I set down the coat hanger beside the car. I had to first pay for my purchase. With all the dents the car showed off, it embodied the character of a car worth about $5,000. Add sentimental value, and I came up with what I thought should be a fair price.

Each parking spot had a number associated with the motel room. The parking number for the Mustang was sixteen. At room sixteen, I heard the television blaring. It meant I didn't have to wake the occupant. *Good.* By the sounds of gunfire, the motel guest must have been watching some action movie or TV show. I knocked and waited. The TV hushed silent, either because the guest turned it off or hit the mute button.

The guest who answered the door turned out to be a beer-carrying muscle man with tattoos inked across his arms, neck, and shaved head. "Yeah?"

"Motel inspector. I'm here to make sure everything is in order."

"Do I look that dumb to you?"

Uh, oh. "Sir?"

"What kind of motel inspector goes to an occupied motel room in the middle of the night? Especially wearing jeans and a T-shirt?"

"Yes, I know I may seem like some guy off the street, but the truth is we investigate motels without the owners knowing, so we can't give away who we really are by wearing suits. I understand this is an inconvenience for you, and I would have come earlier, but you're my last motel of the day. I noticed you were awake, so I chose your room over the others. In exchange for your cooperation, the Motel Umbrella Society Toward A New Grade is prepared to compensate you for your stay at this motel and future motels all over the world."

He narrowed his eyes as if to evaluate me and the offer. The TV must have been on mute because the walls reflected different colored projections, but there was no sound. "You'll just inspect the room?"

"That's correct, sir. I will not be inspecting any of your personal effects or belongings."

He widened the door. "Have at it. Want a beer?"

"Thanks, but since I'm on duty, I better not."

He lay back on the bed and let the TV return to its full sound. As he watched the movie, I made a show of my own, peeking in the bathroom, the closet, the drawers, and the sides of the bed.

"Thanks for your cooperation." I tapped my pockets. "Darn it. I forgot my iPhone. Do you have one? I can transfer the money over via PayPal."

He handed me an old Android cell phone.

"Thanks. What's your PayPal email address?" After logging into my own account, I set up a transfer to his account of $25,000. Enough to buy a new Mustang. He had a pleasant surprise waiting for him when he checked his PayPal balance, that was certain. I handed back his phone. "There you go. That will cover many stays at motels all over the country."

"Cool. Find anything wrong with the room?"

"Just one thing. The mattress tag was missing."

"What mattress tag?" He took a swig of his beer.

"The one that says, 'IT IS UNLAWFUL TO REMOVE THIS TAG.' "

He chuckled and mumbled goodnight.

I spent the next half hour jimmying the Mustang's car door open with the coat hanger and hot-wiring the car under the steering wheel with my pocketknife.

Chapter 60

It was almost 10:30 p.m. when I found Cole at the top of the UC Berkeley Campanile. He sat on the floor of the observation platform picking at his fingernails without really looking at his progress.

I sat beside him. "You gotta stop doing this."

"Doing what?"

"Running away."

He nodded. "You brought her back to the motel, didn't you?"

"Yeah, she's fine, but we had a run-in with a delivery guy who was in a foul mood."

He seemed to get my meaning. "You tracking him?"

"I know where he lives." I wondered what he might know about these murders. "Cole, the guy was a religious fundamentalist and a trained assassin. What kind of combination is that?"

"Sounds like he was a member of the New World Order."

"A secret cabal."

"A group of people seeking the End Times."

"People with power in different fields," he said.

I imagined what such a group could do, each person sticking a finger in different pies. Phone companies, the justice system, police stations…. They could accomplish anything they wished without checks or balances.

I took in one last gander at the view of the University's halls and libraries. "I'm going to head over to the killer's house. Are you going to go back to the motel?"

"Three's a crowd."

"The way this night is going, I won't finish up and return to the motel until morning."

He rubbed his eyes. "I want to stay here."

"Fine. Just don't get caught." I needed a plan. "What do you think I should do once I return to the killer's place?"

He gave me step-by-step instructions on what to look for. As I listened to Cole's plan, I admired his thought process and felt I could trust his strategies.

Chapter 61

Sophia sat on the copper-colored comforter of the motel bed. She thought about what Miriam had said. Was she right? Was the message *only her death can save her* really about Sophia making amends with her mom?

The last time she talked to her mom, it started out as a friendly conversation. Then it took a turn as it often did when talking about Sophia's job reading tarot.

"You're wasting your life," her mom had said. "You got A's in English. You could have been an English major."

"And get what kind of job?"

"You could have been an English teacher for inner-city kids. The pay is good, better than private schools, and they offer health benefits."

"Mom, I don't want to be a high school teacher. I like giving readings to clients. The pay may not be great, but it keeps me living comfortably."

"What about psychiatry? You liked psychiatry. You even took a class in it in college."

"It was a psychology class. And yes, I liked it but I didn't want to waste my time with all their extra classes that were pointless, just to get a stupid degree."

That's when the conversation had gone sour.

"That's it, young lady. I have had enough." Her mom's voice was shrill. "I can't believe you think it was a waste of time. You want to talk about a waste of time? What about all those hours I spent working to make sure your life was comfortable? What about all the days, months, *years* I toiled just to get you through college?"

"Mom…"

"You listen here, young lady. I worked hard for you. And you do what? You throw it all away doing readings, making up people's futures, telling them what they want to hear, so they can go on with their lives and pay you undeserved money."

"Don't you lay that on me. I didn't even want to go to college." Sophia closed her eyes to focus on controlling her shouts. "I just went because you wanted me to."

"I didn't spend good money just to have you prostitute yourself on the street with your cards. Enough. I can't talk to you anymore."

Her mom hung up on her. That had been the last conversation she had with her mom six years ago, and every time she thought about it, it burned her. Sophia deserved an apology, but Miriam had instructed her to apologize to her mom. *The only way to get out of a victim-perpetrator relationship is if the victim apologizes to the perpetrator.* The logic of it made no sense.

Sophia checked the time. It was almost eleven o'clock at night. She took a deep breath, picked up the motel phone, and dialed.

"Hi, Mom? It's Sophia."

Chapter 62

As I crossed the Bay Bridge into San Francisco before midnight, I wondered if the minivan had been towed away. Off the freeway, I snaked through the dark residential areas. Instead of lawns, the two-story houses on the block had thick driveways into their garages. None of the homes looked like they even had a first floor, just garages.

I reached Ira's house. The UPS truck still lay silent on the side of the road, but the Jaguar that had been parked in his driveway was gone. Strong evidence he wasn't home. I slunk low as I approached the door.

The house had all its lights snuffed out. The place seemed dead.

At his doorstep I knocked with a strong fist. "Housekeeping."

No answer.

I used a bump key on the front door and stepped inside. My immediate choice was to either go into the garage or climb upstairs to the rest of the house. Everything was on the second floor. Upstairs showcased the bedroom, the bathroom, even the kitchen, dining room, and living room.

I first went to his bedroom. A crucifix hung above his bed. The rest of the room was bare. This guy probably knew he might have to leave at a moment's notice. I checked the bathroom. Again, almost nothing there except the bare necessities. Toothbrush, toothpaste, hairbrush, hairdryer, shampoo, and soap.

I checked the dresser drawers. A week's worth of clothes, at best. No doubt he had a hidden stash of fake identities and currency from different countries. I didn't think the crucifix fit the profile of an assassin, but it fit Cole's description of some sort of contemporary crusaders seeking to hasten the End Days.

Was he really a trained assassin? If he were trained, my guess was he'd practice a lonely lifestyle, and perhaps owned a dog for a companion and a protector, but Ira didn't have any pets. And even though I studied a lot of self-defense, I couldn't imagine having as much success fighting a trained assassin as I did when I fought him at Cole's house.

If he had a hidden stash of passports, that would shed light on his background. Time to find his stash. I took the stairs down to the garage on the first floor. Couldn't find the light switch, so I paused a moment to let my eyes adjust, and performed my search in the dim room. Opening a tool cabinet, I could barely make out what lay on the shelves. A hammer, a can of something, a screwdriver. Nothing significant here. I removed the hammer and screwdriver, and scrutinized the other contents of the closet.

That's when I felt a poke in the back of my ribs and heard the click of a gun preparing to fire.

A man's voice said, "Good to see you again, Nathan."

Chapter 63

Sophia remained on the phone and paced the motel room, leashed by the telephone cord, waiting for her mom to speak.

"What took you so long, Sophia?"

That was an awful way for her mom to greet her. "Excuse me?"

"It's been six years. What if I had died? What if our last conversation had been that argument? Is that the way you want to remember me?"

Sophia burned. Relationships were a two-way street. Her mom could have just as easily called her. But Sophia knew that if the person she spoke with acted like a selfish child, she needed to be the adult, even if that child acting up was her own mother.

"No, Mom. I wouldn't have wanted that argument to be my last memory of you."

"Then what do you want?"

She took a deep breath. "I want to tell you that I'm sorry. I'm sorry for giving you the impression that I was going to be an English major or a psychologist. I could have told you before I went to college that those jobs were not in my vision." She waited for a response, but none came. Were her words landing in her mother's ears? "I'm sorry for not telling you what my goals were sooner, so that you could understand where I was coming from earlier on."

Again, no response came from her mother.

"But most of all, Mom, I'm sorry that I never showed you how much I appreciate your concern for just making sure I was happy."

Sophia heard her weep.

"Yes, Sophia. All I wanted was for you to be happy."

"Mom, I am happy now."

"I know. I just—"

But the words never came. Sophia's mother just cried into the phone.

"I love you, Mom."

Chapter 64

I turned to face Ira in his dark garage and froze as he kept the gun aimed at my chest.

He asked, "Where is she?"

"Susan Boyle?" I kept my hands low and out of his range of vision as I unscrewed the screwdriver from its handle. "I don't know. Ever since she wowed the world with her voice on 'Britain's Got Talent,' I just assumed she'd be spending the rest of her life doing world-wide music tours." With my face just inches away from his, I managed to slide the shank of the screwdriver into the barrel of his gun. "But it seems like she's fallen off the map."

"Sophia Patai," he growled. "Where is she?"

"She's fine." I sucked in my gut enough to slide the head of the hammer between my stomach and the muzzle of his gun. He didn't seem to notice. "She's been studying neuro-llama programming or some such thing. Let me ask you this doozy of a question. What would you like?"

"*Where,*" he demanded. "*Where* is she?"

"My guess is somewhere between obliviously happy and scared for her life."

He sighed. "You're wasting my time. Before I kill her, I'll tell her you died a coward. Any last words?"

"Yeah. I wouldn't shoot if I were you."

He fired and the bullet forced the screwdriver to ricochet off the hammer at my chest. With the gasses having nowhere to go, the gun exploded in his hand. The way the side of the hammer's head punched against my belly, I'd soon have me a nice bruise on my chest. A helluva lot better than a bullet puncturing my lung.

Ira doubled over clutching his hand. He made funny sounds, the kind of sounds that meant he was either constipated or in a lot of pain. I guessed the latter. Catching his attention, I wielded the hammer in my left hand to give his eyes something to fear, and punched him in the gut with my right. I didn't want to kill him, just incapacitate him.

He tried to kick me. I grabbed hold of his leg and threw his leg over, causing him to lose balance and fall to the floor. I ran for the front door. No good. He'd bolted it with a key from the inside. I ran upstairs to the rest of the house. He clomped up the steps behind me. I had seconds at most. I dove into the bathroom and locked the door. He was probably going to come after me with another gun.

I took out my pocketknife and cut off the cord near the hairdryer's handle. I trimmed the ends and kept my fingers on the insulation as I plugged the cord into a wall socket.

He must have finished climbing the staircase by now. Listening for his steps, I heard nothing. Was he stealthy? He managed to surprise me in the garage, so he must have been. Did he know where I was hiding? As soon as I saw the door handle turn, I touched the wires to the doorknob.

The door handle rattled and shook. I imagined the rest of his body just outside the door also shook from taking in over a hundred volts. I wasn't sure how long to electrocute him without killing him. If I stopped now, he might recover quickly and have enough energy to follow through with killing me. If I electrocuted him for too long, the stopping of his heart could be permanent. Whatever happened, I had to make sure he didn't die. He was the only lead I had to find the one who hired him. If he died, the information would die with him.

I pulled the wires off from the doorknob, unplugged the cord, and listened.

Silence.

Was he bluffing? Luring me out from hiding?

I unlocked the door.

The silence remained.

No, Ira's not dead. He's just waiting for me to make a mistake and open this door on my own.

I waited for the knob to turn. As soon as I saw any movement, I'd lock the door again.

The knob remained still.

I shouted in my head not to fall for his tricks. *Don't do it. Don't open the door.* The wait lasted an eternity.

I opened the door.

Shit.

He was dead. A chill ran through me like I had seen this before.

Chapter 65

Ioverlapped my hands and pushed down on the center of Ira's chest. After counting out thirty compressions, I pinched his nose and blew two breaths into his mouth making sure his chest rose. Again, thirty more compressions and two breaths. And again. *Dammit, breathe!*

After several attempts, there was still no response. I gazed upon the lifeless assassin. He lay in the hallway, his eyes vacant and wide open. I checked his pants pockets. He carried his wallet and a small, black notebook full of odd names and telephone numbers. By the unfamiliar area codes, I wouldn't have been surprised if the book were encoded.

I pocketed the black book and examined his wallet. His driver's license identified him as Mike Carter, not Ira Hughes. No credit cards or library cards. Just a sandwich club card to a place called Sammiches. Ten stamps and the next sandwich was free. The card had nine stamps. I felt a pang of guilt for robbing him of his chance at a free sandwich. Ridiculous, I know, but that was how I felt.

I thumbed through the wallet further. Sixty-seven dollars. I pocketed that. Found a security card for some sort of business building. Non-descript. I wanted to take a credit-card reading attachment to my smartphone and see if I could figure out what the card was for, but my smartphone was out of commission for now and my burner phone didn't have such fancy capabilities. Probably didn't matter. If I ran the card through the reader, I'd probably just get data encrypted beyond anything I could decipher.

I flipped through his wallet again.

Bingo. An ID card for his job.

Chapter 66

With the sun rising in front of me, I had to drive over an hour and a half to get to the assassin's supposed workplace in Downtown Oakland. According to his job's ID card, Ira worked as "Mike Carter" in the Accounts Payable department of an office on Harrison Street. The tall building housed the administrative offices for a nearby hospital. He worked there as a cover for his real employment, whoever his true employer was. By the time I reached the office building, the workday had already started. I stood outside working out how to get past security. A guy in a suit walked in my direction finishing a call on his cell phone.

"Excuse me, sir?" I stepped in front of him. "My wife's in the building, and she's supposed to meet me here. I don't want to have to fill in all the visitor paperwork. Do you think I could make a quick call on your cell to call her down?"

"Sure." The man handed me his phone, and I thanked my lucky stars I looked trustworthy.

"Thanks so much." I turned away and dialed.

A lady answered. "911. State your emergency."

Wondering what the fine was for calling in a non-emergency, I whispered, "Hi. I'm standing next to someone who's been bragging about how he just planted a bomb at 1801 Harrison Street."

I hung up and returned the phone to the nice gentleman. "Thanks. May you never be fined by the police."

He scowled at my comment, pocketed his phone, and went on his way.

In two minutes, people poured out the front doors. I needed to get inside the building without looking like I was working my way upstream against the flow of employees exiting. I turned to face the same direction as everyone else and moved sideways in a zig-zag motion to edge closer to the doors.

The workers complained. "Another fire drill," and "I was just in the middle of finishing my last file for the day," and "What's a guy gotta do to not have his work interrupted?"

I added my own soundtrack. "These fire drills keep happening right when I'm close to getting a new high score in solitaire."

I kept shuffling sideways on a backwards course, passing through the front doors on a zig, passing the security on a zag. I slipped past the stairwell everyone poured out from and sneaked into an elevator. Fortunately, the alarm system was old enough for the elevators to stay in commission during an emergency. I examined the assassin's ID card again. Accounts Payable Development Department, twelfth floor.

Inside, the elevator music dripped all over. It was a fruity instrumental version of a song I didn't recognize. I sang along, anyway.

Cletus, where are you now? Your pizza is waiting for you.

I bought you a new telephone, and programmed the pizza place on speed dial.

Pizza. Pizza. Order out anytime you choose.

Cletus, get your pizza. It's pizza-time.

My lyrics sucked, but I still thought it could be a hit someday.

At the twelfth floor, I exited the elevator and checked the area. I was alone. Now for the next question. Where on the floor was his cubicle?

Chapter 67

Detective Bobbie Graff arrived at the police station in the morning before the other officers. She set her Starbucks coffee on her desk, draped her coat on her chair, and got settled. What was the time difference? Three hours ahead? She called the Pentagon switchboard.

"Lieutenant General Richard Stone, please."

"Who may I say is calling?"

"Detective Bobbie Graff of the Berkeley Police Department."

"One moment, please."

Graff listened to the silence as she waited to be connected to Richard Stone's line.

"This is Richard Stone," a voice said.

"My name is Detective Bobbie Graff of the Berkeley Police Department, here in California."

"Detective." He spoke with a cheerful tone. "What can I do for you?"

"I'm calling because there was a request for me to stop investigating a case that I understand came from you."

"That could be. I have a lot of cases I oversee so it could be any one of those. What was the case involving?"

"A gentleman by the name of Yoseph Schwartz. He was murdered at Live Oak Park in Berkeley by a gunshot to the forehead. Sir, does that sound familiar?"

"I think I do remember something about that case. One second and I'll see if I have the file."

Graff didn't have to wait long.

"Here it is. Ah, yes. I remember this one. Yes, it would be in everyone's best interest if you focused on other cases and leave this one up to us. We have it under control."

"Begging your pardon, sir, but since when does the Department of Defense take an interest in civilian homicide cases?"

"This is more than just a civilian homicide case, Detective. Please stay out of it." The Lieutenant General sounded on edge.

"But I need to know why," Graff pressed.

"You don't need to know anything, Detective." His voice hardened. "Focus on other things. Forget this case, or yours won't be the only life that is at risk."

Graff wondered if she heard him correctly. "I'm sorry, sir, but for a minute there that sounded like a threat."

"That is exactly what this is. If you want your friends and family to continue their merry lives, I suggest you stay the hell off that case."

The line went dead.

Chapter 68

I **scanned my surroundings. According to signs** by the elevator, the twelfth floor of the Downtown Oakland office building had several departments, but the way the arrows pointed, the sign for the Accounts Payable department might as well have said, "Go toward that overall general direction…we think."

My best bet was to locate Ira's boss, the head of Accounts Payable. Wandering past the corner offices didn't help. The doors just had nameplates. No indication of which department those offices supervised. I moved to the nearest cubicle and examined the phone. Almost all the numbers on speed dial started with 883. No doubt those numbers were the business prefix.

I took out the assassin's coded book of phone numbers. A few of the numbers started out with the encoded prefix 368. I tried subtracting 368 from 883 without carrying any numbers. I got 525.

$$
\begin{array}{r}
883 \\
-368 \\
\hline
525
\end{array}
$$

That looked familiar.

I examined the assassin's ID cards. They all showed his birth date as 5/25/1983. I reviewed the nicknames in Ira's black notebook. One phone listing read, "King." If "King" were his office boss, the nickname would make sense, but the King's phone number didn't have the encoded prefix 368, so it was not an interoffice number.

I perused the nicknames in his notebook which *did* have 368 as the prefix. I found a "Guinevere." An office hottie, perhaps? I checked the other nicknames with that phone prefix. None of them sounded like a moniker for a supervisor.

Maybe I was working this all wrong. If Accounts Payable was the assassin's fake job, he probably hated it. No way he would consider his boss "King."

I noticed "Jester" had the 368 prefix, 368-4939, so I added Ira's birth date to the listed number without carrying over any numbers.

$$
\begin{array}{r}
368\text{-}4939 \\
+525\text{-}1983 \\
\hline
883\text{-}5812
\end{array}
$$

The answer gave me an interoffice number 883-5812. I dialed from the cubicle. The sound was faint compared to the alarm, but I could still hear it. In the northeast corner office, a phone was ringing.

I left the phone off the hook and followed the ring. It led to a president's office. Somebody named Rosa Clark.

I stepped inside the office, lifted the phone receiver and hung it up to make it stop ringing. The place was a mess. She left her suit jacket on the floor. Piles of papers and files covered her desk, and the computer was riddled with stickers of happy faces.

I groaned at the prospect of having to dig through the mess to find what I needed. But if she had been a neat freak, she might have been able to detect my presence with just a single paperclip out of place, so I thanked my good fortune, took out my imaginary shovel, and started to dig.

After opening a few drawers and flipping through the mounds of papers, I soon found what I was looking for. A list of employees' names along with their extensions. I followed down the list until I found the assassin's alias, "Mike Carter." The extension was 8539. I dialed it and heard a ring coming from a nearby cubicle.

As I went to the assassin's cubicle, I passed several office party photos posted on a corkboard. At the assassin's desk, I picked up the receiver and hung up his phone. The alarm became the sole sound again, filling the floor with its scream.

I returned to the photos pinned to the corkboard in the hallway. In the pictures, Ira always stood in the back corner. He wasn't even very tall. By the looks of it, he separated himself from the rest of the employees. Did this guy have any friends? The more I learned about him, the more I felt like I was learning about myself.

As the police officers filled the station that morning, Graff opened the case binder for the open investigation of a robbery at a liquor store on San Pablo Avenue. She had cases other than the Yoseph Schwartz homicide to work on, so following orders to drop the homicide didn't leave her with nothing to do.

She reviewed the timeline of the robbery, but had trouble focusing. When Lieutenant General Stone had said she should stop investigating or else those close to her would be in danger, she right away thought of her father. Her father was in no danger. He was dead. When Bobbie was 14 years old, her father was killed in the line of duty. He was investigating Bruce Crane, a wanted criminal. Her father got too close to finding Crane. Crane shot her father twice in the chest and had never been seen since.

At that young age, Bobbie's outrage over losing her father burned like a fire in her chest. She committed the rest of her life to putting away anyone who had the idea that they could commit murder and get away with it. She had considered studying law, but working in courtrooms didn't suit her. She needed to be face-to-face with those arrogant criminals, needed to go after them herself. Having been a street cop for several years and having put away perps of all flavors, the fire for revenge dwindled and was now just a glowing ember in her gut. The only time the rage came back was when she had to deal with high-class criminals who flaunted their undue power with arrogance.

Lieutenant General Richard Stone was arrogant. Bobbie Graff felt the glowing ember ignite inside and blaze.

Chapter 69

At the assassin's cubicle, I broke into his locked desk with a letter opener. Nothing in the drawer but a single calling card. *Donny's Caterers.* Why would that be the only thing in his desk? The card had a phone number, but no other information. No area code that he recognized. No address.

I called the number.

"Donny's Caterers." The female voice sounded down to business. Neither friendly nor pleasant. "Give us your location."

Give us your location? Odd greeting for a caterer.

"How do, Ma'am?" I spoke with my best southern twang. "My cousin said you fixed him up something good at his wedding with all your special grub and whatnot. Every guest was as happy as a pup with two peters, is what he said. He suggested I give y'all a call."

"Uh, I'm sorry but we're booked for the rest of the year."

"Oh, that is a shame. But I have delighted in talking to you. Who may I ask do I have the pleasure of speaking with?"

She hung up.

That was no caterer.

I wrote an encoded text to the rabbi. *Have you heard of Donny's Caterers?*

After sending the text, I jiggled the mouse to Ira's sleeping computer. The screen flickered on and asked for a login and password. I tried a few possibilities like his alias and birth date, but after three tries the computer locked me out and told me to contact the administrator.

I received a text message from the rabbi and decoded it. It read, *Why? Do they do kosher?*

If the rabbi didn't know, maybe Cole would.

A gruff voice called out, "Hey! What are you doing?"

A policeman approached me with a hand on his holstered gun.

Chapter 70

At the Berkeley Police Department, Bobbie Graff did a search on her computer for everything she could about the lieutenant general. Who the hell was this guy?

She found very little information at the Pentagon website. The man's name was Richard Stone, a three-star lieutenant general in the U.S. Army, a few steps removed from the President of the United States.

Graff tried the criminal record database. As expected, nothing came up.

She tried the Total Army Personnel Database to see if she could get more info. Born in Massachusetts, the lieutenant general had received an extensive list of outstanding achievements, awards, merits, and accomplishments. There seemed to be no dirt on this guy.

Her captain made a beeline toward her. She clicked off the screen and flipped open the case binder.

He put his hands on his hips. "You're in early."

"Just wanted to get my work done."

"What are you working on?"

"The liquor store robbery."

He didn't seem impressed. "You've dropped the Live Oak Park homicide?"

"Just as you ordered."

"Mm, hmm. So turning off your computer screen just now has nothing to do with the homicide?"

Shit.

"Don't answer that," he said. "Just promise me your work won't ever blow up in my face."

"Cross my heart, hope to die."

"Fine. I'll let you get back to work."

He left her desk and she exhaled her relief. Turning the monitor back on, she checked the internet for Richard Stone's name. Too many popped up. She tried "Lieutenant General Richard Stone" and several results appeared, but as expected, they were websites about military accomplishments, medals, and so on. Graff wanted to see what went on earlier in the man's life. Before he became a lieutenant general.

She made a note of his parents' names and did a search for "Richard Stone" and his parents' phone number. Only a few results. Mostly lists of attendees and memberships to religious Christian events and affiliations. The affiliations to memberships of Christian groups seemed to increase over the years. Then, sometime after making Lieutenant General, all memberships stopped.

Either the Lieutenant had a sudden loss of interest in religion, or he was hiding it.

Chapter 71

I **put on a big smile as the police officer, hand** on his holster, approached.

I said, "Hi, maybe you can help me out." I shook the policeman's hand. He still had a look of uncertainty about him. "I was supposed to meet Ms. Rosa Clark. She's the President of Accounts Payable, but no one's here."

He eyed my torso, probably wondering why a guy would wear jeans and a short-sleeved shirt to an office building. "Where's your visitor's sticker, sir?"

"Oh, that. It went on lopsided so I peeled it off my shirt and the darn thing took off so many threads. I couldn't get it to stick back on. I tossed it out."

"Sir, do you hear that ringing?"

"Yeah, is the elevator stuck?"

"That's an evacuation alarm for a bomb alert."

I clapped my cheeks. "Oh, my goodness!"

"There's been a call about a bomb here, and we need the place evacuated."

"I'll leave right now."

"The problem is, sir, we're going to have to take you to a safe zone and hold you for questioning."

Uh, oh.

"You see, we have to consider the possibility that someone triggered a false bomb alert just to get easy access to the building."

Dammit! "Okay, officer. Lead the way."

As he walked me toward the stairs, I weighed my choices. If I stayed with him, he might just ask me questions, which would be fine. I could easily overcome those. But he might also check my pockets. I could just say he doesn't have the right to search my belongings without a warrant, but then he'd take me "downtown" for further questioning. Never mind that I was already downtown. My other choice was to comply with all his requests, cooperating like a good citizen, but then he'd see the assassin's book of coded phone numbers, IDs, and, most alarming, Ira's work ID. What if they took me to the police station? The worst that could happen? They could have me in custody, establish that I had the work ID card of "Mike Carter," and find out "Mike" was dead. I'd have no chance of being invited to the Accounts Payable office parties.

As we approached the stairs, I suddenly propelled myself forward, running out the stairwell door.

"Stop!" the cop yelled.

As I descended, I calculated the number of stairwells, elevators and exits a building of this size had. Probably four stairwells, three elevators, two exits, and one way out.

The steps of the guard sounded above me in the concrete stairwell. He squawked into the walkie-talkie. At the ninth floor, I shoved open the door to the floor. At one of the elevators, I popped in, hit the button for the first floor, and popped back out letting it ride empty.

In another stairwell on the opposite side of the building, I stepped down to the eighth floor. No doubt the security and police had all the stairwells and main elevators covered, carefully climbing each stairwell with guns at the ready.

That's why I took the freight elevator. Had to use a bump key to get it open, but it did its job.

Down at the staff-only side of the basement, the elevator brought me to the dumpsters in the underground parking lot reserved for special employees. No cops. I walked out the car ramp entrance of the garage. A number of people on the sidewalk noticed me coming out of the parking lot, so I held the burner phone to my ear.

"Hi, Hon." I used a loud voice. "Now I can hear you. I was saying that there's some alarm, probably a fire alarm, so we all have to evacuate the building." I paused. "I know, right? Ridiculous." Most of the onlookers turned away from my conversation, but a man in a suit still watched me. "You just better make sure you wear those chaps I love so much, you bad boy, you." I winked at the man, and he turned away.

Chapter 72

I parked the Mustang a short distance away from the motel since I planned on driving it again. No sense in letting its owner find it. Then I'd have to steal another car. At ten in the morning, I walked back to the motel room and let myself in. The noise woke Sophia up. Her eyes were red. She jumped out of bed and embraced me.

"What's wrong?" I held her close, relishing her warmth. "Were you crying?"

"I patched things up with my mom."

"That's good, isn't it?"

She didn't reply, just continued to hold onto me. The room smelled like cleanser. She must have tackled Echelon's fragrances.

I pulled away from her. "I need to make a phone call. You okay?"

She nodded and stepped into the bathroom.

I decoded the "King's" phone number by adding Ira's birthdate to the number listed in Ira's coded book of phone numbers, and called the "King" from the landline in the room. If I was right, the number would connect me to Ira's boss.

"Hello?" a man's voice said.

"Hi, this is Barry Leiden with your cable company, and I regret to inform you that your cable connection will be discontinued unless all charges are paid in full."

"I always pay the bill on time. You must be mistaken."

"Yes, we have indeed received regular payments from you, and we appreciate it. Unfortunately, the payments did not cover all the charges."

"What? What charges were missed?"

"I'm sorry, sir, this is very embarrassing, but your charges for seeing certain movies weren't paid for."

"What movies?"

"Let's see, we have *Great Sexpectations, Wuthering Nights,* and *All Quiet On the Western Cu—*"

"Now hold on a second. I don't watch that trash."

"Yes, sir. It's quite common that another member, usually a son, has been watching shows without the parents' knowledge."

"I don't have a son, I live alone, and I'm telling you *I don't watch that trash.*"

"I'm terribly sorry. I should have checked that I have the right account in front of me. Who am I speaking with?"

"Richard Stone."

That made sense. The "King's" phone number in Ira's book referred to Richard. "And your billing address?"

"75…Wait a second. Who is this?"

I hung up, triumphant in figuring it out. Richard Stone. King Richard.

Chapter 73

Lieutenant General Richard Stone hung up the phone and immediately picked it back up.

"Get me a trace on this number." He read off the number of the last call made to his phone. "Check on all calls made from that number in the last two days."

Before Richard could return to his stack of papers to process, someone knocked at his office door.

"Come in."

Richard sniffed. The stocky, gray-haired employee had a flatulent air about him. "Sir, someone called the check-in line as if it were a caterer."

That presented a problem. If someone called the caterer line, it meant the calling card had fallen into the wrong hands. The caterer number was a direct line to Special Project HQ.

"Any idea where the call originated?"

"1801 Harrison Street, Oakland, California. Twelfth floor. Ira Hughes's desk. He doesn't answer his cell phone, and we can't get a fix on his position. His phone must be off or busted."

Richard tapped his pen against the desk. None of Ira's behavior indicated that he planned on going rogue. He must have been either locked up or dead. If he was dead, then who killed him and made the call?

Richard's phone rang. He answered, waving the smelly employee to go away.

"Sir, the number you asked us to trace is from a Berkeley motel, and there was only one other call made from that line in the past two days."

"To where?"

"It was made to one Delilah Patai in New Jersey."

Richard recited the name a few times. Where did he hear that name before? Patai.

He knew where. Patai. Sophia Patai was still alive.

"Thank you." He hung up the phone.

If Ira was out of the picture, the time called for a much more talented assassin. Richard knew just the man. Eric Redding. Redding may not have been a member of the Order—and it was risky to hire outside the Order—but he always got the job done.

Richard phoned his secretary. "Send out an alert to Eric Redding. He may take a few hours to get back to us. When he calls in, transfer him over to me."

"Yes, sir."

A few minutes later, another employee knocked and entered his office.

The employee spoke too slowly for Richard's tastes. "You said to let you know if anyone did a search for your name."

Richard waited for the employee to finish, but he took too long. "And?"

"A Detective Bobbie Graff has searched the internet, the criminal database, and the military database for your name."

"Any other searches?"

"Yes, she did a combined internet search for both your name and a 'Yoseph Schwartz.' "

Richard nodded. She wasn't backing down. "Get me a list of her family members, known associates, and their addresses. Now."

"Yes, sir."

Alone again in his office, Richard called his ex. "I'm sorry, Elizabeth. I'm going to be busy tonight."

"Holly's turning eighteen. You promised her you'd come over for her birthday party. You know what? Never mind. I'll tell her you had another emergency at work."

"Thanks, Elizabeth."

"For some reason, she still loves you with all her heart. I don't know how she puts up with your broken promises. When are you going to take responsibility, Dick?"

Richard stiffened at how she said his nickname. *That bitch.* "Elizabeth—"

"Wait. Stop. I know what you're going to say. Your responsibility to protect the nation is more important than our daughter."

"As awful as it sounds, that's exactly it."

"I hope your logic helps you sleep at night." Elizabeth hung up the phone.

Richard remembered when Holly was born. The first

time he held her in his arms, he swore he'd work at being the best father a girl could have. What happened to that promise?

He turned to the framed photo on the wall of himself in full uniform, shaking hands with the President of the United States.

Promises change. Like the Christmas decorations that promise peaceful times, they all come down when Christmas is over, and reality hits. But more than losing the decorations of fatherhood, he had to take down the decoration of husband, too.

Staring at the photo, Richard admired the three silver stars on his epaulettes designating his lieutenant general rank. Some decorations came first.

Chapter 74

While Sophia washed up in the bathroom, someone knocked on the motel door. I peeked through the window blinds. It was Cole in his "Hell on Wheels" T-shirt, holding his skateboard.

I opened the door. "Finally decided to come back?"

He shrugged. "I was bored."

"Here. Take a look at this." I handed him the card I had found in Ira's desk.

"Donny's Caterers?"

I described the phone call I made, how it sounded like anything but an actual caterer. I took back the card. "Any idea who they are?"

"Who knows?" He sat beside Echelon who slept in a tiny bundle on the bed, and scratched his puppy's ears. "As a hired assassin, the number could have been his contact, but…"

Sophia called out from the bathroom, "What did you say?"

Cole looked up. "That your girlfriend in there?"

"Yeah. I'll introduce you in a minute. What were you saying?" I sat on the other bed.

"It's just odd that the first thing they asked for was your location. Could the location be their way of identifying the assassin?"

I shook my head. "That wouldn't make sense."

Sophia stepped out of the bathroom. "What do you mean?"

Cole explained. "If assassins were identified by their locations, that would suggest there were several assassins under the same umbrella organization, but assigned to different targets."

I patted the bed for Sophia to sit next to me and asked Cole, "What kind of umbrella organization?"

"Could be a private organization, some kind of retired military group making money as hit men."

I nodded. "I suppose that's possible. These hits are religious-based. A rich, religious zealot could hire such an organization to fulfill some delusion of a prophecy."

Sophia took my hand. "What are you saying?"

"What Cole is saying is that a religious freak may have hired a bunch of ex-military to carry out killing the thirty-six righteous."

"Who's Cole?"

He stopped scratching Echelon and got up from the bed. "Ignore her. She's crazy."

"What are you talking about?" I asked him.

"She's no good to us." Cole sauntered over to the dresser.

"Nathan?" Sophia looked worried.

I realized I had forgotten introductions. I gestured to Cole. "Sophia, meet Cole. Cole, meet Sophia.

Sophia's eyes darted between Cole and me.

"You're the last two alive of the thirty-six," I explained.

Cole ran his fingertips along the surface of the dresser, then swiveled abruptly to face me. "I told you, you should never have brought us together."

"Ignore him," I told Sophia. "He's just jealous of your good looks."

Sophia took both my hands and squeezed them. "Nathan, listen to me carefully. There's no one there. It's just you, me, and Echelon."

Chapter 75

I couldn't believe it. As soon as Sophia had said no one else was in the room with us, Cole vanished. Just disappeared in an instant.

Couldn't be. No. That's impossible.

I ran outside to the car. Sophia called after me, but I ignored her and drove off, following the route to Thanan. The freeway signs I thought had said "Thanan" didn't say such a thing. They said, "Fremont." I drove to Toys R Us based on familiar landmarks. The parking lot was bustling with cars this time. I parked in the same parking space, noticing how far the space was from the store. If the parking lot had been empty before, why had I previously parked so far from the store?

Inside heralded clerks at every cash register and long lines of customers waiting with full carts of toys. No laughing clerk. No television sets to watch. Children pounded this place with noise, hammering in sounds of screams and laughter.

I sought the aisle that carried the skateboarding equipment. Couldn't find it. Closest thing I found were a few skateboards on a shelf, not a full aisle of skateboarding paraphernalia. Nearby, a boyish man with the store uniform restocked the shelves.

I called out to him. "Where's the skateboard aisle?"

"Right here." He nodded at the three skateboards.

"No. The full skateboard aisle with the accessories and extra wheels and all that."

"Sorry sir, this is all we have in the way of skateboards." He pointed to the three skateboards again.

Dammit. I looked at the skateboards, searched the ground for answers, then asked, "Where do you keep the Magic 8 Ball?"

"Aisle five."

I went to the aisle and after a few minutes of scouring the shelves, I found it.

Holding the toy in my hands, I muttered, "Is Cole alive?"

I shook the ball. It read, "Try again."

"Is Cole alive?"

I shook the ball and it read, "Try again."

My shoulders dropped. I looked down the aisle. Looked back at the 8 ball. "Where's Cole?"

I shook it.

It read: No.

As I stood in aisle five of the toy store, memories flooded back to me.

Two days ago, when I'd heard the sound of gunfire, I had yelled to Cole, "Come on. We need to move."

Cole had first grabbed his puppy.

"Now!" I urged.

We sped out of the basement. Cole ran to the bodies of his parents out in the exposed hallway.

I tried to stop him, but the gunner shot him. Cole fell clutching his side, screaming. He must have been hit in the arm.

He must have been hit in the arm, right?

No. The truth came to me. His chest was bloody. No way he could have survived that.

"Go, Cole! Run!" I yelled.

"Take care of Echelon," Cole said. He wasn't talking about making sure I got his dog out of the house. He was talking about after he died. *Take care of Echelon.* Those were his last words. His dying wish.

From then on, the visions I had of him, the conversations, they were all in my head. My sick way of dealing with his death.

Chapter 76

In his office, Richard Stone entered a command on his computer, but the machine didn't respond. *For crying out loud.* Not patient enough to give the computer time to process, he punched a finger into the off button. The screen popped to black.

Richard took a deep breath, in then out, and leaned back in his chair. Any time now, he'd hear from Eric Redding.

He turned to the photo of his daughter and took comfort in knowing his tasks would help her soon experience true joy. Memories ambushed his thoughts. He and his six-year-old daughter Holly had been strolling through the evening carnival, her tiny fingers hanging on to two of his own. The smell of popcorn and cotton candy had lined the paths, while festive circus music whistled through the outdoor speaker system.

"What do you want to do next?" Richard hunched over to make sure she heard him. They had just left the Ferris wheel and were passing the shooting gallery when Holly pointed to it.

"I want to do that."

"The shooting gallery? Why do you want to do that?"

"Cause that's what you do. Right, Daddy?" Her simplistic view of his work amused him.

"I don't go around shooting things, Holly, but it's true that I have fired a gun."

"I wanna be like you, Daddy."

He chuckled. "Well, I'm not sure it's the best thing for you. I don't think you'd like my job. But we can play on the shooting gallery, okay?"

"Okay." She rubbed her eye with her fist tucked in her sleeve.

"Just don't tell your mom."

His sweet little girl nodded at him.

He gave her two tokens and instructed her to put them in the slots to activate the gun. He had to lift her in his arms so she could get a clear line of view of the red and white bull's-eye targets. A few older kids played beside them. One kid shot a bull's-eye target next to a can and when he hit the target, a sound of air releasing shot out, *Pssht!* The can followed up a wire until gravity brought it back down again. The whole display simulated shooting a soda can so that it popped up into the air. Another kid hit a target by a vase of fake flowers. The full bouquet spun in a circle like a top.

Richard had to help Holly hold the fake rifle steady. Though lighter than a real rifle, the toy still weighed too much for her. The gun was attached to the counter with flexible, metal piping. The piping must have wrapped around wires making the gun's electric signal work like a

TV remote control. The bull's-eye targets picked up the signal.

"Aim for the closer targets, okay? They're bigger and easier to hit," he instructed.

"Okay."

With some help at holding the rifle steady, she managed to fire the gun at a can's target. The gun made a clicking sound and the can popped up into the air.

"Did it!" she cried out.

"Yes, you did it." He bounced her in his arms.

"I want to try the ducks."

"The ducks?" Richard didn't want her to become disappointed. Not yet. Not at a carnival. Somehow bad emotions felt worse when everyone else around was happy. "I don't know, Sweetie. Those are hard. The targets are farther away. They're smaller, and they're moving."

"Then you do it. I want to see what the ducks do."

Richard smiled and set Holly down. She peeked over the edge of the counter to watch. Richard took the rifle in his hands and firmly positioned the shoulder butt against his shoulder to minimize recoil, though it wasn't necessary. There was no blow back from this toy. He lined the sight at the end of the barrel and counted the seconds it took for each duck's target to fall into his line of fire. Two…three… target acquired. Two…three…target acquired. He exhaled. Two…three…pulled the trigger. *Pshht!* The metal cutout of the duck tipped over backwards.

Holly shrieked with glee.

Richard smiled and picked her up again to let her fire the remaining shots.

Richard's memory of her faded when his desk phone rang. It was his secretary calling to connect him with Eric Redding.

"Eric, I've got an assignment for you. A target."

"Go ahead," Eric said.

Richard gave him Sophia Patai's name and physical description, and read off her current location.

Eric confirmed the name, description, and location. "I'm in the area."

"Then get it done tonight." Richard hung up the phone.

He thought back once again on that day with Holly. The carnival had been a success. He had even managed to win her a big, purple bear. At the end of the day, while driving Holly home, Richard broke the news to her and wondered if she understood what he was telling her. She clutched the stuffed bear in her arms as if she needed someone to hug.

"You're breaking up with Mom?"

"It's for the best."

Holly didn't say anything.

Richard glanced at her. Her nearly invisible blonde eyebrows bunched into a tiny knot. She was trying to understand.

"It's got nothing to do with you," Richard said. "You're not the reason we're splitting up."

Holly looked up at him, as if checking to make sure what he said was true.

He felt awful. He took a deep breath to keep his voice from breaking. "We both love you very much, but I'm not able to be there for the family. We feel it's unfair for all of us to pretend that I can stay a part of the family."

"Don't be sad. You'll always be my Daddy."

Richard's heart cracked. "And you'll always be my little girl." He stroked her hair.

Chapter 77

I returned to the motel room. Sophia sat beside me on the bed, holding me, stroking my back. No one else occupied the room now. Just Sophia and myself. She probably knew what I was thinking. Knew it had been a delusion.

I took my meds, didn't I?

I had. Though it might have been a delusion of my disorder, it might have also just been my brain firing the necessary neurons to avoid dealing with the trauma of Cole's death.

I couldn't look Sophia in the eye. "Why do bad things happen to good people?"

She didn't respond right away.

What kind of world lets a good kid die? I didn't get it.

Sophia finally spoke. "What do you want, instead?"

I rolled my eyes. "I want *good* things to happen to good people."

"Let's make this a little more specific. What do *you* want?"

"I want good things to happen to me."

"What would having that do for you?" she asked in a soft voice.

"It would let me live in happiness."

"What do you expect to have by living in happiness?" She rubbed small circles on my back.

I expect to spend the rest of my life with you, Sophia. I turned to face her. "I expect to live in comfort. No murder, no sickness, no overcooked eggs."

"Overcooked eggs?" She smiled.

"I'd settle for no murder or sickness."

She nodded. "Okay, so what would you have to sacrifice to have a life of complete comfort without murder or sickness?"

That was one hell of a question. "What do you mean?"

"Knowing you, you'd have to sacrifice taking initiative."

"I still don't follow you."

"I know you, Nathan. If there were no starving people in Africa, you never would have constructed the water purification plant. If the supposed thirty-six righteous lived happily without any threats, you never would have come to their aid."

I said nothing.

She tilted her head, locking her eyes on mine. "If I were still safe and sound, you never would have returned to my side."

She was right. When bad things happened, I took action. Back when I didn't know murder or sickness in my daily life, I had been a computer programmer living each day on a monotonous schedule. Even then, I wasn't happy.

Sophia continued. "We choose our own lifestyle. We'll do whatever it takes to keep our present lifestyle. It can be as simple as the primitive part of your brain, your critter brain, noticing that you've survived something and wants to keep you in situations where you've already proved you survived." She took my hand. "In this case, the critter brain thinks that any new situation—even a situation of health, happiness, and comfort—is a situation it may not be capable of surviving."

"You're saying that since my critter brain knows I can survive dangerous, even painful situations, that's the only kind of situation it seeks to stay in."

She squeezed my hand. "Right. So the question is, are you willing to step out of your comfort zone and live an unfamiliar lifestyle of surrounding yourself with healthy and happy people? Are you willing to risk losing your ability to take initiative?"

I nodded. One of Erik Erikson's psychosocial stages in life was Generativity vs. Stagnation. In a weird way, my life didn't follow one or the other. It enveloped both. By constantly generating ways to help and protect people, I remained stagnant in my lifestyle and didn't leave my comfort zone.

Chapter 78

After Sophia comforted me, I was still angry. The sun had gone to bed, but I wasn't ready to do the same. I stomped to the bedside drawer to get some twine.

"What are you doing?" Sophia asked.

"I'm taking the dog out for a walk. Watching him take a dump usually gives me a sense of relief. Maybe it'll help."

The drawer was stuck. I gave it a strong yank. The drawer tumbled to the floor sending the twine and Bible to the floor, too.

I picked up the Bible and shouted, "If Genesis was really written by God, He was an idiot. What dolt says the Universe was made in seven days?"

Sophia looked baffled. Probably more by my choice of conversation than by the question itself.

"I don't know," she said. "Why don't you ask the rabbi?"

I knew the reason she wanted me to talk to him was not to get an answer, but to make sure I talked out my anger with someone.

I tied a stretch of twine to Echelon's collar and escorted him from the room, slamming the door behind me.

I didn't care about the whole phone-texting-in-code thing. Waste of time. Outside, I walked Echelon along the stretch of grass beside the motel rooms. I called the rabbi directly from my burner phone.

"Rabbi, your god's an idiot. Your all-knowing being that wrote Genesis makes the Universe just six thousand years old, not billions."

"Nathan?"

"Yeah, it's me."

"I thought you wanted to communicate by code only."

"Forget that. What the hell kind of god doesn't know how old his Universe is? The Bible says the Universe is under six thousand years old."

"According to whose watch?" The rabbi asked.

"What?"

"Nathan, if I were standing on the sun and you were on Earth, and according to my watch one year passed, how much time on Earth would have passed?"

I breathed in and out. It was a standard question in physics. "A year and sixty-six seconds."

"Exactly. Why is that?"

"Because of general relativity. More gravity means the rate of time goes slower."

"And how many Earth years do you suppose would be the equivalent of the first twenty-four hours standing at the edge of the Universe during the Big Bang?"

Shit. With all the gravity present at the Big Bang, the number of Earth years was probably millions. Even billions. If someone sat at the edge of the Universe during the first few days of the Big Bang, a few twenty-four hour periods for him would take billions of Earth years.

I didn't say anything.

"To have a chat about Biblical interpretation? That is why you called, Nathan?"

I didn't know how to respond.

"Nathan, I am always happy to have such discussions, but what's your real reason for calling?" he persisted.

I thought about Cole. One of the thirty-six righteous, supposedly. Dead for no good reason.

"Cole's dead."

"Mein Gott! Oh, Nathan. That's horrible news."

The rabbi spoke further, but I couldn't pay attention. I remembered Cole's face, his determination and zeal when speaking about his crazy conspiracy theories. The way he made bigger gestures the more excited he got.

There was a pause on the line. The rabbi had stopped talking, so I asked, "Why do bad things happen to good people?"

"Nathan, that is such a good question. I'm afraid there is no simple answer."

"Try me."

"Some say we should be grateful for the time we *have* had with the loved one, instead of feeling resentful for losing time we could have had. Another consideration is that each soul has a purpose, a lesson to learn in their lifetime. For some, the lesson is learned early on in life, their purpose achieved and they pass on. For others, the impact and result of having a loved one die *is* their lesson that allows them to bring strength to others."

Sounded more like excuses than reasons. "Death isn't the only way good people are hurt." I thought about people injured in falls, broken arms and sprained ankles, people who lost their homes and their jobs. I thought about anyone who's been yelled at, scolded for no good reason, hurt by words strong enough to leave a scar.

"Do you know the book of Job?" The rabbi pronounced the name *Joe-b*.

"Heard of it. Don't really know it."

"Job was a good man who praised God, but Satan the accuser convinced God that Job's righteousness only existed because Job was living the good life, and if Job had hardships, he wouldn't praise God anymore. It was a conditional love, Satan told God."

"I thought Judaism didn't believe in the Devil."

"In Judaism, Satan is not a devil, but an angel."

"A fallen angel?"

"No. Just an angel."

I shrugged it off. "What's the point?"

"The point is that Job lost his crops, his animals, and even his wife. Everything that gave him happiness was taken away from him."

"What did he do?"

"He cried out to God demanding to know why God did this to him."

"And what was the response?"

"The response was cryptic."

Anger filled me so much, I was certain I'd say words to the rabbi I'd later regret, so I hung up on the rabbi without a goodbye.

I breathed in.

Breathed out.

Got an uncoded text from the rabbi: *I'm here if you need me.*

I texted back to him: *Thanks. Need time.*

Anger still wrestled with me. I wanted to yell, but settled for a small tug-of-war game with Echelon when he chomped down on the twine and tugged, tail wagging.

Chapter 79

Eric Redding drove the last block with the headlights off. He pulled into the parking lot as far as he could from the target's motel room and stepped out of the car with his cane. He hobbled over to the office where a golden retriever greeted him.

"Well, hello there, boy." Eric eased himself down to sit on the floor and gave the dog a good rubbing. "What's your name?"

"That's Charlie." The balding front desk clerk wiped the counter.

"Charlie, eh?" Eric continued to pet him. "How old is he?"

"He's getting into his adulthood, now. Twenty-eight dog years."

"He's a good boy. You are, now, aren't you?" He laughed as the dog licked his cheek.

"He sure does like you," the clerk said.

"Yeah, he's a good boy. Say, do you have a Sophia Patai staying here? I'm supposed to meet her."

"Let's see." The clerk checked the computer screen. "I'm sorry, sir. No one here by that name."

"Maybe she's with my friend. Do you recognize her face?" Eric held up a photo as he continued to sit on the floor and pet Charlie.

The clerk walked over to where Eric was sitting and looked at the photo. "Yes, I have seen her. I've seen her with the gentleman that's staying here."

"Nathan Yirmorshy?"

"Let me check. I know my customers by their room number, not by their name. Bad habit, I know." The clerk scrutinized the computer screen once again. "Yes. Mr. Yirmorshy. That's the man. Want me to call him?"

"No, thank you. I'll just go to their room. Which one is he in?"

The clerk smiled. "Normally I don't share that information, but Charlie's taken a liking to you. Any friend of Charlie's is a friend of mine. Mr. Yirmorshy's in room twenty-eight."

"Excellent. Thanks so much." Eric positioned his cane to get up.

"Do you need help there?"

"No, thank you. I actually don't need the cane, but it eases the trek." He pushed himself off the floor and stood upright. He was about to leave when he stopped at the door. "Do you take your dog out for walks?"

"We usually go down University Avenue to a park just off Sacramento."

"How often?"

"Eight a.m. and eight p.m. every day. Why?"

Eric checked his watch. "He looks a little like he's itching for a walk, and I see he's due for one in about twenty minutes, so that's perfect."

I led Echelon along the back of the motel where grass conquered the cement. Through the office window, I saw the desk clerk chatting with the very man who pinned me against the wall at the sandwich store. The bully sat on the floor petting the clerk's dog. Apparently he thought dogs deserved better treatment than humans. I couldn't argue with him on that point.

By the time Echelon finished doing his business, the man with the cane had left. I circled to the front of the office and walked in.

The clerk's eyes lit up. "A gentleman was just asking about your friend."

"My friend?"

"The woman. Sophia…Patty?"

"Patai." My arm jerked when Echelon tugged to sniff the clerk's dog. "How did you know about her?"

"I didn't until he showed me a picture. I recognized her because I saw you with her walking to your motel room."

"You told him which room we're in?"

"Well, he spoke of you like he knew you. Even mentioned you by name."

"You told him which room we're in?" I asked again.

He shrugged, and dropped his gaze to the floor. "Yes."

Oh, no.

Chapter 80

Eric Redding prepared the plastic explosive at his car. He kept the C4 in its cellophane packaging and carefully poked it with the detonator's leads.

The great thing about C4 was its stability. It wouldn't explode if dropped or if a bullet hit it. It wouldn't even explode if exposed to fire or microwave radiation. Only a blend of high heat and shockwaves could trigger the explosive. One could safely handle C4 as long as it wasn't hooked up to a detonator.

With the explosive ready, he cradled it out of the car, leaving the car door open. As stable as C4 was, Eric had no interest in risking a jolt to his body by slamming a door shut while carrying a bomb. He left his cane in the car and limped to the target's location a few yards away.

Holding the C4 steady, he scanned for a proper place to install it. Under the window? Too conspicuous.

Behind the bushes? Still too visible.

Then he saw the perfect place.

***

I kept an eye on the bully's slow steps from his car to the motel. Generally, attacking someone who's holding a bomb is not the best idea. People who did that sort of thing were no longer around for you to say, "Kudos! Job well done."

He stepped at a snail's pace, heading toward our motel room.

I sneaked to his car. The front door was left ajar. Made sense. Not easy closing a car door while carrying a bomb. I let go of the twine attached to Echelon's collar so that I could creep fully into the car. That turned out not to be a good move. The dog was getting away, exploring. I put him in the back seat and searched the car further.

I opened the glove compartment. No information. The car was a rental made out to a Simon Randiman. Probably an alias. I noticed the cane he had left behind. That could help. I took out my knife and sliced open the rubber bottom of the cane. After digging out a good-sized hole, I took off my shirt and cut off a piece of the fabric. I cut the palm of my hand. *Man, that stings!* Blood seeped out. I soaked it up with the shirt piece.

In the distance, the bully was returning at a steady limp. I tucked the bloody cloth into the base of his cane, making sure the wet fabric bulged out at the bottom.

Did he see me? Not yet.

I crawled out of his car and squeezed my way through other vehicles before hiding behind a Volkswagen Bug.

He hobbled back and slid into his car. The bully drove away oblivious to the puppy peeking out from his back window.

Goodbye, Echelon.

Chapter 81

I ran for the motel room and searched outside.
Not many places to hide a bomb. Time was against me, though. No reason for the stranger to delay detonating the explosive, as far as I could tell, so I needed to find the bomb fast.

I searched behind bushes. Nothing.

If I were a bomb set to go off soon, where would I be? I wouldn't need to hide in a never-viewed spot, just some place where I wouldn't be spotted in the next few minutes.

I checked the ice chest.

There it was.

Defusing it should be a breeze. No sense for the bully to add hidden trip-wires, motion sensors, and extra fail-safes unless he expected the bomb to be found. That would be like buying bells and whistles for a car whose destination was a junkyard.

This bomb was simple. It had a timer set to go off in seven minutes. I pulled out the leads from the explosive C-4 packets. Successfully defused.

I exhaled. Took off my torn shirt and wrapped it around my bleeding hand. I carried the C-4 and detonator into the motel room.

"What's that?" Sophia asked.

"A bomb."

"Very funny. Why's your shirt off?" Her eyes popped open wide. "What happened to your hand?"

"I walked into a door."

She craned her neck to see behind me. "Where's Echelon?"

I eased the bomb onto the counter. "Good question."

I checked the timer. Though it still ran a countdown, it was no longer connected to the C4 to do any damage. Four minutes left before the stranger would expect to hear an explosion.

I sliced off a piece of the C-4 and hung it from a sprinkler on the ceiling. By hanging the piece of C4 from the ceiling, the blast would do more surface damage than structural damage, breaking glass and mirrors without affecting the walls and building's foundation. The explosion would look more severe than it actually was.

"What are you doing?" Sophia asked.

"Convincing him of his success."

One minute left. I reattached the leads of the timer to the small slice of C4. The bomb was ready.

I grabbed Sophia's hand. "Come on!"

We ran out of the motel into the parking lot. The bomb destroyed the windows in a ball of flame. Car sirens squealed.

Our inked, muscled neighbor came outside and shouted, "What the hell was that?"

"Sorry," I said. "Did we wake you?"

Chapter 82

Richard Stone finished reviewing a threat analysis report when Eric's call came through.

"It's done."

"What's done?" Richard asked. "Not the job."

"Yes, the job. Why else would I be calling you?"

Richard chewed on his lower lip. If the operation had been completed successfully, the whole world would have known about it. As it was, the day still moved along like any other. Either Sophia wasn't dead, or the Rabbi's list contained the wrong thirty-six righteous. Did the rabbi have the wrong thirty-six?

No. Richard couldn't believe that. Not yet, anyway. So what went wrong?

"Hold on a second." Richard tucked the phone under his ear. From his briefcase, he pulled out a manila folder, the words "Project MEG" printed on it. He opened the folder and flipped straight to the part covered by the Israeli government's investigation, which, thankfully, the Israelis had agreed not to release to the media. Reading over the reconstructed events, the mention of Nathan's gunshot wound proved he wasn't invincible. Like everybody else, Nathan could never survive an explosion. But Sophia just might.

Before pursuing the matter of target number thirty-six, Richard knew the time had come to take care of a pest.

"All right. I've got another target for you." Richard tucked away the file back into his briefcase. "Afterwards, I want to talk to you, but not over any phone line."

"I'll make the flight arrangements tonight."

Chapter 83

Eric Redding waited alone inside the shadows of the target's living room. He clutched a plastic bag, which contained the ice pick. A sound of a key unlocking the front door announced the target's return. The owner of the house whistled as he entered, closing and locking the door behind him. The target removed his jacket.

Eric gripped the plastic-wrapped ice pick in his hand and rushed the target.

Before the target had any response to seeing him, Eric hammered the ice pick into the upper chest of the target with the palm of his other hand. Judging by the position of the wound, Eric knew he had succeeded in puncturing the lung. It wasn't the heart, but it would do. Eric yanked the ice pick out of the target's chest, removed the plastic bag, and let the weapon drop to the floor.

The target tried to maneuver into the living room for some reason. Who knew why? People always had a tendency to do irrational things in moments of panic. Eric charged the target and pushed the man into the living room window. He had pushed so hard, the glass broke and the target fell backwards, a large glass shard impaling the target.

The target moved for just a bit longer with spasms and jerks. Then it was done.

On the drive over to Cole's house, I told Sophia how I witnessed the bomber chatting with the motel clerk, how I saw him plant the explosive by our room, and how setting off a piece of the C4 was necessary to make him think he'd successfully killed us.

We entered Cole's house through the back door, having to duck under black and yellow tape which read, POLICE LINE DO NOT CROSS. I took a deep breath, hushing away the memories that whispered. Sophia followed me downstairs to the basement.

"So what happened to your hand?"

"I was all out of bread crumbs, so I had to improvise to leave a trail."

She looked like she was trying to wrap her head around that one. "Okaaayyy, and Echelon?"

"He's our Trojan horse."

Sophia shook her head. "Wait a minute. If he's our Trojan horse, doesn't that mean we should be hiding inside of him?"

"Not us. Information." I flipped on Cole's GPS tracking device for the dog. A map came to view on the screen and showed a red dot crossing the California-Nevada border at a terrific clip.

Sophia moved in for a closer look. "What is that?"

"Either our limping man took Echelon with him on a plane or this puppy is an Olympic marathon runner."

Chapter 84

After spending the night at a different motel in North Berkeley, Sophia and I went to breakfast at a diner on the corner of Sacramento Street and Dwight Way. The red-haired waitress wearing a dark green dress and doily thing around her low collar gave us our menus and winked at me.

Sophia pointed to the GPS in my hand. "Where's Echelon now?"

"Still moving. Somewhere in Virginia."

The waitress appeared. "Ready to order?" She gave me a big smile and didn't look at Sophia. What was her game? She had a young face. Was she fresh out of high school and missed the life of kissing boys in the gym?

After we ordered, the waitress brushed against my shoulder and winked again, completely ignoring Sophia.

"Do you know her?" Sophia asked.

"Never met her."

She wrinkled her nose at the waitress as if trying to figure her out. Then she returned her attention to me and told me a high school memory of hers. Sophia's eyes sparkled as she shared how much she learned about herself in art class, her love of Van Gogh's vibrant hues, her dissatisfaction with washed out watercolors.

It didn't take long for our food to arrive.

"Caesar salad." The waitress placed the salad in front of Sophia. "And fish sandwich with fries." She bent over revealing a hefty amount of cleavage her doily couldn't hide. Her breasts had tan lines showing a clear distinction between brown and white. When I saw the smirk on her face, I realized she was testing me. Seeing if I'd look at her chest instead of focusing on her face. "Let me know if you need anything else."

Sophia placed an elbow on the table and rested her chin in her palm. "You do realize she just gave you the Test."

"I know, I know!" I put up my hands in surrender. "And I failed."

"I don't think she feels that way."

I glanced at the waitress. She smiled and gave me another wink.

I had a bite of the fish sandwich. It tasted incredible. Instead of lettuce, cabbage piled high inside, and there was sour cream and lime juice in place of tartar sauce. After a handful of fries, I saw the red dot on the GPS stopped moving.

I zoomed in on the map for Echelon's precise location. "Oh, crap."

"What's wrong?"

"Check out where Mr. Three Legs took Echelon." I pointed to the screen.

She gasped when she saw the five-sided building.

Chapter 85

Eric Redding found a parking spot under significant shade. His new companion would be quite comfortable. Finding the dog in his car in Berkeley had been a surprise, but not an unpleasant one. Meeting the front desk clerk's golden retriever had been a reminder of how much he wanted a dog of his own.

"I'll be right back, boy." Eric pulled up on the parking brake. "I'll keep the window open a crack for you."

The puppy hyperventilated, tongue hanging out, and gave a happy wag of his tail. Eric took his cane and stepped out of the car to see the boss.

I chewed on one of the last fries.

Break into the Pentagon? That'll be a trick. How does one break into one of the highest security buildings in the US? Especially post-9/11?

I thought about the entrance ways. I had one thing going for me. I wasn't smuggling in any weapons.

Visitors from all over the world came to see the Pentagon, right? There must be some sort of tour that takes place there. Getting in with a tour would be one way. Another would be to see if I knew anyone who worked there.

Fine. Getting in was going to be simple. Now what about breaking out? Didn't a metro train stop near there? What about tunnels? There had to be escape tunnels, right? Or was that just for the White House?

Sophia finished her salad, leaving a few withered leaves to one side of her bowl. It gave me an idea. Before I had a chance to hash it out with Sophia, the waitress placed the bill on the table.

"Let me know if you need anything else." She squeezed my shoulder and left smiling.

I slapped some cash on the bill's tray.

"Ever been to the Pentagon?" I asked Sophia.

"Never."

"It'll be my first time, too."

As we headed for the diner's exit, the waitress watched me with bedroom eyes. Sophia noticed. She faced me, grabbed both sides of my head, and planted a big kiss on my lips. My heart hammered at the surprise attack. Sophia gave the waitress a victor's mocking grin and led me out the door pulling me by the hand.

I was still dizzy from the kiss.

Chapter 86

On our nonstop flight from San Francisco to Ronald Reagan Airport in Virginia, I sat in between Sophia and a tall guy. Aside from his short-cropped hair, everything about him was long. Long face, long fingers, long torso, long legs. Mr. Longfellow had just put away his smartphone and pushed his seat back to get some shut-eye on this five-hour flight.

I tapped his arm. "Mind if I borrow your smartphone to use the internet? I forgot to bring mine."

He gave me a calculating glance.

"I promise not to run off with it." I gestured to our cramped quarters.

He chuckled and handed over his phone. "Just don't flush it down the toilet."

"Shucks. You're on to me," I joked.

Longfellow rolled away from me in his seat. I opened an internet browser and made reservations for a motel. I used my PayPal account to purchase masks and luminol, and punched in the motel address for delivery. I then did another internet search.

"What are you doing?" Sophia asked.

"Looking up my old high school friend Jerri Gaines. Last I heard she was working at the Pentagon."

"She? Your high school friend Jerri was a she? Just how friendly were you two?"

By her tone, I could tell she wasn't jealous. She just got a kick from teasing me.

"We did a lot together," I said. "We were science lab partners."

"Any other kind of partners?"

"Yeah, we co-wrote erotica for lepers under a pen name. Ah! Found her phone number." I examined the online yellow pages listing. "Well, how about that."

"What?" Sophia peered over my shoulder.

"She's a captain. Captain Jerri Gaines." The idea amused me. Last I saw her she wore jeans and a T-shirt that read, "Eat the rich." I never pictured her as the kind of person who'd become a captain.

"So did you two write any titles I've heard of before?"

"*Fifty Shades of Plague.*"

I called Jerri's number.

I wasn't supposed to make a voice call during the flight, but I knew the phone signal wouldn't interfere with the airline's communications. Cell phone technology had advanced to avoid the interference issue. Airlines still prohibited voice calls because the loud conversations annoyed the other passengers.

Me? I needed to make the call. The opportunity to annoy other passengers was just a bonus. I yelled over the thrum of the plane's engines. "Jerri? This is Nathan Yirmorshy."

"You gotta be kidding me. How the hell are you?"

"I'm not a captain like you, Ms. Captain America."

"Shut up," she laughed. "I remember always having to call you to help me understand the science homework. You were so good with science. So what are you doing these days?"

"Oh, same old, same old. You know, save Africa, prevent the end of the world, the usual."

"You always were a joker."

"Yeah. Listen. My wife and I are coming to D.C. and I thought it would be great to visit you at your workplace."

Sophia's eyes popped when I said the word *wife*. I shook my head *no* to let her know it was just a way to ensure our meeting with her. Jerri would so want to know how the school's biggest geek before geek-was-chic landed a wife.

"Your wife, huh? I'm speechless. I didn't think you were the type."

"Do I say 'thank you' to that?"

"It's a compliment," she reassured me. "Is she pretty?"

"Very," I said eyeing Sophia and wiggling my eyebrows.

Sophia scowled, as if struggling to interpret what I was talking about.

Jerri said, "I'd love to meet her. When will you need a visitor's pass?"

"How's the day after tomorrow at 2:00 p.m.?"

"No problem. I'll inform the security of your visit, so they can add your names to the list."

I imagined all the alarms that alerting the security might set off. "You don't have to do that. Our names are already on the visitors list. We planned this way in advance. Why don't you meet us at the Metro Entrance, and we'll see you after we get through security."

"That should work. I can show you two around, and afterward I'll take the both of you out to my favorite Italian restaurant. How does that sound?"

"You know, Jerri, that sounds great, but we already have dinner plans that evening."

"No worries. It will be good to see you."

I ended the call and asked Sophia, "Ready for a private tour of the Pentagon?"

In the morning at the Berkeley Police Department, Detective Bobbie Graff took off her belted jacket and was about to hang it up when Jimmy Belmont said, "Get your coat back on."

"Why?"

"Another homicide."

"Terrific." Graff threaded her arms through the sleeves. "Where?"

"1023 Arlington."

"Why does that address sound familiar?" She tossed the address around in her head, but couldn't place it.

Chapter 87

Bobbie Graff followed the officers at the crime scene toward the victim's large, bungalow house. "Fill me in."

"Vic was stabbed by an ice pick."

"T.O.D.?"

"The coroner has the time of death between one and four o'clock this morning."

They entered through the front door. A plastic sheet covered the victim.

The first-on-scene officer put his hands on his hips. "The victim was found leaning backwards out the living room window. Best we can tell, there was a struggle. The perp stabbed the vic with the ice pick and the vic staggered back or was pushed into the window, breaking it. The shard through his chest increased his bleeding, and he died shortly after."

Graff tried to reconstruct the struggle based on the position of the jostled furniture and fallen framed photographs. A photo on the floor caught her eye and chilled her.

She turned to the officer. "What was his name?"

He pulled out his notepad and flipped through to the right page. "The vic was one Lee Crawford, white male, thirty-seven years old."

Graff felt dizzy and marched out of the crime scene to her car.

Jimmy Belmont followed her. "You okay?"

She knew immediately who had killed Lee. "I can't be here."

"Why not?"

"I'm a suspect. This is the guy I've been dating for the past few days."

Belmont had an apologetic face. "Geez, Bobbie. Do you wanna wait until we're back at the station before I question you?"

"No, I'm good." Her stomach churned, but the faster they eliminated her as a suspect, the sooner they could put all their focus on finding the real perp. "Ask me now."

"Okay." Belmont pulled out his notepad. "How well did you know the vic?"

"My sister set us up on a blind date. We've been dating for the past two days." Graff considered the advantages and disadvantages of telling Belmont about Lieutenant General Richard Stone, how the lieutenant general threatened the lives of her loved ones.

"Do you know if he has any enemies?"

"We didn't get that far in the relationship to find out. So no, I don't know." If she told Belmont, police assigned to the case would look into it.

Belmont scribbled in his notepad. "I'm sorry, but I have to ask this."

"No reason to apologize."

"Where were you last night between one and four a.m.?"

"I was asleep. Alone. I have no alibi." Graff was certain Richard Stone would have had someone do the dirty work. Even if the police figured out who killed Lee, Stone would make it near impossible to connect himself to the homicide.

No, she decided. For now, it wasn't worth telling Belmont about the lieutenant general. If she did tell him, Stone might have another loved one of hers murdered.

Chapter 88

After dropping off Sophia at our Washington D.C. motel, I went to a sports store and found the skates department.

The sales lady there was reading a magazine and chewing gum.

"Excuse me," I said.

"May I help you?" She kept her focus on the magazine.

She wore a red vest as if to say, *Look at me! I work here! Ask me your questions!* But really, what *her* vest was saying was, *Check out this stupid piece of cloth I gotta wear for the job. Don't talk to me. This piece of godawful red linen was not my idea. I just gotta wear the damn thing.*

"I'm looking for detachable inline skates," I said.

"Shoe size?" Her gum smacked as she spoke. Other than my voice, she seemed oblivious to my existence. Her bored tone made it clear that her gum and magazine interested her more than my shoe size.

"Twelve and a half."

She stopped chewing and saw me through the corner of her eye, jaw dropped.

Then she turned her head and peered straight at me. She looked at my shoes, at my crotch, at my face, and smiled, resting her cheek in her hand.

"I bet it is." She stared at my face for a good long moment, chewing her gum, smiling, and brushing her hair behind her ears. "What's your name?"

"Napoleon."

"My name's Leticia." She held out her hand accompanied by the sound of several bracelets clinking around her wrist.

I shook her hand.

She traced the neckline of her shirt with her finger. "So you like sports, huh? Outdoor or indoor?" Another wink.

I scratched the itch at the back of my neck as she smiled and waited for an answer. "Well, if you call breaking into the Pentagon a sport, I guess that would be indoor."

She didn't laugh. Just kept smiling and chewing her gum. "You're funny." She chewed her gum. Stopped. Scanned me up and down again. "Mmm, mm." Came back to my face and chewed again. "So how can I help you?"

"Detachable inline skates?"

She blew a bubble, smacked it with her tongue and grinned. "I'll be right back."

She walked away, then looked over her shoulder. "Twelve and a half, right?"

"Right."

"*Oh* yeah," she said to herself a little too loud.

She came back a few minutes later holding a large shoebox. "Size thirteen. They're adjustable." She handed me the box. As I took it, she placed her hand on top of mine and whispered, "My number's inside the box. Call me," she said and added with lust, "Napoleon."

I chuckled and walked away, scoping out the departments that sold paragliders and torches.

Bobbie Graff sat at her desk trying to work the liquor store case, but she couldn't concentrate. As a suspect in Lee's homicide, she'd have to trust her fellow officers to find the perp and eliminate her from the suspect list to be allowed to investigate Lee's case. Once they found a lead suspect, Graff would be clear to join the investigation. She'd check for any connection between the lead suspect and Richard Stone.

Jimmy Belmont came to her desk. "I've got good news and bad news."

"What's the good news?"

"You've been cleared as a suspect. And since we're so short-staffed, the captain is willing to overlook the potential conflict of interest. You're officially assigned to the case."

"That was quick. What happened?"

"We got prints off the ice pick's handle." He handed her the case file.

"That fast? Results from prints usually take weeks to process." Graff flipped through the file's contents glancing at transcripts of interviews with neighbors, reports of the coroner's preliminary findings, and photographs of the scene.

"Yeah, well, considering we had an officer trying to shirk her duties by posing as a suspect, we felt it best to teach her a lesson and whip her back into shape. We put a rush on those prints."

"Jimmy, I could kiss you."

"I don't think my wife would like that, but maybe she's open to a three-way."

"So what's the bad news?"

"Those prints?" Belmont leaned over and pointed to the results in the file. "They belong to Nathan Yirmorshy."

Chapter 89

lugged my skates, paraglider, and portable torch out of the taxi and stopped at a butcher near our D.C. motel. Had to pick a number. The counter was currently at eighty-five, mine read eighty-nine. A few people browsed through the store, but only one lady looked like she was waiting. A prim and proper type. A frail woman with a long straight skirt and pursed lips.

I checked my number again. Eighty-nine. I wondered what the significance of number eighty-nine was. I realized looking for significance in numbers where there wasn't any had to be the surest way to paranoia and dropped the whole thought.

"Eighty-six?" one of the workers called out. No one replied.

"Eighty-seven?"

No response.

"Eighty-eight?"

The lady waved her number. "That's me."

Darn.

While the first clerk busied himself with helping the lady, the other clerk—the one that appeared to be in charge—finished with another customer and went to the counter. "Eighty-nine?"

"Whoohoo!" I jumped up and down. "Bingo, bingo, I won, I won!" I did a touchdown dance and ran up to the frail woman who looked at me in shock. I raised my palm in the air. "High five."

She didn't budge. The clerks were laughing, though.

I stepped up to the older clerk and spoke with a calm voice. "How ya doing?"

"Good, how can I help you?" He worked at hiding a smile.

"Do you guys still use those meat hooks to pick up slabs of meat?"

"You mean boning hooks? Yeah. Those things look pretty scary, but they do the job."

"I'll take two."

"What?"

I crumpled my number and tossed it in the tiny bin of used numbers on the counter. "I'm going to need two meat hooks."

"Sorry, sir. They're not for sale."

I took out my wallet. "Give you two hundred dollars for each."

"Bingo!" he laughed.

Chapter 90

"**N**athan Yirmorshy didn't do it," Bobbie Graff told Jimmy Belmont as she examined the case file.

Belmont put his hands on his waist. "What makes you say that?"

She slammed the file shut and sighed with frustration. "Yirmorshy's not a contract killer. And while I don't know the name of the killer, I do know the name of the man who ordered the hit."

"Whoa. What do you mean?"

"Chasing Yirmorshy is just what he wants us to do. I know who had Lee killed, and it wasn't Yirmorshy."

Belmont pulled up a chair. "Walk me through it."

Graff laid down all that happened: the information she learned at the kosher diner, how Yoseph's likely killer had a conversation with a man named Richard, how the captain took her off the case by order of a man in the Pentagon, a man also named Richard. One Lieutenant General Richard Stone.

"Whoa, whoa, whoa." Belmont held his hands up. "You're suggesting the Pentagon sanctioned these homicides?"

"Someone at the Pentagon seems to know about it."

Belmont scribbled in his notepad.

"What are you doing?"

"As short-staffed as we are, I'm still going to work at finding a few more guys to help investigate this Richard Stone." He stood and returned the chair to its proper spot.

She felt such a relief knowing that someone was on her side. "Thanks."

He walked with a brisk step to other officers. "Thank me after we get this guy."

Chapter 91

Why? *Why did Cole have to die?*
I hailed a cab and dumped the inline skates, paraglider, and torch in the trunk. In the taxi, I gave the driver the motel address and kept silent as I watched the clothes stores and cafes and parking lots whisk by my window. My mind whirred with all that had happened.

Richard Stone, Richard Stone, Richard Stone, a man in the Pentagon, a man who is a killing man, a man who hires killers, he is who he is who is he, a killer, a religious man, a religious killer, a religion killer, a man of secrets, a secret man, a man of end times, a timing man, an end of man.

The streaking colors created by passing the people and stores melted into paint strokes across the cityscape. Dizziness washed over me. I put my hand up against the front seat to prevent myself from falling forward.

The thirty-six righteous, destroy them and the Almighty gets out a hammer and destroys the Earth with a whack, a wholloping whack, a whack attack, unless the thirty-six who die are not the thirty-six righteous, not the real thirty-six righteous, just ordinary people, ordinary people with mothers and fathers and spouses and siblings and sons and daughters, ordinary people killed by a madman, an insane man, and God doesn't care, doesn't care a bit, thirty-six ordinary people, not worth His attention, not worth His time, and may all those who lost their lives be damned, all those family and friends of the dead be damned, damn them all, too insignificant to matter in God's mind.

The dizziness got worse. I closed my eyes and shouldn't have. I felt as if I were free-falling on a rollercoaster ride. Eyes open again, time shifted. The taxi's meter counted the distance in dollars, but moved slowly. Though the taxi plowed fast down the street, the road stretched like taffy ahead of us, and I wasn't sure if we made any progress moving forward at all. I pounded my fist against the metal window frame of the taxi, over and over.

~

For everything to be all right, Sophia needs to be safe.

For Sophia to be safe, Cole needs to still be alive.

For Cole to still be alive, I need God to hear my voice.

For God to hear my voice, I need my voice to ring out loud enough.

For my voice to ring out loud enough, I need Satan to sing my song to God.

Satan, oscillate my metallic sonatas!

Then, my voice will ring out loud enough.

Then God will hear my voice.

Then Cole will be alive.

Then Sophia will be safe.

Then everything will be all right.

~

The driver shouted at me. "Hey, stop that pounding."

I relaxed my arm.

Dammit. I've been up all night and haven't taken my meds. I just hoped I'd get to the motel in time before paranoia kicked in. Not much good to anyone if I accused the driver of being a conspirator in Cole's death. I still didn't understand why Cole had to die.

Why?

Richard Stone rapped his fingers on his office desk considering what to do next. Eric Redding sat across from him watching him. From Eric's debrief, he realized Sophia and Nathan could not have survived the blast.

Richard remembered when he got the call twelve years ago. It was to his cell phone.

"Yeah?"

"Lieutenant General Richard Stone?"

"Who's this?"

"This is opportunity knocking. The only one that will matter in this miserable life of yours."

"Who is this?" Richard demanded again.

"This is the only membership you need, if you want to make a difference. It has come to our attention that you, now in a high powered position in the Pentagon, have affiliations with a church you attend regularly, and membership to various Christian causes."

Richard bristled. "Whoever this is, listen carefully. I'm a busy man, so I will hang up this phone right now unless you get to the point in the next three seconds."

The voice chuckled. "All right, Mr. Stone. I'll get to the point. Call me Jonah. I recruit Christian servants fit to join our community of powerful people. Have you heard of a society called The New World Order?"

That call twelve years ago had changed the course of his life. Now his every day ran with direction and meaning with sacred projects. Project 36 hadn't fulfilled the goal of achieving the End Times, but it hadn't been a failure. As Thomas Edison once said, "Many of life's failures are experienced by people who didn't realize how close they were to success when they gave up."

Project 36, a necessary step to move closer to success. Now, it was time to move on to the next project.

An employee came to the door. "More searches for your name, sir."

"Detective Graff?"

"No, sir. These were done by other Berkeley police officers."

No doubt spurred on by Graff. She is a thorn in my side.

After the employee left, Richard produced a printout of all the information he had on Graff. He handed it to Redding. "Here's your next target. Make it look like an accident."

"Got it." Eric took the documents and hobbled out of the office.

Chapter 92

I **arrived at the motel in one piece. Fortunately,** so did the taxi driver. There's nothing more embarrassing than the police arresting you in front of your girlfriend while you're trying to explain how you had to beat the taxi driver senseless because he was actually an alien spy from the insect planet Garuck.

I managed to avoid giving in to my bipolar paranoid delusions. No armed police. No surprised girlfriend. No alien insect taxi driver in a hospital's intensive care unit.

As soon as I walked through the motel door, I dropped my purchases to the floor and hugged Sophia.

She didn't resist. "Are you okay?"

"Yeah. I just need to take my meds and get some sleep."

"Another episode?"

"Either that or our planet will soon be invaded by taxi drivers."

In the bathroom, I flicked off the sanitized paper hat from an empty glass, filled the cup with water, and downed my dosage of Depakote.

Sophia stepped beside me holding Cole's GPS device. "I think Echelon's on the move again."

The red dot blinked angrily over Utah. "Our explosives pal is going back to California. Probably to finish us off."

"You think so?"

"That'd be my guess. I had hoped he'd thought we were dead, but apparently he must have figured out he failed his mission." The taste of dust filled my mouth. A common sensation when I've gone without my meds for a time. I slipped past Sophia and flopped onto the bed. "Too bad we won't be around to give him a proper Yirmorshy welcome."

Sophia kicked off her shoes and cuddled next to me. "You sure you're okay?"

"I will be." My mouth felt stuffed with dirt, as though I were being buried alive. I pushed the perception away and let my drowsiness sink in. "If anyone calls asking for Napoleon, tell her your boyfriend is sleeping."

Chapter 93

In the morning, something tickled Sophia's nose. It felt like the bed sheet. She kept her eyes closed and brushed it away, letting sleep take her back to its seductive state of quiet and warmth and serenity.

The bed shifted a bit. Was Nathan getting out of bed?

It shifted again. Sophia reached out an arm to feel for Nathan's body. She felt empty covers. He must have been getting out of bed.

It shifted again.

"Nathan?" Her tired voice drawled out the name despite her best effort. She needed more sleep.

The bed felt like it dropped.

"What the—?" She managed to open an eye. She lay on the mattress, which now rested directly on the floor beside the rest of the bed. He must have dragged the mattress off of the bed with her still in it.

"Go back to sleep." Nathan lifted up the box spring and leaned it against the wall.

Sophia felt discarded by being dropped to the floor like another piece of his equipment. She propped her head up on her elbow. "What are you doing?"

"Preparation."

She watched him wrestle with the bed frame, unhooking the metal beams that functioned to hold up the box spring. Was he having another episode?

"Preparation for what?" She tried to sound calm. "Fighting taxi drivers?"

He chuckled. "I'm no longer interested in the fad of fighting taxi drivers. That kind of thing is just so... yesterday."

He brought the metal pieces of bed frame to the bathroom and came back kneeling like a knight in front of her, his warm hand caressing her cheek.

"I'm okay, now. What I'm working on is to stop Richard Stone from hurting you. I probably won't even need all this equipment, but it's good to have a backup plan."

He kissed her and Sophia felt relieved and comforted and protected.

"Go back to sleep," he whispered. He picked up the torch he had bought the day before, stole into the bathroom, and closed the door behind him.

Sophia put her head back on the pillow and drifted at the amusing thought of the neighbors hearing Nathan breaking the bed to pieces, and wondering what activities she and Nathan must be engaged in.

The sound of Nathan's torch in the bathroom blared like an espresso machine. Sophia groaned and put the pillow over her head to muffle the noise.

***

I applied the final touches to the inline skates. Now each skate's wheels were sandwiched between two flat sheets of metal taken from the bed frame. When worn, the skate's wheels could no longer touch the ground. The metal sides raised each skate a few inches off the ground. Good.

When I stepped out of the bathroom, Sophia was sitting at the small table. She sipped from a nearly finished glass of orange juice, a ravaged bagel and cream cheese breakfast splayed in front of her. A second setting of juice and bagel tempted me at the seat across from her.

I wiped my wet hands. "You're awake."

"Yeah, well, remind me never to rent a room next to an auto mechanic."

"Sorry about that, chief." I nodded to the food. "That the motel breakfast?"

"Mm-hmm." She wiped her lips with a napkin. "Come join me."

I sat down. "Why do they call it a continental breakfast? I think of a continent and I think huge, massive, overpopulated. The size of the breakfasts they offer is more of a tribe than a continent. A tribal breakfast."

She smiled. "At least it's complimentary."

I nodded. Picking up the bagel and cream cheese sandwich, I opened and closed the two slices of bread like a mouth and gave the sandwich a high voice. "My, but you're looking exceptionally stunning this morning, Sophia.

Usually, you're breathtaking, but today you look absolutely stunning. What's your secret?"

She laughed.

"You're right. It's complimentary." I took a bite of the sandwich.

The phone rang. I froze. *Who knows we're here?* The phone sounded a second ring. The diminishing echo of the ring hung in the air.

"Are you expecting a call?" I asked.

She shook her head.

The phone rang a third time.

I stood and raised the receiver to my ear. I listened for a voice.

"Mr. Schroedinger?"

I exhaled. It was the front desk. I had registered under the name Schroedinger.

"Yes?" I said.

"We have two packages for you. Just arrived express mail."

"Perfect. I'll pick them up later today." I hung up and frowned.

Sophia searched my face. "What was that all about?"

"Our key to sneaking into the Pentagon arrived." I sat and gulped down the rest of the juice. "I'm tired of taxis. Give me an hour. I'll be back with taxi-free wheels."

Chapter 94

After taking out a substantial sum from a Western Union, I scouted the neighborhood on foot for a car with a "for sale" sign. I needed to be in a part of the neighborhood where guys frequently sold their cars. From my experience, certain kinds of people regularly sold their cars and bought new ones because they thought the cars were a reflection of their status.

I turned into the slummier side of the town. From a single vantage point, I spotted three cars with "for sale" signs—a Cadillac, a Mustang, and a Thunderbird. A bulky man sat on his front porch holding a smartphone too tiny for his fingers. He twitched his hands at irregular intervals, pressing the keys on the phone. Probably playing a game.

I had a weakness for Mustangs, so I stepped closer to the Mustang convertible to call the number advertised. I dialed and the bulky man's phone rang.

As he answered, he noticed me, a stranger, standing by his car. "Yeah?"

"I want to buy your car."

I hung up and so did he.

He shuffled over to me like a cowboy ready for a gunfight, but his smile told a different story. "You got a good eye for cars, mister."

I didn't have time to get friendly and become his boyfriend. "What's wrong with your car?"

"What?" He looked genuinely offended.

"Before I buy your car, right here, right now, I want to know what's wrong with it."

"Man, there ain't nothing wrong with my 'Stang. It's a V8. Can go from 0 to 100 in ten seconds. Up to 155 miles per hour, the AC is primo. It even comes with surround-sound speakers and a bass booster for your CDs."

"Don't get me wrong. I want your car." I tried to figure out a way to make sure the car had all the necessary features, like working brakes. "Let me put it this way. Say I call the other two guys in your block selling their cars. If I ask them what's wrong with your car, what are the things they'd both mention?"

He stopped to think on that for a second, then sulked. "The temperature gauge don't work. The car had an over-heating problem a couple months ago because of a bad temperature gauge sensor. I removed it and tossed it out. Never got a replacement, but now the car don't overheat no more."

"That's it?"

"That's it, man."

"I can live with that." I checked his advertised price and handed him cash. "That's $8,000 for the car. You married?"

"Yeah."

"Here's $200 more. Take her out on a date. Somewhere special."

"Really?" He beamed. "You're the best. I know just the place. Been wanting to take her there for years."

I believed him. He gave me the keys, and I drove the car a few times up and down his block, finding out all I needed to know. The brakes worked.

Chapter 95

Sophia felt the fresh air hit her face. She whooped and screamed in the passenger seat as Nathan drove the Mustang on the freeway with the top down. Nathan didn't seem to mind. He was smiling wider and seemed happier than she had seen him in the past few days. They sped out of the city and into the country. Nathan had told her the journey plan: to head west on the I-66 and take the I-81 South. The high-rises gave way to houses, the houses to fields, the fields to forests, and the forests to the Appalachian Mountains. He snaked around through the woods higher into the peak of Big Walker Mountain until they reached a clearing.

Sophia stepped out of the Mustang and swooned at the surrounding summer grassy fields, the scent of pine trees, the view of the canyon just past a nearby cliff. A few rugged men in shorts and T-shirts worked at preparing their parachutes. The men's legs were tan and muscular and solid.

Hooked up to a parachute, one of them ran right for the edge of the cliff. The rectangular, nylon sheet billowed with wind and raised from the ground pulling him up high before he could reach the cliff's drop. He swung and swayed forward over the edge, then gently floated downward.

She grabbed Nathan's arm. "You're not planning on doing this, are you?"

"No, of course not."

She relaxed her grip, relieved.

"We're jumping together."

"What?"

He unpacked the parachute and spread it on the ground. "Relax. This is a tandem paraglider, so it can easily handle both our weight."

This was crazy. "Please tell me you've been trained in the Air Force and know everything there is to know about parachutes."

"Paragliders. The chute is actually called a canopy." He shrugged. "I've done extensive reading on the subject."

Sophia started walking away. "Nuh-uh. I don't want any part of this."

Nathan jogged up to her and grabbed her hand. "I had a friend who was big into paragliding. He often took me with him and taught me how. You're in good hands." He led Sophia back to the canopy.

"You sure?"

"I'm sure."

"You're full of surprises." Sophia felt butterflies in her stomach as she watched him assemble the straps to metal links. She was actually going to run off a cliff. "Is there anything else I don't know about you?"

"I'm a zombie who moonlights as an accountant." He fiddled with some straps. "I wonder which way is front?"

That didn't exactly inspire confidence. The butterflies in her stomach grew hands and fingers and tickle-tortured her nerves.

Nathan saw her face and laughed. "I'm kidding."

Sophia gave him a playful punch in the arm. He strapped himself to the canopy and had her stand in front of him with her back to him.

He strapped her to him. "On the count of three, we're going to run together to the edge of the cliff. You'll feel the canopy pull us backwards and into the air. As we get off the ground, sit in my lap. Ready?"

What the hell are we doing? "As ready as I'll ever be."

"One."

This was crazy.

"Two."

She didn't even know why this was necessary.

"Three!"

Against all her intuition, she ran with Nathan forward to the cliff's edge. The ground began to escape from her feet as she felt herself lifted.

Nathan's voice rumbled against her. "Sit back in my lap."

She tucked herself against Nathan, and the canyon once in front of her now spanned below her, a stunning drop of emerald pine trees and grassy fields and rhododendron bushes. The wind blasted against her face and chilled her body. She felt as though she were flying.

Nathan pulled cables steering their flight. "How're you doing?"

"It's incredible," she shouted over the wind. "Amazing!"

They rose higher. She didn't think that was possible. She thought parachutes just helped jumpers float down, not up. Maybe it had something to do with the shape of the canopy compared to the circular ones she'd seen more often.

She felt Nathan's chest solid behind her and took it all in, being with her beloved under a canopy with the entire world and their future at their feet. She couldn't tell if her heart pounded from the jump or from Nathan taking charge of protecting her.

After a full day of paragliding, Sophia and I returned to the motel. We stopped at the front desk.

"You have some packages for me? Room 108?"

"Absolutely. I'll be just a minute." The clerk left and came back carrying a box big enough to hold a basketball and a smaller box on top. "Here you are, Mr. Schroedinger."

As Sophia and I walked to our room, she asked, "What's inside the big box?"

"Remember how you pushed aside the withered lettuce leaves from your salad?"

"Yeah, so?"

"So these are realistic masks of withered faces." I unlocked the door. "Think you can act like an old woman?"

Chapter 96

Evening smothered the Bay Area, and Eric Redding had another target to hit. He considered himself a man willing to step out of the white and into the grey. He took on assignments most professionals turned down. American civilian targets, for example, and illegal alien targets. Not just foreign tyrants. Handfuls of people in the U.S. with regular jobs and ordinary lives spent their free time planning terrorist attacks and needed to be stopped.

This assignment was different.

The target named on the printout was one Detective Bobbie Graff. He had read the documentation on her, and unlike the other target's files, which had no information on their contribution to society, hers had pages of commendations. Whatever threat she posed to national security wouldn't be mentioned in the printout, anyhow. The purpose of the documents was to relay addresses and phone numbers, not the profile of the target's quality of character. He had to trust that her threat to the nation mattered more than her effectiveness as a police detective.

On first appearance, the house sat perched like any other on the block. The neighborhood conveyed a suburban white-picket-fence kind of place where all the residents had good-looking gardens and no blight. A place to be cautious because it was also the kind of neighborhood that had a neighborhood watch. There may be good citizens ready to report anything out of the ordinary, so the hardest part would be entering her place without being seen. Worse than that, he spotted a motion detector guarding the door, so if he moved any faster than a shuffling old man, the light would broadcast his presence.

He'd have to move slowly.

Wearing all black clothing, including a ski mask, he moved with his cane as though through molasses. It took a solid fifteen minutes to reach directly underneath the motion detector. He sprayed the sensor with hair spray, ready to run if the light went on.

The light stayed dark.

He waved his hand under the sensor, ready to run.

The light stayed dark.

He exhaled and took out his lock picks.

Picking a lock quietly can be relatively simple with the right tools. Just combine a tension wrench and the appropriately shaped pick into the lock.

The assassin clicked the door open and pushed gently. A chain lock stopped the door from opening further.

***

Detective Bobbie Graff lay awake in bed putting herself in Lieutenant General Stone's shoes. If Richard Stone wanted someone dead, what steps would he take to set up the homicide? What paper trail might he leave? What phone records would give him away? She knew he'd be too careful to write down anything incriminating, and he likely used secure phones with untraceable records.

Graff didn't want to think about it. She needed to get some sleep. She shifted in bed and yanked the covers over her shoulder. Sleep didn't come. She flung the covers off her, expelling an exasperated sigh.

That's when the detective heard someone at the front door toying with the chain lock.

Chapter 97

In Eric Redding's experience, chain locks could be opened with ease. The trouble came when trying to open one without making a sound. In hotel rooms where the bed lay right by the door, opening a chain lock was stupid. Unless you knew the target slept soundly and not even gunfire could wake them up, opening a chain lock made too much noise to be an option.

Eric had one thing going for him in this situation. The front door opened nowhere near the bedroom. Getting that chain unlocked wouldn't make enough noise to wake someone in the upstairs bedroom.

Eric leaned his cane against the porch wall. He took out a rubber band, opened the door as far as it would go, and wound one end of the rubber band around the sliding disk of the chain lock. The other end, he stretched and wrapped around the tip of the door's inside lever.

He closed the door, the rubber band relaxed by sliding the chain to the open position, and the chain fell out of the track.

Standing outside, Eric screwed on the gun's silencer. The sidearm was only meant as a backup. This death had to look natural. No gun wound, no suspicious explosions. He kept a vial of arsenic at the ready in his pants pocket, a virtually undetectable and often overlooked poison in autopsies. The simplest execution would have been to lace her foods in the kitchen, but people were unpredictable. They throw away foods they don't want, or they might have guests over for dinner. The only way to be sure the target ingested the poison was by directly placing it in her mouth.

He opened the door, retrieved his cane, and entered. With quiet steps, he climbed the staircase along the left wall, and kept his gun pointed in front of him. He surveyed the layout of the upstairs floor. Usually, the bathroom was the second or last door down. The first door would be a bedroom, either hers or a guest room. That third door would also be a bedroom. Hers or the guestroom. The door to the first bedroom was open a crack. Peeking in, he made out bulges under the covers.

The bedroom was hers. Definitely.

He prowled into the room, leading his entry with the gun through the narrow opening of the door. The door slammed onto his arm. Eric cried out, his arm crushed between the door and doorway.

"Police," a woman shouted from behind the door. "Drop your weapon!"

"Okay, okay. Just let go of my arm."

"Drop your weapon now before I shoot it out of your hand."

Shit. Who was in the bed? The bedroom light flipped on. Were those pillows under the blankets?

Eric weighed his options. If he dropped his gun it could be traced to him. A bad option. Then again, if he dropped his gun, she would either kick the gun away or bend over to pick it up. Considering she anchored the door against his arm with her foot, he bet she'd bend over to pick up the gun. A moment of being off balance. An opportunity to retrieve his gun and escape. A good option.

"You win. I'm dropping my gun." He let the weapon hang between his thumb and index finger and let go. The gun hit the floor with a thud. Timing it right, when he felt some ease off the door and off of his arm, he pushed back hard on the door. The door hit home with a whack and opened enough for him to see the woman fall to the floor. Dropping his cane, he jumped upon her and with one hand pushed her armed hand out of the way, and with the other punched her in the eye.

The punch landed with a crack. *That should put her down.*

But he hadn't counted on her free hand. She grabbed hold of one of his fingers and twisted it back. Eric screamed. She landed a knee in his groin and spikes of pain impaled him.

Best to leave before things got worse.

He placed all his remaining energy into throwing her across the room. Unfortunately, she had a hold of his ski mask. Ripping off his ski mask, along with some of his hair, she flew to the other end of the room and hit the wall. He took the opportunity to grab his gun, snatch his cane, and get the hell out of there. His escape triggered the neighbor's porch lights to flicker on. Once inside his car, he revved the engine and was gone.

Chapter 98

Detective Bobbie Graff came into work the next day with her body voicing a cacophony of aches and pains. She hadn't bothered covering the black eye and bruised face with makeup.

As she approached her desk, Jimmy Belmont beamed. "Congratulations, Detective."

"For what?"

"I didn't know you got married."

"Funny." She eased into her chair, a shooting pain striking up her spine.

"So what happened to you? Had a few too many and fell down some stairs?"

"My pet cat and I had a disagreement."

"I see." He lifted a page to a file he had in front of him. "So did you give in and buy him that bell and feathers on a string?"

"No, he gave in and bought me the bell and feathers on a string. It's really fun."

An officer plopped a package on Graff's desk. "The mailman just dropped this off for you."

As the officer left to hand out other mail, Graff examined the return address of the package. Her heart sank. It was from Lee. A note scrawled on the brown wrapping paper read, *Sorry, no nunchucks.*

She ripped open the package and inside lay a wooden box. Flipping up the lid, she found that Lee had bought her a set of Wusthof steak knives.

"What's wrong," Belmont asked.

"Nothing." She snapped closed the lid and stuck the box in her drawer. Wiping her eyes dry, she winced. The bruise around her eye still hurt.

Belmont held a pile of files upright and tapped their edges in alignment against his desk. "So what really happened last night?"

"Someone broke into my home and tried to kill me."

He dropped the files. "What the hell? Are you serious?"

"I'm fine. Still alive, nothing broken."

"I should be more worried about the other guy, right?"

"Right." She logged into her computer.

"Where is he?"

"I got stupid. Let my guard down and he escaped."

Belmont shook his head. "I bet you didn't report it, did you?"

"I'm fine," she said again.

"You stubborn.... Look at it this way, what if he tries to kill you again? What if he tries to kill someone else?"

That stopped Graff in her tracks. *What was I thinking?* "You're right. I'll write up the report."

"I'll do it." Belmont typed on his computer. "Walk me through it."

Graff told him the exact time when she heard a noise coming from the chain lock on her door, how she stuffed her bed with pillows, and how she loaded her sidearm and waited for the intruder until it came down to a fist fight.

"Did you get a look at the guy?"

"He had a ski mask on."

Belmont sighed. "Of course he did."

"But I got it off of him, along with some of his hair."

"That's my girl. Let's get you to the sketch artist."

Chapter 99

While we ate lunch at a diner, I thought about what the rabbi said. How he reinforced the idea that God wrote the book of Genesis. I didn't want to believe in some almighty being. Cole was just a kid. What god would allow him to die so young?

"Imaginary penny for your thoughts," Sophia pretended to place a penny on the table.

I picked up the imaginary penny and weighed it in the palm of my hand. "I don't know if I want to talk about it."

"Please?" Sophia used a sing-song voice. "I'll be your best friend."

"Too late. You already are."

"So tell me."

"Heads or tails?" I positioned the imaginary penny on my thumb ready to flip it.

"Heads."

I made the hand gesture to flip the coin, pictured the coin flying up into the air, and back down. I motioned as if catching the coin and slapped it onto the back of my hand. I took a peek at the coin. Then smiled at her.

"Well," Sophia asked. "What is it?"

"Take a look." I lifted up my hand revealing the imaginary penny.

"Heads! I win!" She leaned closer, her head propped up with her elbows on the table. "So what were you thinking?"

"I forgot."

She nudged me in the arm.

"I was thinking about how the rabbi compared the six days of creation in the book of Genesis to the Big Bang, but really, with the Big Bang's expansion of the Universe, there is no need for a creator."

"What do you mean?"

"After the Big Bang, there's no need to create something from nothing. The stars form themselves, the planets form themselves, life evolves by itself. Nothing else needs to be created."

Sophia poked at her grilled chicken salad with her fork. "So?"

"So I just needed to get that out. There really is nothing to the whole Genesis story."

"Aren't you going to hear the rabbi's side of the story?"

I didn't say anything.

Sophia tucked her hair behind her ears. "You're not one of those people who decides something without hearing what the other side has to say, are you?"

Her words made me think of that old expression. *If you can only afford one newspaper, get the one with the opposing view.*

I took out my burner phone. "Fine, I'll call him."

I punched in his number. He picked up on the first ring. After he answered, I told the rabbi my perspective.

"The growth of the Universe after the Big Bang doesn't need a creator. There's no need for six days of creation."

"Actually, Nathan, when you read the text carefully, it's just three."

"What's just three?"

"There are only three days that *HaShem* created anything. The first day, Genesis says, HaShem created the heavens and the earth, He created all the matter in the Universe. Like the moment of the Big Bang."

I chomped on a fry. "Fine. I'll buy that. It would explain how the Universe became something from nothing. What about the rest though? Nothing else needed to be created after that. The formation of everything follows through naturally."

"There are only two other times in the entire Torah where HaShem creates something. The first time was the creation of the Universe, and the second time was on the fifth day, when He created the *nefesh*, the life force in all living things. From there all living things could evolve into other creatures."

"But life can evolve from anything," I pointed out. "Read any biology textbook, and it'll show how Stanley Miller was able to build life forms by imitating the beginnings of the Earth."

"He made amino acids, not life."

Semantics. "Fine, I'll buy that, too. Let's say the jury's still out on whether or not life can evolve from nothing. What's the third thing? The third time that the Torah mentions creation."

"On the sixth day, HaShem created the *neshama*, the soul of humans. The very thing that separates us from animals. While there were hominids wandering around, they were not human in the sense of being capable of thinking with a critical mind and morals until nearly 5800 years ago when HaShem gave them the neshama, the start of the bronze age, and that's when you see the progress of the species expand exponentially. The start of Adam and Eve."

I thought about it. There were some flaws with using logic backwards. If the Bible were to claim the whole Adam and Eve thing happened 3000 years ago, the rabbi could have just attributed it to the start of the iron age. What he said didn't prove anything. The only thing he proved to me was that Genesis didn't necessarily contradict science. Still, it bothered me that I couldn't unequivocally falsify the creation story. Falsifying it seemed the easiest way to disprove the idea of an Almighty Author. And I didn't want to believe in a god who would let bad things happen to good people.

"Thanks, Rabbi." I hung up.

"Well?" Sophia asked. "What did he say?"

"I'll tell you later." I stuffed my mouth with a bite of my sandwich before Sophia could interrogate me further.

Chapter 100

Sophia admired the variety of trees they passed, maple and oak and beech and hickory, as Nathan drove toward the Pentagon for their meeting with his friend Jerri. Nathan pulled over at a mall.

"What are we stopping for?" Sophia asked.

"I need more cash." He pointed to a Western Union nestled between a souvenir shop and a jewelry store. "I'm also going to get tickets for getting into the Pentagon." He pointed to a travel agency a few doors down. After he kissed her lips, he gazed into her eyes and smiled. "I'll be back soon. Turn on the radio to keep yourself company."

"Okay."

Alone in the car, Sophia didn't bother with the radio. Her heart fluttered like crazy. It was ridiculous, really. She was just going to *pretend* to be married to Nathan for their visit with Jerri, but the idea of it made her head spin.

She fiddled with the sapphire on her ring finger, her birthstone, the ring that Nathan gave her as a parting gift before he'd left for Ghana.

When he gave her the ring, she felt the commitment, even if he meant it only as a parting gift. The ring became a solid reminder of his love for her. It saved her and comforted her during the months Nathan had been away.

But when was this relationship going to get as real as the ring? Nathan never addressed the possibility of a commitment.

This dance of indecision became too much for her. She needed to know their relationship wasn't temporary. She needed to know that they could be with each other as boyfriend and girlfriend. If it meant he had to have a place to stay, all the better. He could stay with her. Not that there was any room, but it could work. She needed it to work. Either he took the next step to spend more time with her or…. Or what? Could she really end it? Just to give herself the freedom to find a man more willing to commit? As much as it was the right thing to do, she couldn't picture breaking up with Nathan. But she needed to say something. She needed to tell him to stay with her, or end this relationship.

Twenty minutes later, Nathan got back in the car. He carried a paper bag with the souvenir shop logo on it.

Sophia shifted in her seat to face him. "Nathan, I need to ask you something."

He ripped the cellophane off of a CD of classical music. "Sounds complicated. Should I be frightened?"

"This is important."

He put the CD in the player and selected a track, but put the disk on pause, clearly respecting her need to speak without anything interfering.

She took a deep breath. "I need to tell you that I don't think I can handle being away from you anymore. I need you to be closer. I need you in the Bay Area. I need to see you and feel you and be with you."

He smirked.

"Nathan, I'm serious. If you can't find a place to live, then you can stay with me."

Nathan scowled as if he were trying to picture where, in Sophia's voting-booth-sized apartment, he could put his things.

"Just…we can figure something out," Sophia insisted. "So what do you say? Will you move to the Bay Area?"

"We'll talk about this later." Nathan taped to the windshield a large photograph of stunning brick windmills from Holland. "For now, we need to prep for the meeting with Jerri."

Sophia sighed, about to protest Nathan's dismissal of her question. Then she saw Nathan pull out a jewelry box from his coat pocket. The logo showcased the name of the nearby jewelry store. Sophia gasped.

Nathan played the track on the CD. The moving melody of the string piece "Air" by Bach caressed her skin and heart and tears.

He looked sheepish. "I planned to whisk you away to Amsterdam and ask you this once we got there, but I couldn't wait any longer."

She placed a hand over her trembling belly.

"Sophia." Nathan took her hand and stared into her eyes. "You are the only one I've felt comfortable with sharing everything about myself. And now that I know you're willing to take the tough times along with the good times, I want to make your life as good as I possibly can."

She wiped away the tears, but couldn't control her breathing and laughter and sobs.

"Sophia," Nathan said as he removed the ring from the box and slipped the diamond-studded band around her ring finger. "Will you marry me?"

"Yes! Yes!" Sophia embraced Nathan and just repeated her response over and over and over. Yes. Yes. Yes.

Chapter 101

We parked at the Pentagon City Mall parking garage. The day was hot enough. Spending an hour inside the car to put on our masks would have been torture if it hadn't been inside a garage and on the day of our engagement. Everything about a day seemed better when getting engaged. People should do it more often.

Sophia appeared to be having the time of her life as she played with the makeup on my face to make the mask have a seamless fit. When it was my turn to work on her mask, she kept smiling.

"What?" I smoothed the mask out at her neck.

"I've never had this much attention before. I feel doted on. I like it."

"Well, we have many years ahead of us. I guarantee you'll be so tired of me gazing at you, you'll beg for alone time."

"That'll never happen," she said.

An hour later, we finished applying our makeup, exited the car, and started our ten-minute trek to the Pentagon Metro Entrance. We had to walk through a tunnel under the I-395 freeway to get there. On the way, I told Sophia the plan. I stuffed my tools in a purse I had picked up at the souvenir store and gave the purse to her. We soon emerged out of the tunnel into the South Parking Lot, a parking area reserved for Pentagon employees.

"Hide your hands," I said. "They're too pretty to belong to an old woman."

She balled them up into gnarled-looking fists. I liked the effect and did the same. We hunched over and complained to each other with old, scratchy voices.

"Oy, Harold! How could you forget something so important?" Sophia asked.

"What do you want me say, Helen? You want me to say I'm sorry? Okay, okay. I'm sorry, Helen. I completely forgot."

From the corner of my eye I saw a young couple in loose clothes noticing us. They looked like hippies. Not the kind of people I would expect to visit the Pentagon, but it played in our favor. We needed a spontaneous, adventurous couple.

"Oh, look Helen. They look like nice kids." I waved them down as if making the movement was the hardest thing to do with my body.

They approached with inquisitive smiles.

I held out the tickets I purchased from the travel agent. "My wife and I were going to take a cruise on the Potomac River. I thought the cruise started next week, but it actually starts this afternoon."

The young man looked like he understood. "You want us to drive you there?"

Sophia croaked. "Oh, Harold. Isn't he a dear?"

I nodded. "Antlers and all. That's very kind of you, young man, but Helen and I are too old to rush and make the cruise. Besides, we're already here, and I've always told my wife how much I wanted to see the Pentagon, haven't I, honeybunch?"

Sophia nodded. "Ever since we got engaged."

The hippie woman with dreadlocks smiled.

"You're such a cute, young couple," I said. "We wondered if you two would like to have the tickets and go on the cruise yourselves. It's a lovely tour. Dinner is included, there's sightseeing, music, dancing. You'll have a wonderful time. The tickets are completely transferable."

The young man's eyes widened, and the woman jumped up and down squealing.

He took the tickets from my hand. "This is awesome. Thank you so much!"

"Our pleasure. Could you do one thing for us?" I handed him a piece of paper and pen. "We'd love to hear how your trip went. Could you write down your names and addresses and phone numbers? I'll mail you a letter to let you know what the Pentagon was like."

"No problem, man." He scribbled his name and contact information, then passed the paper along to his girlfriend.

We wished them goodbye and hobbled to the Metro Entrance of the Pentagon.

Chapter 102

Hunched over, we slogged inch-by-inch to the entrance. The wig itched like spiders crawling over my scalp. The fake hearing aids that came with the mask felt uncomfortable. When Sophia reached the guard, he asked for her two forms of identification. She turned to me. I took her hand and stepped closer to the guard.

While communicating in sign language to Sophia, I spoke with a loud voice. "I'll take care of this."

I hoped the guard didn't know sign language. I had signed the only phrase I knew: *No, thank you. Shellfish gives me gas.*

The guard asked, "Name?"

"The same as what?" I croaked.

"Your name, sir," he said louder.

"Yes."

Pointing to the name on his security badge he mouthed the words, "Your name?"

"Oh! You want our names. Of course. How silly of me." I gave him the names of the young man and woman who took our cruise tickets down the Potomac.

He checked off our names from the list of the day's visitors. "ID?"

The guard seemed somewhat distracted. Probably keeping an eye on the line extending fast behind us.

"What?" I asked.

"ID!"

"Heidi?"

"Your ID, your identification!" Some of the other guards looked at him shouting at an old man. Causing a scene in the Pentagon in front of tourists? Not good for the guard. He sighed and took out his own driver's license. "This. Show me yours."

I squinted. "Never seen him before. Sorry." The line behind us got longer.

"Yours! Show me yours!"

I examined the ID again and then opened my mouth, pointed to the picture and smiled. Pointed to him. "That's you!"

He closed his eyes and groaned.

"You know what? You remind me a lot of my grandson." I leaned on the counter as if preparing to share a long story.

"Sir, I – need – to – see – your – I – D!"

"No, silly. Not Heidi. His name is John."

An older guard came up and asked what the trouble was. When the first guard explained it to him, the second asked me, "Sir, may we see your ID?"

"You, too? His name is John, not Heidi. He's a marine in the 74th Special Infantry Division. One time he came over for Christmas in his complete uniform."

The second guard held his palm up to stop me, and asked the first, "They're on the list?"

"Yeah," the first one said. "I already checked them off."

The older guard nodded. "The line's getting long. I'll pull these two aside and take care of them myself."

"Thanks," the first guard said.

"Sir," the second guard addressed me and gestured to the metal detectors, "just go on through."

"Don't mumble, son. Speak up."

"Go on through!"

"You're going to? Going to do what?" I followed his hand. "Oh! 'Go on through.' I'm sorry. I'm beginning to think I'm getting hard of hearing."

The older guard with gray hair smiled at that remark and met us at the other side of the detector.

I asked, "May we use the restrooms?"

He nodded. "I'll take you there and we can get your IDs worked out afterwards."

I put a hand to my ear.

He waved it off. "Never mind. Follow me." He presented the direction of the restrooms with his hand.

Chapter 103

Once past the security, I found myself astonished by how many vendors occupied the entrance. There were gift shops and sandwich shops and pharmacies and fast food chains. There was a post office, an electronics store, a hair salon, and a jewelry store. I didn't think of the Pentagon as a place to go shopping, but I guess even the military needs to be active consumers.

As the security guard escorted us to the restrooms, we passed Jerri who was peering over the crowd of incomers, probably looking for me. The security guard stopped outside a couple of doors with the international symbols for male and female. He gestured for us to go ahead. Sophia and I hobbled our separate ways.

In a men's room stall, I ripped off the itchy mask, glad to free my face of it. I tossed the mask and fake hearing aids in the garbage and washed my face, making sure all traces of makeup were gone.

Two o'clock. Time to meet up with Jerri.

I took a deep breath, relaxed, stood up straight and left the restroom as a tourist, passing the security guard. Not too fast, not too slow. A few yards away, I stopped in front of a fast food store and acted as though I were studying the menu. Sophia caught up with me, grabbing my hand. A quick glance at the gray-haired security guard, and I could tell by the way he leaned against the wall opposite the restrooms with his arms crossed that he expected a long wait.

We left the fast food restaurant to meet Jerri. Sophia never stopped looking at me with a big smile on her face. She kept kissing me every several steps we took. The whole display embarrassed me, the way everyone was watching, but I also loved seeing her so happy.

Jerri greeted us with surprise. "I didn't see you come in." She was still her short self, but had lost quite a bit of weight, and she had her hair pinned up, probably to fit the military look. "You're as tall as ever, and this is your wife Sophia, is it?"

"Yes," Sophia smiled wide, letting go of my hand to shake hers. "Good to meet you."

Sophia took my hand and kissed my cheek again.

"Wow," Jerri said, "It looks like you two really are in love."

"We're married," Sophia giggled.

"So Nathan tells me," Jerri scowled at her. "Isn't that often a side-effect of having a husband and wife relationship?"

"You'll have to excuse the way Sophia and I act in public," I said.

"Yes," Sophia said, "because we are very much in love."

Jerri scowled some more.

"And we're married," Sophia added.

"I think she knows that, dear." I hated having to use the 'D' word.

"That's okay," Jerri said. "She reminds me very much of my wife."

Now Sophia definitely got wind of why nothing serious happened between Jerri and me.

"And I agree, Nathan," Jerri said. "Sophia is indeed very pretty."

Sophia turned to me with surprise, and I got another kiss on the cheek. Why did her affection feel so good? Such things were supposed to make me sick.

Chapter 104

Jerri took us through her favorite historical displays. We saw the Hall of Heroes and the USAF History with model airplanes. We saw the USAF Portraits of Veterans, the POWs and the MIAs. We saw the Army Living History exhibit and the Disaster Relief exhibit, the Women in the Military and the 9-11 wing.

"I'll never forget that day in September." Jerri had a distant look on her face with a hollow spirit. "I had a friend in the Army Communications department who died in the crash. Laura Francisco. She and I used to have lunch together every Friday, you know, to celebrate the weekend." A sad smile crossed her lips. "She used to do this thing where she'd guess how my wife and I would spend our weekend. She'd always get it wrong, but that didn't stop her from trying." Jerri clasped her hands and rubbed her thumbs together as if working to ease a pain. "Now every time Friday comes around, and it's lunch time, I lose my appetite." She took a deep breath and sighed. "Come on. You have to see the purple fountain before you go."

She brought us to the eighth corridor on the mezzanine level. Crowds of people gathered around the water fountain, which was encased behind a glass wall. The fountain, made from purple porcelain, had a dark plaque behind it conveying the mystery of the fountain's existence. According to the plaque, no one knew the true story of the fountain's origin.

Sophia clutched my arm. "I love it."

Jerri gazed fondly upon it. "Isn't it wonderful?"

Didn't see what the big deal was. It was just a water fountain. I shrugged and instead enjoyed watching Sophia get a kick from the purple fountain.

Just after four o'clock, when we were done, Jerri offered to show us out, but I managed to insist that we do it ourselves.

As we wandered down the halls, I found a janitor's closet and kissed Sophia goodbye. It was the longest kiss we ever shared.

"Be careful, okay?" She gave me her purse with the tools.

"No problem."

I watched her walk down the corridor, then I entered the closet. The hardest part was waiting.

Chapter 105

I crouched in the corner of the janitor's closet and after about fifteen minutes Sophia called me on the burner phone.

"You get out okay?" I asked.

"No problems. So now what?"

"Now just keep me company until five o'clock, when most people are gone for the day, Mrs. Yirmorshy."

"You got it, mon chéri. Sure is hot outside." She paused for a moment. "Anything you want to chat about until five o'clock?"

"Hm." Nothing came to mind. "Know any twenty-minute songs?"

She sang, "Twenty thousand bottles of beer on the wall. Twenty thousand bottles of beer—"

I chuckled.

"Aren't you going to stop my song?"

"No. I like the sound of your voice too much."

"How about I sing it to you tonight as a lullaby?"

"Works for me." I adjusted my sitting position to get more comfortable.

"Any ideas for our honeymoon?" she asked.

"When this is all over? I figure I owe you a trip to Amsterdam."

She screamed.

I sat up and nearly dropped the phone. "What's wrong?"

"Nothing's wrong, everything's perfect! Amsterdam, the Rijksmuseum, Rodin, Rembrandt, Van Gogh, all the masters are there. And the Anne Frank House and the canals and windmills and coffee shops."

"It'll be something to see, alright." I unscrewed the spray nozzle off a bottle of window cleaner.

"And I'm sure you won't want to miss a little stroll through the Red Light District."

I forced myself to say the obligatory words. "Why would I want to see that when I have you?"

"Don't tell me you're not even the slightest bit curious."

I sighed. "Guilty."

"Thought so. Don't worry, we'll have plenty of time for you to dote on me."

"Like I said, I'll be doting on you so much you'll get sick and tired of it."

She laughed. "I'll never get tired of it."

She couldn't see that I was smiling.

Chapter 106

After five o'clock when most people packed up and left for the day, I got off the phone with Sophia and wandered the corridors. I hiked as close to the Metro Entrance as I could without getting caught. Had to make sure there was no one around.

Once I felt safe, I took out the "water bottle" from Sophia's purse and attached the spray nozzle to it. Took out my key ring with the fluorescent black light on it. I sprayed the floor with the luminol and shined the black light.

Nothing.

I tried the E ring in the other direction. Sprayed, applied the light.

Nothing.

I needed to find a path. One that led directly to Richard's office. Best thing to do? Try another entrance. I decided against the Metro Entrance. Pretty sure the man I was tracking rented a car. My research of the Pentagon revealed that a person could walk between any two points within the Pentagon in less than seven minutes.

Time to test that claim.

I cut through the concentric rings to get to the North Entrance. Detecting old blood stains is not as difficult as one might think. Blood can be found over a year after the stain is made. The tricky part is making sure the stain is made in the first place. The stain itself may last, but blood can congeal in just a few hours. A pool of blood or a wadded-up bloody rag on the other hand can take as much as twelve hours to dry.

I reached the North Entrance in about nine minutes. Finding the most remote corridors to make my way slowed me down. I tried a path leading from the North Entrance. Sprayed. Applied the light.

Bingo.

Glowing circles formed a trail. Blood. My blood. From the bottom of a cane.

Though Joe Peterson the security guard received the warning hours ago of an elderly couple somehow slipping through the security gate, he had been advised that the threat was a low-risk threat, so he took the low-priority status very seriously.

Dinner time.

He tired from eating his watch-your-heart healthy lunch bag dinners. He would never tell his wife that, though. Opening the brown bag, he took out the note from his wife and read it. It always said the same thing, and it always made him smile. *Be good, but only because the government is watching you. When you come home, be as bad as you want.*

Having been nourished by the love, he threw the rest of the bagged dinner away and opened the take-out bag from McD. The smell of fries didn't just make his own nose happy. His coworker Sean took a dramatic whiff and turned away from the security monitors.

"Joe, you have got to let me have some of those fries."

"Take as many as you want." Joe let his coworker reach in the bag. As Sean retrieved a fistful of fries, Joe noticed a bizarre scene on the monitor for corridor five. "Uh, Sean. You are not going to believe this." Joe pointed to the screen. "Check it out."

They both stared at the man with a purse huddled over with a spray bottle and weird flashlight.

Joe called it in to the nearest security guard.

Sean tilted his head. "What's he doing?"

Chapter 107

The trail of blood spots led to an office. I peeked through the door window. Someone was still in there, but packing up to leave. Earlier on, I figured I could use a bump key to get in. No good. The lock required a sliding card key. No way I could break through that. I waited on the side of the door that best hid me for when the door opened.

When he exited the office, I caught the closing door, slipped in, and stayed in the dark until time elapsed and I didn't hear any more footsteps outside the door. I felt certain he had gone for good.

I flipped the light switch. The office was smaller than I had expected. Just a desk with a chair. On the desk perched a computer screen and beside it lay metal trays serving as the inbox and outbox. Scanning the mail confirmed the office belonged to Richard Stone. The key player in all of this. The "King."

I scoured the room. The drawers had envelopes and staples and pens and other insignificant office supplies. If he was a member of the New World Order, he didn't bring any membership paraphernalia to work with him.

I took in the full room again. Noticed the speaker above him. Probably for security announcements. I pulled out of Sophia's purse the compact screwdriver I had bought from the souvenir shop. Putting Richard Stone's chair against the wall, I reached the speaker and unscrewed the screws from the plastic grid cover.

Changing a speaker into a makeshift listening device is quite simple, really. Just adjust the wires so that they include a small microphone and Bob's your uncle, or your transvestite aunt. The electricity from the speaker takes care of the rest.

I wired a two-way transmitter to the speaker and added the microphone from a set of Sophia's earphone buds. Doing so gave me the ability to send signals as well as receive them.

RING! My phone. Damn thing near scared me off the chair. "Yeah?"

It was Sophia. "Nathan, get the hell out of there. A swarm of security is hovering at the front gates. I think they've caught on to you."

How? I groaned. *Of course. There must be hidden security cameras.* "I'll be out in a sec."

After screwing the speaker's cover back in place, I stepped off the chair and taped the detonator, set to go off at my call, under Richard's chair.

Chapter 108

In the scorching afternoon sun, Sophia had spotted two guards running to the Metro Entrance. By the way the guards put all their attention on the doorway and spoke into their walkie-talkies, they looked like they were hunting someone down.

After warning Nathan on the phone, she ran to the guards waving her arms.

"My husband is in there. Don't hurt him!" She explained to the guards, "My husband is in there. I think he's wandering around. I think that's who you're looking for."

One of the guards spoke into his walkie-talkie. "I have someone up front that says her husband is the one wandering around inside the building."

"I think my husband is having a delusion. He and I came in to visit a friend of his, but he hasn't taken his meds. He's got bipolar disorder and sometimes thinks he's a spy."

The guard stared at Sophia with a blank unreadable expression on his face.

A gentleman with thinning blond hair stepped close. "Hi Ma'am, I work here and couldn't help overhearing your story." He turned to the guard and showed him his ID. "Let's listen to this young lady. I believe any intel we can get on the intruder—"

"He's not an intruder!" Sophia said.

"Of course. I beg your pardon." He then addressed the guard again. "Any intel we can get on her husband could be useful in finding him and getting him to safety. Please listen to all that she has to say and pass it along to the other guards."

"Yes, sir." The guard turned to Sophia. "Is he armed?"

"He's not armed. He's not dangerous. Please don't hurt him. We came to see Captain Jerri Gaines. Arrest him and you can check his medical background. Just don't hurt him."

The guard examined a sheet of records on who worked in the building. Found the captain's name and asked, "What's your husband's name?"

Sophia gave him the name of the young hippie who by now was enjoying a cruise on the Potomac with his girlfriend.

The guard spoke into his walkie-talkie, sharing the name Sophia had given him. "Do not fire on the intruder. I repeat, do not fire on the intruder. His wife says he has a medical history of…"

"Bipolar disorder," Sophia said.

"Bipolar disorder. Unarmed. Not dangerous. He thinks he's a spy. The wife recommends arresting him. We can do a background check to confirm the story later."

The guard asked Sophia for her name and cell phone number. She gave him the hippie girlfriend's name and her burner phone's number. With that out of the way, she thanked the guard and the kind stranger.

The kind man with the thinning blond hair adjusted his suit. "Why don't we go around the corner here? We can sit down and chat while waiting for your...husband did you say?"

"Yes."

"Excellent. There's a table just around the corner this way." He pocketed his ID and while withdrawing his hand from his pocket, his wallet slipped out and fell to the ground.

"Sir, you dropped your wallet." Sophia picked up the leather fold and noticed a photo of a young girl with a blue bow in her long, blonde hair. Her eyes were big. Her toothy smile suggested she had just found a cookie jar to raid. "Is this your daughter?"

He took the wallet and admired the picture alongside Sophia. "Yes. Way back when."

"How old is she now?" Sophia kept one eye on the guards at the entrance as she and the blond man strolled further away from them.

"Eighteen, but she still has the same innocent eyes and mischievous smile."

"You must be very proud. What's her name?"

"Holly."

Chapter 109

***H**ow the hell am I going to get out of here?* I kept moving. Better to be changing my location than to stay in one place. I veered toward the Metro Entrance. All the while, I knew security observed my every move.

Cameras were everywhere, they knew what I looked like. Or did they? What would their description be of me? A lone man with a purse in a blue collared button-up shirt and dark slacks? What were my options to change all that?

I couldn't blend with the tourist crowd. It was after hours. The crowd was gone. I couldn't sneak out. Cameras were watching my every move. What's worse, guards were closing in on my position. I couldn't change clothes. I had nothing to change into.

The vendors at the fast food stores were finishing their day. They cleaned the grills, they mopped the floors, they told each other jokes, and they checked the clock.

I slipped into the bathroom, tossed the purse, and hoped my luck would have a good day. Sure enough, one of the young fast food clerks came in, the name Derek stitched on his red polo shirt.

I gave him a hearty smile. "Derek, would you be willing to part with your clothes?"

His eyes popped wide. "What?"

Real smooth, Nathan. "That came out all wrong. Let me explain. For years I wanted to see the Pentagon and now that I have, I lost track of the time and didn't get a chance to buy a souvenir from the gift shop."

"So you want my clothes?"

"Just your shirt and visor."

He said nothing.

"Sounds bad, doesn't it?"

He nodded. "It really does."

I pulled out a stack of twenty-dollar bills. "Would five-hundred dollars make it sound any better?"

He handed me his visor and pulled off his red shirt. "Do you want another shirt and visor? My friend Larry would probably be willing to part with his."

"Thanks for the suggestion." I unbuttoned my shirt, shrugged it off my shoulders, and handed it to him along with the cash. "You better take this. Not very professional walking shirtless in the Pentagon."

I donned the fast food uniform, thanked him, and left the restroom. I made a beeline for his store and saw one of the workers wearing the same uniform making his way to the Metro Entrance. The name Larry was stitched to his shirt.

I walked alongside him. "You Larry?"

"Yeah."

"Your friend Derek mentioned you." I made small talk and kept up our conversation as I strolled with him out the Metro Entrance.

Chapter 110

Sophia followed the blond gentleman. "Where are the tables?"

"Just around the corner." He pointed to the Pentagon's edge.

The setting sun invited a cold breeze to fill the air. It bothered Sophia that she wasn't close to the Metro Entrance anymore. She reminded herself that Nathan could call her if he made it out unseen.

Sophia felt in a daze.

The blond man said, "To who?"

"What?"

"Don't listen to who?"

Sophia scowled. "What do you mean?"

"You just said, 'Don't listen to him.' So I'm just asking who…"

"Oh, I must have had a small seizure. Sometimes I say things without knowing I'm saying them." Did the Shekinah have anything to do with the seizure? Sophia shrugged it off. "Thanks again for your help."

"Don't mention it. My father had bipolar disorder himself. He told me all sorts of stories. Sometimes it was hard to tell what was real and what was all in his mind. Every time he spoke, he spoke from his heart. Whatever he said must have been true in his world."

"So did you end up like most kids who don't listen to their parents? Did you not believe anything he said when you were a teenager?"

"No, I still believed in some of the things he said. Others, I either recognized were too ludicrous to be true, or I chose not to believe them, true or not. For example, I didn't believe in his story of how the government was covering up UFOs."

They turned the corner and Sophia didn't see any tables.

The man said, "But I do believe in the thirty-six righteous."

Sophia gasped and turned to face him.

He stabbed her with a knife in her gut. Pain burrowed a path through her body.

"Goodbye, Sophia Patai."

Richard spotted a citizen in a suit nearby. He withdrew the portable knife, folded it back into its credit card shape, and pocketed it.

Sophia collapsed to the ground. That drew the civilian's attention, so Richard called out, "Quick, dial 911! Some crazy man knifed this woman."

Richard pretended to apply pressure to the wound to stop the bleeding as the man made a call in the distance.

Instead, Richard applied pressure beside the wound to get it to bleed out more.

But the civilian got off the phone and rushed over. "Let me. I know first aid."

Richard watched helplessly as others gathered around to see the civilian tear off strips of clothing to bandage the wound.

Richard grit his teeth. *Come on, die! Die!*

Chapter 111

Imanaged to get outside far enough away from the entrance to be out of sight from the guards. I didn't see Sophia, so I called her on the burn phone.

A man's voice answered. "Hello?"

I tensed. "Who is this?"

"My name's Jeff Samson, and I understand you are looking for the lady who owns this phone."

"What happened to her?" My words came out louder than I intended.

"She's been hurt, but I've treated her wounds, and an ambulance is on its way."

I noticed some heads turned toward the far corner of the building. "Where is she?"

"We're on the southeast corner of the Pentagon. Are you nearby?"

I ran to the small huddle of people. A siren screamed its way closer. Pushing through the crowd, I found Sophia in a pool of blood, a stranger treating her wound.

I fell to her side. "Sophia, wake up." I clasped her hand in mine and stroked her cheek. "Stay with me. Wake up."

Her eyelids fluttered. "I'm not...tired." She pushed out her words with weak breath. "I'll never...be tired of it."

"Of what?" I gripped her hand tighter and stroked her hair. I had to keep her talking until the ambulance came. "Tired of what?"

"Of you," she whispered, a glimmer of life fading from her voice. "Doting on me."

The emergency medical technicians pushed me aside and took control of any chance left of her survival. They asked her their questions, they put her on their gurney, they wailed their siren. She was gone before I had a chance to say goodbye.

Chapter 112

Hospitals always depressed me. **People** arrived without an ounce of joy, and hours later left the hospital in a daze, either from the shock of realizing their true predicament, or from being too drugged to know the difference. But somehow, the friendly support from the nurses always made the ordeal tolerable.

The nurse at the front desk was a chubby woman, and by the way she held her chin high, she seemed too busy giving the patients the attention they needed to be bothered by any self-esteem issues.

I made eye contact with her. "My name's Nathan Yirmorshy and I'm here to see Sophia Patai."

She consulted her computer. "Relative?"

"Fiancé."

Sympathy crossed her face. She whispered in a conspiratorial tone, "Have a seat over there and I'll make sure the doctor speaks with you."

I sat. The emergency waiting room resembled an airport gate for a flight no one wanted to take. In one corner, a teenager played a video game on his tablet. Opposite him, a girl sat wearing what looked like a prom dress, by its pink frills. Beside her an overgrown teenager in a tuxedo draped the chair with his head back, in a deep cavernous snore.

After ten minutes, someone called my name. By his white coat, I knew it was the doctor.

"I'm Yirmorshy."

"Sophia is currently being treated in the ICU. She had a shallow knife wound. We've already stitched it up."

My gut felt like I had swallowed sandbags. "Is she going to be okay?"

"She lost a lot of blood, but we're giving her a transfusion. She seems to be responding."

I nodded.

He never broke eye contact with me. "At this time it would be a good idea to contact her family and let them know she should be fully recovered in a few days."

"Will do," I lied. Other priorities demanded my attention.

Priorities like saving Sophia's life.

After I drove near to the South Parking Lot of the Pentagon, I put in the ear bud and tuned to the frequency of the listening device. I heard Richard talking. Based on his pauses and no one audibly responding, I guessed he was on the phone.

"Listen, Jonah. Like I said before, Project MEG was a waste of time, in my opinion. It was wishful thinking that lasted decades. Project 36 may be a long shot, but it's simple to carry out. We've already closed the first 35, there's only one left. We've gone this far. We must finish the project."

Silence.

"No, I'm not going to wait on training another assassin. I'm going to hire one of the people here."

Silence.

"Yes, I know the assassins here aren't members, but it doesn't matter. You assign a target to them, claim the person's a traitor to the country or a danger to national security, and they'll terminate whoever you want."

Silence.

"My mind's made up, Jonah. This should be an easy target. She's already wounded. She isn't going anywhere."

I removed the ear bud. Would Sophia ever be out of danger? I had to take down Richard Stone.

Chapter 113

Nurse Walcott sat at her desk enjoying the slow shift. Just one suicide attempt and one knifing. If the rest of the evening stayed this slow, she'd be happy.

The phone rang.

"Victoria Hospital, Mary Walcott speaking, may I help you?"

"Is that Sophia lady dead yet?"

"Excuse me?"

"That woman with the knife wound. Is she dead yet?"

"She's being treated in the ICU now, but we anticipate she will soon be transferred to the recovery ward for continued observation."

"That bitch isn't dead yet? If she's not dead, I'll come over there and kill her myself, do you hear me? I'll kill that bitch myself!"

Nurse Walcott's heart drummed. "Sir, who may I ask is calling?"

"The guy that's going to slice that bitch in two." The man hung up.

Walcott dialed the number for the police. Her hands were shaking as she waited for them to pick up.

"Arlington Police."

"This is Nurse Mary Walcott calling from Victoria Hospital. I just had a threat made to one of the patients here. The threat was made by phone to a patient that was attacked with knife injuries. I'm calling to request police protection."

"Fax in the official request, and in the meantime we'll send a patrolman to your location."

Relieved, she jotted down the fax number he gave her and thanked the officer.

I shivered, but felt I'd done good. Making that call to the nurse, making those threats, I had no doubt Sophia would get better protection. All I wanted to do right now was to get myself ready for when she woke up.

Chapter 114

Andrew McGraw had a simple task that morning. Visit a patient and kill her. When the lieutenant general told him his target was wounded and unconscious in the hospital, Andrew had to wonder just how much of a threat to national security she could really be. And to kill by any means necessary? That meant he didn't need to make it look like she died of natural causes. It could be a messy kill. Gun, chainsaw, even guillotine would satisfy the lieutenant general.

Andrew arrived at the hospital holding a bouquet of flowers. Everyone stopped a moment to stare at him. Hard to resist noticing a guy carrying flowers, even if it was a common view at a hospital. He scanned the waiting room and saw a few kids, a guy in a red shirt, a man holding a weeping woman in his arms. Andrew did a double take at the man in the red shirt. The man had an almost completed pyramid of empty coffee cups.

"Nice pyramid," Andrew said to him.

"Thanks." The guy nodded to his bouquet. "Nice flowers."

Andrew smiled. "For my sister."

"She okay?"

"I hope so." Andrew turned to the nurse.

"Hi, I have flowers for Sophia Patai."

"They're lovely," the nurse said. "I'll hold on to them for her."

"I can't drop them off myself?"

"I'm afraid we don't allow flowers in ICU. And she isn't seeing visitors right now, but I'll take the flowers to her when she's able to receive them."

Damn! "Thank you very much."

Andrew handed her the flowers and paused to think about what to do next.

"Yeah," the man with the pyramid of cups said. "They wouldn't let me visit my fiancée, either."

"She okay?"

"Better be." The man straightened his shirt. "If she dies, I'll kill her."

"That'll teach her," Andrew said. "Well, I better make a phone call."

Andrew left the building.

Richard wondered if today would be his last day at the Pentagon. With the elimination of target number thirty-six, would it be everyone's last day here on Earth? Would all Christian souls be taken to a better place? A perfect place?

The day seemed like any other. It was hard to believe that the End Times were near.

The office phone rang and Richard answered.

"It's Andrew. They won't tell me her room number. Do you know it?"

Richard chided himself for not thinking of it before. *Of course he needed that info.* "I'll call you back."

Richard called the hospital and managed to be connected to Sophia Patai's doctor. Speaking directly to doctors had its benefits. Doctors had less concern than nurses over following security protocols in the hospital. "Who am I speaking with?"

"This is Dr. Gordon," the doctor said.

"I'm sorry, I didn't catch your first name?"

"It's Henry. Who is this?"

Richard typed "Henry Gordon" into his database and found the phone number, residence, birthdate, social, and details that would make the good doctor blush.

"Is this the Dr. Henry Gordon who lives at 271 Cherry Lane?"

There was a pause on the other end of the line. "Yes. Who am I speaking to?"

Now that Richard had established proof of having immediate access to knowledge about the physician, he said, "You have a patient. A Sophia Patai."

"Yes?"

"When do you expect her to regain consciousness?"

"Sir, if you could tell me your name—"

Richard raised his voice. "I need to know when."

After a moment, the doctor replied. "Hard to tell at this point."

"Ballpark?"

"Anywhere between a day and a week. Very hard to judge with the amount of blood she lost."

"Okay. What room is she in?"

"I'm sorry, sir. I'm not allowed to give out that information."

Richard had to play the blackmail card, after all. "Henry, I see that you stay at the Hotel Rouge every Tuesday night. Now maybe your wife Maryanne knows about your weekly excursions, but what would your daughter Penny in Emerson Preparatory School have to say about it?"

Richard waited for the doctor to respond. After a long stretch of silence, Henry said, "Room 223."

"Thank you." Richard hung up and called Andrew back with the target's room number.

Chapter 115

Andrew McGraw returned to the hospital nurse. The target's room was located in the Intensive Care Unit. No visitors could get to her room. Authorized access only. If he walked through those doors, the nurse would try to stop him, she'd call security, security would take several minutes to get to the right floor, and they'd chase after him.

Challenging, but doable.

He walked past the desk toward the ICU's swinging doors.

"Excuse me," the nurse shouted. "You can't go in there, sir."

Andrew barged through the doors. He could hear the nurse shout words like "restricted," and "stop."

He followed the room numbers and looked for room 223. The nurse probably had her hands on a phone by now, calling security.

Then he heard the nurse follow after him. "Sir, this is a restricted area. Somebody, stop that man!"

A male nurse stepped in front of Andrew. "I'm afraid that's as far as you go, sir."

Andrew smiled and punched him in the gut. The man doubled over, and Andrew pounded one hard on the male nurse's back. The nurse fell to the floor. Others came to the nurse's rescue. Andrew adopted a quick stride and took out his gun.

Screams echoed through the halls along with shouts of "He's got a gun!" Like Moses at the Red Sea, the path magically cleared for him.

He continued to follow the numbers to 223. *The room should be straight down this hall.*

That's when he saw the guard. No, it wasn't even a guard. It was a policeman. An armed policeman with a gun pointed straight at Andrew.

"Don't move! Police!"

Andrew got annoyed. *The lieutenant general didn't tell me a policeman guarded her room.*

Killing a traitor was one thing. Killing a police officer? Well, that was a whole different can of patriotism.

Andrew put his hands up in surrender. "Okay, I'm setting down the gun."

Andrew held the gun's barrel with his thumb and forefinger to show he had no intention of pulling the trigger. He slowly crouched to the ground. When he saw the telltale sign of relief in the police officer's stance, Andrew spun and fled in the opposite direction.

"Stop," the policeman shouted. Andrew heard him call for backup.

When Andrew turned the corner, he figured he was safe. An officer would never fire a gun in a crowded hospital.

Andrew ran for the back stairs. He found the stairwell door and pushed it open. The door slammed back into his face. Andrew dropped to the floor, stunned for a second, an instant headache emerging. That was no accident. Someone had pushed the door hard into his forehead.

The door opened again and Andrew recognized the man with the red shirt from the waiting room.

Andrew clutched his forehead, confused. "The pyramid guy?"

While I used my body to hold the stairwell door open, I grabbed the assassin by the collar and rolled backwards onto the floor, lifting him with my legs and flinging him down the first flow of steps.

I pivoted to see him leaning up against the far wall on the landing halfway down the flight of stairs. I didn't see his fall, but he must have rolled knowing how to fall down stairs without hurting himself.

I peered down at him from the top of the stairs. His gun had fallen and now lay beside me. I left it on the floor. If he was a trained assassin, no way he'd leave without his weapon.

I waited for him to come get it. I had the advantage. Didn't matter if he looked like he weighed a bit more than me, I was above him. The height gave me the advantage of potential energy. Dropping a bowling ball on your foot will cause different degrees of pain depending on whether you drop it a millimeter above your foot or a mile above your foot. My added height gave me more energy to fall and land on him in a way that could cause him weeks of grief.

He didn't come back up to get his gun. He stood his ground waiting. Probably waiting for my attack so he could defend himself with an attack of his own. I had to distract him. Surprise him somehow.

"Richard sent you?" I asked.

He looked surprised. While he worked out how I knew Richard, I grabbed the railing and did a sideways cartwheel with legs bent. I spun at a shorter radius to get higher angular momentum going, and applied the potential energy by kicking my feet into his face.

The guy's head flung back and hit the cement wall. Somehow, he stayed upright, staggering back. Before I could land another hit on him, he punched me hard in the nose.

Pain shot through my head. I didn't understand how he could have responded so quickly after such a kick. He must have turned off all his pain and focused on the problem. He grabbed me and shoved me down the stairs.

I fell, each stair a punch to my body. At the foot of the stairs, I stood on wobbling knees. If I wanted to recover, I had to do what he did. I shook off all the pain and focused my mind on calm, peace, readiness.

Now he had the advantage, and his smile said he knew it. One flight above me, he had the potential energy to cause serious injury if a hit landed on me, and the experience to make it lethal. But instead, he applied another surprise I should have anticipated. He walked up the steps and retrieved his gun.

He returned to the platform above me and pointed the gun at me. "Now get out of my way."

I stood my ground, my eyes watering from the stinging pain. "You're not going to shoot."

He froze. He must have figured out how I knew he wasn't going to shoot me, because he engaged the safety on the gun and put the firearm in the small of his back. I witnessed the way he avoided shooting the police officer outside Sophia's door. If he wasn't going to kill a police officer, he wasn't going to kill a random civilian either. This assassin had a moral code.

He sighed, and then lunged in the air at me holding his fist in his other hand and leading with his elbow. If that elbow point landed on me, all of his weight would be focused at a single point. Like dropping a bowling ball attached to a knife.

Easier to dodge a point, though. I twirled and hammered a knuckle-pointed fist at his neck. He landed at my feet, but not without feeling the force of my knuckle crush his throat. Nothing fatal, just extremely unpleasant.

I wrapped my arm around his neck, hindering the circulation of blood to his head.

He gasped, "Who are you?"

"A carbon-based life form. You?"

He passed out before he could respond.

Chapter 116

After the police cuffed the assassin and took him away, the hospital staff set me up with a room to wait for a doctor to treat my splintered nose. It's one thing to know that a broken nose hurts like hell, it's quite another to actually feel it. I could barely see anything, the way my eyes teared from all the pain.

I made a call while I waited for the doctor.

"Rabbi, it's Nathan."

"You think it's safe to call?"

"Yeah," Even with all the resources Richard had, listening in to conversations on burner phones wasn't one of his luxuries. "The powers that be aren't quite as powerful as all that."

"What do you need, Nathan?"

"What if—?" How to put this? "You believe in the thirty-six righteous, right?"

"Yes."

"But I'm guessing it wouldn't surprise you if I don't."

"Not a bit," the rabbi said. "Most people I know don't believe in the existence of the lamed-vav tzadikim, the thirty-six righteous."

"But let's say it is true, just for the sake of argument."

"Easy enough."

"What if your list was wrong? What if it turns out that another thirty-six righteous are still out there?"

"Then if everyone on my list dies and nothing happens—no earthquakes, no floods, no volcanic eruptions—either the murderers will believe there's nothing to the legend of the thirty-six righteous after all, or they'll seek out a new list of people to kill."

"What if you tell them you had it wrong? That the list you made didn't have an accurate tally of the true thirty-six righteous, and it was just your best guess?"

"I see what you're getting at, Nathan. If they believed me, they might stop coming after Sophia. But how do you convince them of that? How do you convince them that Sophia is not one of the thirty-six?"

I pinched my nose harder to still the throbbing pain. "The problem is, Rabbi, every assassin I stop, they just send another one. Even if I stopped the guy who's sending the assassins, he's just a player in some no-girls-allowed club. Their society is going to keep sending assassins, unless they think Sophia isn't one of the thirty-six righteous."

"I understand, Nathan. But I'm afraid that when I put her name on that list, I was sealing her death."

"So what do I do?"

"I honestly don't know what you can do, Nathan, except pray. And hope HaShem hears your prayer. That's probably not what you wanted to hear, but it's the only solution I have. Pray, and listen to what God tells you."

I hung up. Great. Listen to God. I could do that. Had

plenty of experience hearing voices in my head when nobody was around.

So they would keep coming for Sophia until they killed her. And all I could do was pray to God. And listen.

I needed another solution. I stuck a hand in my pocket and felt Sophia's iPhone. I took it out and turned it on. In the memo app, a list of recordings she had made spilled across the screen. Those recordings were perhaps the only things I had left of her voice. I played the shortest one. I heard her say, "Remember to send Miriam a birthday card…. Oh! And remember to listen to this message before Miriam's birthday."

I smiled. Flipped through the other memos, scanned them, and saw one crazy long one. It lasted thirty-six minutes. I played it.

Still ignoring the "No Cell Phones" sign in the hospital, I called Detective Bobbie Graff and wondered if she'd remember me, once I mentioned my name.

"Nathan, you have to get to the Berkeley Police Department right now. You're a suspect in two murders and the sooner we clear you, the sooner we can put all our attention on finding the real killer or killers."

"Two murders?" That didn't make sense. "I'm guessing one of them was Yoseph Schwartz. Who was the other one?"

"I can't talk about it over the phone. Come to the station, and let's sort it out."

"I'm afraid I can't do that. I'm in Virginia, so it would be a long walk."

"What are you doing in Virginia?"

I pinched at the throbbing pain at my nose and had an idea. "For that second murder victim. Did the weapon have a wooden handle?"

"I'm almost too afraid to ask how you knew that."

"It did have a wooden handle? Figures." I told her about the limping bully I met at the sandwich shop, how he forced my hand around a wooden handle of some tool I couldn't see.

"He limped? That sounds like the same man who attacked me in my home."

"You were attacked?"

"I'm fine. Sounds like we should put all our resources on this limping man."

I ran a hand through my hair. "Whoever he is, he's just a worker bee following orders."

"You wouldn't happen to know the name of the queen bee, would you?"

"A lieutenant general at the Pentagon. Richard Stone."

Graff cursed.

"Know him?" I asked.

"Forget it. I'm not sure we could ever get enough evidence to arrest him, much less convict him."

"I have an idea, but I'll need your help." I told her about Richard Stone's role in what he called Project 36. Told her about Sophia and our visit to the Pentagon, Sophia's knife wound and the hospital fight. Told her what the best solution could be. Distract, confuse, and deceive. If it was a good enough strategy for the government, it was good enough for me.

After I explained my plan, she sighed. "Okay. I'll call the doctor and get a plane ticket."

After my hospital care, I spent the rest of the evening at the metro stop, Rosslyn Station, marking all the points where the security cameras were, where all the guards ran their watch, where all the alarm doors were, and where all the flow of traffic went during rush hour. I memorized the timing, and I placed the explosives.

Chapter 117

In the morning, Richard Stone watched the news on his computer. "A man whose identity is still unknown at this juncture has been arrested for charging into a hospital with a gun. Authorities are still unclear who he is or why he came in carrying a weapon, but believe it is related to a knifing that occurred outside the Pentagon."

"Dammit." Richard closed the news browser.

"Hey! Richard," a man's voice said.

Richard looked above him. It was the loudspeaker.

The voice continued. "I always pictured God speaking with a booming voice from the sky, casting down judgment."

What the hell? If that was Nathan Yirmorshy's voice on the speaker, then he must have tampered with the speaker. Nathan must have been inside the office.

Nathan said, "I've heard a lot of voices in my head, but I've never heard a booming one coming from the sky. You, on the other hand, deserve to hear God's voice. You deserve to hear Him cast judgment upon you."

Richard had half a mind to tell Nathan to piss off, but figured it would have been as effective as shouting at a radio. Nathan probably wouldn't hear him.

"Richard Stone, I am your god and I find you guilty. You are guilty of murdering innocent people. You are guilty of murdering Cole. You are guilty of attempting to murder Sophia. You shall die and burn in Hell for all eternity."

Richard snorted at Nathan's empty threats.

"A word of advice, Richard. If you ever blow up someone's motel room, just be sure all the explosives are used up and not repositioned under your seat. I hope you're wearing sunscreen, because you're about to burn. Five...four...three..."

Richard checked under his seat and saw a detonator and phone taped to the chair.

I gotta get out of here.

He jumped from his seat and leapt to the front of his desk.

"Two...one...Dialing!"

BANG! BANG! BANG! BANG! BANG! BANG! BANG!

Still crouching at the desk, Richard's heart hammered fearing the worst, but he didn't feel injured.

"Yes," the voice continued. "You, too, can enjoy the pleasures firecrackers can bring. Available now at your local souvenir shop."

Two guards rushed in, "Are you okay sir?"

"I'm fine."

One of the guards sniffed. "What is that smell?"

"It's nothing. Leave me alone." Richard stood and felt the cold on his pants.

The guards stared at the puddle on the floor. One of the guards turned, stifling a laugh.

Richard retrieved some napkins from his desk drawer and wiped the crotch of his pants. "Get the hell out of here."

The guards left. Richard slammed his office door closed. The phone rang, and Richard answered. "Who is this? Is this you, Nathan?"

"Good one. You got it one guess."

"What do you want?"

"I want a meeting with you. Alone."

"Why? You gonna kill me?"

"As I just demonstrated, I could have killed you now, but I didn't."

"So what do you want?"

"I know what you're trying to do. And I want to prove to you that Sophia isn't one of the thirty-six righteous. The rabbi had his list wrong."

"The thirty-six what, now?"

"Nice try," Nathan said. "I'm going to prove to you you're wasting your time."

"Considering you'd do anything to make sure she stays alive, that proof would have to be rather unbiased."

"It is."

Richard couldn't believe he pissed his pants over firecrackers. "Where and when?"

"At Virginia Square Metro Station, 5:15 p.m."

"I'll be there."

After hanging up the phone, Richard called the Counter-Terrorist Unit for an APB on Nathan Yirmorshy.

Believed to be armed and dangerous. Plans to bomb Virginia Square Metro Station during rush hour.

While Nathan is busy with them, I can take care of Sophia myself.

Chapter 118

I **wore all white clothing and waited for Richard** on the westbound platform of the Virginia Square Metro Station in case he showed. As expected, there was no sign of him but I did see people with government-issued ear buds approaching.

On one side of me, a guy in a suit sidestepped closer. On my other side, another approached me without looking directly at me. Their timing was perfect. Perfect enough for me to cross the rails.

To the gasps of several onlookers, I jumped off the platform into the subway rail system, hopped across the rails, and jumped up onto the eastbound platform. The suits had no qualms jumping in after me until they saw the train approach. Then they hustled back to their side of the station.

When the eastbound train stopped, I boarded and hoped they'd follow standard procedure. Call in the direction of my train and have people ready at the next station to take me down.

I maneuvered to the back of the train and forced a window open.

As I climbed through, one of the passengers asked, "What the hell are you doing?"

I ignored him. Pulling myself through the window, I climbed to the top of the train car. It was dirty as hell. I crawled forward toward the next car. Dirt and grim covered my face, hands, and clothes. The train was oily and hard to hold onto.

Distraction complete.

Richard paced his office. He knew that killing Sophia himself had only a few challenges. Getting inside Sophia's hospital room didn't concern him. What concerned him was leaving the scene without being connected to her death. After all, he couldn't ignore the possibility that Sophia *wasn't* one of the thirty-six righteous. If that were the case, well…he just had to be sure no one pinned the murder on him.

Richard didn't have his firearm, but it didn't matter. He needed something less conspicuous. He scanned his desk, examined a few sharp objects—a letter opener, a to-do list paper spike. He then looked at his empty hands and smiled.

Special Agent Jim Colfax instructed the guards, "Get everyone out of the station. Our suspect is taking the train from the Virginia Square Station to this one, so he'll be on the eastbound platform."

The guards evacuated Clarendon station. People grumbled as they were forced to find other routes to get home.

Colfax pointed at the spots along the platform where the train's doors would open. "When the train arrives, I need all the doors covered."

Agents spread out evenly among the estimated position of the train's doors.

A stale wind blew harder through the tunnel. The station echoed and rattled. The train was coming closer.

Chapter 119

I kept inching forward on top of the train, moving closer to the front. Sliding on my back this time, the tunnel's ceiling passed above my face with such speed, it was disconcerting. I could reach up and my hand would get torn apart. Almost at the front car. I ran my hands through my hair. Grease came off. I was a mess.

Special Agent Jim Colfax scanned for the suspect dressed all in white as the train pulled in to a stop. The passengers had shocked faces when they saw all the agents holding their weapons at the ready.

"See him?" Colfax called out.

No response.

When the doors opened, Colfax guided each passenger toward the exit. The other agents did the same. "Everyone stay calm and come out one at a time."

As the passengers headed toward the exit away from potential harm, other agents asked them if they had seen Nathan Yirmorshy. The passengers were shown a picture and asked if they recognized the man.

After getting nearly everyone off the train, Colfax heard the announcement on the walkie-talkie.

"Someone said he saw the suspect open the window in the back of the train and jump out."

"He jumped out?"

"Correction, he climbed out. To the top of the train."

"Keep guarding your positions," Colfax called out to the others. He pointed to one of the agents. "Come with me. We're looking for a guy dressed all in white."

Colfax had to see if the suspect still lay on top of the train. He might have planted the bomb there.

Once the train had stopped, I descended from the top of the train onto the railroad tracks. I climbed onto the platform while the agents were busy getting everyone off the train. I huddled over, my clothes now black with grime and grease and my hair disheveled. I probably looked like a homeless man. I joined the masses and walked toward the exit, shoulders slumped in an attempt to look the part. Thought I was home free. Thought I didn't have to put plan B into effect.

Then I saw the agents asking everyone if they'd seen someone. And they were holding my picture.

Special Agent Jim Colfax examined the opened window at the last car of the train. Back on the platform, he said to the agent, "Give me a hand."

The agent made a foothold with interlaced fingers, and Colfax stepped on to be lifted up to the top of the train where he could get a good view.

Nothing there. No suspect and no sign of a bomb. Then he saw a man's silhouette running down the tunnel toward Court House, the next station.

I headed for Court House station. If they saw me, they'd get their agents to meet up with me, ready for my arrival. But they'd be too late. I ran through Court House station, getting a bunch of perplexed stares from the passengers waiting at the platforms. I guess they weren't used to seeing a man run along the tracks. I arrived at the planned position, the biggest curve on the track, and retrieved the in-line skates I'd hid there. I attached the skates to my shoes.

A voice shouted, "There he is."

The words came from a man in a dark suit pointing at me from the Court House platform. He descended onto the tracks. I waited beside the tracks of the eastbound train. Two others joined the first agent, running along the westbound train tracks, which ran alongside the eastbound tracks.

Where was my train?

The agents were getting closer, just a few hundred feet away. Fortunately, the eastbound train made its way toward me. I waited against the wall at the biggest curve in the rails, where the train moved at its slowest speed.

Squeezing against the subway wall, I watched the train pass inches away from me. I squinted expecting a blast of air in my face, but the train moved at too much of a crawl to generate any wind. I raised the meat hooks at the ready. As the last car passed, I hooked onto the train and jumped onto the rails. The inline skates with metal plates attached alongside the skates' wheels locked onto the rails. As expected, the train accelerated at a slow enough rate so that it didn't pull my arms out of my sockets. Glancing back, I saw the agents had given up chasing after me.

The train pulled me along.

My feet vibrated like crazy. The train squealed its noise with a piercing echo rumbling through the tunnels. My train skates kept rolling. Humid wind hit me and I had to squint. I leaned to the side. The tracks ahead swerved slightly, left and right, creating the illusion of the tunnel shifting side to side.

The train pulled me deeper into its burrow.

Hooked to the subway car, I traveled underneath Wilson Boulevard and winced at the shrieks of the train. My legs wobbled, the muscles not used to this strange workout. The train brought me all the way to Rosslyn Station and slowed down. As the train came to a stop, my body rolled up and pressed against the back of the subway car.

I tossed aside the hooks and took awkward steps off the rails. I clicked the skates off my shoes and climbed onto the Rosslyn Station platform. As I took a calm stride to the escalator, an agent with a crew cut spotted me.

Damn!

I pushed past the people riding the escalator. I doubted I would get a mention in anyone's diary for favorite person of the day.

Agents pursued me. I climbed up to the Rosslyn Metro Mall. Inside, among the bustling food court, I ran across to the connected twenty-two-story building. Had to go through an employees-only door.

"He's going upstairs," someone said.

He said it. He didn't yell it. It meant he was calling for backup through his walkie-talkie and not calling out to people behind him.

Agents could be flocking to my position any moment now. I could be running straight into capture.

Ignoring caution, I plowed further up the stairs. My leg muscles ached at the climb. I had to catch my breath every four flights. Fifteen more flights of stairs to the roof. I hiked the final flight and pushed out the stairwell door. On the roof, I ran to the ledge and grabbed the pack I had left there.

I wasn't alone. Behind me, the agent with the crew cut paused at a ventilation shaft and pointed his gun at me.

"Federal agent! Don't move!"

I started to strap on the pack and called out, "Get away from there."

"Put your hands in the air and get on the ground." He stepped closer to me but was still situated too near the ventilation shaft. Other agents appeared from different points. My 9 o'clock, my 12 o'clock, and the first one still yelling at me at my 2 o'clock.

I raised my hands in the air and yelled with as much belligerence as the agent. "Get the hell away from that ventilation shaft!"

All three agents moved closer to me. When they were clear from danger, I flicked the switch on the remote detonator and crouched.

The small piece of C4 I had placed in the ventilation shaft barked an explosion. The agents fell to the ground. Just the distraction I needed.

I finished putting on my pack and jumped off the roof. My canopy opened. I steered away, gliding over D.C.

Not the smartest thing to do in restricted airspace, but it bought me time to reposition myself at an advantage.

Confusion complete.

Chapter 120

Special Agent Jim Colfax spoke into the walkie-talkie. "What the hell was that noise?"

An agent responded. "He set off an explosion in the ventilation shaft. No major damage."

"What about the suspect? Where the hell is he? Did you capture him?"

"Suspect got away. He parachuted off the building."

Shit. The lieutenant general was not going to be happy.

I glided above the Potomac River, descending to the shoreline off the Mt. Vernon Trail. With a strong yank, I pulled the canopy down to the ground, out of the way of the wind. Removing the harness, I left the paraglider by the river. I trekked to my car parked off the George Washington Memorial Parkway, got in, and changed out of my greasy clothes. After putting on hospital surgical scrubs, I gunned the engine and drove toward the hospital.

I hoped I wasn't too late.

***

Richard Stone arrived at the Intensive Care Unit and showed his government ID to the nurse. "I'm here to see Sophia Patai. I understand there was an attempt made on her life, an incident that could have something to do with her injury at the Pentagon."

The nurse didn't question Richard's authority. "Right down the hall. Room 223."

Richard thanked the nurse and continued through the doors labeled "Notice: Only authorized persons to enter this area."

He showed his ID to the police officer outside Sophia's door and entered her room. The blankets covered her completely, apart from her head and neck. She was asleep and looked already dead. *I can help that process along.*

Richard gently raised Sophia's head and removed the pillow from underneath. Then he placed the pillow on top of her face and applied a smothering pressure.

Chapter 121

I arrived at the hospital and dashed to the ICU, passing the front desk. For some reason, the nurse wasn't there to stop me from entering the authorized personnel doors. I ran to Sophia's room, heard an extended tone coming from her room, and when I rushed in, I gaped at the machine's flat line.

The doctor had his fingers at Sophia's wrist, checking her pulse. He gave a slight shake of his head and flicked off the heart monitor. A nurse pulled the bed sheet over Sophia's head. The whole room turned pale and died.

I scanned the scene to see who occupied the room. Besides the doctor stood two nurses, two police officers, Detective Graff, and Richard Stone.

Richard wore an apologetic face that almost looked genuine. "I'm sorry, Nathan. We all hoped she would pull through and the doctor did everything he could."

I leapt upon Richard, choking his throat. "*You* did this. You killed her."

The two police officers pulled me off of him.

A scream ripped out from my chest. "I'll kill you!"

I couldn't see anything but Richard. I couldn't hear anything at all. Maybe Detective Graff was telling me to calm down. Maybe I was fighting against a police officer's grip. Maybe I was screaming so loud my voice split apart. I just didn't know. Not until I drew a breath.

By that time, Richard was rubbing his throat. "Arrest him for assaulting a federal agent."

Cold cuffs clicked around my wrists tight behind my back.

Even as they shoved me out of the room, I shouted out all my breath could carry. "You have a death wish? I'm going to kill you!"

The burn in my eyes. The burn in my throat. The burn in my heart of a love lost. It was all so much louder than I could scream.

Chapter 122

Two hours later, I paced inside a jail cell. I had requested to see Richard Stone for one last face-to-face meeting. The police officer had told me that Richard agreed.

The police led me to a private room and cuffed me to the table.

I thought about the cell I had put myself in. I, Nathan Yirmorshy, was no longer a free man. It amazed me how a split second decision could control the rest of one's fate. A split second of anger could put you in a cell. A split second of poor judgment could put you in a casket, just like it did to Cole.

What a waste of life.

Cole wasn't the first to tell me about government conspiracies. Back when I attended high school, my friend claimed President Roosevelt knew about the impending attack on Pearl Harbor and let it happen so that the Americans would get angry enough to fight the Germans.

My friend had laughed as he told me about Roosevelt's complicity in letting the Japanese bomb Pearl Harbor. He said, "I don't think the U.S. should get involved in any foreign wars. Even World War II."

I crossed my arms. "You talking to me? Not if you had your way. If the U.S. hadn't stepped in to help put a stop to the Nazis, my mother wouldn't have survived, and I would never have been born. I wouldn't be standing here today listening to your crap if you had your way."

That shut him up. Distract, confuse, and deceive. Distract the Americans by allowing an attack on Pearl Harbor, confuse them into thinking Pearl Harbor was a surprise attack, and deceive them into believing the U.S. had to fight the Nazis as well as the Japanese to retaliate for Pearl Harbor. If Roosevelt really applied such a strategy to get the U.S. into war, he saved my life and the lives of millions. What if the same could be said for 9/11? Distract, confuse, and deceive. It was one hell of a strategy.

The door opened and a policeman escorted Richard into the windowless room. The officer informed Richard to knock when he was through talking to me. The lieutenant general nodded his understanding and the policeman left us alone.

Richard sat across from me. "What do you want to know?"

"The thirty-six are dead. There are no fancy lights. There's no heavenly discotheque. You just killed thirty-six innocent people. Good innocent people. For no reason."

"Look, Nathan. The truth is no one is sorrier than I am. I expected the world to reach the Rapture. Can you imagine if everyone lived in a world of peace? One without hunger? One without war or poverty? Everyone gets what they need. Every day. And everyone lives forever."

I said nothing.

"Nathan, this reality exists. And it's a worthwhile goal."

I said nothing.

"Don't you see, Nathan? I *had* to give the order to kill those thirty-six people. I'm sorry this led to you losing someone like Sophia. But she will be remembered in all our hearts for the sacrifice she made in pursuing the most heavenly goal there is."

I said nothing.

"You have to understand, Nathan. Sacrificing a single life to save many lives is a noble cause."

"You're in a smokeless fire."

Richard looked confused. "What are you talking about? What fire?"

I raised my shirt, baring my chest.

His face turned red and his veins puffed out from his neck. "Is that a wire?"

"You're wrong, lieutenant. Sacrificing one's own life to save many is noble. Sacrificing someone else's life to save many, that's murder."

A policeman came in with Detective Graff and said to the detective, "I'll let you do the honors."

Graff yanked Richard's hands behind his back to cuff him. "Richard Stone, you have the right to remain silent…"

"You can't do this," Richard shouted. "You have no idea who I am. You have no idea what I'm capable of."

With only one wrist cuffed, he fought Graff to the floor, took the gun from her holster, but froze before moving any further. Graff had what looked like a steak knife tight against his throat.

She squeezed the knife against his neck. "Give me a reason!"

Richard let the gun fall to the floor. Graff finished cuffing him before taking him away.

Deception complete.

Chapter 123

All Richard knew was that he would have a visitor. Life certainly played its cruel tricks. Just hours ago, Richard had visited Nathan when Nathan was chained to the table. Now Richard was chained to the table at the windowless room of the police department. A cruel twist of fate. Richard half expected Nathan to be the mysterious visitor, coming to gloat.

But when the door opened, Richard saw a welcome face.

"Jonah, thank the good Lord you've come. You have to get me out of here."

Jonah sat across from Richard and watched the door close. "Of course, Richard. We're going to do everything we can. You haven't said anything stupid, have you?"

"What do you mean?"

"About the Order. You haven't been talking, have you?"

"Of course not, who do you think I am? I've kept our secrets safe. The only thing I did was tell my daughter that Nathan Yirmorshy tricked the police into arresting me.

She's going to let my ex and my lawyer know I'm locked up, then they can help me out."

"That's good, Richard." Jonah stood up and walked behind him, placing a comforting hand on Richard's shoulder. "I knew we could trust you. You're a good man."

"Just get me out of here, Jonah. I need to get that Nathan Yirmorshy fellow. He has to be put down."

"I'm afraid I can't do that. Sophia Patai was on the list of thirty-six righteous and you handled that. Nathan Yirmorshy, on the other hand, never made the agenda."

Richard felt Jonah jab him in the neck with a needle. Cold fluids flushed from his neck to the rest of his body. Richard's chest pumped pain.

Jonah's voice was calm, so different from the panic that thrashed through Richard's mind. "I'm sorry about this, Richard. The Order no longer has any use for you. I tried to persuade them to let you live, but they convinced me that we just can't risk it. I'm sure you understand."

Richard cursed himself for not seeing this fate sooner. He could have warned the police that someone would be coming to kill him. He could have asked for better protection. He could have done something, anything to prevent Jonah's attack.

Breathing became impossible. Richard struggled for air, fighting against the chains. He couldn't even scream.

At his dying breath, he heard Jonah pound on the door. "Someone help him! He's having a heart attack!"

Chapter 124

Detective Graff drove me across the Potomac River on the 14th Street Bridge to the U.S. Marshals building on Constitution Avenue.

We walked through the front entrance.

She glanced over to me and said, "I need to fill you in. Your name is Carl Best. You work as a bank teller at First Federal Bank in Amsterdam, New York…"

We entered a conference room.

Graff continued, "with your wife, Sarah Best."

Sophia rushed into my arms and we kissed.

Graff said, "I'll just leave you two alone for a minute." She closed the door behind her.

"You okay?" I asked.

"Yeah. It was hard holding my breath, but as soon as I disconnected the heart monitor like the doctor showed me, the sound of the flat line was enough to make Richard stop choking me. I was able to fake the rest pretty easily. How'd you come up with a plan like that, anyway?"

"I heard your memo. 'Only her death can save her.' It told me what needed to be done. I'm just glad you were conscious for the doctor to tell you how to play your part."

Detective Graff knocked and walked in. "Here's part two of your request."

She escorted Rabbi Elihu Silverman into the room. He looked as happy as I felt. "Nathan, Sophia, I am so pleased to see you are okay."

Graff held up a set of crystal champagne glasses and a bottle of red wine. "I got you two a wedding gift." She turned to address the rabbi. "There's not much time, Rabbi. Can you get on with it?"

"Of course. I brought the *ketubah* and the *chuppah*."

Detective Graff scowled. "Translation?"

The rabbi explained as he handed me a pen. "A ketubah is the wedding contract, and a chuppah is the wedding canopy."

Before I signed, I asked the detective, "What name should I sign?"

"Your new name," Graff said. "Carl Best."

"Best?" the rabbi asked. "What kind of a name is Best? What's wrong with Cohen or Manishevitz? Even Lipshitz is a step in the right direction."

I signed as Carl Best and Sophia signed as Sarah Best. Detective Graff and the rabbi signed as witnesses. They held the canopy above our heads as Sophia walked around me seven times, and the rabbi recited the seven blessings.

She was my universe now.

The rabbi filled one of Graff's champagne glasses with red wine. Sophia and I drank the symbol of happiness.

"We must remember the destruction of the ancient temple." The rabbi wrapped the glass in a handkerchief and placed it at my feet.

I said, "I've always wanted to do this." I smashed the glass with my foot and it shattered inside the handkerchief.

"*Mazel Tov!*" the rabbi shouted.

"I want to try." Sophia placed another glass at her feet and stomped on it.

Graff looked appalled. "Those champagne glasses weren't cheap, you know."

As I drove Sophia—Sarah—north to our new home in Amsterdam, New York, she pulled some envelopes out of a plastic bag.

"What are those?" I asked.

"My mail. Detective Graff picked it up from my place and said it would be the last mail I'd ever receive as Sophia Patai." She flipped through the letters. "Junk, junk, junk…. Here's something. A card from somebody."

I took my eyes off the road and glanced at her. She peeled open the envelope, tugged out the greeting card, and read the card silently. I wondered who sent the card. A relative perhaps? She wiped tears from her eyes.

I felt a chill and continued to glance at her. "What's wrong?"

"Nothing," she said with a smile. "It's from Leah. A friend. I thought I disappointed her, but she sent me this card." She traced the edges of the card as though she were touching a priceless jewel.

I placed a hand on her knee.

"It means she forgives—" Her voice choked. She gulped a breath. "I guess if she's able to forgive me, I can follow her example and learn to forgive myself."

I nodded. Even if I didn't know why Sophia thought she had to forgive herself, I understood what she was going through. I felt responsible for Cole's death. Forgiving myself was *my* goal, also.

I remembered Cole and how he gave me the strategy necessary to save Sophia. Now he was dead. Why did bad things happen to good people? I may never know. But I did know that *good* things happened to good people, too. And in my heart, I knew that Sophia was all the good I ever needed.

Why do bad things happen to good people?

Essays and Interviews

Introduction to the Responses

If you have recently lost someone close to you, my heart goes out to you. No one should have to endure such suffering. There's no reason for it. It's horrible and terrible. What you don't need at this time is some philosophical discussion on why bad things happen to good people. What you need to do now is close this book and grieve.

I remember my college days when I attended the Hillel at Cal State Northridge. I met and spoke with a young woman who lost faith in God because her brother had died. I offered several reasons for why God might have allowed such a thing. She didn't respond well to my suggested reasons.

Now I know why.

Ever since I discovered Rabbi Harold Kushner's sermon, which is now printed in the following pages, I have regretted the things I told that young woman. She didn't need answers. She needed comfort.

The following responses are not meant to be read by men and women currently suffering from the pain of losing a loved one. Such hardships require time for grieving, not answers. These interviews and essays, instead, are offered as a scholarly discussion for chavurot or book clubs, or even for personal curiosity. I should also mention that the opinions and ideas expressed in the novel do not reflect those of the contributors.

I felt honored getting the opportunity to speak with these rabbis and reverends, and I gained tremendous insight from them.

I hope you gain the same.

Rabbi Harold S. Kushner

There are not many synagogues in this country where God is talked about seriously. For most synagogues, it's a lot more tempting to talk about synagogue budgets, to talk about Israel, to talk about politics, and never to get around to God and some of those theological issues upon which everything else is grounded.

The question is the question of tragedy, and human suffering, and people having things happen to them that they don't deserve, and the lengths to which we will sometimes go to make sense of things that I suspect don't make sense. Let me take just a moment to tell you a story that I heard recently. It's the story of a very simple unpretentious pious little Jewish man by the name of Ginsberg who goes through life saying his prayers, and being honest, and helping people.

One night, God appears to Mr. Ginsberg in a dream and says to him, "Mr. Ginsberg, according to my records it turns out you are the most pious man in the world. You are my most faithful follower. I think you deserve a reward, I will grant any one wish that you ask of me."

In his dream, Ginsberg hears himself responding and saying, "God, I'd like to be rich. I'd like to know what it feels like to have a lot of money. I see people buying fancy expensive things, I've never done it. Make me rich."

Ginsberg wakes up in the morning not sure if this really happened or if it was just a dream. He picks up the paper and finds out he's won a million dollars in the lottery.

He's ecstatic, God has answered his prayer, made his wish come true. What is the first thing he does? He goes downtown to this fancy barbershop, he has his hair styled, he has a manicure. He goes into an elegant men's clothing store, buys a fancy continental suit, a silk shirt, a forty-dollar tie, looks at himself in the mirror and he feels so wonderful. He's enjoying every moment of being able to buy these fancy things. On the way out of the store for good measure he buys himself a cashmere overcoat, a pearl gray fedora hat. He walks out feeling absolutely on top of the world.

He looks across the street and he notices this dealer in imported cars, and he says, "I'll cross the street, and I'll buy one. I'll buy two."

He starts to cross the street and is hit by a speeding truck. The truck runs him over, knocks him flat. With his last dying breath Ginsberg looks up to heaven and says, "God, this is how you treat your most obedient follower in the whole world? You tantalized me with all this good stuff for one hour and snatch it away? How could you do this to me God?" A voice comes out of heaven and says, "Ginsberg? That was you? I didn't recognize you."

Let me tell you what's been happening to me since my book came out, When Bad Things Happen to Good People. I find that I can't check into a hotel or take a cab carrying a copy of my book to an interview without the clerk at the hotel, the taxi driver looking at it and saying, "Hey, mister. You've written the story of my life."

I'm finding out everybody has a story to tell. Everybody is baring this burden of misfortune, of grief, of tragedy. I was in New York one day, I took a cab back to the airport. Talking to the taxi driver I think I detected an Israeli accent. I tried speaking in Hebrew, he responded in Hebrew.

For twenty minutes going out to LaGuardia Airport, we're talking in Hebrew. What am I doing in New York? I tell him I've got a book coming out. What's the title? I tell him and he tells me the following story.

This Israeli taxi driver was born in Jerusalem, his father was an Orthodox rabbi. He was known as one of the saintly rabbis in Jerusalem. One year, on the first day of *Sukkot*, on a holiday, the rabbi was walking to officiate at a brit, at a circumcision. He had to walk because it was *Yom Tov*, it was the holiday. And as he was walking he was hit and run over, killed by a car. The driver and his brother had to drop out of school to help earn a living for the family. Whatever career plans they had, they had to discard.

The driver told me this happened fifteen years ago. He has not been in a synagogue since the day of his father's funeral. He told me he was so angry. He had been raised to be a traditional Jew. He felt so furious, he felt the unfairness of what happened to his family. He has not been able to go into a synagogue since. I hear stories like that all the time. I officiate at funerals, I hold the hands of people in hospitals. I listen to congregants pour out their story of anguish and sickness and unfairness, and I can't help feeling that so often it's the wrong people who get sick, and the wrong people who die young, and the wrong people whose marriages fail, and the wrong people whose businesses go bankrupt.

In addition, my wife and I suffered the tragedy of the loss of our son at age 14. Since he was 3 years old, we lived with the knowledge that he would not live beyond his early teens. We lived with the knowledge that he would never really grow up. He had that very rare disease that causes accelerated aging in children. We felt very angry. We felt betrayed and cheated. We were religious people, honest people, working to serve the cause of Torah and God's purposes. How could a tragedy like this happen in our family? It didn't make any sense.

If we were in any way going to continue as people who would believe in God and in Judaism, we had to come to some kind of understanding. Beyond that, when we contemplated the sickness and the ultimate death of our son, do you know what I found out? I found out that all the answers I had been giving as a rabbi didn't work. What I had been telling people to comfort them was not very comforting. "Don't take it so hard," "It will work out all right," "It's not that terrible." "There must be a reason for it." "Don't be so upset." "Who are we to try and read God's mind?"

People said to me what I had been saying to them for years. And for the first time I realized how hollow these answers were, how inadequate they were, how they really did not help the person. All they did was say to you, "You have no right to feel angry."

Harriet Schiff—whose son died at the age of ten during heart surgery and who has written a marvelous book called *The Bereaved Parent*—told me the story of what happened after her son died. Her rabbi came over to her, put his arm around her and said, "Don't worry, Harriet. You'll be all right. God never gives us heavier burdens than we're capable of bearing."

Do you know what her response was to that? She remembers to this day. Her response to herself was, "If only I had been a weaker person, Robby would be alive. This tragedy would have happened to somebody else."

Whether we realize it or not, so many of the answers we give strenuously try to defend God at the expense of the victim.

In one way or another we say to the person who has suffered, "It's your fault. You deserve it. There were good reasons why it happened to you."

Which is by the way another way of saying, "There are reasons why it happened to you, and not to me."

It's what we call blaming the victim. If the girl wasn't so provocatively dressed, the man wouldn't have assaulted her. It's her fault, and not the criminal's fault. If the Jews hadn't been so pushy and prosperous in Germany, the Nazis would not have made them the victims. Blame the Jew, and don't blame the Nazi. To the person who has suffered, we add another dimension of suffering by saying there was a good and valid reason why this should have happened. We do it because we want to make sense of the world.

But the conclusion I came to was that sometimes the world simply doesn't make sense. Things happen for which there is no reason, for which there is no good moral reason. The conclusion I came to which made it possible for me to go on believing in God, to go on counseling people, urging people to pray and to believe and to be religious, was that when these things happen it's not God's doing. I found I had to choose between a powerful God who was not kind, and a kind God who was not powerful. And I had to say to myself, "Which is the authentic religious quality? Do I want to believe that power is God's essential attribute, power is divine? Or do I want to believe that kindness and justice and compassion are divine?"

If I want to teach people to be God-like, what does that mean in the Jewish tradition—I want them to be powerful, or that I want them to be kind and fair and helpful and compassionate? Which is the authentic Jewishly religious quality? If we look at what happens in this world and we can't believe that God is both powerful and just, which would we rather believe? To me there's no question, that Judaism would rather affirm God's justice, God's fairness and God's compassion rather than affirm God's power. Because if God is powerful but not fair, but not kind, where do we get our kindness? Where do we get our instinctive sense of righteous indignation, of compassion when we see children languish and die, when we read about young parents being wiped out in a senseless crime?

Can't we believe that the anger we feel is God's anger working through us? That the tears we shed are reflected in the tears God sheds? He doesn't want these things to happen but there are some things which are even beyond God's power. I think I could document in Jewish sources, in the Book of Job and passages in the Talmud, that there are some isolated voices in Jewish tradition that would solve the problem of bad things happening to good people by saying, "It's not God's doing." What sort of things happen that God doesn't cause? If human beings want to mess up their own lives, if human beings want to mess up the lives of people around them, we are free to do that. That's what it means to be human.

God isn't going to pull any strings and isn't going to press any buttons to make sure we only do good things. If we choose to be good, honest, faithful, helpful, we get the credit for moral choice. If we choose to be weak, selfish, deceitful, destructive, we take the responsibility. Sometimes bad things happen to good people because people are very cruel to each other. For me the Holocaust is not a theological problem. It's a very raw and painful human problem but not a theological problem. Where was God at Auschwitz? I must believe that God was on the side of the victims, not on the side of the Nazis. If I ever thought that God was on the side of the Nazis, that he wanted this to happen for whatever exalted purpose, I tell you I would have trouble worshipping a God like that.

I was in Chicago doing some radio and TV appearances for my book. And on a call in a radio show somebody said, "Rabbi Kushner, can't you accept the notion that

God caused your son to have this disease and to die so that you would be a more sensitive spiritual leader, so that you would write a book which thousands of people will be helped by?" This is in Chicago, remember. I said to the caller, "Ma'am, do you remember John Gacy?" John Gacy was that mashugana who killed 22 boys and buried them in the basement of his Illinois home. I said to the woman, "Suppose John Gacy's defense attorney, instead of pleading insanity, had pleaded theology which is a branch of insanity. Suppose John Gacy's lawyer had gotten up in court and said, 'Why did Gacy kill those children? To teach parents to be more careful where their children play, to teach parents to be grateful that they have healthy children at home, to let us be more alert to some things that happen in the world. Gacy killed the children in order to teach us some high exalted purpose.' Would anybody for one second take that line of defense seriously? Absolutely not. Why then should we take it seriously when people say exactly the same words about God? That God wants innocent people to die so that we will learn some sort of moral lesson from it?"

Why do bad things happen to good people? Sometimes we are victims of the laws of nature which make no exceptions for the fact that we're nice or that we're necessary. Laws of gravity, laws of illness, the harm that bullets and automobiles and germs do—these treat all people alike. My big argument against the insurance companies who call the flood or the earthquake an act of God, I don't think it's an act of God. It's an act of nature. Nature is blind, nature is amoral, nature doesn't know the difference between a good person and a bad person. The forest fire burns away, the earthquake churns away and doesn't know who gets in its path. They're not the act of God.

The act of God is when a human being whose been selfish and apathetic his whole life risks his life to save his neighbor from a forest fire. The act of God is when a devastated community picks itself up to rebuild itself after it's been wiped out by an earthquake. That's where I find God. If God does not cause the tragedy and if God can't prevent it, what good is he? He moves people to help. He makes some people doctors and nurses, researchers and therapists who ease the pain of tragedy and loss and bereavement. He moves friends to come over and counsel and support and sustain the bereaved and the afflicted. And most of all where is God when tragedy strikes? I want to do a little bit of an exercise with you.

There is one chapter of the Bible that every one of you know by heart, the 23rd Psalm. I want to show you something in the 23rd Psalm you may never have seen before. Martin Buber talks about the difference between an I-it relationship and an I-thou relationship. That is, when do you treat somebody as an object? "What can he do for me?" When do you treat him as a person, as a subject in an authentic relationship? I want you to pay attention as I read you the 23rd Psalm. When does the Psalmist talk about God as "He"? When did he talk about God as "You," "Thou"? Buber said the difference between philosophy and religion, philosophy talks about God, religion talks *to* God.

And the difference between them is the difference between reading a menu and having dinner. Philosophy is very educational, only religion nourishes the soul. When is the Psalmist being philosophical talking about God, when is he talking *to* God?

"The Lord is my Shepherd, I shall not want. He makes me lie down in green pastures. He leads me beside the still waters. He restores my soul. He guides me in straight paths for His namesake. Yea, though I walk through the valley of the shadow of death, I will fear no evil or Thou art with me."

When things are going well for us, when everything is fine and we're healthy and wealthy, God is a subject fit for theology. We talk about God, "He," "Him."

What are His qualities, what are His attributes? Is He imminent, or transcendent, and all these things we had to learn about in college. When we find ourselves in the valley of the shadow of death that's when God stops being the subject for theology and becomes very very real to us. Then for the first time this abstract concept which we talked about in synagogue becomes "Thou," becomes an authentic force in our lives. What convinces me that God is real is when I see ordinary people doing extraordinary things in time of tragedy.

I'll tell you a true story. I more or less jog. Last Father's Day, my 15-year-old daughter gave me a t-shirt to wear when I jog, on the back of which she imprinted the verse Isaiah 40:31.

If you check out in your Bible what is Isaiah 40 verse 31, it reads, "Those who trust in the Lord will have their strength renewed. They shall run and not grow weary." That's my slogan when I jog. Sometimes it works, sometimes it doesn't work, but that's what I believe.

Much more importantly though, that's my slogan when I function as a rabbi and I try and hold people's hands, and help them, and support them. People who trust in the Lord find that their strength is renewed. Where does a person get the strength to do the things that you and I have all seen people do?

If somebody had said to my wife and myself 18 years ago, "You're going to have a son who will look different from normal children, who won't be able to go out in public without being stared at and laughed at, who will have all sorts of pain and discomfort and infirmity, and who will die when he's 14 years old, can you handle that?" I would have said, "No way. Absolutely not. I know my limits, I cannot take something like that." Yet we took it, and we loved him, and we enjoyed every day we had with him. Where did we get the strength that we did not have the day that Aaron was born?

Where do parents of a retarded child get the strength and the patience to wake up every morning and get their son out of bed, and dress him, and feed him, and try and teach him things that they tried to teach him a month ago knowing that there will never be a happy ending to the story? Nobody, *nobody* starts out with that much love and that much patience. It must be that when we use up our initial store of love, God replenishes it for us. Where does a woman get the strength and the courage to go twice a week to visit her mother in the nursing home who is dying of Parkinson's disease?

It's a painful ordeal, and she hates going there, and she hates what she sees when she gets there. And it drives her crazy, and it hurts her to see what her mother is becoming.

But twice, three times a week she goes. Nobody starts out with enough love to do that twice a week, 52 weeks a year, for year after year unless God is replenishing our store of love when we use it up. For me, that's what God represents. He doesn't cause the problem. He doesn't wake up every morning and decide whom to afflict with Leukemia, and whom to send the heart attack, and what plane should crash, and what city should be devastated by earthquakes.

That's not the God I believe in. Those things happen for other reasons which have very little to do with God. I find God in the resolve of the widow who's never signed a check in her life but takes over her husband's business. Of the man who says, "Rabbi, what do I have to live for?" and finds something to live for. Of the brilliant, gifted doctor who decides to dedicate himself to research so that fewer tragedies will happen to good people. That's where God becomes real for me.

The question was, "Why do bad things happen to good people?" Have we answered it? Have we explained this notion of what God does, and what we should not blame God for? I don't think I'm teaching you a diminished, a limited God. I think the God I'm teaching you is much more powerful than the God you may have heard about in Sunday School, because it takes much more power to rebuild than to destroy, much more power to sustain the widow and the orphan than to cause them to become widows and orphans in the first place. But when we have said that, have we answered the question, "Why did this happen to me?" Have we answered the question, "How could God let this happen to an innocent person?" I'm not sure we've really answered it.

Even when we have covered all the squares and the game board, and we're very proud of our intellectual cleverness, I'm not sure we've really answered the question because, you see, the word "answer" has two dimensions of meaning. An answer can be an explanation, a solution, and I'm not sure in that sense there is an answer to the question. But an answer can also be a response. I think we can respond to the question, "Why me?" even if we can't explain it. And the response is to go on living. Rabbi Harold Schulweis taught me something very important. He taught me that the question, "Why did God do this to me?" is not really a question. It's a cry of pain. And we misunderstand it when we think it's a question about God.

I visit the victim of an automobile accident in the hospital, and she looks up at me from her hospital bed and she says, "How could God do this to me?" And I misunderstand her totally if I think she's asking me a question about God, and I try to explain to her why God did this, or what God's role in it might be. It sounds like a question about God, "Why did God let this happen to me?" I have to decode it first. What she's really saying is, "I'm a good person. Why do I hurt so much?" When your child falls down and scrapes his knee and comes to you crying, that's not a time to give him a lecture about forces of gravity and centers of balance. Hold him on your lap, and wipe off his bruised knee, and dry his tears, and comfort him. Talking to him about taking care of himself and watching where he steps? There will be a time for that later.

The question, "Why did this happen to me?" is not really a question we answer by explaining or defending God. We respond to it by reassuring the victim, "You're a good person. You didn't deserve this. You're a good person. I feel so bad for you. I'm sorry it happened to you." I've been very helped and very comforted by Archibald MacLeish's play *J.B.* It's a modern telling of the Book of Job, the classic story of bad things happening to an innocent man. For the first two thirds of McLeish's play he retells the story of Job in a modern setting. A good, honest, pious man loses everything. His children are killed, his business fails, he loses his health. At the end of the Biblical story there's a happy ending.

God says to Job, "It was all a test to see if you would be faithful. You passed the test, I'm going to give you twice as much wealth, twice as many children. You'll be better than you ever were before," and Job is grateful. At the end of MacLeish's play there's a happy ending for a very different reason. In the same way I think the author of the Biblical Job realized it, McLeish realizes how unsatisfying that answer is. For God to say to Job, "It was all a game, a wager. I'll make it up to you." How does MacLeish end the story? Job forgives God. He forgives God for not being perfect enough to protect him. He forgives the world for being such a cruel, painful, imperfect place. Job goes back to his wife.

Despite what the world has done to Job and his wife, they're going to go on living in it. They want more life, though life has been cruel. They're going to go on loving each other and their love, not God's generosity, is going to create the new life and the new children that will make their lives fuller. Job forgives God. His wife says in the beautiful lines with which the play virtually ends, "The candles in churches are out. The lights have gone out in the sky. Blow on the coal of the heart and we'll see by and by." In other words you won't find the answer you're looking for, not in philosophy and not in science, and not even in religion. You'll find it in your own heart. In a cold and dark world, blow on the coal of the heart and let's see what little warmth and light we can find there to share with each other.

Ultimately the question, "Why did God do this to me?" a question that focuses on the past, a question that really can't be answered, has to be asked and then left out there and replaced by a succeeding question. The question it seems to me would be something like this. Can you accept the fact that the world is not fair and can you love it anyway because it's probably the only world we have? Can you accept the fact that people have hurt you by not being perfect, by not always knowing what you needed, and not always being alert enough to give you what you needed? For that matter, can you accept the fact that God is not perfect? And can you love God even when you found that out—just as you once did when you were young, and you had to learn to love and forgive your parents for not being as strong and as wise as you needed them to be? Can you love God when you found out that he couldn't protect you from the world's unfairness? And if you can, can you recognize your own ability to love, and your own ability to forgive and to go on living? Can you recognize these things as qualities that God has given us so that we can live bravely and meaningfully in a less than perfect world? Blow on the coal of the heart and we'll see by and by.

Harold S. Kushner is Rabbi Laureate of Temple Israel in Natick, Massachusetts, where he lives. His books include the huge bestseller *When Bad Things Happen To Good People* and *When All You've Ever Wanted Isn't Enough*.

Reverend Amber Belldene

Thanks for inviting me to share my thoughts about this. They are my educated theological opinions, but they are my own. I don't speak for all Christians, or the Episcopal Church.

I'm honored to speak with you. Has anyone come to you about their pain asking, "Why did I deserve this?"

Well, I have had that experience a few times in pastoral counseling with people, but I would say most of the time when I've been with people at someone's bedside or in planning a funeral or something similar, that wasn't the question people asked.

However, a lot of my work as a priest has been with children and young people, at Sunday school and youth group. And there, that is a huge question for young people who are trying to figure out what they believe about God. They want to understand why bad things happen if God is in charge of the world and why God made our world this way. Why is there suffering? Why isn't this a perfect world?

So when I teach about the Bible and about who God is, I end up answering that question a lot, and not as much in counseling situations.

One thing that's very frightening to us as human beings is the idea that we are not in control, that anything random can happen to us. So the narrative of, for example, reward and punishment—that this bad thing happened to me because God is punishing me for misbehaving—that narrative is completely woven throughout the Bible. We want to impose that kind of order on things because it's frightening to think bad things might happen to us randomly.

I've seen in my pastoral work as a priest and from my own experience as a human being that many of us are inclined to look for the ways that our suffering is our own fault and we blame ourselves for it. The truth is, sometimes it's just not. Sometimes shit happens.

Still, we ask ourselves: How am I in control of this? How is this my fault so I can make sure it never happens to me again?

This modern human impulse can also be seen in the Bible. In many stories it seems to me that's what the figures are doing. They're scared to death and they're looking for some way of imposing a narrative on their experience. Some kind of cause and effect sensibility in order to feel comforted, hoping if they are better behaved, then bad things will not happen to them.

One of the challenges I have with teaching the Bible and teaching theology is that people have constructed something called a "systematic theology" from the Bible as a text and from the Christian tradition. In my opinion, frankly, Jews have a more helpful tradition because you have the rabbinical teachings and the *midrash*, which are stories about stories about stories. I think that's a better way of addressing it than systematic theology because systematic theology is like trying to create a logical system that explains an inherently inexplicable God.

The thing about the Christian tradition and the Bible—which includes the Hebrew Scriptures—is that the texts came from such a radically different context than ours. So when I teach about the story of Noah and the flood, for example, and I talk about the idea of God being so disgusted with the violence and selfishness of the people that God decides to wipe everyone out and start over again except for Noah—that's just terrifying and it has nothing to do with the God I believe in.

Both the Jewish and Christian traditions have this idea of God as a parent, as a father (or a mother in some of the scriptural metaphors we don't talk about as much). And because I am now—thanks to God—a parent, I know what parental love is like. It is not "I'm so disgusted with you that I'm going to kill you and start over."

So I understand the Noah story to have came out of a religious experience of ancient people who went through something and were trying to understand it. Just like we all do. We all go through suffering and we try to understand it.

So the way that I teach the story of Noah is I invite children and adults to think, "What was the experience the ancient people went through? And why is this the story they told us about?" I do believe God is in that story, and I believe that those people's experience of suffering is sacred. It should be considered because it has something to teach us.

When I read the Bible and I teach other people to read the Bible, I'm always trying to get at, "What can we understand about something so different, and from such a different time and place as the one we're in? What can we understand about it? What is the core of the story as it relates to what we might believe about God now?" It's hard to read those stories and understand what they mean.

I love the way that the rabbis have been reinterpreting the stories for generations and talking about God weeping over the death of the Egyptian army in the Red Sea, for example. Because for a very long time people of faith have been asking, "Gosh, would God really do this? Is that what the God that we believe is in like?"

As we read the Bible, it is good and it is right to follow our own heart and trust the religious experiences we have in the modern world, and to look back at the stories from the ancient world and try to reinterpret them in a way that makes sense to us, realizing how different that context was.

The classic theological question people have asked is whether God is all-loving or all-powerful. When people boil down this question, that's the paradox they get to because to them those aspects of God are mutually exclusive. If God were both all-powerful and all-loving, then there wouldn't be suffering.

On the other hand, some people say logic doesn't constrain God. God is mystical and beyond our comprehension, a being who can be both all-powerful and all-loving in a way we don't understand.

I get that, and a part of me delights in that mysteriousness. But I'm also comfortable accepting that maybe God is not all-powerful. I don't think of God as controlling everything that happens, but as a force of creativity and the power that is Love. So instead of thinking, when a bad thing happens, God somehow caused it or allowed it to happen, I think of God being in those moments of suffering in the way that we respond to help each other.

So God is the force and the power that inspires our compassion and our willingness to give of ourselves and make sacrifices, and serve and help each other.

So when we find ourselves comforted by others, that might be God's way of comforting us and connecting with us.

Absolutely. I'm sure this is an idea in the Jewish tradition, too, but I tend to think of it from the Christian perspective. I think it was St. Francis who said that it's our job to be Christ's hands in the world. And when we embody compassion and generosity and sacrificial love, then we are embodying God in the world.

Let me give an example. I went through a period of infertility before I ended up conceiving my children. After a few years of not getting pregnant, I did conceive and then I miscarried. And that was really, very painful. It was the most grief I have ever experienced.

During that time, I felt like the boundaries around myself and my heart and my identity dissolved, and I felt totally open to the people around me that were loving me and supporting me. I felt carried by those people and by the understanding and compassion I received from them.

My response was to realize that it's my job to return that love into the world. I felt those loved ones and strangers were being God for me and that my job was to hold that, to know what it felt like, and to give it back. I have memorialized that realization by getting a tattoo of the Sacred Heart of Jesus over my heart so that every day when I look in the mirror I see that Christ's heart is my heart and that my job is to love everyone with that same kind of passion.

Reverend Amber Belldene grew up on the Florida panhandle, swimming with alligators, climbing oak trees and diving for scallops. As a child, she hid her Nancy Drew novels inside the church bulletin and read mysteries during sermons—an irony that is not lost on her when she preaches these days. Rev. Belldene is an Episcopal Priest and student of religion. She believes stories are the best way to explore human truths. Some people think it is strange for a minister to write vampire romance, but it is perfectly natural to her, because the human desire for love is at the heart of every romance novel and God made people with that desire. She lives with her husband and two children in San Francisco.

Rabbi Maury Grebenau

In the educational role that I'm in, I've found that this question of why bad things happen is a really important question for high school students. It's a question that bothers them, one they think about and one they want to understand. The Book of Job is traditionally pointed to as the book which speaks about it the most.

I had the opportunity to teach The Book of Job to high school students for a few years in Dallas. We dealt very extensively with this question and some students seemed very engaged by this question. I think that we all feel a yearning to understand how God runs his world.

And when someone comes to you, what is something you might say in response?

The most important way to frame it is that there's a significant difference in terms of dealing with it as an academic question, which has a lot of merit, versus somebody who is personally going through a difficult experience. It's so important to make that distinction. If someone comes to you and says, "I'm going through a difficult episode and I want to know why it's happening," it's not really the time to just go into the sources and talk about the different opinions about why bad things happen to good people.

When someone is in the midst of pain, it's not the time to do that. At the end of The Book of Job, God berates the friends of Job for some of the ways that they were answering that question. When Job was going through difficult experiences, it was not the time for philosophical discourse.

What was it that Job's friends did wrong?

So there are differences of opinion, but there's definitely the sense that they were callous towards Job's feelings. Perhaps Job had done certain things to deserve some of what had happened to him. But his friends were not correct in the way that they pointed that out to him. They're responses are listed amongst the examples of hurtful speech.

The point is that Job's friends were being hurtful. They did not really appreciate Job's situation and did not react as friends should. They did not try to make him feel better or comfort him in his time of distress. Instead, they got right into some of the philosophy, which is important and interesting but it wasn't the appropriate place or time.

Got it. Now, you're pointing out a very good distinction of an academic discussion versus a time when someone is experiencing personal grief. In the case of an academic discussion, what might be an answer to address the question?

Right. Traditionally, we have the basic assumption that God is omnipotent. If we assumed that God wasn't omnipotent and that there were certain restrictions on what God could and couldn't do, then there would not really be a call to ask why bad things happen. Maybe bad things happen because there's no one controlling the outcome, or the one who controls many things is not able to control everything.

But we assume that God certainly can and does control everything. And that brings us to the question. *Ein beyadeinu*, it is not in our hands. That shouldn't discourage us from discussing the topic, but at the same time we recognize some of our own limitations in discussing it. One of the philosophers in the middle-ages said, "If I would know God, I would be God."

We are limited in terms of our understanding. But there are certainly some important ideas that are powerful and that resonate. Maimonides makes an interesting distinction. He says it depends on what kind of bad things we're talking about, the bad things that are brought on to us by ourselves or the bad things that are brought on to us by others.

Sometimes there are things that are happening to us because of poor choices that we're making or because of poor choices that someone else is making, and that actually speaks to how important free will is. It doesn't seem just and doesn't seem fair that somebody else could affect me in a bad way because I don't deserve that.

But free will has such an important place in our tradition that the concept overrides what's fair. Sometimes it might seem unfair, but free will—the idea that we get to choose in this world—is what defines us as human beings.

So God's gift of free choice, free will, allows us the wonderful advantage of choosing our destiny and our goals. But at the same time comes with the potential horrible side-effect of choosing things that hurt us and choosing things that hurt others.

Right.

That's very important. Now for situations of natural disasters, say earthquakes or disease?

So the other source that really resonates with me is Nachmonides. He talks about the nature of God testing people. He grapples with that question, "If God is all-knowing then why does God need to test us? Doesn't He already know what we can and cannot do?"

A *nissayon*, a test, is meant to bring out our potential. As we think back on our lives and see the times that we've been tested, those were the times that we realized our strengths and we realized our abilities that we didn't necessarily even know we had. Through those challenging times, we've had tremendous growth.

Being in New York during 9/11 and the aftermath, I'm struck by some of the disasters that we've experienced. And by some of the other news stories that come out of the national disasters that we're seeing. What always happens is that we see the best of people, and the worst of people. We see the absolute unbelievable selflessness of people, and some the most inspiring and unbelievable stories that come out of difficult situations. People who put themselves in harm's way to help others. People who freely go and stock people's kitchens and give food, and fly across the country and across the world in order to help others.

Great. So any tests that we experience or that God gives us, are not for God to learn from, but for us to learn about ourselves and grow?

Right. I think that's a nice way of saying it.

The word nissayon, or test, is interesting in terms of the Hebrew. There's a commentary that asks, where did that word come from? He said the word comes from the word *nais*, which means miracle. The explanation is that a miracle breaks through the natural and rises above to the super-natural, and a test is really the same. We all have natural boundaries that we sometimes put around ourselves in our own minds, and the test is able to have us break through those boundaries and perform at new heights that we didn't previously realize we could do.

That's beautiful. So in situations where it's not helpful to have these academic discussions with a person who is grieving, what is a proper way to address such a situation?

When people are grieving it's very interesting to look at the customs of mourning that the rabbis have put in place: the wisdom from the psychological perspective that went into these kind of customs where there are specific things to be doing, for specific time periods, and certain things that happen in the aftermath. There's the initial seven days of mourning, and then there's thirty days, and then a twelve-month period after that. Such time periods set for mourning create a sense of needing to work through it.

I think that is the most important factor. Working through it, taking time to remember, and going through that mourning process. It is a critical process. Not only is there no words or answer that would cut off that process, but cutting off a mourning period actually would not be helpful. It should not be cut short. It should be gone through.

And it's interesting also to note that within the laws of the mourning custom, the person who comes to a mourner's home is not supposed to start speaking. They're supposed to wait for the mourner to start speaking, they're supposed to help them where they are, rather than come in and say, "I'm going to explain to you why this happened," or "I'm going to give you a lesson in terms of this."

There's a famous story about a great rabbi who visited another rabbi who was in mourning. The visiting rabbi came and sat down with the mourner, and simply sat for ten minutes without speaking. The mourner didn't start the conversation, so the visiting rabbi didn't either.

They just sat with him, they were with him for ten minutes and then they took their leave. I think that is really the answer. The answer is that when someone's going through pain, be there for them, recognize where they are, and try to meet them there seeing if there's anything you can do for them where they are. Don't try to get them somewhere else so quickly. Allow them to go through the process. There certainly is an end goal, but recognize that the process is important.

That really hits home with me, because I have this almost fundamental desire to make the person feel better, and that needs to be curtailed.

Absolutely. I frequently see that. You want to say something. It stems from our own discomfort with the situation, and wanting to fix it. Though it's not easy to accept, the discomfort can't be fixed. It cannot be fixed. This is a new reality and we need to accustom ourselves to that new reality. And that's something that takes time.

The question of why bad things happen to good people is really a question of seeing God in our lives, and sometimes not seeing God in our lives, and the struggle we have with that. And the imagery that is actually used in The Book of Job in one place, is of the sun shining through the clouds. It's a cloudy day, but you have your rays of sunlight that shine through.

There are times in our life when we feel strongly God's presence, and we see it and we get it and we feel great. But many, many times, it's a cloudy day, and we don't see it. It's not obvious, it's not clear, and those are the difficult times. When you're experiencing those cloudy times, remember those rays of sunlight. Remember those times of clarity, those times when you did feel it, and use that to help you get through the cloudier times.

Rabbi Maury Grebenau received a B.A. in Mathematics (cum laude) at Yeshiva University. He was ordained at the Rabbi Isaac Elchanan Theological Seminary and studied at YU, Yeshivat Ohr Yerushalayim and the Mir Yeshivah. Rabbi Grebenau holds an M.A. in Education from the Azrieli Graduate School of Jewish Education and received additional training through The Principals' Center of the Harvard Graduate School of Education. Rabbi Grebenau taught at the Marsha Stern Talmudic Academy in NY and Akiba Academy of Dallas. He was the Associate Principal at Yavneh Academy in Dallas where he taught both Jewish studies and mathematics. He currently is the Assistant Head of School at the South Peninsula Hebrew Day School in the San Francisco Bay Area where he lives with his wife and three children.

Reverend Amy Roden

I have asked the question "Why do bad things happen to me?" based on some of my own personal trauma that I experienced growing up. Why was I sexually abused? Why was I teased and bullied as a child? Why was I hit by an 18-wheeler, an accident which caused me to completely change my way of living? I know I am a good person. Why did these things happen to me?

My car accident created a course correction of a huge magnitude. After a year of trying to separate from my boyfriend, I had finally gotten rid of him just a week prior to the accident and ended up getting back together with him. He came to my rescue and had to take care of me. It was the fulfillment of a healing agreement. I had previously helped him through a full-scale depression breakdown. It was now his turn to take care of me.

I was faced with not being able to have a job where I did anything of a physical nature. I had to rebuild my body and my mind. I couldn't recall how to tie my shoes, simple math had to be learned all over again. All of this I hid from people. I remember being at my chiropractor's office the day he told me I was allowed to walk 10 min a day. I never thought I would see the day when an adult had to give me permission to walk.

While taking a one-year Intensive Clairvoyant Program at the Berkeley Psychic Institute in Santa Rosa, I realized that this life of struggle happened to me because I chose it. I created it.

When we decide as spirits to take a body on earth, we make our first choices. Who do we want as parents? Which continent, country, state, and city do we want to be born in? There is a lot of competition between spirits to get a body on earth. There are more spirits than bodies available. Spirits will take what many would call some of the worst circumstances in order to get life experience and grow from them.

Before I was born, I chose this life for life experience, personal and spiritual growth. I have to take responsibility and accountability for everything I create. I am a conscious being and *I* choose how to respond to my circumstances, as bad as they may be.

As I learned how to read energy and see past life pictures at the Berkeley Psychic Institute, I was able to pull my energy out of that pain, trauma, and heal. I realized that I chose the sexual abuse of this lifetime so that I could light up the past life pictures, see the pattern, then stop it. The abuse was a catalyst for me to recognize and stop the pattern of abuse my spirit experienced.

I know I am not alone.

Not too far from where I live, a 12-year-old girl named Polly Klaas was kidnapped and killed. I am sure she was a good person. Why did a bad thing like being kidnapped and killed happen to her and her family? Consider what transpired.

Her kidnapping created a planetary search and awareness that had never happened before. It was the first time the internet was used to create global awareness of a child gone missing. A new community was created, and other families came forward to express their children had gone missing and were looking for support. A foundation was created that was committed to supporting other families of missing children and preventing other children from being harmed.

Was it her prenatal choice to be the legacy that would help millions of families? Did she have a huge vision of how she wanted to impact the world? I see her as a spirit so huge and beautiful that she only needed a few years on the planet to create such a huge impact.

Her life experience became the catalyst for creating a positive impact across the planet. She left the earth making it a better place than it was when she had first arrived.

We have all created life experience to make ourselves stronger emotionally and physically. It is how we meet the challenge and how we persevere through it that creates growth. It prepares us for our next hurdles we may create, either in this lifetime or the next.

Reverend Amy Roden is passionate about teaching people how to find their power through simple meditation tools. These tools have helped her transform her traumas into successful creations. Rev. Roden is also a committed life learner. Over ten years she has graduated from many of the programs that the Berkeley Psychic Institute (BPI) offers as well as branched out to learn other healing modalities. From BPI she graduated with an Associate Minister title upon completion of the one year Clairvoyant Program. She went on to earn her Ministers license by completing Ministers in Training and the Teachers Program. She completed the three-year Oracle Trance Medium Program, and is currently the Co-Director of the Berkeley Psychic Institute of Santa Rosa.

Reverend Leslie Nipps

You have a background in physics and then you transitioned. At what point did you start your spiritual journey?

My whole life. Although I grew up as an atheist in an atheist family, I do consider atheism to be a form of spirituality in the sense that spirituality is about questioning what is ultimately real and having some kind of ongoing relationship with what is ultimately real. For atheists, that ultimate reality is material reality and it's revealed by science. I consider that a spirituality.

At some point, after I got ordained, someone said to me, "I don't get it. How could you be interested in topics as varied as physics and astronomy and then clinical psychology and then religion?"

For me, it's been an obvious trajectory. I was always interested in the ultimate questions, the deepest of the deep. It's a bit of an obsession, really. Sometimes I wish I were just interested in carpentry or something simple. But it started out in science, and then it moved into psychology, and then I became more interested in religion. I'm actually coming back a little bit more into psychology and science through Neuro-Linguistic Programming (NLP). Those modes of inquiry are not remotely contradictory. They're really complimentary.

And I like how they critique each other. I've got no patience for the Richard Dawkinses of this world who talk about religion with ignorance, and I've got no time for the creationists of this world who talk about science with ignorance. I think science and religion have good critiques of each other and they both offer important contributions to the human spirit.

Thank you. In your experience and training, has anyone experiencing painful challenges come to you asking why they deserved to suffer?

All of us suffer, and most of us have big questions about it, but not everybody asks *why* they deserve to suffer. It's usually a specific kind of person in a specific kind of situation who asks that sort of question. Usually the ones who ask are the ones who have had a lot of suffering for a long time and they've tried a lot of different ways to fix it, either through doctors or medicine, and it hasn't been fixable.

It's like there's still hope for their life to be different, but it isn't getting any better and it hasn't been for a really long time. Often it's people with a chronic condition that isn't well-diagnosed or addressed. There's a quality of frustration and discouragement and heartbreak that these folks are usually dealing with that leads to that kind of question.

Those are the folks that I tend to be in relationship with through my private practice. And so, the Why question starts getting to be really important, because they feel like they're doing everything that they know how to do to try and make it better.

So, here's the deal: I don't try to answer the question.

And I don't offer any comfort around that question. I don't think there really is any comfort around that question. I address the heartache or the discouragement that's at the heart of it. So what do I do to comfort them? I usually find some way to address the experience of despair or discouragement of frustration. Then, the Why question tends to transform on its own and turn into other questions that will move someone to hope or into action rather than into despair.

In my experience, there are so many more useful questions than why do bad things happen to good people. There was a famous book by Rabbi Harold Kushner, *When Bad Things Happen to Good People*, which is why we phrase the question just this way. But it raises two questions. Do we absolutely know what a bad thing is? And do we absolutely know what a good person is?

All of us have had experiences where something terrible happened and eventually we become grateful for it, and all of us have had moments that we experience as blessings and then later went, "Oh my God, that was the worst thing that ever happened to me." All of us.

For example, I've heard alcoholics stand in front of groups and say, "I'm grateful for my alcoholism." Of course, you don't go to someone who is having an awful experience and tell them they ought to be grateful for it, but when you hear it from someone who says it with authenticity, it's quite a beautiful thing.

For the other half of the question about "good people," who of us is actually totally 100% good? Some of us are more committed to trying to be honorable and good than others seem to be. But the question presupposes that the Universe ought to be fair and that good people ought to be rewarded and the bad people ought to be punished, in which case, we're all kind of screwed, because all of us have done terrible things. All of us. We've betrayed people, we've forgotten people, we've all participated in systemic oppression. If God has created a universe where we're all going to get our just rewards at the end, *none* of us should be looking forward to it.

So, what tends to create hope or action or encouragement or forward movement is a really different set of questions. What does it mean to be in a world in which there's suffering? And how do I want to be in a relationship with it? What do I freely choose in response to this challenge? Where is there support I can get that would make it tolerable? There are bunches of more useful questions.

Any of us might have the question, "Why is something bad happening to me? I'm such a good person." It's an understandable question and it deserves a lot of respect. But for the alleviation of suffering, that question is going to have to transform in some way. And, I think that people know it when they actually ask it. Somewhere in there is a question of, "Is there a better way for me to look at all this?" Again, getting to that point can require spending a whole lot of time going, "Wow, that really sucks. That's really horrible."

And what is the Family Constellation viewpoint?

From the point of view of Family Constellation, there are some kinds of suffering, difficulty, and challenges we *choose* in order to belong to our families. A simplified version of this is the unconscious commitment to be depressed so that you can keep your depressed mother company. There can be a kind of unconscious guilt that arises when we dare to have a better experience of life than our parents or other forebears did. And it also feels like we don't belong so well anymore.

So, out of love for our families and our desire to belong to them, we unconsciously choose to imitate their challenges, or in some way take on their difficulties, in the hopes that it will help, so that our ancestors in the past will not have suffered so much and everybody can have a better experience in life.

Now consciously, we simply experience ourselves as having a difficult experience and it feels terribly unfair. But when people decide to have constellation work done, what they discover is that they're part of a larger system that has unresolved suffering in it, and it is very compelling to join in it. What does it mean for a child of generations of slaves to enjoy his or her freedom? What would it mean for a great-grandchild of those who suffered and died on the Cherokee Trail of Tears to have a grand time in life?

The metaphor I often offer is this: Imagine yourself at a table with all of your ancestors who suffered greatly and you all have plates in front of you, except you're the only one who has a lot of food on your plate, and a voice somewhere says dig in and enjoy. Most of us would refrain. This desire to belong is behind a lot of difficulties in life, things like eating disorders and mental health problems, emotional disorders, or more concrete situations like the difficulty with having enough money or a physical ailment, all kinds of things.

We've all heard the cliché of the guy whose father had died at fifty of a heart attack, and right about when he hits fifty he also dies of a heart attack. Now, we could look at that genetically, but from the Family Constellations point of view, it's an attempt to belong and to be in a relationship with dad.

Have you come across similar situations with the children of Holocaust survivors?

Ooh, you betcha. In those instances, it's almost explicit. I think we've probably all met people here in the United States who had grandparents or granduncles and grandaunts or grandparents who suffered or died in the concentration camps. The descendants often explicitly know that they cannot thrive or live well because it makes them feel too guilty to enjoy and love life and freedom when their forebears couldn't.

In cases of the Holocaust or slavery or The Trail of Tears, after those kinds of big national or ethnic disasters, there's absolutely no way for the families and the communities at the time to integrate and deal with the enormity of the disaster. There's just no way. It's too big. It's hard enough for one parent to lose a child to leukemia, yeah? At this level of mass suffering, it shatters the experience of a community system and so again, the grandchildren and the great-grandchildren feel that suffering, they feel that their forebears have not yet been fully honored, and the pain not yet fully resolved. So the children join in on the task of trying to make it better by having whatever difficulties they have in life.

When people in your constellation work strive to overcome the subconscious method of honoring their ancestors by having these chronic difficulties, what about the chronic issues that are chemically based? I can't imagine that just by feeling better and being open to having a better life than one's ancestors would be enough to resolve physical pain. It seems odd that a mental shift would be enough to overcome those types of chronic issues. Have you seen situations where that was, in fact, the case?

If we've been chronically sick for a long time, it's become part of our identity and we've created a lot of coping mechanisms around that. Yes, it's not a simple thing to shift. Having said that, we are all body, mind, and spirit. Science is well-acquainted with the placebo effect, which is simply to say that we can harness the mind, spirit, and heart capacities for self-healing. Even science is aware that there is an internal healing mechanism, which can support healing alongside medical interventions. And, yes, I have seen people have those kinds of placebo effect, if you want to call it that, from constellation work. Usually, it's an improvement in symptoms rather than a complete remission, but sometimes, that happens, too.

One constellation session isn't likely to heal all of life's problems. Anything like a chronic condition is often reinforced by a lot of different kinds of things. But yes, I've definitely seen constellation work improve symptoms, and improve people's physical health.

So constellation work often works alongside medical treatments.

Sure.

It reminds me of how someone can win the lottery but their mindset is in the state of living a life of poverty, so they spend it all and go back to the destitute lifestyle they're comfortable with. In that scenario, it's not enough to win money. Even though they have a shift in income, they also need the mind shift to let themselves live a wealthy lifestyle.

You bet. In the work that I do we talk about it as an identity thing. So, after years and years of being unwell, one can have the identity of being a sick person. Susan Sontag wrote beautifully about this in her book *Illness as Metaphor* when she got cancer. So, what does it mean to have an inner and deeper health, even while having physical symptoms? We work at the level of identity and by doing so, perhaps we can release the body's natural healing power. We are not replacing medical treatment or anything else by any means.

The reality is that there's a mental aspect to health. And although science hasn't been able to quantify it— because it's not very quantifiable—science certainly acknowledges it.

Yes. And in the case of bad things happening to good people?

What all spiritual traditions pretty much agree on at the most elevated level, is that the universe is not fair. It just isn't. We don't get what we deserve. This is bad news and this is good news.

This is bad news in that things happen that seem out of scale to anything bad you've done in your life. The good news is that we don't get punished when we do really horrible things. Isn't that good news? Just take a second and think of the worst thing you've ever done to somebody, or to yourself, and then be grateful it's not a fair universe.

The Sunday school version of religions don't teach this. They say God likes the good, rewards the good and punishes the evil and blah, blah, blah. But, even in my tradition, which is Christian, when we get past the Sunday

School version of things, we learn that God sends the rain on the good and the evil alike [Matthew 5:45]. Having our mature spirituality is what gives us the ability to appreciate that the universe does seem to be set up this way, a universe set up for free will and choice.

Reverend Leslie Nipps's first calling was to astronomy. She pursued a degree in physics at Cornell University, then completed a degree in the History of Science. She moved on to clinical psychology, and got involved with the community of support for people with AIDS in San Francisco in the late 80s. Accompanying the mortally ill and dying forever changed her life. She pursued the path of priest and theologian, was ordained a priest in the Episcopal Church in 1995, and was a parish priest until 2006. Currently she is a Neuro-Linguistic Programming (NLP) and Family Constellations Practitioner in Oakland, CA, where she helps a variety of clients overcome and heal from painful family and personal patterns that limit their experience of life.

Rabbi Aron Moss

Many are bothered by the fact that people suffer undeservedly. As they should be. Any person with an ounce of moral sensitivity is outraged by the injustices of our world.

Abraham, the first Jew, asked God, "Should the Judge of the whole world not act fairly?"

Moses asked, "Why have You treated this people badly?"

And today we still ask, "Why God, why?"

But what if we found the answer? What if someone came along and gave us a satisfying explanation? What if the mystery were finally solved? What if we asked why, and actually got an answer?

If this ultimate question were answered, then we would be able to make peace with the suffering of innocents. And that is unthinkable. Worse than innocent people suffering is others watching their suffering unmoved. And that's exactly what would happen if we were to understand why innocents suffer. We would no longer be bothered by their cry, we would no longer feel their pain, because we would understand why it is happening.

Imagine you are in a hospital and you hear a woman screaming with pain. Outside her room, her family is standing around chatting, all of them smiling and happy.

You scream at them, "What's wrong with you? Can't you hear how much pain she is in?"

They answer, "This is the delivery ward. She is having a baby. Of course we are happy."

When you have an explanation, pain doesn't seem so bad anymore. We can tolerate suffering when we know why it is happening.

And so, if we could make sense of innocent people suffering, if we could rationalize tragedy, then we could live with it. We would be able to hear the cry of sweet children in pain and not be horrified. We would tolerate seeing broken hearts and shattered lives, for we would be able to neatly explain them away. Our question would be answered, and we could move on.

But as long as the pain of innocents remains a burning question, we are bothered by its existence. And as long as we can't explain pain, we must alleviate it. If the suffering of innocent people does not fit into our worldview, we must eradicate it. Rather than justifying their pain, we need to get rid of it.

So keep asking the question, why do bad things happen to good people. But stop looking for answers. Start formulating a response. Take your righteous anger and turn it into a force for doing good. Redirect your frustration with injustice and unfairness and channel it into a drive to fight injustice and unfairness. Let your outrage propel you into action. When you see innocent people suffering, help them. Combat the pain in the world with goodness. Alleviate suffering wherever you can.

We don't want answers, we don't want explanations, and we don't want closure. We want an end to suffering. And we dare not leave it up to God to alleviate suffering. He is waiting for us to do it. That's what we are here for.

Rabbi Aron Moss grew up in a somewhat traditional Jewish home in Sydney, Australia, and embraced religion after his bar mitzvah. By age 14, he knew he wanted to be a rabbi. He studied in a broad range of yeshivas in Israel and in the USA, including Kol Torah, Karlin-Stolin and 770, where he gained rabbinical ordination. Rabbi Moss worked at a number of educational settings: He was a lecturer at Chabad of Binghamton University; Lecturer and Director of Judaic studies at The Mayanot Institute in Jerusalem; and since 2001, he has been the senior lecturer at Bina Adult Education Institiute. Together with his wife Nechama Dina, Rabbi Moss established Nefesh Synagogue, an instructional and educative synagogue designed to provide spiritual inspiration for mainly young unaffiliated Jews.

Rabbi Tsiporah Gabai

What experience have you had with people coming to you grieving, asking how such bad things could happen to them?

I had people who lost their parents all of a sudden. I had people who lost young children. This big question is difficult to answer. I had one student that was very, very ill, and his father was not a believer, but still, when he was lost and sought out answers, he wanted to be comforted and wanted to know why. What did his little boy do to deserve such a thing? And, that's a difficult one, and we know it even from the time of *Moshe Rabbeinu* [Moses, our teacher] that he asked the same question and could not understand it.

What was the specific story of Moshe Rabbeinu and his struggle?

Moshe Rabbeinu also asked that question. There is a place in the Talmud, in the Gemara, where Moshe is asking *lamah tzadik v'tov lo, tzadik v'ra lo, rasha v'tov lo, rasha v'ra lo?* [Why is it that some righteous people prosper and other righteous people suffer; and some wicked people prosper and other wicked people suffer? – From Brachos 7a] So we know that for generations after that, Moshe Rabbeinu even says to HaShem, "Explain to me the way you act, the way you deal with this world."

I don't think he received an answer, and this is something that—especially with death, I think—this is something that we have to accept. But you're talking about why bad things happen to good people. I don't like to look at it like that. I don't think that bad things happen only to good people. Bad things happen also to bad people. Things happen to people, to human beings. We were born fragile. *Hacol tzafui, v'harishut netunah,* everything is foreseen and the choice is in your hand [Pirkei Avot, 3:15].

So, certain things we must take responsibility for, to guide our life and protect our life. This is our obligation. We need to live a certain way of life so that we will stay healthy and be in a healthy community. So, if somebody's a drug addict and dies from it, we can't blame God and say, why did it happen to him or to her? Everything is foreseen and the choice is in your hand, which means basically, in many cases, we are responsible for things that happen to us, okay? People that are drinking and driving and hitting someone, can you say that God did it? No. It's the actions of human beings that are doing these things, and things happen to bad people, and to good people.

And also I don't believe that people are completely one way or the other. Most people, they have a part of them that is good, and even criminals that are put in jail, when we look into them, they are mentally ill, or things happened in their life, and that's why they are doing what they're doing. So, do they deserve to be in jail? Did the person they hurt deserve to be hurt by them?

HaShem created us, gave us a beautiful planet, gave us laws, and, I believe, gave me ways to live my life and I have to do the best in my utmost effort to live by these laws and try to follow them the best I can. And, if everybody does follow these laws, maybe not that many bad things will happen.

So, by people following Jewish laws or the laws of a country or both, it diminishes the possibilities of bad things happening to people?

Yes. That's right, and also being responsible for one another. For example, when Hitler came to power and killed so many, if people had made themselves aware of what was happening, we could have prevented that.

We can't blame God. We can maybe blame society a little bit. There are things that we can do to prevent things.

Okay, and for situations that we have no control over, like a disease, when people come to you and say, "What did my child do to deserve this?" what's been your response?

The answer is your child did not do anything to deserve this. There are a lot of things that are beyond our comprehensions to understand, and unfortunately we are just human beings and things happen, and it's unfortunate that such things happen, and sometimes, it's very difficult to tell a person it's happened for a reason. When you lose a child, it never happens for a reason. Often, ten years later, people will tell you that they found strength with each other and their relationship, so they found God again, or they learned from this experience and they helped others. But still, losing a child is a terrible thing, right?

Sometimes I believe in *gilgul neshamot* [cycle of souls]. Like reincarnation. In Judaism we have many beliefs. Many times I try to use all the wealth of knowledge that my heritage and my traditions gave us to try to deal with terrible things that happen.

And, some say this *neshamah*, this soul, came to this earth for a period of time. He came to complete this task and leave, you know?

I'm the youngest of nine kids. My father was a rabbi, a Moroccan rabbi, my grandparents were rabbis, and in Morocco they lost many kids. My mother told me she lost five kids. One baby, she lost him right after the *bris* [circumcision]. As a child hearing this story, I asked my father "How can HaShem do that?" My father said, "Look, the neshamah that came was supposed to be born and live for eight days, and that neshamah was supposed to go back to God." Maybe the baby was reincarnated later on in a different child or a different person, so that's sometimes a comfort. For example, the Druze, they believe… you know who the Druze are, right?

Don't they live north of Israel?

They live in North Israel, they live in Syria, in Egypt, and they go by the law of the country. But in their religion, if you ask them how many people there are, they'll say that the number never changes. What does that mean? It means that when a person dies he or she will be born immediately somewhere else. They will give you many stories of kids that act in a way that suggests they were someone else now born again. Now, why did they die in a certain time? We do not know.

But, I always tell my students this wonderful story. A righteous man comes to God and he's very angry. "God, I need to find answers. Why are terrible things happening to my friends? I do not understand your ways."

So, a poor and old man comes to him and says, "I'm Elijah the prophet and you want to find answers, correct?" Elijah the prophet in the Jewish tradition always appears as a poor and old man.

The man says, "Yes, Elijah. I need to understand the ways of God."

"Okay, travel with me, but as soon as you ask me a question to answer why, I'm disappearing."

The man says, "Okay."

So, they travel together and it's raining, pouring. They're going from town to town. Finally, they get to this small village. No one wants to host them. It's night. The villagers don't have room for them, and they are wet, and not very groomed.

So finally, the man and Elijah come to this shack where an elderly couple lives, and they ask if they can spend the night, and the elderly couple who are very poor, welcome them in.

The couple said, "Look, we have only some cheese and milk. We have one cow that sustains us. We sell the milk and we are able to buy bread. The cow is like our child."

The couple gives them their bed, and their food, and for three days they are hosting them.

So, on the third day, just before the man and Elijah are leaving, they're getting up in the morning, praying, and then they hear the woman is screaming.

She screams, "It's a snake!"

The man and Elijah come see that the cow is dead and the woman is crying, "My cow. My cow. The only thing I had left, God is taking my cow away."

A snake bit the cow and the cow died, so the man, the *tzadik*, the righteous man says to Elijah, "You see, now explain to me. This woman was so kind to us and God took the cow from her."

Elijah says, "Look. If I answer the question, I'll disappear."

The man says, "I don't care. Start answering because I don't understand anything."

Elijah says, "Look. The snake was supposed to bite the woman, because today the woman was supposed to die. But because she was such a *tzadikah*, a righteous woman, instead of the *Malach HaMavet*, the Angel of Death, taking her life, he took the cow's life. So, you see, its better that the cow died and not the woman."

A great story.

So, you understand that.

Here's a true story. A story that happened here at this school. On Israeli Independence Day, *Yom Ha'Atzmaut*, one of the teachers was coming. And just as she was coming, she fell and broke her ankle. She couldn't make it. She was in a cast.

So, she calls me. "Can you believe that? I did such wonderful things, and look what God did to me."

I said, "You never know why it happened."

Lo and behold, a week later, she was asleep at home. She was supposed to go to visit her elderly mother in Los Angeles, but because she broke her foot, she stayed at home. Her husband was not feeling good, so he took a medicine that puts you to sleep. Benadryl.

Her daughter also, she had a hard time sleeping, so she also took some Benadryl. All of them were fast asleep. The pilot light in the basement exploded and the house went in flames in two minutes. Luckily, she was there. She had to shake her husband awake, and her daughter. Shake them out of bed. They were able, the three of them, to escape with their pajamas on.

Incredible.

The house burned to the ground because it all exploded. It was an old home in Oakland. So, she calls me the next day and tells me what happened.

I said, "Wow, are you okay?"

She said, "Tsipi, thank God I didn't go to L.A. If I didn't break my foot and went to L.A. this weekend, I would have lost my husband and a kid."

So, sometimes you can look at things this way, and again, as long as you have life, everything else, you know, we can replace. We can say, worse things can happen.

So, you never know why things happen. Sometimes things happen for a reason.

In the Jewish belief of reincarnation, for when the child was to live for, say, only eight days, is there a viewpoint on whether the purpose for the eight days is for the baby's growth, the growth of the baby's soul, or is it for the growth of the people who have the baby?

Okay. So, many times they say it is the purpose for all souls. That baby was born, and had to be born to my parents, for example, because its neshamah, its soul, did not complete its purpose on this planet. In the Jewish tradition, we believe that many times you're going to be reincarnated again and again, until you are a great tzadik. Then you don't have to live in this world, only in the world next to the Almighty, right?

So, they say this neshamah still needed another eight days on this planet. To complete what it needed to do when it lived. As for the purpose for these parents, what did my parents learn from this? I don't know. I know that they were in a lot of pain, but my father says they were the ones that were given the privilege of having this neshamah in their possession for eight days. This righteous person in their family for eight days. So it's a comfort. To people who believe in these things, it's very comforting.

That's beautiful.

So, our belief system helps to deal with pain and with the acceptance of loved ones who suffer. But, of course, again, if it's other things that we can be responsible, then for these things we don't blame God. If a child is growing up in an abusive home, if God gave this couple a wonderful young child and they are abusive or they are drug dealers, or drunk, they are not giving the right environment to this child, you can't blame God for that.

You can't. Everything is foreseen, and the choice is in your hand. So, people have to be aware and careful, and take care of the environment, and of their lives, and their actions, and live by the *mitzvot*, by the commandments, taking care of their health and their community by being aware of what's happening around them, by loving your neighbor as you would love yourself, by remembering that we were all created in God's image and that we're all the same, and that we have to take care of each other and give from ourselves, and then we can prevent a lot of bad things that can happen in the community, or to other people. And yes, there are things that are not within our control. It's nature. It's a part of nature. We are fragile human beings, and that's how we are created.

Rabbi Tsiporah Gabai received her rabbinic ordination, as well as a Masters in Rabbinic Studies, from The Academy for Jewish Religion. She was the first ordained female rabbi from Morocco. She also holds a Certificate of School Administration from the Jewish Theological Seminary in New York. During the years leading up to her transition from growing up in Israel to transplanting herself in Northern California, Rabbi Gabai received a BA in Bible and Jewish History, as well as a teaching credential, from Haifa University. She is currently the rabbi and Head of Hebrew and Judaic Studies at Tehiyah Day School in El Cerrito, California.

Josh Rosenau

The problem of evil is classically posed as a question of why evil should exist in the world if there is an omnipotent, omniscient, omnibenevolent deity. By straightforward logic, one can argue that the existence of evil is evidence against the existence of an omnipotent, omniscient, omnibenevolent deity. As the Stanford Encyclopedia of Philosophy notes, there are a lot of theodicies—attempts to defend the notion of an omnipotent, omniscient, omnibenevolent deity against this argument—and there've been a lot of attacks on those defenses, and nothing's really resolved because this is a discussion where your assumptions *a priori* matter a lot. There being no way to independently test the basic assumption (some god exists, that god is omnipotent, omniscient, and omnibenevolent), the two sides tend to talk past one another.

Theists don't (generally) understand the mindset of atheists, and atheists don't (generally) understand the mindset of theists. They have different unstated premises and so the logic they offer simply doesn't compel the other side.

I don't doubt that some theologians really are focused on *a priori* proofs, and that they really are taking the philosophical perspectives of nontheists seriously. I don't doubt that they really are trying to revise their argument to get at the formal structure of arguments against theism, and to get at the informal perspective underlying those arguments.

Like all generalizations, the ones about theists and atheists understanding each other have exceptions, which don't disprove the broad point. So I'll take the theistic assumption for granted here and there, but only to explore the ideas, and to explore why people might adopt those ideas.

Throat-clearing aside, let's get back to the problem of evil. There are three basic ways to explain why bad things happen to good people. It could be that there's nothing in the universe which cares one way or another, the "shit happens" option. It could be that there's something in this universe that likes making bad things happen to good people, the Loki option. Or it could be that the bad things which happen to good people are in service of some greater good. That last one is where the numerous branches of theodicy come in, and the first two don't technically create a *problem* of evil existing in our world.

Obviously, the first option applies to atheism, but it also covers a range of theisms. The Norse gods and any superhero, for instance, have some influence on the world, but aren't omnipresent, aren't omniscient, and aren't omnipotent. They aren't omnibenevolent, but even if they were, some bad things would happen that they couldn't stop, either because they can't be everywhere at once, or because other equally powerful forces are working against them, or because they do bad things through clumsiness, malice, oversight, or indifference. The God of Job also doesn't seem to be omniscient (or else why would Satan bother arguing hypotheticals with God?), which helps explain why bad things happened there.

Then again, the example of Job also could take the Loki prong. The God in that case (and Satan, who was part of the polytheistic/henotheistic pantheon when Job was written) lets Job's family be killed and his property destroyed just to settle a wager about the nature of piety. It isn't so much malice as a certain indifference to human suffering, and a willingness to inflict suffering for reasons that are hardly justifiable morally (Job, after all, is "blameless" by premise). Of course, in a world without deities, there are still plenty of forces and entities that want to hurt good people, or that punish altruism in other ways. Dropping the theistic assumption doesn't so much resolve the moral questions, but it does make them easier to ignore.

For the third option, there are a few standard arguments. You can argue that this is the best of all *possible* worlds, and that what evil exists in the world is an inevitable result of natural laws (which are, presumably, the best of all possible laws) or of a divine commitment to the greater good of unchecked free will. You can argue that the deity, omniscient as it is, knows that averting evil action X would result in eviler action Y, and so allowing the lesser evil to take place is the best outcome. Or you can argue that there are reasons which are beyond our capacity to understand.

In this realm as in so many others, I side with Darwin, who wrote to Asa Gray:

> *With respect to the theological view of the question; this is always painful to me. – I am bewildered. – I had no intention to write atheistically. But I own that I cannot see, as plainly as others do, & as I should wish to do, evidence of design & beneficence on all sides of us. There seems to me too much misery in the world. I cannot persuade myself that a beneficent & omnipotent God would have designedly created the Ichneumonidae with the express intention of their feeding within the living bodies of caterpillars, or that a cat should play with mice. Not believing this, I see no necessity in the belief that the eye was expressly designed. On the other hand I cannot anyhow be contented to view this wonderful universe & especially the nature of man, & to conclude that everything is the result of brute force. I am inclined to look at everything as resulting from designed laws, with the details, whether good or bad, left to the working out of what we may call chance. Not that this notion at all satisfies me. I feel most deeply that the whole subject is too profound for the human intellect. **A dog might as well speculate on the mind of Newton. – Let each man hope & believe what he can. –***

Certainly I agree with you that my views are not at all necessarily atheistical. The lightning kills a man, whether a good one or bad one, owing to the excessively complex action of natural laws,—a child (who may turn out an idiot) is born by action of even more complex laws,—and I can see no reason, why a man, or other animal, may not have been aboriginally produced by other laws; & that all these laws may have been expressly designed by an omniscient Creator, who foresaw every future event & consequence. But the more I think the more bewildered I become; as indeed I have probably shown by this letter.

Most deeply do I feel your generous kindness & interest. —

Yours sincerely & cordially | Charles Darwin
(Emphasis added)

I don't see how an omnibenevolent being with the power and knowledge to make anything would create a world exactly like the one we're in, but I also don't think I can put myself into the mindset of a (hypothetical) omnipotent being that exists beyond time and space, that was there before the Big Bang and will be there after. Who can guess what such a being might want, or what notions like good and evil and just and unjust might mean on that scale?

Joshua Rosenau spends his days defending the teaching of evolution and climate change at the National Center for Science Education (NCSE). He is a biologist, and author of the "Thoughts from Kansas" blog at ScienceBlogs, where this essay first appeared. He is currently the Programs and Policy Director of the NCSE. The opinions expressed here are his own, and do not reflect the official position of NCSE.

Rabbi Daniel Kohn

My personal experience is based very much on the reading of Rabbi Harold Kushner's, *When Bad Things Happen to Good People*. I read it very early on as a young adult and as part of my rabbinical school studies, and it was very influential in my own thinking.

Essentially, I feel much the same that Rabbi Kushner does which is not a question of God allowing bad things to happen. I don't think God has anything to do with the good events or the bad events. It's like how your parents raise you, they give you lots of advice and support, and you learn different ways of living and dealing with experiences in your life, and then you go out into the real world. When good things happen, maybe you're able to respond in a good way, because that is how your parents raised you to be.

It's like the Oscars or the Grammy Awards that we watch on T.V. You want to praise the influences which have led you to this experience, and hopefully you thank God for the goodness that happens to you even though maybe God had nothing to do with it.

I feel like it's not within a theological realm. Bad stuff happens. Like the little baby bib that I love, the one that says "Spit Happens."

I like the explanation that I've read from Harold Kushner. It's a different department. That's not God's department. You want to praise God for the good? Great, give God credit. God will take the credit. You want to blame God for the bad stuff? Fine. Go ahead, but it's like water off a duck. It doesn't stick, He's got nothing to do with it.

Fine, you can yell at me, like when my kids yell at me for something that happened at school. Okay, fine, I'm happy to listen to it, but there's not much I'm going to be able to do about it. And quite honestly it's for them to learn from and deal with as well. So that's my initial response when it comes to bad stuff happening.

I want to give you my favorite movie quote about God and bad stuff. It comes from the really awful science fiction movie with Vin Diesel called *Pitch Black*.

In it, there's this religious character that is having a conversation with Vin Diesel, the action hero. The religious character says, "Perhaps your problems are because you don't believe in God?" and Vin Diesel says, "Who says I don't believe in God? I just hate the son-of-a-bitch."

And that's been my philosophy. It really has. The one thing that I'll share, which is of a slightly personal nature, is that my wife and I are adoptive parents. We were unable to have children of our own despite many years of efforts. And during that time I blamed God. And you know what? God didn't care. In fact, I was even asked once to give a talk at one of the local national organizations of support for infertile couples called Resolve.

The organization asked people to share their religious perspective, and there were a number of people that spoke before me on a panel. They talked about how grateful they were once they were able to get pregnant or adopt and have children, and they owed it all to God. God was completely involved with them. It was from a very Christian point of view.

And it just left me cold. I could even see people in audience that were not affected by the panelists because those audience members were still dealing with the very awful emotional effects of not being able to have children, and the depression. So when it came to my turn, the very first words out of my mouth were, "God is an asshole."

I started attacking God and just let it fly. The other people on the panel were shocked at that. I was the only Jew and rabbi on the panel and they were all coming from a very Christian point of view. I shared a tremendous amount of bitterness. And after the talk, most of the people came up to *me* to thank me for *my* comments.

Blame God all you want. But God's like a good listener on the telephone. Let it all out. God's your therapist that doesn't say a thing. You get it all out, and then you move on and you deal with it the best way you can. Hopefully, with a lot of positive parenting experiences from your parents. Hopefully, they helped you learn to deal with challenging experiences in life and move on.

I take a more existentialist point of view when it comes to learning from our pain and suffering, which is, we're going to make out of it whatever we make out of it. And that's based more on psychology, not on any theology. Some people are incredibly optimistic no matter what happens to them.

They roll with the punches, and you just look at these people and you're amazed. Like Nelson Mandela, *alaiv hashalom* [may he rest in peace]. I think he's one of the most incredible examples in modern humanity of someone who was able to deal with all of his years of incarceration and not be bitter. The example that he set for the country, and the Truth and Reconciliation Commission he established for South Africa. I mean, what a way to deal with incredible crimes against humanity, and still not be bitter about it.

And yet there are people that get cut off on the freeway in the morning, and that leads to them being rude and frustrated and angry with people for the whole rest of the day for a ridiculous non-reason. So I think it just depends on the psychology of how we happen to be, and whether that's nurture or nature, blame God.

Have you ever had a situation where a person has just lost someone close to them, and they came to you for solace? Did you have any special way of addressing that?

I want to give credit to my congregational rabbi, who is Rabbi Menachem Creditor at the Congregation Netivot Shalom in Berkeley. He talks often about the importance of just being present. Just being there. Not to find any kind of quip or phrase which is going to help people magically feel better. Because it's not going to happen. I recently lost my mother, just over a year ago and the most intense and powerful healing experiences I had were when people would come up to me and they wouldn't say a thing.

They would just give me a hug and be there, and stand next to me, hold my hand, and sigh with me, and say nothing. I found the most intrusive experiences were when people would come to me and they would look at me very seriously and say, "So how are you feeling? How are you doing?"

I was suddenly struck by the wisdom of the Jewish tradition that deals with mourning practices, which says that when you make a *shiva* [mourning] call in a house of shiva, the first seven days of someone mourning, you're actually forbidden, according to the Jewish tradition, to ask how they are, because it's a pretty stupid question. How do you think they're feeling? They just lost somebody in their life.

In fact, the wisdom of that Jewish tradition was actually proven to me with my father. My father is very disconnected from the Jewish tradition and many of his friends are also not part of the Jewish tradition. I was sitting shiva with my father for the first few days of my mom's passing last year and someone came in and had that exact question. They said to him, "So how are you feeling?" My dad just blurted out, "How should I feel? I just lost my wife of 58 years? How do you think I'm feeling? I'm feeling awful. I'm feeling horrible."

And I thought, "Wow, that's exactly the kind of answer that my father should not have ever had to be put in the position to actually express and articulate out loud." That's the wisdom of the Jewish tradition. You don't ask, "How do you feel?"

You just be present.

Rabbi Daniel Kohn is a professional Jewish educator and spiritual leader. He has published numerous articles and books on Jewish education, spirituality, conversion, and classical Jewish texts, including his most recent, *Jewish FAQs: An Internet Rabbi's Answers to Frequently Asked Questions about Judaism*. Kohn is the Rabbi-in-Residence of the Contra Costa Jewish Day School. A third-degree black belt of Aikido and long-time student of Tai Chi, Rabbi Kohn lives in Mill Valley with his wife and their three children.

Acknowledgments

Creating a good book takes a village. Creating a great book takes a village of great minds. If there is greatness in this book, it is owed to the brilliant people who helped me write it.

My wife Beth Barany has been a never-ending source of support and wisdom. She is also the best editor I've ever known. Beth, thank you so much. I wish to express my gratitude to Rabbi Harold Kushner, Reverend Amber Belldene, Rabbi Tsiporah Gabai, Rabbi Daniel Kohn, Rabbi Maury Grebenau, Reverend Leslie Nipps, Rabbi Aron Moss, and Reverend Amy Roden for their contributions in addressing why bad things happen to good people. I am also thankful for the invaluable feedback I received from Steve Manke, Patricia Dake, Dixon Rice, Matt Posner, Julie Morfee, Martin Reisberg, Derri Pollack, and my parents Bella and Ron Barany. They raised my story to heights I could never have reached on my own.

And to all my readers, thank you. I would not be where I am today without you.

About the Author

Ezra Barany started his career of freaking out readers with his suspense and thriller stories in college. In March 2011, Ezra unleashed his first novel *The Torah Codes*, which became an award-winning international bestseller. In his free time, he writes mushy love songs inspired by his wife and book coach Beth Barany. Ezra, a former physics teacher, lives in Oakland with his beloved wife and two cats working on his next book in *The Torah Codes* series. Ezra, not the cats.

CPSIA information can be obtained at www.ICGtesting.com
Printed in the USA
BVOW01s1104060614

355472BV00001B/1/P